# FEAR ME

*Broken Love Series*

BOOK ONE

## B.B. REID

Copyright © 2015 B.B. Reid
Fear Me by B.B. Reid

ISBN-13: 978-1540768315
ISBN-10: 1540768317

Second Edition 2016

Manuscript Analysis & Editing by
Rogena Mitchell-Jones, Literary Editor
Final Proofread by Ami Hadley
RMJ-Manuscript Service LLC
www.rogenamitchell.com

Cover Design by Amanda Simpson of Pixel Mischief Design.
Cover Photo by Jozsa Levente from Shutterstock

# TABLE OF CONTENTS

Prologue......................................................................1

Chapter One...............................................................7

Chapter Two...............................................................15

Chapter Three...........................................................27

Chapter Four..............................................................40

Chapter Five................................................................50

Chapter Six ...............................................................67

Chapter Seven...........................................................81

Chapter Eight.............................................................98

Chapter Nine..............................................................118

Chapter Ten ..............................................................140

Chapter Eleven .........................................................155

Chapter Twelve ........................................................177

Chapter Thirteen......................................................208

Chapter Fourteen......................................................215

Chapter Fifteen ........................................................218

Chapter Sixteen........................................................234

Chapter Seventeen...................................................248

Chapter Eighteen .....................................................261

Chapter Nineteen.....................................................271

Chapter Twenty .......................................................281

Chapter Twenty-One ...............................................296

Chapter Twenty-Two ...............................................316

Chapter Twenty-Three.............................................334

Chapter Twenty-Four ...............................................348

Chapter Twenty-Five ...............................365

Chapter Twenty-Six ...............................375

Chapter Twenty-Seven........................, .........385

Chapter Twenty-Eight ...,.......................395

Chapter Twenty-Nine ...........................403

Chapter Thirty.................................423

Chapter Thirty-One ............................428

Chapter Thirty-Two ...........................446

Chapter Thirty-Three............................459

Author's Note...............................466

Acknowledgments...............................469

Also By B.B. Reid ...........................471

Contact the Author............................472

About B.B. Reid............................473

# DEDICATION

*This book is dedicated to every romance author who fulfilled my romantic heart and fantasies.*

# PROLOGUE

*I HUFFED AND wiped the sweat off my eyebrow for the hundredth time in the last five minutes. The pink toe-nail polish Aunt Carissa helped me paint on this morning glistened in the sunlight.*

*I wasn't having a very good time.*

*"Wanna play hopscotch? I've got chalk. Pink ones too if you like. My mom says girly-girls like pink. Your bow is pink, so you're definitely a girly-girl. I like your bun. You look like a ballerina. Are you a ballerina? Can you show me your moves?"*

*The soft voice above me rushed the words out before I could raise my head. I looked up and stared into twinkling green eyes and a chubby face. She reminded me of my mom's statues that she often called cherubs.*

*"Willow," she stated.*

*I continued to stare.*

*Her wild mane of curly red hair, more like a copper color, was currently pointing in every direction as if it had never met a brush before. Freckles covered what seemed like every inch of her face and framed her big round eyes. Her bright green overalls had a yellow daisy print that she paired with purple sneakers. She definitely had the adorable kid look down.*

*"Hi," I finally responded after the silence became awkward. I could see some of her confidence disappearing when I continued to stare.*

*"What's your name?" she prompted nervously. I wasn't sure I should answer her. She looked like trouble and a long day. I didn't get the chance to answer, though. A lady with equally red hair, but with it carefully swept back to rest on her shoulders, interrupted before I could.*

*"Willow," the lady called out in a stern tone. "What happened to your hair? Oh, never mind. Where is your brother? It's time to go home."*

*"Mooooom," she whined. "How would I know? Buddy's five! He's practically an adult!"*

*I'm almost sure that isn't right.*

*"Willow Olivia Waters," her mother started, turning red.*

*Uh-oh.*

*"Lake," I stated abruptly.*

*They both turned to me, her mother appearing confused while Willow grinned at me triumphantly. I guess learning my name was some kind of victory for her. Weird.*

*I only gave my name as a distraction because, for some reason, I didn't want the other girl in trouble, but now I didn't know what to do as they both stared at me.*

*"Mom, Lake and I will find Buddy, and we'll meet you at the car," the girl rushed out as she grabbed my hand and took off running across the playground.*

*We quickly passed swing sets, merry-go-rounds, and jungle gyms, but I never really saw any of it as she pulled me across the park at top speed. We finally* came to a stop near a set of bright blue monkey bars. It looked pretty scary to an eight-year-old so I could only imagine how the younger boy in denim overalls, crouched over in tears, on top of the bars felt. I wondered how and why he got up there. The monkey bars were meant for kids three times his size.

"Buddy!" Willow called out next to me.

"Willow, help me. I can't get down!"

I could see him shaking from where I was standing and felt sorry for the little guy. I turned to his sister expectantly to see what she would do, but she no longer looked like the vibrant girl I met a moment ago. She looked scared. I nudged her, which seemed to break her out of her trance.

"Well?"

"I can't go up there," she whispered softly. Her rosy cheeks paled as she turned to me with wide eyes.

Great, she's scared of heights.

I looked around for their parents and noticed we were surrounded by trees on the far side of the park away from any adult help. I thought for a moment on whether or not to go and get help, but the little boy was near hysterics, and Willow continued to look around nervously.

What was the big deal anyway? The monkey bars weren't that high. I sighed, knowing I was going to be the one to climb the monkey bars and coax her little brother down.

I knew giving her my name meant a really long day. I started forward and grasped the first bar, ready to climb when I heard him.

"Stop."

I froze and immediately looked in the direction of the unknown voice. I was looking into a stranger's eyes for the second time today. These eyes didn't twinkle, though. No... they were dark and reminded me of the thunderstorms I hated so much. They were scary and mean.

Everything about this moment felt different. I was unable to look away from his startling gray eyes. They were taunting me, daring me to look away and risk the consequences.

I didn't, or rather, I couldn't look away, and I didn't know if I wanted to.

I watched him watch me and suddenly, I wanted to know what he thought of me. I needed to know what he saw when he looked at me. I wasn't entirely sure what I saw when I looked at him, but I knew the reaction we were having toward each other wasn't normal. It was too powerful.

He was leaning casually against the ladder on the opposite side from where I began my climb, but his intense stare said this encounter was anything but casual.

I could tell he was around my age or maybe older. His dark shaggy hair fell forward partially shading his eyes because it was slightly longer in the front.

Little rivulets of sweat lined his angular face and sharp cheekbones that were still slightly rounded with youth. A basketball was lying at his feet so I guessed he had just finished playing.

"I want to go home." I heard the sniffled cry from above, snapping me out the trance I was in. I noticed a few other kids now standing around the monkey bars watching Buddy cling to the bars, but no one moved to help.

There was a smaller boy standing close to him who favored him. He was staring at us, watching our silent exchange. Without giving a response or another glance, I continued on, the moment gone, but the awareness very much present. However, I didn't get my foot into the next bar before he stopped me again— this time with a hand on my right leg. His eyes seemed even darker up close. It made me pause.

How did he get over here so fast?

"No," he said this time. It almost sounded like a growl, but that couldn't be right. People don't growl. But apparently, he could, because he continued speaking in the same forceful tone. "He got himself up there, he can get himself down."

What? He was just a little kid, I thought angrily. But then so were we.

"Look, I don't know who you are or what your deal is, but he needs help, and he is going to get it from me. Got it?" I rushed out when I found the courage to speak. Truth be told, he was scaring the crap out of me.

I immediately realized I had made a mistake. But no, it wasn't the shocked sounds from the other kids surrounding us that made me realize my error. It was his hand tightening and the anger growing in his eyes turning them black.

I looked around and saw Willow in the same spot where had I left her. She was chewing on her lip with a worried expression on her face. I assumed it was for her brother, who had stopped crying and instead, watched us with wide eyes.

Still, I yanked my leg free and continued my climb, quickly reaching the top of the monkey bars. I started to move closer to the younger boy waiting for help.

Don't look down.

I should have looked down.

The split second warning as I reached out my hand to Buddy, when his eyes widened in terror, unlike what I witnessed below, didn't prepare me for what *would happen.*

*Something shoved me and then I was falling.*

*Pain unlike anything I had ever known rushed through me, almost blinding me after I hit the concrete below on my left side.*

*I managed to roll over onto my back and look up. Once again, I met his eyes as they watched my tears fall. He no longer seemed so beautiful to me. He looked like the monster I never knew I needed to be afraid of.*

*"I told you I couldn't go up there." It was Willow speaking from somewhere far away. "Keiran wouldn't like it."*

# CHAPTER ONE

TEN YEARS LATER...

"LAKE!" I SNAPPED out of my daydream as the last bell of the day rang, signaling the end of school and my junior year.

I survived.

I knew why, although I didn't dare speak it aloud foolishly, believing the reason would appear suddenly in front me like a dark cloud.

Be for real, Lake.

I looked over at my best friend, who was looking at me with questions in her eyes. I said nothing, gathered my books and stood by the door. Willow finished collecting the many colorful pens she used to take notes in class. That's just Willow. She's flamboyant in everything she does—no exceptions. The rest of the class along with the teacher had already disappeared. Everyone was equally eager for the start of summer. Willow stood and approached the door with the same mischief in her eyes that was present from the very first day we met.

I closed my eyes briefly. *Don't think about that.*

We silently walked to Willow's purple Eclipse in the parking lot. Of course, it was purple, or it wouldn't be Willow. I watched her from my peripheral, waiting for whatever was on her mind to spill out. I knew I wouldn't have to wait long because Willow was a talker. "So did you hear?" she asked as she stopped just outside the driver's side. I waited patiently, but she hesitated to unlock her door as if she didn't want to let me in.

*No*, I pleaded silently. There was only one thing Willow was cautious about with me, or rather, one person. *Don't bring him up. Don't bring him up.* She continued on, completely missing the change in my body language. One would think, after ten years, we could read each other better, or maybe we were just too comfortable to care.

"No, what?" It slowly became harder to breathe. Sometimes I think I enjoy pain, physically and mentally. *Sick right?*

"The Dark Lord of Bainbridge High returns next year." I met her worried gaze. I guess she isn't as oblivious as I thought.

*She's warning me.* Breathe.

I used controlled breathing exercises to keep myself from hyperventilating whenever he was brought up. Ironically, the habit developed *after* he left last year. After years of allowing him to control me out of fear, you would think I would be skipping with joy after he had left.

I finally controlled my breathing and looked up to find her by my side now, rubbing my back soothingly.

"I'm fine," I said only after I was confident my sanity was intact. "Besides, I have all summer to prepare myself along with your slightly illegal antics to distract me," I stated, attempting humor to lighten the mood.

Willow looked away and began chewing her lip. *Okay...*
My heart was beating fast now—too fast.
My breathing was out of control again as I waited for the final blow to my sanity.
"My parents are sending me away this summer...and he's already here."
I died.

\* \* \*

NO, I DIDN'T die, but it was a close second.
I woke up to find the school nurse standing over me, pressing a cool cloth to my forehead. The principal and gym teacher were sitting with a crying Willow in the corner, attempting to console her.
"It's all my fault," she kept repeating as Principal Lawrence hugged her.
"She's awake," Nurse Kelly announced.
Willow rushed forward as everyone turned to me. "I'm sorry, Lake. I shouldn't have said anything!" I gave her a shaky smile but didn't respond. I couldn't in front of them. Principal Lawrence interrupted to say my aunt had been called and was on her way.
*She's going to ask questions.* I quickly sat up, thinking there might have been time to escape. She would want answers I wasn't ready, and never would be ready, to give. I might have escaped if the nurse hadn't nudged me back with a stern look. "I'm fine, really. Willow can drive me home." I gave her what I hoped was a healthy smile.
"Miss Monroe, our policy requires us to notify parents or guardians when incidents such as these occur. We chose not to call an ambulance because you had a strong pulse and began to come around quickly...and then you started talking.

I talked? Oh, no. What did I say? Was it bad?

Principal Lawrence continued to speak, but I'd tuned her out as I wondered what I could have possibly said in near unconsciousness. My mind went through many scenarios in a small space of time. "Miss Monroe, did you hear me?" she asked impatiently.

"I'm sorry, what did you say?" She huffed as if I were wasting her time. I fought the grin tugging at my lips from her mini tantrum. The staff at school sucked, and I didn't care for any of them, but that was mostly because they turned a blind eye to my tormentor and the reign he had over the school. It was too fucked up for words.

"I said we think you should speak to Mrs. Gilmore." I immediately looked at Willow, wondering if she told them anything to make them want to involve the counselor. She immediately shook her head, knowing what I was asking.

So it was bad.

I was saved from answering by my Aunt rushing into the nurse's office, followed by the flustered school secretary. My aunt could be a worrier.

"Lake!" she exclaimed as she bound forward to grab me in a hug. "What happened, why did you faint? Are you okay? Let me look at you. Hold still!"

I never moved an inch, but my aunt was far from rational right now. She would make an incredible mother, but she never had children or a man in her life despite the fact she was beautiful in every way.

She looked a lot like my mom, her sister—blonde with blue eyes, long legs, great body, and personality. She was also one of those Star Trek geeks who liked anything sci-fi. I guess that's why she is a best-selling fantasy fiction author. I was proud.

We grew close after the disappearance of my parents ten years ago, after...well, it happened during that summer. I don't know if they are dead or if they abandoned me. My aunt is adamant my parents would never leave me willingly. It hurt either way. They were *gone*. Just like that, out of thin air. I found out a month after the playground incident. It had been my birthday, and we'd just left the doctor's office after an X-ray for my arm.

I had been unconscious for two days and suffered a broken arm after *he* pushed me off the monkey bars. It was pretty harsh stuff for an eight-year-old. I never said a word, and neither did anyone else. The adults pretty much assumed I fell off trying to help Buddy. I wonder even now how he could hold so much power at a tender age, but I've learned over time, and after years of torture, there was nothing *tender* about him.

Focus.

"Honey, they want you to speak to the school counselor," my aunt said, but it was more of a question than a statement. Despite our closeness, I never told my aunt anything about what happened to me within these halls, outside these halls, in my nightmares, or *in my dreams*. Knowing my aunt, she would move us away, and I couldn't do that. My aunt loves Six Forks. She says it inspires her. *Whatever that means*. I just know I couldn't take that away.

So I endured.

Ten long years of endurance, and then it would be over, and I could finally breathe and finally live without fear, without control, without the desire for the dark and unobtainable.

Yeah, not going there.

Mrs. Gilmore arrived and immediately introduced herself to my aunt and me. I already knew who she was, but we had never crossed paths before. As I said, I've endured.

"Why don't you two follow me to my office so we can talk privately?" I wasn't ready for this, but what could I do? I needed to know what I said while I was unconscious.

"Willow, why don't you go ahead home? Thank you for staying with her, but I'm sure your parents are worried by now," my aunt suggested. I'd forgotten Willow was there. She nodded and smiled nervously at me. I smiled back but didn't have anything to say, at least not with the current party present.

Mrs. Gilmore led the way to her office as we followed silently behind. *You can do this.* We reached her office and went inside. I took a moment to look around. Her office was homey although a bit messy with papers and files strewn everywhere. My hands were itching to straighten up her office or point her in the direction of the nearest office supply store for a better filing system.

We each sat down and just looked at one another, not sure how to proceed. My aunt was the first to speak after a few moments of tense silence. "Principal Lawrence said she talked while she was about to lose consciousness?"

"Right! Yes, people sometimes do as they regain consciousness, but in this case, it was the nature of what was said." It took everything in me not to scream for her to spit it out when she fell silent again. "You said..." The more her cheeks colored, the more dread built in the pit of my stomach. I swallowed deeply and waited. "Well, you said," she continued, "*Master can't come back.*"

Silence.

Complete and utter silence filled the room once more and only I could hear the deafening roar of mortification and feel the room spin. It had grown so quiet you could hear a pin drop... *down the hall. This can't be happening.* I must have repeated that a million times in my head and few times out loud.

But it happened. I knew it did. My body was wound tight, so tight I thought it might break. *Not if my mind did first,* I admitted. My aunt's gaze was locked on the counselor. I knew it wasn't what she was expecting the counselor to say. Neither did I. Mrs. Gilmore clapped a hand over her mouth as if she couldn't believe she had said it either. *Join the club.*

"Are you...are you sure that's what she said?" my aunt asked.

"Ms. Anderson, I understand your doubt as the situation is a tad disturbing," she responded. *Yeah, no kidding.* "But Coach Lyons was quite sure that was what he heard her say."

Coach Lyons was the boys' basketball coach and one of the school's gym teachers. He was also a fan of my tormentor, who also happened to be the team captain until he left last year. I've never had any issues with the man, but he never cared about anything except making sure his star player stayed happy.

"I have to ask...is there any trouble in the home?" My aunt's back straightened at the counselor's question and implication. I guess she didn't know my aunt had a temper when riled, which wasn't often, but when provoked, even I ducked for cover.

"Excuse me? Are you implying I would actually hurt my niece? Are you insane?" she yelled. "Let's go, Lake. My right hand is twitching." She stood up to go, and Mrs. Gilmore quickly tried to recover the situation.

"Ms. Anderson, please. It is only a routine question we have to ask. This doesn't have any personal bearing on your ability as a guardian. Please, sit down," she pleaded.

Aunt Carissa still looked as if she might jump the poor counselor, so I decided to speak up. "Mrs. Gilmore, my aunt is the best parent I could have asked for. There isn't anything she wouldn't do for me. I am completely safe with her." My aunt's expression softened from my reassurance.

Situation saved.

"I didn't think so," the counselor replied. She gave Aunt Carissa an apologetic smile, and we turned to go, but her next question stopped me in my tracks. "One more thing..."

I turned back around to face her again. "Yes?"

"Does this have anything to do with Keiran Masters returning next year?"

# CHAPTER TWO

"I swear I didn't say *anything*," she told me for the hundredth time. I wasn't home long before Willow arrived at my house for details. I wasn't eager to relive the humiliation, but my inquisitive friend wouldn't let me die alone. *Dramatic much?*

I thought back to the moment she asked me about him. I mentally patted myself on the back for the lame excuse I gave Mrs. Gilmore after she dropped that bomb back at her office.

"I don't know what you mean, Mrs. Gilmore. He and I have never had any association with each other. I hardly know him. I must have simply overheated and fainted."

That wasn't entirely untrue. I felt my body warm even now thinking about him. Sometimes it was too much. "I believe you, Willow. You don't have to keep reminding me." I laughed.

She sat up on my bed and stared at me for a moment chewing on her lip again. That meant Willow was thinking, and Willow thinking is *not* a good thing.

"So what are you going to do?" she began. "I mean,

you can't stay in the house all summer, and we have to go back to school in three months."

"I don't know," I answered truthfully. I wasn't foolish enough to think that just because he's been gone for almost a year that the effect won't be the same. Maybe he won't be interested in tormenting me anymore. *I can hope.*

Willow didn't stay much longer and left after assuring herself that I was okay. I welcomed the chance to be alone and prepared to take a shower for the night. My aunt had already gone to bed. I guess she didn't know how to deal with the situation. I could understand. She didn't ask too many questions for which I was grateful.

I gathered my favorite pink sleep shorts with dancing teddy bears and the matching top before heading to the bathroom. Despite my aunt's success, we lived modestly in a three-bedroom, two-bath home. It was two stories high with a nice sized backyard and pool. For my sixteenth birthday, my aunt bought a car for me, but Willow and I carpooled, switching turns every day. We've been inseparable since we met, despite what occurred that day, although I think she feels guilty for some reason.

I gazed at myself in the mirror as if the reason for the past ten years was within the glass. I was tall with too-long legs that made me feel awkward, especially around other girls who were short like Willow.

My blonde hair fell to the middle of my back, and I kept China bangs because of my mom. She always liked my bangs. My eyes were blue, but in the right light, they appeared almost green. My aunt says they're turquoise. I was lean and tone in the right places thanks to yoga. I wasn't much of an outdoor person, so I was kind of pale, but it didn't bother me. Willow liked to joke that I looked like a Barbie ballerina and was such a girl at times.

I didn't know how else to be. I am me. I wasn't perfect though, not even close. I was diagnosed with dyslexia at a young age when it became apparent that I was having trouble learning by text. And to break out of my 'good girl' image, I got a navel ring a few months ago. I convinced Aunt Carissa to let me get one after many weeks of begging. In the end, she agreed because she didn't want to tempt me to sneak off and get one, so she went with me. The silver lucky charm ring that I currently wore was my favorite.

I quickly ended my perusal and hopped in the shower, eager to end my drama-filled day. Who knows... maybe I won't even run into him.

\* \* \*

SOMEONE WAS LAUGHING at my expense. Not literally, but even if they were, I was used to it. "Shit, bro, I'm out of condoms," I heard a voice announce.

I know that voice.

It wasn't *the* voice, but I knew it, and I knew who usually followed. I held my breath, waiting, hoping, *praying* that I wouldn't be caught, that this wouldn't be the aisle. I was in the local pharmacy picking up my favorite shampoo and did a quick look around.

My focus zeroed in on the topic item, and I quickly hurried to grab what I came for, but time and circumstance were not on my side.

Bottles of shampoo and conditioner tumbled down as I knocked my hand across the shelf. It was like a domino effect as I watched them fall, a few bursting open and splattering my legs and sandals. Seriously, who put condoms and shampoo together anyway?

For a moment, I considered leaving them to run

off, but a misstep landed me in the slick mess across the tile just as a tall form turned the corner and entered the aisle. I reluctantly looked up as the younger, more volatile Masters stopped in front of me.

Keenan.

He was almost a replica of my tormentor, except his face didn't hold the same hard lines, giving him a more boyish, youthful appearance his cousin lacked. Sometimes I couldn't believe they were cousins and not brothers. He was gorgeous, if not more than his older cousin was.

Keenan kept his dark hair stylishly spiked and always appeared tousled as if he were constantly running his hands through it. *Or some girl*, I thought wryly. It was no secret Keenan was the school whore even though he was exclusive with Bainbridge's hottest, most popular girl. She was also a cheerleader. They were the typical teenage couple—hot, popular, and shallow.

His eyes zeroed in on me and paused to take in my situation. He was probably thinking up his best one-liner for a girl in distress, but when he recognized me, a malicious grin slowly spread across his face.

Shit.

"Bro, get over here... this is going to top your fucking day," he called out without looking away from me.

I moved to get away, but Keenan decided to taunt me further. "Oh, no, baby. No need to move... you're already in position to greet my cousin properly." His voice was cold and dripping with venom.

I felt my face burn with embarrassment. I was currently bent over on all fours and quickly looked down to use my hair as a shield.

*Run, Lake, just run*, I pleaded with myself, but I was too afraid to move—caught like helpless prey waiting for the predator to sink its teeth in. I was partially surprised at Keenan's words. While he never went out of his way to be nice to me, he usually ignored me. He idolized his cousin, and so Keiran's beef was his, but his reaction toward me just now was new.

Great. Another fan.

Another form, this one taller, suddenly turned the corner and a large pair of black, leather sneakers immediately stopped in front of me. I slowly raised my head. Some unforeseen force had taken control as my will and common sense fled.

My gaze passed over long legs that I could tell were muscular even through the black jeans that hung low on his hips. He was bigger than I remembered—taller and more defined. His body looked hard and lean under a black Five Finger Death Punch T-shirt that hugged his chest and biceps.

Any hope our separation would diminish the effect he had on me had disappeared once I finally met cool gray eyes. He looked the same as he did a year ago except his previous shaggy black hair was now cut short. His jaw was also stronger and his face more angular.

Our first reunited moment told me everything I needed to know—he still hated me. Those beautiful eyes never lied to me. Even when his lips said I was nothing in the past, I had come to know his eyes well.

I couldn't do this. It was too soon.

Maybe if I disappeared quickly, I could escape with my feelings intact. With my new plan in mind, I jumped to my feet, forgetting about the slippery mess under me, and I was falling again. This time, I crashed into his hard body. My humiliation just wouldn't end.

"Oh, look Keiran—she fell for you. Was it love at first sight?" I heard Keenan's snide voice somewhere off to the side.

I closed my eyes, wishing for the ground to open up

and swallow me, but then I felt strong hands grab me. They felt large and heavy against my frame, and I bet, if I looked down, his hands would completely circle my waist.

I sucked in a breath, prepared for him to shove me away in disgust or anger, but it never came. Confused, I chanced a look up at his face. He was standing at least six inches taller, the top of my head reaching just under his chin. My hands were planted lightly on his chest while I stared up at him.

The simmering heat in his eyes threatened to boil over and made me think he was having the same reaction I was. But that couldn't be right. Not when he despised the very fact that I even breathed. I know because he told me so almost every day for the last ten years.

There was anger in his eyes, but there was also...confusion? I could understand my own because we've never been this close, never before touched like this. I could smell his scent as it washed over me—strong, male... virile. It was an aphrodisiac. His eyes lowered with what could be mistaken for lust, but I knew better. This was the beginning of a verbal attack. I recognized the signs over the years.

He leaned closer, his hands tightening around me while he inhaled deeply. "Fuck," he growled, speaking for the first time since he entered the aisle and came back into my life. His voice caused my body to tremble as always. Or was I just shaking in fear? I couldn't tell the difference.

Keiran turned his head to his cousin, still holding onto me. "Leave," he directed to him. Keenan slowly straightened off the shelf he was leaning against and left with a smirk.

He watched his cousin walk down the aisle until he turned the corner, and only then did he turn his gaze back to me, letting it pass over my body slowly. He looked as if he'd been starving and I was his feast.

Definitely not ready for this.

He looked around quickly, but no one else was around. The only employee in the store was probably still outside smoking a cigarette, I thought grimly.

Suddenly, he flipped me around until I was pressed against the shelf. I froze, but then came to my senses and tried to push myself off, but he was quicker. He grabbed my hands with one of his larger hands, bringing them up over my head. I felt his chest press against my back as he leaned in close to my ear.

"I've had a lot of time to think about what I would do once I caught you alone."

I tried once again to free myself, anger rising as he held me against my will... In a *pharmacy*, of all places. I've allowed Keiran to torment me over the years, but I promised myself I would never allow him to touch me or physically hurt me again.

His arm wrapped around my waist as I continued to struggle, frustration building inside me as he locked my body to his. I finally found the courage to speak. "Let me go or I'll scream," I threatened. He chuckled, but I had the feeling he didn't find the situation humorous.

"Yeah?" he taunted. "Scream and I promise you I will make your life a living hell. The shit I've done to you before was child's play. I can give you much worse and shatter your perfect, porcelain world, and you will know real pain. Scream."

The force of his threat shook my body, his words coming out viciously, and I felt his grip tighten further. I hoped I wouldn't find bruises in the morning.

"What do you want?" I asked although, I was pretty sure I knew what it was.

This wasn't everyday bullying. He was after something.

So I waited, anticipating his response. I felt his body tense right before he flipped me around to face him again, our bodies now aligned while he still held on tight.

"I've watched you…" He leaned closer, our lips touching lightly in an almost kiss. I felt a warm hand slide beneath my dress and stop just before my thigh. I suppressed a moan, surprised at the quick reaction of my traitorous body. "I've watched you, and I've studied you," he began again, breathing deeply. "I memorized you. I know what makes you hurt… I know what makes you sad… I know what makes you cry. And all your deepest fears, I *will* know. I'll take your so-called strengths, and I'll make them your weaknesses."

If Keiran scared me before, he terrified me now, I admitted to myself as a tear burned a hot trail down my face.

"I've got a whole year with you," he stated, finally releasing me. I slowly slid down to the floor, my legs too weak to hold me up. "I'm going to break you. But most importantly, I'm going to make you pay."

\* \* \*

10 YEARS AGO

"I HATE YOU," he whispered.

I was tugged to the ground by the pretty ballerina bun that my aunt helped me do that morning. My hair fell around my shoulders, and I cried out in pain when he stepped on my hand. "B—but why?" I could barely speak through the sobs and trembles that wracked my body.

"Shut up and stop crying. You'll get me in trouble if someone hears... you don't want me to hurt you, do you?"

I shook my head and looked up at him fearfully. He wasn't that much taller, but to me, he seemed like a giant. Maybe since I was sitting on the floor because of him.

I had just come out of language class. I was distracted by the bad marks I had received on my essay about what makes me happy. I guess Mrs. Peterson didn't like that I wasn't happy... not anymore. Not since my parents disappeared. Every day I had hoped it would be the day they would come to rescue me.

Maybe they're lost, I thought. Mommy said she would 'see me soon' when she left so she had to come back. Mommies were supposed to keep promises, always.

Not long after my parents failed to show up, Aunt Carissa decided to enroll me in the local school. My first day was today, and all day, I'd been wondering about the mean boy who pushed me off the monkey bars. Earlier, I had seen him again for the first time during recess. Our eyes met across the play area, and I knew he recognized me. The empty look in his eyes filled with hatred when he saw me. Just as he started forward, the bell rang, and I practically ran for safety. I wasn't expecting to see him again so soon, but he found me. Little did I know, this would become our ritual.

"Why are you still here," he asked scornfully.

"My—my parents didn't come get me yet." I felt a fresh set of tears forming when I thought about how much I missed them.

His eyes narrowing caught my attention, pushing aside thoughts of my parents. "Why?"

"I don't know. Ma—maybe they're lost?" I don't

know why I was asking him, but a small sign of hope would help me feel better.

"Maybe they're dead." He snickered.

"Don't say that!" I shouted and balled up my free fist. He watched my fists clench tighter with mocking eyes.

"I bet they're dead," he taunted further.

"No," I moaned.

"Or they left you behind..." My shirt was now stained with my tears as they released from me uncontrollably. "Jeez, you're just like her," he said with an annoyed tone. He frowned and kicked my hand away with his foot in disgust.

"Who am I like?"

He ignored my question and his frown deepened, making him looking meaner. "I'm going to do it one day, you know," he prompted in a hateful tone.

"Do what?" I asked shakily. His fists balled as he stared down at me with angry eyes. I suddenly got the feeling that I needed to get away, so I started to back away from him. I scooted across the floor while he followed after me.

"I'm going to kill you. Just like I killed her. It's the only way."

\* \* \*

OVER THE YEARS, Keiran would remind me of his promise. He'd unleash his subtle threats on me to scare me and it always worked. Keiran could always get inside my head with little effort. Willow called it a mind fuck. I called it torture.

I turned into my driveway on autopilot. My mind still couldn't define what had just occurred at the pharmacy.

He touched me.

I foolishly hoped for the past year that he would move on... or not come back at all. My heart lurched at the thought of never seeing him again even when I knew it wasn't possible. He still had to finish his senior year that he also thinks I stole from him.

I was sick and disgusted with myself for feeling the way I do for someone who hates me almost violently. I was too afraid to ask at the time what he was planning to do, but I didn't need to. Keiran was dangerous enough, but when provoked...

I shook off the thought and briefly considered telling my aunt about Keiran. I wasn't sure I could handle him like this, but I didn't know how far his hatred ran so I couldn't involve her.

I felt well and truly isolated.

I entered the house and called out for my aunt. She gave a hollow answer in return, and I knew what time it was. I found her in the living room watching re-runs of Sons of Anarchy. I think she had a thing for Charlie Hunnam.

She and Willow did some serious drooling whenever he came on the screen. I had to admit his rugged swagger was sexy. He reminded me of someone dark-haired, ruthless, and hotter.

I flopped down on the sofa next to her and looked at the clock. It was just after noon on a Saturday, and I had nothing exciting planned. Willow had left the week before for an eight-week summer college program. My girl was focused—quirkiness and all.

"Lake, you know you can talk to me about anything, don't you?" she asked without taking her eyes off the screen.

*I knew this was coming.* "Yes, I know, Aunt Carissa." We still haven't discussed what happened at school.

I was glad she wasn't looking at me. If I met her eyes, all the pain and heartache of the last ten years would come pouring out.

"Do you want to talk about him?" I whipped my head around to face her unable to hide my reaction.

"Him?" I asked in a shaky voice.

"Keiran Masters. The counselor from school mentioned him." The look she gave me let me know that she didn't buy my story about heat exhaustion, but I couldn't tell her the truth either. My aunt wasn't ready to hear about what Keiran had done to me over the years. It was still a hard pill to swallow each time I would remember. "Lake, I trust you," she continued when I didn't answer and the silence grew thick with tension, "I just wish you could trust me."

She got up and walked away, and I immediately felt like crap. She thought I didn't trust her, but that couldn't be farther from the truth. I didn't want this. I didn't want to hurt her, but I had to protect her.

Who will protect me?

# CHAPTER THREE

SUMMER PASSED WITHOUT any more run-ins with Keiran. Six Forks was a good size town, but I must admit, part of the reason was because I had hid out in my house for the past two months. Willow was wrong. I could hide, so I did. But now it was the first day of school, and I couldn't hide anymore.

*Senior year*, I thought jubilantly. Senior year meant the last step, taking me closer to moving on and escaping the fear I lived in every single day. He didn't come looking for me, and I assumed, once again, it was a tactic to scare me. After all, he'd promised to kill me for ten years now.

My phone beeped signaling I had a text message. I checked my phone seeing that it was Willow: Don't come outside!

I stared down at my phone, puzzled. Willow being weird was normal, but why wouldn't she want me to come outside? I walked over to the window to see what the reason was and nearly fainted when I looked out the window. The way my heart was pounding caused me to drop my phone. I did not expect what I saw.

He was leaning against his blacked out muscle car and looking very much like the typical bad boy in black cargo pants and a dark gray, short-sleeved button-up that probably matched his eyes.

How did he know where I lived?

I'm sure it wouldn't be hard to find where I lived, but why would he come here? This was too close to home. *No pun intended.* Willow was standing by her car as well, eyeing Keiran warily. My gaze was fixed on him, debating what I should do, when suddenly he turned his head and looked straight up at me through my bedroom window. I jumped back immediately and tried to calm my racing heart and the somersaults my stomach performed.

I weighed all my options, hiding being the most desirable possibility, but I knew I couldn't leave Willow out there alone with him. He never terrorized her or anyone else but me, but what would he do if I didn't come out? I knew he wouldn't just go away. It was obvious that he came here for something. I made a decision and grabbed my backpack and headed downstairs. He made me a prisoner in my home the entire summer, but I couldn't hide out here any longer and he knew that.

I reached the door and stepped outside, feeling as if I was on death row and this was my final walk. I reluctantly walked over to him but only close enough to talk to him without Willow overhearing. As I drew closer, I admitted there was something dangerously irresistible about him. It drew me in even when I wanted to run away. If only I could figure out why…

"Why are you here?" I asked before I lost my nerve.

His eyes lazily traveled over me in a way that made me feel both insignificant and naked. I was wearing white jeans and a dark red top that hugged my torso and flowed to my waist. The top made me feel feminine and sexy. I knew I was making a statement when I put it on. I just wasn't sure what I was trying to say.

He used both hands to push off his car, the momentum bringing his chest to mine all too quickly. I sucked in a breath and felt my body shudder just as it did in the pharmacy when he first touched me.

"Lose the girl," he said loud enough for Willow to hear. It took a moment for me to realize what he said because my mind and body had both shut down in submission.

"But she's my ride to school," I answered.

"Get rid of her," he repeated. The look on his face warned me not to argue.

I reluctantly turned to Willow, who was openly glaring at Keiran. I never told her about the incident at the pharmacy. She'd only been back for a week now, and it was an unspoken agreement between us that Keiran was a taboo subject. Not only that, but Willow seemed different since she'd been back. She was still my Willow, but I knew something happened over the summer. I was fond of looking into people's eyes. They told more than the lips ever could—they told the truth. Willow's eyes had changed. They held something that I didn't recognize, but they also held something mine did—pain.

"Will, I'm going to drive to school today. I'm sorry you came all the way here for nothing." I gave her a small smile, hoping to reassure her.

"Lake, we live less than a mile apart and your house is on the way to school. What's going on?" I could hear the suspicion in her voice.

"Nothing, I just have stuff I need to take care of immediately after school. I'll see you in class, okay?" She caught the look I sent her to drop it, so she huffed and got into her car after sending Keiran another glare.

I waited until she disappeared down the street before I rounded on Keiran. "Please don't do this," I immediately begged.

"Get in the car," he ordered. I blinked up at him a few times to process the idea of me in Keiran's car... alone... with him.

"Thanks, but I can drive myself to school."

There was no way I was getting into that car with him. We would be too close—breathing the same air. I was already painfully aware of him from a distance. I didn't need to torture myself.

I dismissed him by turning back and heading for my car. I guess that's how I ended up over his shoulder and tossed into his car the next moment. He was in the car before I could right myself. While reaching for the handle, I heard, "I don't have the patience, Monroe." He snapped the words out harshly, and I quickly ditched my plan to make a run for it.

*Oh God, he's going to kill me*—kill me and toss my body in a river. *I seriously watch too much Law & Order.* I can see the words on my headstone now:

*She lived a miserable life full of fear*
*and abandonment issues. Maybe it's good she's dead.*
*After all, this was all we could give her.*

"Listen, I know what happened a year ago, and I know how it looked, but I'm telling you, I had nothing to do with you being arrested!" I yelled, uncaring that I just raised my voice at Keiran freaking Masters. My fate was already sealed.

He didn't reply, but I could see a muscle tick in his jaw as he pulled out of the driveway making my nervousness increase tenfold. Six Forks has a lot of wooded areas, secluded so no one could hear my screams. We

were driving for about ten minutes. All th~B.B. REID
holding my breath. We reached one of the six ıc was
the road that made up the town. I was near panickin&
when he turned down the road leading *away* from the
school.

Oh, God. Oh, no... Shit!

"Let me out," I was visibly shaking now. "Let me
out... let me out of the fucking car!" I screamed as we
headed down a long road that led to nothing but more
trees.

He parked when we were out of sight and shut off
the car. He ignored my tantrum as he got out of the car,
heading around to my side. I frantically grabbed my
phone from my bag to call for help while cursing my
stupidity for getting into the car with him in the first
place. He ripped open the door, grabbed both of my
arms, and slammed me up against the side of the car.

"I'm going to make this quick and I'm going to say
this only once because something tells me your little
friend won't hesitate to call the police if you take too
long to show, so listen up." I just stared up at him wondering if this was really happening. "You framed me—"

"I swear it wasn't me..."

He quickly wrapped a hand around my throat in
warning. "You're done talking," he sneered. It was more
a statement than a question. I looked away as the intensity of his stare burned through me. "Eyes on me." He
refused to make this easy for me. "I have a score to settle and it directly involves you and *only* you."

I felt his thumb rub my neck softly, but he dropped
his hand as quickly as it happened leaving me wondering if it really did.

"You won't make a move without my knowing. Any
time you eat, drink, or *breathe*, I will know." I stared at
him as if he'd grown two heads. "Every moment is

*EAR* your thoughts, your hopes, your dreams are all *me*. I will always know where you are and what you are doing. You are *mine*... at least for the next year." He smirked.

"Who do you think you are?" I asked, my anger overriding my fear. Of everything he could have done, I never expected this. It sounded like slavery. I still didn't understand why he didn't kill me and get it over with. He's been playing this cat and mouse game for years.

"I am the guy whose freedom you stole." The clipped tone of his voice cut into my nerves. I could tell from the tick in his jaw that he was losing control. "For an entire year, my free will was taken from me and you *will* feel how I felt."

I still didn't understand what he was asking for and what purpose he would need to take away my freedom. He wanted control, that much was apparent, but he wanted something else, too. I could see it in the burning heat in his eyes.

"What do you want?" I swallowed back the fear and ignored the dread settling in the pit of my stomach.

"You and I both know what it is that I want." I shook my head in denial though I was starting to have a clue. I had nothing else that he could possibly want, but the look in his eyes was unmistakable.

He stepped closer and placed his forearms on either side of my head, resting them on the hood of his car. My back was pressed against the door, and I was caged in by his hard body and drowning in the cool smell of his body wash. His tall body blocked everything beyond him from my view so I could see nothing but his broad chest.

"I want the one thing that is keeping you so fucking innocent. I've wanted it for a long time, Monroe, and you are going to give it to me."

"And if I refuse?" I looked up into his eyes that were almost black with lust. He didn't really expect to... Did he? His smile was sinister and completely without humor. My heart began hammering against my chest, and my stomach twisted up into a tight ball of tension.

"Submit to me... or your aunt will disappear just like your parents did."

\* \* \*

HE'D DO IT. I knew he would. I didn't know how, but I knew. A shiver ran through me as I entered the school in a daze. I thought of Keiran as a bully—nothing more, nothing less. But now I knew there was something far darker below the surface waiting to come out.

And I was the dumb twit who released it.

*He never actually said he would kill her. But what else could he mean?* He would kill my aunt if I didn't give him what he wanted. I thought back to our conversation on the way to school.

"Why are you doing this?" I forced the question out. Did I really want to know?

"What would stop you from framing me again, this time putting me away for life? I hate you, but you know that already, and I don't trust you, so I need to keep an eye on you." I closed my eyes against the confession that he hated me. Yes, I did know, but hearing him say it was more painful.

"You could just leave me alone," I suggested.

He looked amused as he said, "That's not going to happen. You still have something I want."

I walked down the hallway in silence, unsure of what to do next. Keiran was out of my league and too big of an enemy for me to fight and win. I thought back to 'her'—*she* was the one he'd killed. She was the reason

I was afraid now. But who was *she?* Did she die because she fought back? These were the questions that have run rampant in my mind for ten years. It was the reason I lived willingly in the dark shadow of his hatred.

"Give me your phone." I nearly jumped out of my skin at the sudden sound of his voice behind me. I was so lost in my thoughts that I completely forgot he was following behind me. Keiran wasn't a person to easily forget, but it was also fair to say he had me out of sorts.

I dug my phone out and handed it over. When I looked up, I caught him staring down where my hand disappeared to in my back pocket. I cleared my throat, but he took his time shifting his gaze from my ass when I held out my phone.

He finally looked up and stared at me unapologetic as he took my phone. His eyes were heated, and I saw the blatant lust as I felt a flush spread over my body. Nothing about today was normal. Was it really possible to desire someone you hated?

"Why isn't your phone locked with a security code?"

"Oh, I... don't have much activity through my phone," I stated sheepishly. I only had Willow and Aunt Carissa as constants in my life... there was no one else, and he knew that.

He stared at me for a moment before looking back at my phone. He was taking his time, so I got the impression he was searching through it. *What was he looking for?* I heard a vibration after a few minutes then he pulled out his phone and silenced it.

"Why do you still have Peter Simpson's contact information? Any contact or *relationship,*" he sneered, "you have with him ends today. Make this the last time I tell you."

"I haven't even spoken to him in a year since you—"

I stopped when I realized he was ignoring me and remained silent while he finished invading the privacy of my phone. There were a few other numbers in my phone from guys I had saved out of politeness, but never used. It wasn't until after Keiran went away that any guy would show me any attention and even then, only in complete secrecy.

Once word got around that Keiran was coming back, the offers stopped. I even had a few guys ask me to delete their number those last few days of school. I didn't understand why, but now I had the feeling it was because they were afraid of Keiran. But why would Keiran care about guys asking me out? He wouldn't care enough to do something premeditated.

"What's your first class?" he asked, handing my phone back.

"English IV with Mrs. Connors."

"Let's go. We're late. He walked in the direction of the senior hallway.

"No shit, Sherlock," I mumbled. He turned his head slightly as if he heard but turned back without saying a word. I breathed in relief I had escaped my slip-up unscathed.

I reached the classroom twenty minutes late much to the displeasure of the teacher. She shot me an annoyed look before motioning for me to take a seat. The other students seemed to be focused on me a little too hard, and I wondered what had their attention.

I shrugged it off and sat down in the first empty seat at a table next to a guy whose name I think was Josh. That's when I realized Keiran was right behind me. I never considered we might have the same class considering he missed his senior year.

*So that was what had the other kids' attention.* Keiran and I had apparently entered the classroom *to-*

*gether.* I nervously looked around and could see a few of them speed texting while others continued to stare. I knew by the end of the period the whole school would know about what should have been an insignificant and ordinary piece of information, not gossip. Only day one and there was already a rumor spread about me.

Great.

I was taking out my notebook when I felt Keiran's hand grab the back of my neck and lift me, none too discreetly or gentle, from the seat. He then grabbed my backpack and marched me to the back of the classroom where two empty seats were. The teacher, of course, was oblivious to his manhandling because her back was turned to the board.

The medium-sized tables were two-seaters and seemed intimate now that I knew it would be ours. I never imagined us ever sharing anything.

"Unless Mr. Masters and Ms. Monroe are teaching the class, please face the front and do try to pay attention," Mrs. Connors huffed out when she turned to find that the other students attention were fixed on us rather than her lesson.

The entire class was sneaking peeks at us until Keiran leaned forward from his sprawled position to rest his forearms on the table to shoot them all warning glares, and suddenly, they were all scrambling to turn around. It was the one time I was grateful for his power within the school. I didn't want the attention, especially when it involved Keiran.

I felt my phone vibrate with a text from Willow: Tell me the rumors aren't true! What is going on?? You and Keiran?!

Willow's social status was not much better than mine was. Although she didn't have an enemy like Keiran, if the news had already reached her that meant the entire school already knew. I looked up at the clock—five minutes.

That's got to be a record.

I started to type out my response when Keiran deftly plucked my phone out of my hand, checking the message before pocketing it. I gaped at him. *He just took my phone!*

"Ms. Monroe, please pay attention. If you cannot, I will have you removed from the class," the teacher announced. I heard snickers around the class mainly from a few of the popular girls sitting together in front of us.

My embarrassment doubled when Keiran shot the teacher a look that had the color draining from her face. She fumbled over herself and then resumed teaching the class. *Whoa, the teachers are afraid of him, too?* That didn't give me much hope for enlisting help. I wondered who else was afraid of him.

The rest of class passed without much excitement, and I was surprised to find Keiran was actually studious. He took notes although he didn't engage in any of the discussion. I didn't either, but then again, I never really did. I had conditioned myself to stay hidden at all times even when he wasn't around. It was a messed up way to live, but he left me no choice.

\* \* \*

BY THE END of English, I was eager for my next period, which was physical education. I was pretty sure I wouldn't have a class with Keiran because athletes weren't required to take physical health and with Keiran playing for the basketball team again he is excused. The schools made physical education a yearly requirement at all levels as a way to promote health awareness.

He stopped me before I could walk off for my next

FEAR ME

class and said, "Let me see your schedule." I handed him the card, and he scanned it before handing it back to me. He then grabbed my chin and raised my face to his to stare down into my eyes. "You tell no one about this, not even your friend." I looked away from him defiantly, but he only gripped my face tighter. "Don't test me on this, Monroe. You won't like the consequences."

I nodded then asked, "Can I have my phone back?"

He looked as if he wanted to refuse, but then he dug my phone out of his pocket and handed it over. He followed me all the way to the gym where I had volleyball. I was looking forward to it for two reasons. Willow and I enjoyed the game, so we decided to take it together, and Keiran wouldn't be there. The only downside was there were only females in this class, and every one of them was in love in Keiran. I headed for the locker rooms to get changed. As I was storing my phone in an empty locker, I noticed I had a message:

Behave.

I frowned at the cryptic message until I read the name or rather the initial 'K.' He must have gotten my number when he was digging through my phone earlier. I wondered for a moment what I should say before I decided not to respond and tossed my phone into the locker. I changed into my gym uniform while cursing my current predicament and myself.

"All right, you, cough up the good stuff and no funny business, capiche?" I couldn't help but laugh at the bad impersonation of a mobster and turned to face my best friend...who was *actually* holding a toy gun.

Her antics never stop.

"Hey, who's holding the gun here? No laughing." I stifled my laugh and waited for her to continue.

"Now a little birdie tells me you and the dark lord showed up to class this morning and were making cute

and cuddly in the back of the class. Tell me my Intel made a mistake. I don't want to have to off any tops if you know what I mean, but I have to protect my interests. You are one of my best, Don Lake."

To someone who didn't know Willow, they might think she was just clowning around, but I heard the message loud and clear. She was scared for me and wanted me to remember I'm her best friend, and she was there for me if I needed help.

I wanted to confide in her, but I knew Keiran's threat wasn't exclusive to my aunt... He would use anyone I loved to get to me. I couldn't let that happen, so I just hugged her to me. Willow and I were like sisters where it counted and could feel each other's pain. I let a tear fall as we embraced.

"Lake, you can't keep secrets from me. You have to be honest! Tell me what's going on with you," she sobbed and broke down in frustration.

"You first..."

# CHAPTER FOUR

I FINISHED THE game with an over aggressive spike that had some of the other girls raising an eyebrow, but so what? We won the match. Most of my anger was coming from the fact Willow wasn't speaking to me. She even chose an opposing team, which was huge for us. We did everything together, and now it felt as if there was a wedge driven between us. I couldn't lose my only friend, but I also couldn't believe she was hiding something but wanted *me* to bare my demons. I shook my head in frustration. *What the hell happened to her this summer?*

I now had confirmation that something was wrong. She closed up after I hinted that she was keeping secrets. Willow was an open book—a free spirit. She knew who she was and wasn't afraid to show the world. Unlike me. I hid. After showering, I rushed to catch up with Willow, who had finished before me and left without saying a word. We had lunch period together this year, but I didn't know if she would show up since we normally avoided that area.

When I rounded a corner, my mouth took a

nosedive, and I blinked just to make sure I wasn't hallucinating. Willow's lips were freaking attached to a tall, muscular guy. He had a strong arm wrapped around her waist while a large hand palmed the back of her head as he devoured her lips like a starved man. They were oblivious to my presence and continued to feast on each other, so I stepped back around the corner to give them privacy. When I heard a low masculine groan, I peeked around to watch them again. His hand was lowering to grab her ass and lift her into his groin. She moaned, which seemed to make him hungrier.

Willow had the body of a siren that could bring men to their knees—all voluptuous and womanly, but she always griped that she needed to lose weight. If she saw the lustful stares that she often got, especially when she wore her unusual getups, she wouldn't feel that way. She was a knockout.

"Wait," Willow softly protested. He only pulled her tighter, unwilling to let her go. She looked so small in his arms. "No!" She tore her mouth away, gasping for breath. "I told you I can't do this anymore. It was a mistake." When she pulled away, my mouth dropped along with my heart now sitting in the pit of my stomach. I pulled my head back around the corner to regain myself and prevent a mental meltdown. *It couldn't be him. She wouldn't...*

"A mistake?" he asked, sounding amused. "What was? When I fucked you or when you fucked me back?"

"Don't, please," she pleaded, causing me to peek back around the corner.

"Why not? What we shared was real, our whole summer was *real*."

"I won't be your play thing. That's all you want."

He growled in frustration and took a menacing step forward crowding her against the lockers. "How the *fuck* would you know what I want? You don't even know me."

"You're right. I don't know you," she spoke firmly. "And I don't trust you."

"I don't care," he barked. "I get what I want." He left the warning hanging as he stalked away.

What a douche.

I wanted to comfort a sobbing Willow even though I felt sick and was angry with her. I couldn't tell her who to date, but then I never thought it would be with the enemy. Regardless, I knew I had to be there for her. We could talk about what I saw later. I stepped forward, ready to console my friend, but was suddenly hauled back by an arm that felt like steel wrapped around my waist. My back felt the impact of the hard chest, and I was held arrested, my body molding to the muscular body holding me hostage.

"What are you doing?" Keiran's harsh voice spoke into my neck. I didn't see or hear him approach so I assumed he must have come up from the other hallway.

"I was just—" I stopped when I felt his other arm wrap around me. His face was still buried in my neck as he brought me close like a lover would. Despite my shock at how natural it felt to be in his arms, I closed my eyes, relishing the moment and forgetting who we were and what this was.

This wasn't reality. It was a fantasy. It felt too good to be real. All it took was one wrong move and this fantasy would quickly turn into my worst nightmare. His lips brushed my neck, and his thumb swept under my shirt to caress my stomach, making butterflies erupt.

"If you try anything, you will be sorry," he whispered. The malice in his voice was like a bucket of ice water thrown in my face, and suddenly, the feeling of his hands and lips on me felt like the kiss of death.

"Let me go," I demanded. I was angry, but I wasn't sure exactly what made me angrier. He shoved me away and when I almost fell, I glared at him, but his back was already turned as he walked away as quietly as he'd come. I followed behind at a slower pace so I could recover from the last five minutes. *Fucking hell.*

\* \* \*

THE CAFETERIA WAS alive with upperclassmen milling around in various cliques. I usually avoided the cafeteria, choosing to spend lunch in the library or anywhere Keiran wouldn't be. It was usually his routine to torture me either at the very start or at the end of the day and to ignore me during the middle. Still, I thought it was safe to be invisible during that time just in case he ever felt extra sadistic.

I chased around answers for why Willow wouldn't tell me about this summer as I looked around for her. When I didn't immediately see her, I knew it meant I would have to risk going further. With Keiran out for my head, I was more on edge than ever. All morning, I'd been wondering if he was actually serious about taking my virginity for revenge. At least...that's what I thought he was saying.

The idea that Keiran desired me sexually when he hated me so fiercely was impossible to believe. He has to be using sex as a way to humiliate me. It wasn't about desire. It couldn't be.

I circled the entire cafeteria looking for Willow when I realized whose table I was unknowingly approaching, and before I could avoid it, our eyes connected, and I suddenly got the feeling he had been watching me the entire time. I quickly turned around to head back in the opposite direction.

"Stop."

I froze on the spot. The sound of his command took me back ten years to the playground where I first laid eyes on him. I slowly turned back around to face him and his table of mindless followers.

"Have a seat," he ordered and pushed out the chair in front of him with his long leg.

"You seriously don't mean for her to sit here, do you? But we hate her." The catty girl currently sitting on Keiran's lap and staring daggers at me was Anya Risdell—head cheerleader and all-around bitch. *I'm sorry, was that mean?*

"Yes, I mean here. If you have a problem with it, you can go sit at another table," he replied coldly without taking his eyes off me.

I was still standing a few steps away, thinking of a way to get out of entering further into the lion's den. When his eyes flickered from me to the chair and back, I reluctantly sat down in the designated chair, letting my displeasure show. He looked only a second away from causing a scene, and I remembered all too well the last time he caused a scene in the cafeteria. *Don't go there.*

I felt numerous eyes staring at us curiously. Keenan was sitting at the table along with their other friend, Quentin, who they called Q. He was a lot like Keiran— silent and brooding. He never really had much to say and sort of moved in silence. No one had ever seen him with a girl on his arm either, and so there was a quiet rumor around school that he might be gay. *People are idiots.*

A couple of other guys and girls were sitting at the table as well, but they were all jocks and cheerleaders. *Give me a break.* Sheldon Chambers, Keenan's girl-friend, was at the table as well. She seemed to be the only person not giving me hostile looks. Instead, she was looking at me curiously from her seat next to Keenan.

"Who were you looking for?" Keiran asked breaking me out of my inner musings.

"No one."

He became eerily silent as he watched me from lowered lids. His face looked like it was carved out of stone as he clenched his jaw muscles. "Is that a lie?"

"No," I lied again. I didn't owe him an explanation of anything I did.

"We'll see," he replied smoothly, but I heard the threat in his words and saw the promise in his eyes. I knew I had made a big mistake by lying, but it was too late to do anything about that now. My mind was occupied with Willow and what I had heard just minutes before.

Sometimes, I wondered if his empty threats were just that—empty. But the look in his eyes would always warn me that they weren't. *So what held him back?* I had been enduring his tricks and torments for ten years. It wasn't anything I couldn't handle with only a year left and my freedom right around the corner. I was going to make it.

"So, Lake. How do you like the fact that Keiran is back? I'm sure he has a lot of catching up to do with you. I can't wait," Anya cackled, and her robotic friends laughed with her.

"I don't think he'll have much time to do anything if he's too busy using you. I heard it was his favorite hobby." There were a few muffled laughs and snickers around the table from the guys, and Anya turned a deep shade of red.

Normally, I would just ignore Anya, but the frustration of dealing with Willow and Keiran this morning had me a bit touchy. Looking away, I discreetly texted Willow for the third time. I had to think of a way to get out of here and away from the firing squad.

When I returned my attention back to the people at the table, I noticed Anya was still glaring at me. I met her stare and lifted an eyebrow in mock challenge. Her lip curled as she leaned forward and spoke words I definitely wished I could have slapped right back down her throat. "Didn't you and Jesse Fitzgerald have a thing last year? I mean, you two were pretty cozy for a while, but who could blame you. He was a major hottie. So what happened to that? You finally get a boyfriend and couldn't keep him?"

The table grew deathly still as silence descended after Anya's question. A few guys shifted in their seats and looked at Keiran nervously, which was weird because *I* was the one he was looking at like he wanted to kill. I avoided his gaze and looked down at the empty space on the table.

Jesse was the only other person I could have ever called a friend. He was a military brat who moved here with his family after Keiran left. After a month or so of school, we crossed paths when I'd been stuck in the mud after a hard rain swept through Six Forks. I was having bad reception and couldn't call my aunt for help or a tow truck and no one was around. I stood there for maybe fifteen minutes trying to get a signal when I heard the rumble of a bike pull up next to me. I remembered looking into the second most beautiful set of eyes I'd ever seen. They didn't give me the familiar jolt that Keiran's did, though. I instantly recognized him as the new kid, but he was more than that, too.

Jesse had quickly ascended the ranks at Bainbridge and had an endless supply of girls chasing him, so when he befriended me, it nearly caused an uproar within the school. People constantly tried warning him away, including me, but he never paid any attention. Pretty soon, a rumor started that Jesse and I were an item, but it couldn't be further from the truth. We were hanging out often and managed to grow close when his father was suddenly deployed. His mother felt better being closer to family, so they moved back north halfway through the year. I had him for six months and then he was gone.

"Hey, Keiran, listen, man, we were going to tell you—" one of the guys spoke up. Before he could finish, a fight between two guys broke out on the other side of the cafeteria. Chairs and tables were flipped over as a stampede formed to get a closer look, quickly turning the cafeteria into a stadium.

Just then, Willow walked through the door with wide eyes and looked around. When she saw me, her eyes grew larger, and she rushed over to me.

"Gosh, Lake. I'm mad at you for five seconds, and you try to commit suicide." The group at the table took one look at her in her dark green overalls and lopsided bow and erupted into laughter, but she didn't spare any of them a glance. "Let's get out of here," she said taking my hand. I didn't waste any time arguing and jumped up from my seat before Keiran could stop me again.

* * *

"SO WHAT HAPPENED this morning when Keiran took off with you? That was scary." We sat down in our seats, waiting for our French class to start after hiding out for the rest of lunch period. I'd been looking over my shoulder ever since Anya dropped the bomb and I had run away from him.

"Willow, I told you I needed to drive to school—"

"You forget people talk, right? Especially, when it involves Keiran, so try again."

I took a deep breath and thought of what to say. Willow was pissed I had just lied to her, but what could I do? I couldn't tell her the truth.

"Oh, you know... he just wanted to start the year off traditionally. I'm sorry, Willow. I just didn't want you to worry." That much was the truth at least.

She stared at me before shaking her head and pulling out her usual assortment of colored pens. I needed to change the subject and fast.

"I'm also sorry for accusing you of keeping secrets. Whatever is wrong, you can come to me when you're ready. I won't pressure you. Best friend?" I wasn't really sorry for wanting to know what was going on with my best friend, but I wasn't willing to hurt her over it.

She looked at me with relief on her face, and I felt like an ass. "Best friend," she relented. "I'm sorry too, Lake. I've been a butt. Hey, want to do something later? I have to work tonight, but we can see a movie tomorrow night."

"Sounds great. How did Pepé take you being gone all summer?" Pepé was Willow's ferret that she named after the cartoon skunk Pepé le Pew.

"I still can't get him to play with me. The little shit sure can hold a grudge. He just gives me the stink eye. It kind of reminds me of the she-witch, Anya." I laughed. I never believed an animal, especially a ferret, really had personalities, but Pepé certainly was a character. "So...are you and Keiran really dating?" she asked.

I hesitated, feeling like I was suddenly under a microscope. Willow knew all about Keiran believing I framed him. I still haven't told her about the pharmacy, and I couldn't tell her about his threat.

"As if Keiran would really date you. Unbelievable." Willow and I looked up to find Anya and her posse standing over us.

"Oh, no, it's the hussies of Bainbridge High," Willow retorted.

I choked back a laugh. "Is there something we can help you with, Anya?"

"Yeah, stay away from my boyfriend." She shifted her hip and smacked her overly glossed lips. "Keiran doesn't want you, and it's pathetic seeing you follow him around all day. He doesn't need a lap dog."

"Boyfriend? Does Keiran know this?" Willow asked sweetly.

"I'm not talking to you, weirdo. I'm talking to this loser. Keiran just wants to use you because everyone heard how you give it up so easily, but he's mine."

"I'm sorry he never mentioned you, but I'll keep that in mind." I turned to Willow, who was biting back a laugh. When Anya continued to stand there, I faced her again. "Was there something else?"

She rolled her eyes at me before stomping off with her army of skanks following. "Can you believe that chick? You would think Keiran's penis was made of gold, the way these girls act." Willow scoffed. I looked at her in shock. *Yeah, definitely something up with her.*

# CHAPTER FIVE

I HAD BEGUN to think school would never end. I almost shit a brick—excuse my language—when Keiran had walked into fifth period along with his closest cohorts. For an hour, I felt the chill and tension at my back all the while praying for the period to end quickly.

Willow dropped me off at home, and I immediately noticed my aunt's car in the driveway. I released a low groan knowing there would be questions about my day. Besides Willow, my aunt was someone I hated lying to so I was hoping to avoid this talk altogether.

"Lake, how was your first day as a senior?"

Stressful.

"It was good. I don't have any serious classes besides English and French." *That's good, Lake. Keep it going.* With any luck, I could bullshit my way through this conversation.

"Well, that's great. So...did anything happen?'

Shit.

She was fishing, and I knew what she was fishing for. Ever since I had fainted in the parking lot, she'd get a worried look in her eye whenever school came up. I had worked so hard over the years to keep my school life away from home, and now it seemed everything was coming to light.

"No. It was pretty uneventful. Some guys got into a fight today."

"It wasn't over you, was it?" A teasing smile spread her lips as she watched me.

"No. Nothing like that."

"One day. You're too gorgeous not to have it happen."

"Aunt Carissa, I don't find the idea of being fought over like table scraps appealing."

"And that's what makes you such a strong girl." She kissed my forehead and resumed preparing dinner as if she hadn't just sent my world crashing.

I wasn't strong. I was anything but. I'd let a single guy isolate me my entire life, and now he was after me in the worst way, and I was too afraid to stop him. After the playground, he'd made it his personal mission to make me fear him. His threats were always done in secret though, and I never knew when they were coming. I touched my neck, absently thinking about the most terrifying time he threatened me...

\* \* \*

THREE YEARS AGO

*"BUT I DON'T want to go in there with you. Please don't make me." I had been walking down the empty hallway, on the way to the bathroom. Everyone had class, including me, so I wasn't expecting to run into Keiran. Literally. We rounded the corner at the same time and collided, causing me to fall on my rear while he*

*watched me with cold eyes.*

*"Shut up. I'm sick of your whining. I haven't even done anything to you yet," he gritted in a deep voice. Not long ago, his voice had become rougher, making him even scarier. It also made me feel strange in another way, but I didn't know how to explain it. My aunt did tell me that our bodies would start to change after puberty so maybe that was it. He had just turned fifteen, after all. Gosh, I hope my voice won't become like that when I turn fifteen in six months. Boys already didn't like me.*

*He pushed past me, into the janitor's closet, then gripped my wrist and yanked me inside before shutting the door and closing us in with the darkness. My breathing became uneven as I started to panic from being enclosed in such a small space with him.*

*"What do you want?" I wanted my voice to sound strong, but it trembled along with my body. There was only the sound of his erratic breathing, so I squinted to see what he was doing.*

*"Open your shirt," he ordered. I instinctively crossed my arms over my chest and took a step back, but the shelves behind me told me there was nowhere to go.*

*"What? Wh—why?"*

*"Why what?" he snapped.*

*"Why do you want me to open my shirt? You'll see my—"*

*"I won't see anything, stupid. It's fucking dark."*

*"So why—"*

*"Just do it," he said impatiently. I was fourteen and already self-conscious about my body, especially because I knew what my shirt hid. I was a late bloomer, so my breasts were new to me, and I wasn't all that comfortable with them. My hands dropped to*

the buttons on my shirt. After the first button, it became harder and harder to continue, but somehow, I did until the sides of my shirt were lying open.

"I—I'm finished," I whispered. I heard him suck in a ragged breath and just as he did, I could feel something cold and sharp against my neck before it trailed down to my chest and stomach and up again. A knife? Did he really have a knife?

"Do you feel that?" I could feel his breath on my skin and knew he was close. The hard point was now teasing one of the hard tips on my breast, and I shivered involuntarily.

"Yes."

"What is it?" he asked.

"A knife." My voice was small as I answered him.

"No," he said softly. I felt a sharp knick and winced silently in pain. "That's your life coming so close to ending. Soon, Monroe."

\* \* \*

I REMEMBER GOING home later that day and finding dried blood on my shirt and skin and realized he must have cut me. I often wondered if it was by accident or intentional. After that, I never chanced going to the bathroom alone.

"So are you sure you'll be okay staying by yourself for six weeks?" My aunt's next question snapped me back to the present.

"I'm sure. This is big, Aunt Carissa. You shouldn't miss it."

"I just feel awful about missing your birthday."

"No worries. You know how I feel about my birthday."

"Oh, honey..."

FEAR ME

"Really, it's fine." I shifted from my feet, hoping she wouldn't bring them up. "Are you still mad at Susan?" Susan was my aunt's agent and friend. They'd been through thick and thin since the start of her career.

"No. She pulled some strings and got Europe included in the tour schedule, so all is forgiven now."

"That's awesome!" I swallowed against the pain in my throat while trying to hide the anxiety I felt over having her leave. *What if she left and never came back like they did?* I shook it off and headed for the stairs, thinking I should get a head start on my homework assignments. Bainbridge gave out syllabi with pre-planned assignments and readings to prepare us for college. This would pretty much be my routine since I didn't have a social life.

When I reached the landing, I made a beeline for the shower, deciding to wash the day away first. After showering, I wrapped a towel around my body and headed for my room, flipping the light switch on as I entered. I immediately saw him lounging on my bed and felt my heart leap out of my chest. Thankfully, I didn't scream, or it would have alerted my aunt.

"Close the door," he said. I tensed at the angry and predatory tone of his voice. As I shut the door, I couldn't help but feel as if I was locking myself in with the devil himself. "Lock it." The sound of the click as I turned the lock was deafening as it echoed throughout the room. "Come here."

I faltered. I couldn't get that close to Keiran with only a towel between us for protection. My gaze shifted around the room as I tried to think of a way out of this. I was hoping by now that he would have gotten over the cafeteria. I definitely didn't expect to find him in my room.

"There are no second chances with me, Monroe.

We both know what will happen if I have to come get you."

My feet carried me toward him while my mind was screaming and clawing the floor for the door. *You can do this. Maybe he just wants to talk... yeah, and bears don't shit in the woods.*

I stopped at the foot of the bed and tried not to think of what seeing him sprawled across my bed was doing to me. His dark hair and skin contrasted deeply with the pale yellow blankets on my bed. He also made my queen sized bed seem incredibly small. He slowly sat up straight and planted his booted feet on the carpet. The look he gave me next could almost have been mistaken for seductive, but I knew better.

"Closer," he whispered, and then gestured to the space between his legs. Breathing was nearly impossible now as I inched the rest of the way over, clutching my towel tighter around my body. He looked relaxed, but I knew he was ready to pounce at any moment.

"Ho—how did you get in here?" I stumbled over my question when he drew his legs in forcing me to step closer within his legs.

"You have sixty seconds to tell me everything about Jesse Fitzgerald and what the fuck you were doing with him."

He completely caught me off guard, and I stuttered out, "I'm not sure what you mean..."

I was happy my relationship with Jesse was something that Keiran would never be able to take away or taint because he was already gone. He also didn't have the right to question me about him or even sound...jealous. "He's a friend."

"Did you fuck him?"

"And if I had?"

"I would kill him—and you."

FEAR ME

The room grew silent as I searched for words, a reaction, something. Whatever I'd been expecting him to say, it wasn't that. The angry possessiveness in his voice was unexpected along with the tingle I felt low in my belly. Not only that, but Keiran had just threatened my life again. Did he really hate me so much he would actually kill me?

"We never did anything. We were friends. I'm entitled to have them."

"Only for as long as I am willing to let you. I think you seem to forget who it is that controls you. I can fix that."

"How exactly do you plan to fix it? You can't control someone." I was bluffing, and I knew it. He did control me. He has for ten years, but I wouldn't let him see that he'd already won.

"Simple." He shrugged. "You're going to stop being friends with Willow."

Complete and utter desolation spread through me like a wildfire. My temperature rose until I was on the verge of passing out again. I continued to back away until my back was against the wall, literally and figuratively. He rose from my bed and stalked after me as a predator would stalk its prey.

"But she's my best friend. She's all I have."

"Precisely."

"Why are you doing this?" I whispered in defeat. "I thought you wanted..."

"Oh, I want and I will take..." He toyed with the corner of my towel, and my trembling increased until I was visibly shaking. "This is only the beginning. I told you I would make you pay, but it's going to be slow. I want to take my time with you."

Before I could say anything, a knock sounded on the door, breaking us out of the moment. Keiran's head turned toward the door before slowly turning back with a cold look on his face.

"Keiran, no, please don't," I whispered in dismay. He would hurt my aunt if she interfered.

"Lake, are you okay? I thought I heard something." I stared at Keiran, begging him with my eyes. .

"Get rid of her," he ordered but didn't move from his position in front of me.

"Uh, yes, Aunt Carissa," I called out, willing her away from the door. "I—I'm fine. The window blew the door shut." I looked over at the window that was tightly shut. The white curtains looked undisturbed making me question how Keiran got into the house.

"Are you sure you're okay, honey?"

"Yes, I'm fine. I'm still getting dressed."

"Okay, well, listen. I've got an early start in the morning, so I'm going to head to bed. Are you sure you will be okay staying by yourself for six weeks?"

With everything that was going on, the safest place for her to be was far away from Six Forks where Keiran couldn't touch her.

"Of course, Aunt Carissa, I'll be fine. I have Willow if it gets lonely." I choked on the words because I didn't know anymore how true those words were. Keiran's hate for me ran deeper than I thought with no hope of an explanation.

"If you're sure. Goodnight, Lake." I heard her soft footsteps walking away and slumped against the wall in relief. When her bedroom door closed, I chanced a look at Keiran, who was watching me with a calculating look on his face.

"Where is your aunt going for six weeks?"

"A book tour and far away from you." I wanted him to know that for now, my aunt was untouchable, but instead of seeing any sign of anger or defeat, he smiled and stepped closer, pressing me into the wall. He braced his hands against the wall on either side of my head and leaned down to whisper in my ear. "And so you think that makes her safe?"

"For now." There was no way he could get to her if she were out of the country.

"I see."

His right hand dropped, and I thought he was going to step back until I felt his fingers grip my thigh, lifting it up to wrap around his waist in one smooth movement. I clutched my towel to keep it from falling while silently pleading with him not to do whatever it was he was about to do. All the confidence I had moments before washed away.

"I can feel the heat from your pussy burning through the towel." He paused and moved his hand further up. "I bet if I ripped this shit away and touched you, you would be wet. Should we find out?"

I whimpered as my body reacted to his threat. It caused a familiar ache deep inside me whenever he was near, except this time it was stronger. His eyes darkened as he pressed harder against me.

"This business between us has taken a dangerous turn, and I have no intentions of stopping. I'm going to enjoy stealing away what you cherish most and will make you love it while I do." His voice was barely restrained animal lust as his hand slid further up to rest at the apex of my thighs.

"If you had even the smallest idea of all the things I'm going to fucking do to you, you would run and run fast." I shook my head weakly and pushed forward as I licked my lips and met his eyes, letting him see the need he was creating inside me. "But then... I wouldn't let you get far."

He suddenly pushed off the wall and scrubbed a

hand down his face, his normal blank mask in place as if the last sixty seconds hadn't just happened. Without another word, he moved to the window. *So he did come through the window.*

I watched him go and had the fleeting thought that desire and fear were the same. *Was that screwed up or what?* He lifted the window and paused, gazing out into the night.

"There isn't a worse threat out there to you than me." His shoulders tensed, and I held my breath, waiting for him to continue. "Do as you're told," he gritted, disappearing into the night.

\* \* \*

MORNING CAME TOO soon. It was my birthday. I was now eighteen and miserable. I'd forgotten my birthday was coming until Aunt Carissa reminded me last night. Ever since the pharmacy, my mind was stuck in one place. Keiran.

I hated my birthday, though. It was the day I found out my parents weren't coming back. I stopped thinking of it as my birthday and instead, considered it the anniversary my parents became dead to me. *They left.*

I'd come downstairs expecting my aunt to be gone, but found her waiting with my favorite dessert. I was a sucker for ice-cream cake. She tied balloons to the bar stools and had streamers everywhere, and I laughed at her when she blew on those blow out things that sounded like an elephant with a cold.

"Happy Birthday, Lake!" she jumped up and down much like a big kid, which was sort of embarrassing, but I loved it.

"Thank you, Aunt Carissa. This is great."

"Oh, honey, Willow was supposed to be here, but

she's running late. Something about Peepee hiding her keys."

"*Pepé*," I laughed, correcting her. "He is still mad at her for leaving for the entire summer." He was a sneaky little guy but cute as a button... for a rat.

"Shame. He'll come around. No one can stay mad at Willow for too long." That was true. Willow had a gift for winning people over except for the ones who thought she was a freak. It was more about the way she dressed than it was about her.

"I'm making your favorite mixed-berry pancakes, so I hope you're hungry." I was hungry though I never ate much in the mornings. My appetite usually developed later in the morning, but today was different considering I skipped dinner after Keiran had left. I went straight to bed, too emotionally wrung out to hang.

"Starving."

"You should be." She turned from pouring the batter into the skillet and gave me a hard look. "You didn't eat the dinner I prepared last night." I knew my aunt enough to know when she was questioning me without actually asking a question.

"Uh, yeah. I was too tired after my shower and decided I wasn't all that hungry, so I just crashed." She nodded her head but continued staring me down until she finally turned to flip the pancakes. "I thought you were leaving early?" I asked, taking the attention off me.

"No, I said I had an early start. I had to be here at least this morning to make you pancakes, so I chose a later flight. Tara will be driving me to the airport on her lunch break."

The doorbell stopped me from answering, and I hopped off the stool to open the door. Willow usually just walked in so I wondered who it could be this early.

I opened the door and immediately slammed it back.

*Oh, God. Oh, no. Oh, God. Oh, no.*

"Lake, who was that?"

"Aunt Carissa, won't the pancakes burn?"

"The pancakes are done. Who was that?" she asked more sternly.

"Paperboy?" I lifted a shoulder but knew guilt was written all over my face. She rolled her eyes and nudged me aside to open the door.

Her eyes widened in surprise before she whispered, "Oh, my." She turned to me with accusation in her eyes and a huge grin. "And who are you?" she asked when I refused to explain why Keiran was on our doorstep.

"Keiran Masters." His deep voice rushed over me causing goose bumps to cover my skin. "I go to school with your niece."

My aunt hid her surprise well, but I knew she re-called his name. "Well, you aren't a friend. I would have seen you before, "she bluntly stated, and I suddenly had the urge to hide her from Keiran. She didn't know the danger she was in just by being this close.

"No, ma'am, I'm not her friend," he answered truthfully. I could feel his eyes boring into me even as I avoided eye contact.

"Too bad. You're cute... enough." I almost snorted. He was gorgeous, and she knew it. My aunt was baiting him.

"I'm glad you approve," he smoothly replied.

"Not quite, so come in so I can see more." She walked away, heading for the kitchen and leaving us standing in the foyer alone.

"Why are you here?" I whispered vehemently. I wouldn't let him anywhere near my aunt. He merely smirked at me before shouldering his way past me.

"Didn't you hear? Your aunt wants to see more," he

threw over his shoulder before disappearing into the kitchen.

I pulled at my hair before pushing the door shut and following them into the kitchen. Keiran was already settled into a seat as if he belonged here. I made a sound of frustration when I saw my aunt pushing *my* pancakes onto a plate for Keiran. She looked at me in surprise while Keiran wore a smug look on his face.

"Lake, did you just growl at Keiran?" *No, actually I was growling at you.* "Sit down and stop being rude. It's your birthday. Keiran, did you know that today is her birthday?"

"Sure," he mumbled around a mouth full of *my* pancakes.

"Well, maybe you two can celebrate later. I feel so bad I have to leave today. Keep her company for me, won't you?" She winked at Keiran, and I rolled my eyes.

"I'll keep an eye on her," he agreed. My aunt smiled, completely oblivious to the deception in his words. He made eye contact with me, holding my gaze until I looked away.

"Ooh, I have to finish packing and leave for my flight. It was nice to meet you, Keiran. Don't let me down." With that, she disappeared up the stairs, leaving me alone with Keiran again.

"Let's go," he commanded. I grabbed my backpack to follow him out the door and sent Willow a quick text to let her know I was leaving and would explain later. Willow knew when not to push. Sometimes.

"Why did you come here? You could have called to let me know you were coming." He ignored me until we were seated in his car, and then he shrugged.

"I wanted to meet the woman whose life you held in your hands."

"Do you really believe your plan will work?" I asked

mockingly. If he didn't think I was afraid of him, maybe he would leave me alone. It was a long shot but worth a try.

His jaw clenched before he hauled me over the gearshift and into his lap, wrapping his hand around my ponytail. "I will do everything in my power to make it work. You see, I have nothing to lose...but you do."

"Maybe you do, but you just don't care," I argued.

"Then that makes me a very dangerous man."

* * *

IT WASN'T EASY trying to ignore Keiran when he was part of most of my day—by force and circumstance. I was still fuming over the stunt he pulled this morning. Most of the day was gone. Lunch and French had come and gone, and I'd just arrived at art class. I was setting up my station when Keenan walked in with Trevor Reynolds. I felt a cold chill run down my spine when Trevor and I made eye contact. I flipped him off when he continued to watch me with a smug expression. When his face fell, I turned away satisfied. *What a jarhead.*

I didn't recall him being in my class yesterday so he must have changed courses—though I didn't take him or Keenan for art people. When Keenan disappeared into the supply closet, Trevor chose that moment to saunter over to me.

"How's it going, Lake?" he asked cheerfully.

"Fuck off." I didn't bother to spare him a glance.

"You may want to be a little careful with how you speak to me." He leaned down to whisper into my ear. "Unlike Keiran, I don't hold a secret torch for you. I will end you."

I finally looked up to meet his glare with one of my

own. "I don't know what you mean. Keiran wouldn't hold a torch for me unless it was to burn me alive with it."

"You might be right..." There was a Cheshire grin spread on his lips as he walked away to sit in his seat.

Keenan came out of the supply closet with a giggling brunette following. I had one guess at what they had been doing. I just shook my head. He really had no shame. I snorted and turned back to the poster in front of me and thought about Trevor's unnecessary threat.

Keiran would never listen to me anyway. I looked too guilty. The day Keiran went away and left my life for the first time was a day I would never forget...

\* \* \*

ONE YEAR AGO

"ARE YOU SURE you're okay? We can totally bail if you want." I smiled at Willow because she really was a good friend. The day before, Keiran had humiliated me in front of the entire cafeteria when I asked to speak to him.

"Thanks, Willow, but you are not using me to get out of your Biology exam."

"Ugh, don't remind me. Ms. Thompson is such a beyotch. I swear she fails me on purpose."

"Willow, you made an A- on an assignment one time because you skipped a question."

"Whatever, she's still a witch. Hey, did you ever find your cell phone?"

"No, but I'm sure it will turn up." My cell phone disappeared the day before after the scene in the cafeteria.

"Maybe someone stole it."

B.B. REID

It was possible.

I remembered sending Willow a text in third period before heading to the bathroom. I thought I left my phone on my desk and didn't realize it was missing until fourth period when Willow asked why I didn't respond to her text.

After searching my backpack, I went back to the restroom to check there and then even asked the lost and found committee, but it never turned up.

"Maybe. I'm going to search again and ask around before I report it missing."

We pulled into the school parking lot, and I immediately noticed the flashing lights. There were squad cars and a gang of students gathered around, watching the school anxiously.

"Whoa, did someone die?" Willow asked.

"I don't think so. There aren't any ambulances."

We quickly approached the large crowd to see what was happening. I wasn't prepared for what I saw. Just as I breached the wall of students, I caught sight of Keiran being led in handcuffs to a squad car. Another police officer followed with small bags of what looked like marijuana in Ziploc bags.

"This is bullshit!" I heard and saw an enraged Keenan emerge from the building followed by a furious Dash. They both looked as if they were ready to kill. I've never seen the two of them with as much as a frown on their face before.

"Son, you might want to calm down and step back before we arrest you, too," an officer stated.

"Fuck you, let my cousin go. That shit was planted!"

"You pigs are making a grave mistake. I will have your badges by the end of the day." That came from Dash, who was standing nearby deceptively calm.

"Mr. Chambers, we are only doing our jobs." With that, they placed Keiran in the back of the car.

Later that day, I was doing homework at home when the doorbell rang. I opened it to find Keenan and Dash on my doorstep with fierce expressions. To say I was surprised was an understatement.

"Um, hi—" I was about to ask why they were here when Dash cut me off.

"Cut it, this isn't a social call."

"We know you sent that bullshit tip to the authorities and planted the drugs, bitch." This came from Keenan, who looked to be only one wrong move or word away from strangling me.

I shifted nervously, wishing my aunt were home. "We are giving you one chance to go down to the station and tell them you planted the drugs."

"I don't know what you are talking about. I did no such thing." I tried to shut the door, but Dash quickly lodged his boot in the door.

"Money talks, so we have good word that it was your cell phone that called the station...and you left your name. Not very smart," Dash mocked.

"I told you I had nothing to do with it. Leave before I call the police."

"No need to be scared, little lamb," Keenan's voice lowered. "Keiran wants to deal with you personally."

# Chapter Six

Later in the day, I walked into fifth period with Keiran trailing behind. He had been standing outside the door talking to Quentin as I walked up. When I entered the classroom, he wordlessly followed me in.

I discreetly looked around for Willow as I sat in the same seats as the day before. I had to talk to her and see if she was okay. She wasn't in volleyball, French, or lunch, and she hadn't answered my texts. I didn't even know if she ever made it to school. I sat down in my seat and texted Willow again.

Could Keiran have done something to her? "Monroe, come sit here."

"I'm fine right here." The silence that followed was more intimidating than if he had yelled and screamed, and I knew now was not the time or place to piss him off. He wouldn't care about the other people in the room. It would just be another opportunity to humiliate me.

I sighed and gathered my books to move to sit next to him. Keenan and Sheldon walked in a moment later with ruffled clothing and secretive grins on their faces as they made their way to the back, but sitting in the row in front of us.

"Mr. Masters and Ms. Chambers, it would behoove you to make it on time to class next time. Tardiness will not be tolerated."

"Sure thing, Mr. Lawson, but I don't think people say 'behoove' anymore," Keenan joked. The class erupted into laughter causing Mr. Lawson to turn red.

"Keenan, quit it," Sheldon scolded.

"Yes, dear."

I watched the couple as they settled in. Keenan was tickling and poking her, making her giggle. He always found reasons to touch her, and I had noticed the way he looked at her. He seemed to adore her despite his unfaithfulness, which I didn't understand. Sheldon was beautiful, and I felt sorry for her.

"Hi, I'm Sheldon. Lake Monroe, right?" Sheldon smiled at me as she sat down with her bag. Her eyes were bright amber, and her hair was a light shade of blonde. I always thought she looked exotic and admired the athletic build she got from cheerleading.

"Uh...yeah. Hi," I replied but didn't return her smile. I was still wary of Sheldon—she was, after all, popular, gorgeous, and had an amazing rack. *Shit, now I sound like Keenan.* I often caught Keenan motor boating them for everyone to see.

She seemed nice enough but didn't seem all that smart when it came to men. Keenan was a slut and made no secret about it, yet she stayed with him. I didn't understand that type of commitment although I never had a boyfriend thanks to Keiran.

"Senior year. You excited?" she asked. *You have no idea.* I nodded my head politely but said nothing else. I couldn't see why she was talking to me much less sitting next to me. "So you and Keiran, huh? You two an item?"

she waggled her eyebrows suggestively.

Keiran had been talking to Quentin, but I knew he heard her question when his conversation with Quentin stopped, and his attention shifted to me. I couldn't rebuff him, and I couldn't tell her the truth either. His smirk told me he was enjoying the power he had over me.

I was saved from responding by Willow entering the classroom. When she spotted where I was sitting, she sent me a questioning glance. I forced a smile but sucked in a breath when she walked over to me.

"Happy Birthday, Lake," she said cheerfully as she leaned downed to kiss my cheek. Just as I was about to respond, Keiran seized my chin in a hard grip and turned my face up to him.

"If you want to be cool, then you can't talk to her anymore. We talked about this. You have to drop your dead weight."

My world came crashing down at the double meaning in his words. Silence passed between us as I stared at him with hate in my eyes.

"Lake?" Willow's voice trembled, and I knew she heard him. He meant for her to hear.

I wanted to turn and reassure her. I couldn't let him do this. I couldn't let him take away the only two people I had to love. Did giving up one really mean saving the other? Despite my doubts, I knew I couldn't risk it. He'd won. He knew the moment I submitted because he finally let go of my face.

My gaze dropped down to my notebook in front of me, but I didn't see it. I didn't see anything. All I could feel was the weight of my best friend's stare and the hurt I had just caused her. She wordlessly walked to our normal seats and sat down. Only then did I allow my gaze to rise, and it immediately landed on her slumped shoulders. Whoever had said choosing between right and wrong was easy was a damn liar.

\* \* \*

DROP YOUR DEAD *weight*. I played the words over in my head repeatedly as I stood in front of the bathroom mirror. I didn't like who I saw looking back at me.

I was mortified.

I hurt Willow.

I never hurt Willow and Willow never hurt me. Once class was over, she practically ran out the room, and I couldn't stop her.

I finished cleaning up and tossed away the many tissues I used to cry my pain into. I never thought when I woke up this morning that any of this would happen. He said he would take her away from me, but I didn't believe him. There was a lot I didn't want to believe. Like the fact that Keiran was going to use sex and control to destroy me, and I had to let him.

I knew Keiran would consume me if I let him have me. I wouldn't be able to survive what he was planning without experience.

I finally left the bathroom to find Keiran leaning against the wall across from the bathroom door with one foot perched on the wall with his hands in his pockets. I stared at him and he stared back. When he crooked his finger, motioning for me to come to him, I gave into temptation. He stood up straight and fisted his hand in my shirt bringing my chest flush with his.

"Whatever bullshit you're telling yourself to escape what's going to happen between us, drop it. I've already told you how it's going to be. You want it just as bad as I do and I... will... have... you. End of discussion."

It was safe to say that I was in deep shit.

\* \* \*

I TRIED ONCE again to reach Willow in the hour I'd been home. I figured there was no way he would know I talked to her, but when I didn't get an answer after the fifth or sixth time, I grew frustrated. I had allowed Keiran to tear us apart without lifting so much as a finger.

"Screw it," I grabbed my keys and headed downstairs, ignoring Keiran's warning not to leave. He dropped me off after school and immediately left. Aunt Carissa was gone now for her tour, and the house felt incredibly empty without her.

I stepped outside and locked up, but an eerie feeling had me looking around nervously. I instinctively searched for a particular black muscle car, but when I didn't spot it anywhere, I shook off the feeling and hopped into my car. Willow lived just around the corner in the neighboring cul-de-sac.

I was at her house a couple of minutes later and noticed her car outside. Her parent's car was gone so I knew she was home alone. Buddy probably wasn't home as usual. He was a freshman but had already moved up in ranks at Bainbridge and earned the title as one of the hottest—even senior girls chased him. We had grown close over the years, and he was like the little brother I would never get. I swallowed down the unwanted feeling of bitterness and rang the doorbell.

A few minutes passed, but no one answered. Refusing to let my only friendship die, I tried the doorknob. The door surprisingly opened, so I entered, checking the living room and kitchen before moving upstairs.

"Willow?" I called out when I reached the landing. I could hear low sounds coming from her room as I moved forward. When she didn't answer, I feared there was something wrong, so I pushed the door open. "Willow?"

I walked in and instantly wished I hadn't.

I could barely make out Willow on the bed covered by a large male body. Her legs were wrapped around his hips. Her head was thrown back, and her eyes closed tight. She was gripping the muscular buttocks of the guy who had her pinned to the bed as her breasts rocked in rhythm with the headboard banging against the wall. Her passionate cries were mixed with his lustful groans as he pounded her, forcefully. It was a wonder I couldn't make it out clearly before. Suddenly, his head turned toward the door, and he immediately spotted me as I stood frozen watching them.

Dash Chambers. Keiran's best friend. His name tasted bitter on my tongue.

He continued his furious pace—never missing a beat as he watched me watch him with a smirk. Willow had yet to notice me as he continued to pleasure her, so I stepped back quickly, quietly closing the door. I ran down the stairs and out the door. I couldn't believe that I caught them like that.

So it was true... she *was* sleeping with the enemy.

\* \* \*

"HEY, CHARLIE," I greeted when I walked through the front doors.

"Thanks again for covering the shift. I know it's your birthday."

"No, problem. Sorry, I couldn't get here faster. "

"Please tell me it was finally because of a guy?"

"Not quite..."

"Well, honey, that's not a no! Congratulations!" Charlie began jumping up and down, clapping and drawing unwanted attention.

"Can we please not do this again?"

"Forgive me for being worried about your love life when you aren't. At this rate, all I see in your future are tabby cats and bowel problems. Can you imagine what that could do to a person?"

I listened to Charlie's rants while he followed me behind the service desk and into the employee den. I had to threaten him with bodily harm when he tried to follow me into the bathroom stall. He finally went away, muttering about clueless teenagers, and I quickly changed into my uniform shirt.

I picked up this job at the gym last year after Keiran had been gone for about two months. I remember feeling as if I had lost a vital piece of my life, and so I picked up a few hobbies at first but couldn't stick to them. A few weeks later, on my way to the local burger joint, I saw an ad in the window of the local gym and applied. Charlie had taken one look at me and started to bemoan my lack of a love life. He guessed I either didn't appreciate men or was hung up on someone who hadn't noticed me. If he only knew. I tried to explain I was only sixteen and had the rest of my life to make a love connection, but that nearly brought him to tears.

"You poor thing. It's worse than I thought. You're hired. I have to help you. This is my one true purpose in life."

And I've worked here ever since. It was a nice distraction and gave me a chance to save some money for college. I didn't have a clue where I wanted to go then, but as long as it was far away from *him,* I would survive.

I clipped the headset they made us wear on my jeans, clocked in and headed out to make my rounds. There was nothing like spending a few hours inhaling the aroma of sweat and watching lonely housewives lust over the half-naked, sweaty men. The gym definitely had its perks.

Charlie was back on the floor, pretending to oversee things while discreetly checking out the men as they worked out. He was a full fledge homosexual and proud of it. He also had the biggest heart and was a decent mentor in all things men though he called himself a failure because of my single status.

Later into my shift, I was deep into the membership accounts, sifting through accounts that were overdue and marking them for later, when I smelled lemons. A satisfied smile covered my face, as I looked up at the woman responsible. Mrs. Fletcher frequented the gym, even at the age of sixty-eight, though she mostly walked on the treadmill and stair master. She sometimes brought me lemon cookies.

"Good afternoon, dear. I brought you some treats." She set the paper bag on the counter, and I immediately snatched them up.

"How are you, Mrs. Fletcher?" I asked while stuffing a chewy goodness into my mouth and wishing for a cold glass of milk.

"Slow down before you choke. There are more in the bag," she scolded.

"Oh, I know. I just want to eat enough before Charlie gets a whiff of them. He almost ate my whole stash last time."

"Where is Charles? I need him to come set up the death trap for me."

"Well, hello," a deep, silky smooth voice greeted.

We both turned to the attractive, middle-aged man who had just walked in. He was also a frequent gymgoer though I've never seen him actually work out.

*Maybe he's here to check out the men, too.*

I briefly wondered if Charlie would be into older

men. He'd just turned thirty, and this man looked to be in his mid to late forties.

"Oh, hi, Mr. Martin. What brings you in today?"

"To exercise might be the correct answer," he countered with a small smile.

I smiled apologetically and took in his usual, well-kept appearance and dark wavy hair. He was tall with a muscular frame that wasn't bulky, and he was always polite and charming. I always wondered if he was married but never asked. If he weren't gay, then I could consider introducing him to my aunt. But if he wasn't a Star Trek fan, then you can forget it.

He turned to smile indulgently at Mrs. Fletcher, who was staring up at him. "Hello, Mrs. Fletcher. How are you today?"

"I'm fine, thank you." Her tone brightened further at the attention, so I studied the two to gauge their familiarity. I wasn't aware they knew each other.

"Always nice to see you."

"You're too kind." She blushed and reluctantly left when Charlie, who had just finished setting the treadmill and had waved her over.

His attention was now directed at me, and I felt the pressure of his gaze. "How are you, little lady? What's new?"

"Fine, thank you. Nothing much," I lightly replied, attempting casualness.

He continued to stare as if waiting for something. I shifted uncomfortably, feeling the familiar need to hide. For the past year, he had come to the gym and did much of the same. He would ask questions about me and about school. One time he even asked if I was dating anyone. I remember the panic I felt when I thought he was hitting on me, and it must have shown because he apologized and left the gym abruptly.

He finally handed me his membership card to swipe after a few moments. "You know, we have a promotion going on if you refer a friend to the gym, you get half off the next month's membership fees. You can even use a wife or child—"

I paused at the anger that flickered in his eyes at the mention of a wife and child. I couldn't describe it, but it wasn't warm and fuzzy like people who have families usually get.

"I won't be bringing anyone," he replied in a brusque tone. It was very different from the charisma he usually displayed.

"I'm sorry if I offended you, I—"

"Nonsense." His smile was forced and didn't quite reach his eyes. "It is me who should be sorry. My wife died some years ago. I haven't quite gotten over her death."

I immediately felt like an ass, not only for bringing up bad memories, but the thoughts I was having about him. "Then please accept my apologies, Mr. Martin." I offered a smile and handed back his card.

"I can tell you are a very special girl, Lake. Such a shame," he stated and then walked away. My smile immediately dropped as I watched him disappear into the locker rooms.

\* \* \*

THIRTY MINUTES INTO my shift, I was cleaning the front windows and bobbing along to the music when I felt the breeze from the outside summer air as someone walked in.

"Welcome back. We are currently running a special promotion. If you refer a friend, you get half off the next month's fees."

"Excellent. I'm sure Keiran would be very interested to know a certain someone works here." I heard the gruff voice of the snake as it made my skin crawl.

I quickly turned in the opposite direction to escape when his hand clamped around my upper arm. "Not so fast, mouse," he taunted while pulling me back toward the reception desk. He freed my arm and grinned down at me. "I'd like to apply for a membership."

Trevor handed over his ID with a smug look, and I reluctantly accepted it, keying in his info for the application. I could feel his eyes on me as I did. Once I finished, I handed his card back and kept a wary eye on him as he tucked it back into his pocket.

"So?" he asked with a raised brow.

"So, what?"

"Does he know you work here?"

"What's it to you?"

"Just protecting my interests."

"You mean your ass? Because if he finds out—"

"He won't, and you are going to keep your mouth shut," he warned. "What do you care anyway? He already hates you."

"Because it's a lot more personal now, and he actually has a reason to hate me. He's already threatened me because of you," I whispered harshly. He slashed his hand in the air impatiently.

"I don't care. Keep your mouth closed, or I'll threaten you, too."

He stalked away, heading for the weights, and I couldn't help hoping a weight could fall and just smash his brain in.

It wouldn't wake me up from this nightmare, but it would definitely make me laugh. *Now who's the sadistic one?* I wouldn't tempt fate in such a way because I wouldn't be able to live with it on my conscience. It made me once again remember the fateful day everything turned to shit.

* * *

16 MONTHS AGO

"KEIRAN MASTERS TOOK over the team! He's officially the team captain now."

"I heard Trevor is pissed. What do you think he will do?"

"What can he do? Keiran is too badass for Trevor to take on."

"Well, I'm glad Keiran is the captain. He's a little scary but so much hotter, and maybe we will actually make it to the Championship this year."

I listened to the giggling girls gathered around the lockers next to me. I couldn't help but listen considering the subject.

I needed to stay alert if a quick getaway was needed. I sighed when I realized this was just another Keiran Masters pep rally. Their unending rambling as they praised his good looks and popularity was making me nauseated, so I tuned them out and finished storing my books in my locker. When I was done, I debated if I should risk lunch today. After Keiran had some girls toss a pot of chicken fat over my head for shits and giggles, I avoided the cafeteria even if it meant I had to starve.

"Oh, gosh, he's coming this way." A member of the fan club giggled. My heart started pounding fast as I quickly closed my locker to get out of dodge.

"Hi, Trevor." Another one giggled.

I relaxed a little and released the breath I was holding when they greeted Trevor. My relief was short lived though, when Trevor bypassed the trio without responding and headed toward me with purpose. He'd never done anything to me personally, but he was still popular and a jock. I was too far down the food chain to think this was going to be a friendly social call.

I was apprehensive, but surprisingly, he didn't scare me. Only one person scared me, and thankfully, he wasn't in the vicinity, so I stood my ground waiting for what was to come. He stopped and scanned my face thoroughly. *He probably doesn't even know my name,* I thought and almost rolled my eyes.

"Lake, right?" *Wait, did I say that out loud?*

I continued staring without a response. Maybe I should tell him he had the wrong person since he didn't look sure of who I was. He looked over at the trio of girls who were still standing close by glaring at me when I remained silent.

"Lake Monroe?" he tried again.

"That's her," one of the girls offered. He continued to ignore her but grabbed my elbow and pulled me down the hall behind him.

"Look, I need to talk to you in private. I have a proposition for you," he said while dragging me into the library. We passed by tables and computers and then into the bookcases until we reached an alcove. I finally found my voice once he stopped and I was sure I wouldn't trip and plant my face on the floor.

"Listen, I don't care what he says. I don't perform sexual acts for money, so if that's what your proposition is about, you're wasting your time. I'm sure there are plenty of girls willing to do it for free so, please, let me go," I huffed out furiously.

I constantly received money and lewd notes in my locker asking for sexual favors after Keiran spread rumors last year that he saw me giving Peter Simpson oral for money in the hallway after school and then offered to do him for twenty bucks.

"I'm not after that."

"Oh, yeah? Then what are you after?"

"We have a mutual enemy, and I know how to get rid of him."

# CHAPTER SEVEN

"YES, AUNT CARISSA, everything is fine. How is Canada?" Whatever she said, I never got to hear. As I walked through the door after work, the phone was ripped out of my hands. Then, as I was being tossed on the couch, I watched it hit the wall, but thankfully, it didn't seem to break. *What the—?*

"You seem to be hard of hearing."

I looked up at Keiran standing over me expecting to find him angry, but instead, he was standing and talking as calmly as if he was discussing the weather. Truth be told—that scared me even more.

"I had—"

"Shut up. Why did you go see Willow?" *So he had been watching me.*

I lifted my chin and looked him square in the eye. "Because she's my best friend, and thanks to you, she's my only friend, but she is mine, and you don't get to take that away."

Aside from my aunt, Willow was the most important person in my life and the only one I loved. I used to love my parents, or what I could remember of them, but as long as the truth of their disappearance evaded me, I would continue to have mixed feelings. Parents abandon their kids all the time.

When he stalked toward me, I scrambled to get away, but he was quicker and dragged me kicking and screaming to him at the other end of the couch. He sat down, pulled me into his lap, and then wrapped my legs around his waist. His arm banded around my waist, and I flinched when he fisted my hair in his hand and yanked my head back. His nostrils flared, and I shivered from looking into icy eyes. It's like I could feel everything he felt.

"Is that what you think you are to her? Her *friend?* She won't even tell you about Dash. What else does she keep from you, huh? You're not her friend... She doesn't even *trust* you." A sound of regret and hurt ripped through my throat.

Didn't Willow trust me?

I didn't want to believe it, but why else wouldn't Willow talk to me about Dash? Nothing else made sense because we'd always shared everything... or at least, I thought we did.

"That's not true." I shook my head in denial, but the bad seed he planted in my head had already taken root.

"Isn't it? I can see the doubt in your eyes. Did you know he took her virginity this summer?" he said with an evil grin. "I do. I know when he did it. How he did it. And how many times he's done it. And do you know why I know?" I shook my head as best as I could with his heavy hand controlling it. "Because I told him to do it."

*What? No, no, no. This can't be happening.* Not even Keiran could be that cruel, could he? He finally released his hold on my hair and used his hand to trace the erratic pulse beating in my throat.

"Why?" My voice was little more than a croak as I searched his eyes for a sign he was lying or joking. He held my gaze as he brought his face closer. His lips touched my neck and began trailing bites down my skin.

"Because it would hurt you," he said between bites, and I sucked in a breath. "He's going to use her and make her fall for him... and then he's going to break her heart."

*The hell he is.* "Why are you telling me this?"

"Because there is nothing you can do to stop what's already done. He's just waiting for my go-ahead to complete the final act. Of course... that doesn't need to happen... but it all depends on you."

I swallowed down the bile that had risen up. "You don't need to do this. You can have me—"

"And I will."

"So why haven't you?" I snapped.

He cocked his head at me curiously and bared his teeth. "Is that a challenge?" he growled, pressing up into me. I gasped at the contact from the hard-on he did nothing to conceal. "Make no mistake, there is nothing more I would rather do right now than bend you over this chair and introduce you to my cock the right way, but business first, and then we fuck." I didn't know what pissed me off more—what he said or the way my body reacted to it. "I see the look in your eyes, Monroe. You can keep up the good girl act, but we both know what I would find if I touched your pussy right now."

"The only thing I feel toward you right now is contempt..." I leaned forward until my nose was touching his. "...make no mistake about that."

I was flat on my back before I could blink, and then my jeans were being ripped off my hips. Panic took over as I grabbed onto Keiran's wrists, but he effortlessly broke out of my grip and turned the tables by pinning my wrists against the cushions with one of his. A second later, he shoved his other hand down my panties, delivering an unexpected swat to my pussy before his fingers slowly slipped inside of me. He immediately withdrew them and used his now dripping fingers to strum the little bundle of nerves until I was gasping for air. Only then did he plunge his fingers into me once more, causing my body to bow off the couch. His grip tightened to keep me from escaping the pleasure he was forcing on me. After only a few teasing strokes of his fingers, a violent tremble shook my body.

"How can it only be contempt you feel for me when all I feel is you coming on my hand? I barely touched you..."

"No." I shook my head against his claim. He watched me quietly until the shaking subsided. Whatever just happened left me feeling weak. When he shoved away from me to sit upright, I quickly pulled my jeans back over my hips, feeling embarrassment flood my senses. I couldn't meet his eyes, but I knew he was watching me from the other end of the couch.

"Now... back to business." His blank face and callous attitude over my first sexual experience had me choking back my ever-present tears. It was a common occurrence around him. He rolled his eyes, and he pulled out his phone. "As I said when you came in—you seem to have a hard time hearing me." He began dialing on his phone, and then a video feed of an older man with long blond hair pulled back in a ponytail appeared on his screen. "You got her?"

"In my sight as we speak."

"Good. Someone needs to see." He crooked his finger and patted his lap with a satisfied look on his face. I reluctantly slid over, but when I refused to sit on his lap, he hauled me over. I wrestled with him until he placed a restraining hand around my neck and whispered low, "Move again, and I'll spank your ass."

"You got a feisty piece there, don't you?" the guy commented lustfully. A black look crossed over Keiran's face as he turned back to the camera. The guy suddenly looked nervous and cleared his throat while apologizing. The screen suddenly switched, and I was looking at the glossy background of a bar. I could see the name of a well-known, five-star hotel chain plastered on the wall, and then something, or rather someone, caught my attention.

My aunt. Sitting at the bar with her agent.

I knew immediately what Keiran was showing me—what he was *telling* me. Without saying anything, Keiran ended the call, and the video feed of my aunt disappeared.

"One phone call and she disappears. There are a lot of places a person can disappear. I should know. I did."

"What do you think I'm going to do?" I cried with anger and emotion filling my voice. I was yelling by the time I spoke the last word. Fear for my aunt overshadowed my need for self-preservation.

"I don't know. You surprise me at every turn, and I have to say, I didn't think you had it in you to fight me. Planting those drugs in my locker? Brilliant. The execution was sloppy as hell though, but not to worry... I'll show you how to get back at someone properly. So here's what you're going to do."

* * *

I WALKED INTO school with my head low, watching the tile floor and my feet as they quickly carried me to English. My phone rang for the umpteenth time since I left my house this morning, and I closed my eyes to quell the pain. *Don't answer it, Lake. Just ignore it. You can do this.*

I quickly stored my extra books in my locker and hurried for English. I couldn't be late. Being late meant something else would be taken away from me, and though I didn't think there was anything left, I couldn't risk it. He would know exactly where to strike. He always did.

I made it to the classroom with no time to spare and was careful not to make eye contact with my tormentor. He was sitting in his normal seat, and I headed for the one assigned to me. The one he told me to sit in. I kept my head down, staring at the table and ignoring the silence. The class was completely empty and school wouldn't start for another half hour.

"Take your hair down," he ordered from a few rows behind me. I slowly unwound my hair from its bun on top of my head and let my hair tumble down my back.

"What happened this morning?"

I tried to hold back the tears immediately threatening to spill over. "I told her."

"*What* did you tell her?"

"To stay away from me."

"And?"

"Not to contact me."

"And has she?"

"Please, she doesn't understand—"

"Has... she... called... you?" I nodded my head, unable to speak. I kept seeing the hurt and confused look on her face this morning when I broke her heart and mine.

"Why Willow? You don't need to do this."

"Don't I? She was the only thing left standing between you and me."

"And now that she is gone? What now?"

"I get to play." Apprehension shook my body at the underlying threat in his words.

"What—"

"No more questions. There is nothing you can say or anything you can do that will deter me."

"How long are you going to do this?"

"Until I've had enough and not a second before."

"Can I ask you something?"

"I suppose."

"You were only supposed to do six months. Why were you gone for a year?"

He was silent for a while, and I figured he wouldn't answer when he finally spoke. "Dash's parents and my uncle pulled some strings, and I received a reduced sentenced, but inside, I got into a few fights on a regular basis. I guess you can say, I had a lot of tension to work off. I ended up with seven months tacked on to my original sentence that accumulated over time. Why is that your business?"

"I think it has everything to do with me. Don't you?" My voice dripped with sarcasm, and I was almost sorry he couldn't see it on my face.

"Now is not the time to grow a pair of balls, Monroe. We are alone here for at least another fifteen minutes, and there is nothing keeping me from you right now except my goodwill."

"I'm sorry." I really wasn't.

"Don't be sorry. Be careful. I want you to do something for me."

"What?"

"Take off your panties." I felt my skin pale as I squeezed my thighs together unconsciously. He couldn't be serious, could he? "Time is against you, Monroe. The sooner you do what I say, the better for you it'll be."

My hands were at my panties, pulling them down from under my dress before he could finish talking. After last night, I was learning to take Keiran's threats seriously. The material was at my feet, and I quickly grabbed them and looked around nervously. Teachers and staff would usually be at school before students were, and Mrs. Connors could walk in at any moment.

"Bring them to me." I rose from my seat and turned to walk to his table. "On your knees." My footstep faltered, and I looked at him across the room.

"Excuse me?"

"Get on your knees and bring me them to me, and since you can't seem to keep your mouth closed, you can gag yourself with them first."

He watched me with a cold look in his eyes. Needless to say, I obeyed him and stuffed my panties into my mouth, and then sunk down to my knees all the while keeping my eyes on him.

"Good girl. Now crawl to me. Slowly."

My hands touched the floor, and I was now on all fours as I made my way to him. He was sprawled lazily in his chair with one leg bent, and the other stretched out, looking entirely too comfortable. *I hope he doesn't make me do something crazy like lick his shoes. Hell no.* The tension was thick in the room as well as the anticipation of what he would do once I reached him. I tried to distance my mind from the present and think of happy places, but that didn't work. I didn't have happy places. He never let me.

I stopped by the table and waited for his command. He watched me from his perch on the chair like a King looks down on his peasants.

"Stand up," he finally said. I rose to my feet, surprisingly graceful, and I saw the brief look of pleasure in his eyes before he hid it.

"Take off your shoes." I slipped my gold sandals off my feet and looked at him curiously. What was his game? "Get on the table and face me." He was sitting close to the table but didn't make room for me, so I when I slid onto the tabletop, my feet ended up resting on his legs.

"Spread your legs and rest your feet on the table edge and before you try to overthink it, let me remind you that we now have ten minutes max before someone comes walking through that door."

A feeling of uneasiness and desire swept through my body at the same time, and I could feel the familiar quake start at my toes and work its way up. My panties were in my mouth so we both knew what he would see when I opened up for him. I closed my eyes briefly before opening them again. I placed first one leg and then the other on the table, keeping my legs as close as possible.

"Don't fuck with me," he barked.

I spread my legs wider for him and closed my eyes again, feeling his gaze travel over me. The silence in the classroom was haunting me, making me nervous, when it should have done the opposite. The hiss that came from him broke the silence, and I felt his hands palm my knees before slowly moving down my thighs. Up and down, he softly rubbed my skin. My body was rigid on top of the table, but the more he touched me, the more the stiffness faded away as my body consented to his touch while my mind cursed him to hell.

"There has been one thing on my mind since I left you last night, and I think you know what it is. I need to make you feel that again. I need—" He paused to take a breath. "I need to see it."

I need it, too.

FEAR ME

He took my panties from my mouth and stuffed them in one of his many pockets. "Place your hands flat on the table, behind your back and don't move them no matter what I do to you. Do you understand me?"

"Yes." My voice was unsteady. I tried to obscure the moan that passed through my lips, but the smirk on his face told me he heard as I watched my tormentor of ten years gaze between my naked thighs with lust and purpose in his eyes.

"I want you to tell me what you feel. I want to know everything and don't hold back. I'll know if you do. This ends when you come and not before. Are we clear?" I nodded instead of speaking. I didn't trust my voice when he touched me. "Good. Now ask me to make you come."

I hesitated though I couldn't deny the eager anticipation I felt. Not to mention the nervous thrill I got from being touched and exposed like this in the middle of our classroom.

"Please... make me come..."

He smirked and lowered his head. "My wish is your command."

His face disappeared between my thighs, and the first swipe of his hot tongue on my aching pussy caused me to suck in every bit of available air. *What is he doing to me?*

It was much more than I could handle, and still, it didn't feel like enough. My first instinct was to grab onto him, but I remembered his order and dug my nails into the wood of the table as he continued to lick me. The foreign feel of his tongue on me was like a hot, wet massage that I never wanted to end.

"I don't hear you," he said. I cursed those few seconds he took his mouth away from me. But when he plunged his tongue inside my walls immediately after, a scream erupted from me.

"What... are you... doing?" I moaned brokenly. "I can feel you... licking... sucking... touching me."

He worked his tongue on me relentlessly and soon my hips began to roll and press into him for more. When his thumb began to stroke my clit, I leaned back, using my arms to support my weight. The sounds of pleasure that broke from my lips filled the room, mingling with the sound of the rocking table as I moved wildly on top of it combined with him tasting me, eating me,.

"You... have... to stop. I can't—"

A menacing growl came from him when I begged him to stop and to spare me from what he was doing to my body. His talented mouth was turning me inside out as he latched onto my clit. I wasn't myself anymore. That much was clear. There was someone else on top of that table letting him take what he wanted and enjoying it. The open-mouthed kisses he placed on my lower lips made my body shudder, and then he plunged his tongue inside me once again.

"Right there," I moaned.

I didn't think about the broken nails I would find when this was over. Instead, I embraced the madness he was creating inside me as I fought not to touch him. In the deep recesses of my mind and conscience, I was mortified at how I came apart so easily. I was letting him win. But worse than that, I was letting him know I liked it.

*I'm going to enjoy stealing away what you cherish most and making you love it while I do.* I heard his words in my head from the other night. He kept his word, as he was known to do. I did love it.

"So fucking hot," he muttered. I was about to respond when I heard the telltale sounds of cars pulling up and footsteps in the hall.

"Oh no. Keiran—"

"Don't say my name," he snarled.

"But they're coming. You have to stop," I moaned. "Please, we'll get caught," I protested again while I pressed forward sending his tongue deeper inside me.

"You know what I want. Give it to me," he ordered.

His hands were now massaging my ass, and I looked back at the door to see a few heads through the small window passing by. The pace of his tongue increased, and I felt my walls clench around his tongue.

"How?" I cried in frustration as the rhythm and pace of my writhing hips increasing.

"Beg me."

I hesitated though my body screamed for me to do just that. Could I really beg for something I shouldn't ask for?

"Make me come, make me—"

The force of my orgasm overpowered my words as I came with a silent scream that rocked my body and threw common sense out the window. His mouth remained on me through my orgasm, and afterward, he pressed lingering kisses on my heated skin. Just as the first bell for first period rang, he lifted his head and stared at me with a dark look in eyes.

"You taste sweeter than you pretend to be."

\* \* \*

HOURS LATER, I was rushing out of French to avoid Willow and to wait for Keiran. Part of our agreement from last night was that I had eyes on me at all times, preferably his. I guess that's why Keenan emerged out of nowhere and said, "You're with me. Keiran's busy."

"Oh, that's okay... I can just walk myself," I volunteered.

"Not happening," he replied shortly before he marched away, assuming I would follow. I did.

We ran into Sheldon on the way to class, and I watched her prance up to Keenan, who wasted no time embracing her. "Hi, handsome. I missed you," she giggled. Keenan kissed her enthusiastically while grabbing a handful of her ass. Public displays of affection were the norm with these two.

"I missed you more, beautiful. We still on for tonight?"

"Yeah, can't wait." She looked up and noticed me, a grin spreading across her face. "Hi, Lake. How's it going?

"Great, thanks." I still wonder why she is so nice to me since she is part of Keiran's camp.

"Oh, I almost forgot. Happy belated birthday!" She noticed my puzzled look and stated, "I overheard Keiran telling Keenan. What did you—"

"Okay, babe, I'm walking Lake to class for Keiran," he quickly interjected and walked off, leaving behind Sheldon, who now looked confused.

"Why couldn't Keiran take me to class?"

He turned his head to look at me and lifted an eyebrow. "Why do you care?"

"I just think it's a little much. I can find my own way to class."

"Yeah, well, we've seen how treacherous you are and how far you're willing to go. You framed my cousin, princess. You did it to yourself."

We reached the class, and he motioned for me to go inside, but I hesitated. "Keenan, listen. I had *nothing* to do with it. I lost my cell phone, or it was stolen—I don't know, but I didn't frame him. Please, you have to believe me."

I didn't know why I was pleading my case to Keenan, but after what happened this morning, I was desperate. The way I gave in and responded to Keiran scared me. I wasn't supposed to like what he did to me. Keenan didn't immediately blow me off, which was promising. Instead, he searched my eyes before he sighed and shook his head.

"Not my call, babe," he stated before walking into our class with a shrug.

\* \* \*

BY THE END of Art class, I was praying for the last eighty minutes of school to pass quickly. Seeing Keiran for the first time since this morning had brought a permanently heated flush to my skin because my perpetual blushing just wouldn't end. He stared at me for a long time when he entered the classroom after I had already been seated. Keenan had once again walked me to class so I hadn't expected to see Keiran again today. The sound of my moans as he forced pleasure on my body still echoed in my ears. And then there was remembering the feeling of his mouth on me...

Willow had just entered our fifth-period classroom looking harassed, and when Dash entered behind her, I knew why. It looked as if he were holding her backpack hostage. She said something to him and held her hand out, but he shook his head and headed toward us with her backpack in tow.

Dash sat down on my right, leaving a seat open between us and plopped her backpack in the chair. He relaxed in his seat while glaring at her. She stood in the doorway looking as if she wanted to cry. *Why was he messing with her?*

I opened my mouth to curse Dash out when I felt

Keiran grip the back of my neck and whisper, "Not your business," in my ear. *The hell it isn't!* I ignored him and tried once again to help Willow, but when he applied pressure to my neck, I started to see spots. "What... did I... say?" He spoke slow and calm. The effect was much more intimidating than if he had screamed the words at me. I relaxed back into my seat and reluctantly nodded. "Good girl."

He released my nape and began rubbing my neck with the pad of his thumbs. I was annoyed that I gave in to him, but I had to admit the massage felt good. Willow was my friend, but I couldn't help her if she wouldn't let me in—although it might have had something to do with the fact she was sleeping with my tormentor's best friend.

Willow sucked her teeth and sat down with us, murmuring something about 'practically kidnapping.'

"Lose the attitude, angel," Dash scolded.

*Angel?* I was tempted to take back my promise to her and demand to know what was up with them. I caught his eye and noticed he was playing with the ends of her hair and twirling it around his finger. He shot me a cocky look before turning to face the front of the classroom.

Sheldon turned to face us again and smiled at Willow. "Hi, I'm Sheldon," she held out her hand. Willow shook it and introduced herself. "Are you and Dash dating?"

*She really doesn't waste any time.* She pretty much asked me the same thing yesterday. I felt my eyes narrow as I wondered what her motive was.

"No."

"We're friends," Dash added.

"Not in this lifetime."

Sheldon looked at Dash, her twin brother, for an

answer, apparently not believing Willow. "We hang out," he confirmed again.

Sheldon then took in Willow more closely and remarked, "Wow, you look hot," she said as she shamelessly admired Willow's body. "I love your curves." Willow wore a red and black, plaid skirt with a dark purple button up and black combat boots. It was tame compared to what she usually wore. I could see the lust in Dash's eyes even now, as he stared at her.

"Babe, are you lusting after her?" Keenan laughed.

"Totally. Oh, cool... my first lesbian crush." She winked at Willow making her laugh.

The tension between us was even thicker than in French earlier when she tried to talk to me, and I rebuffed her. I wouldn't put it past Keiran to have someone watching. He wielded a lot of unnecessary power around school and wasn't afraid to use it.

Fifth period didn't end as fast as I hoped, and when I walked out of the classroom with Keiran, I let out an involuntary groan. Anya was waiting in the hallway, and immediately, she snaked her way into Keiran's space, pushing her breasts against his arm.

"Keiran, where have you been. I haven't seen you all day," she whined. A flash of annoyance that he didn't try to hide appeared on his face.

"Around," he replied shortly without sparing her a glance. His gaze was focused on me, and when she took notice, she scowled at me.

"Did you know Lake is saying you two are dating? How pathetic." I didn't bother to defend myself against the lie, and instead, shook my head at how easily she let the lie spew from her lips.

He sent me a smirk before stating, "She should know better... she knows I'm not dating anyone. See you later, Amber." Anya gasped in outrage while the other kids snickered at him for calling her the wrong name. He shook her off before sending me a look and walking away. I followed, feeling every bit the lap dog that Anya claimed.

"I didn't, you know," I stated after we walked a good distance.

"Didn't what?"

"I didn't say we were dating. Willow asked the other day, but before I could answer, Anya overheard and interrupted," I explained.

"Doesn't matter. You're mine for now. That's all anyone needs to know."

"What does that mean? I'm yours? I belong to no one."

"The fact that you're with me now says differently."

"But by force."

He stared down at me for a moment. "Is it?" he questioned with a smug look. I wanted wipe that smugness off his face with a retort, but he continued on before I could respond. "By force or free will, you belong to me until I'm done with you."

"And then what?" I couldn't help but ask.

"Hey, Bro," Keenan interrupted, appearing out of thin air. I didn't even realize they were following us. "We need to start practicing soon before the season. We have to get your game back up," he said with excitement.

"My game must be up because you still can't beat me," Keiran retorted. Keenan stopped and began cracking his knuckles.

"So how do you want to do this?"

"Fifteen minutes. First to ten."

"Oh, yeah," Keenan grinned.

"Oh, no" Sheldon groaned.

# CHAPTER EIGHT

"SHIT, THAT'S A foul!" I watched in horror as Keenan took a blow to the nose from Keiran's elbow. They had been exchanging blows since the first pass. Keiran had just suffered a kick to the gut from Keenan after he knocked him down and stole the ball.

This was basketball?

What I thought would be a friendly game between cousins was an intense and violent match... and it just so happened that a ball was involved.

We were in their backyard, which was spacious enough for a decent size court. So far, the game was tied at eight points, and the closer they got to the end of the game, the more violent they became. I winced at an imaginary pain as Keiran's jaw was clipped with a strong right hook, but he maintained a hold on the ball. His next move was too quick. One moment the cousins were squared off and the next, Keiran was dunking the ball, winning the game.

"You're still slow," Keiran gloated.

"Fuck you," Keenan laughed. They shook hands before limping off the court, both sporting scrapes and bruises.

Keiran locked eyes with me, still grinning and my heart stopped. I'd never seen Keiran happy before. I don't think I've ever seen him smile... well, not a genuine smile anyway.

Keenan disappeared inside the house yelling for Sheldon and leaving Keiran and me alone.

"You know you didn't have to watch. You could have gone into the house with Sheldon," Keiran stated.

"Oh, um. I wasn't sure—"

"Jeez, Monroe, I brought you here, didn't I?" He shook his head before gesturing to the house. "Come on," he ordered.

"Why? So you can chain me up in your basement?" He turned back to face me, cocking his head to the side.

"Don't give me any ideas, Monroe, or you'll never make it out of here. The only reason I haven't chained you in my basement is because I know you'll be missed." His grin was malicious as he stared at me. "I can guess how much your aunt loves you," he said with disdain. "And I know how much you must love your aunt... that's why you are going to do whatever I say and whatever I want. So start by getting your ass in my house."

He stood back to glare at me until I walked through the door. We entered the house through the backdoor and made our way down a long hallway until we reached the staircase. He grabbed my arm and pulled me up the stairs.

"Wait. Uh, where is your uncle?" I asked nervously.

"Gone... and he won't help you," he smirked before pushing me into his bedroom and slamming the door shut behind us. I looked around Keiran's room, taking it all in, but I only focused on the large bed dominating the room. "Have a seat," he directed.

"I think I'll stand."

"Now."

I was still standing when he pulled his shirt over his head giving me my first look at him shirtless. The sight before me had me in awe, and I didn't realize I had taken a seat when my legs grew weak. Sweat glistened across his chest, and I could see a single rivulet run slowly over the hard ripples that were his abs before it disappeared into his shorts.

I licked my lips unconsciously, wanting to chase that dewdrop with my tongue. He had the body of every teenage girl's dream. I suddenly felt hotter than hell and fidgeted.

"Looking at me like that will get you fucked, Monroe." I ended my perusal and glared at him even as I felt my cheeks heat in embarrassment because he had caught me ogling him. "You think you deserve my bed?" he asked and arched his brow.

I assumed he was talking about sex and was about to remark that I never asked for it when he nodded to where I was sitting *on his bed.* "Get up," he ordered before I could hop up. I didn't want to be on his bed any more than he wanted me there. He motioned to his desk chair, and I took the seat. "Stay here."

He left out of the room, and I got comfortable and took in my surroundings. His room had a blue, black, and gray color scheme with built in shelving on the left side of the room. It held various trophies and photographs of him, Keenan, and Dash. What I didn't see were any pictures of his parents or uncle. It made me wonder where his parents were and how he came under his uncle's care. Yesterday, he mentioned how he had disappeared, and I realized I had no clue what he meant, but I knew it couldn't be good. I looked around more and noticed the basketball hoop hanging on the backside of the door. An all-black basketball rested on the floor near it. On the wall, there were a large flat screen television and various gaming systems and disc hazardously lying on the floor.

I walked over to the large black dresser to inspect the contents on top, but it only held spare change and watches and other knickknacks. My eye, however, caught his cellphone laying there with a message from 'Blake' lighting up the screen.

Good to go.

When school was over, he took my phone from me so there was no way for me to call for help if I needed it. I don't know why I picked up his phone after reading the message repeatedly, but I immediately regretted it when the door burst open.

I jumped and dropped the phone on the floor. Keiran had come back. He was staring at me until his gaze traveled to the floor, and his jaw clenched when he noticed his cell phone.

"What are you doing?" He closed the door behind him slowly, and I took a deep breath.

"Nothing. I—"

"Who were you trying to call?" He was walking toward me slowly, and I went to take a step back, forgetting the dresser was behind me blocking my escape.

"Oh, um..." I faltered, not knowing how to talk my way out of the crap I had just got myself caught in. He released a tired breath and shook his head.

"Sit on the floor over there." He pointed to a spot near his nightstand.

"I can explain—"

"I'm not interested in your explanations."

I gave in just like he knew I would, if the self-satisfied smirk was anything to go by, and sat in the spot he designated. When he bent over his nightstand, I inhaled his scent. I admired his dark locks and plump lips before I could stop myself, but the sound of metal had my gaze flying to what he held in his hand. I'm sure my eyes were close to popping out of my head as I gaped at the object in his hand.

Handcuffs. Freaking handcuffs.

"What are you doing with those?"

"Handcuffing you."

"No, I mean why do you have them in the first place?"

"I'm saving them for a rainy day. These are new actually. It's like a 'thinking of you' gift because I was *thinking of you* when I bought them."

He quickly cuffed both hands to the long thin handle on the nightstand drawer so that my body was now bent in an awkward position unless I faced the nightstand completely with my back to the door.

"I'm not an animal," I argued, but when I heard the click of the door, I realized he was already gone.

\* \* \*

Minutes later, there was a soft knock on the door, and then it opened. Light footsteps rushed in my direction and then I heard Sheldon's soft voice ask, "Are you okay?"

"Yes, I'm fine," I said sarcastically. I dropped my gaze down to the dark wood but felt her gentle fingers pick up my chin, forcing me to look at her as she sat on the floor next to me.

"Did he hurt you?" Her voice and eyes were full of concern, which surprised me.

"Yes," I answered truthfully, "but not in the way you think."

Keiran always had the power to hurt me without lifting a finger, and on the days he was feeling particularly sadistic, he would take from me relentlessly until I had nothing left to give. Over the years, I learned the signs, and while I knew there was no escaping him, I was able to bounce back quicker.

"Lake, what are you doing here with him?"

*Letting him punish me.* "Why?" I asked instead.

"Because you two don't have the best history. I mean, why does he hate you?"

I let out a dry laugh. "I wish I knew."

"Keenan won't tell me much. He only said it began a long time ago, but I already figured that. I was there sometimes when he teased you. It was awful."

I shrugged. "I survived it."

"Sometimes, surviving isn't enough." She was wrong. It was enough. It had to be.

I stared at her flawless face and bright eyes and knew she had never experienced a day of hardship in her life. She had her parents, a boyfriend, and an endless supply of friends, and not to mention, both money and status. While I didn't begrudge her happiness, we didn't have anything to talk about.

"I really appreciate you checking on me, but I don't think I should talk to you." She tensed, and I realized my mistake. Sheldon was sharper than I thought.

"Did he threaten you?" *Yes.*

"No." She looked at me skeptically.

"Are you lying to me?" *Yes.*

"No."

"Are you here on your own free will?" *No.*

"No." *Shit.*

"I see." When she stood up in a hurry, I panicked. "Wait! I meant yes, I agreed to come here."

"Why are you covering for him? You're obviously in trouble," she hissed as she gestured to the handcuffs.

"Please, Sheldon. You don't understand. Leave it

be."

"Make me understand," she demanded.

"I don't know how! Why do you care anyway? You're his friend and Keenan's girlfriend.

"I can handle Keenan," she argued.

"But can you handle Keiran?"

"Keenan won't let him do anything to me."

I wasn't so sure about that. Keiran said he had watched me, but I've watched him, too. His presence affected everyone around him. They either wanted him or admired him, but they all feared him.

He was unstable as a kid and violent at times, often fighting or attacking, unprovoked. After his fights with other boys, he would immediately seek me out and rip me apart with vicious, verbal attacks or hurtful pranks. That lasted until we were thirteen when his fighting ceased altogether. By then, everyone either avoided him or went out of their way to be friends with him.

He was controlled now and less volatile. Always cool, always silent. He rarely ever spoke except when I was in the vicinity, but when he did, everyone listened, including me.

The only person who didn't seem to be afraid of Keiran was Dash. Maybe that was why they were best friends. I didn't doubt Keenan could hold his own, but I also think his love for Keiran blinds him. The only time Keiran had acted like a normal teen was when Keenan and Dash surrounded him. They complemented each other. Dash was the charmer, Keenan was the rebel, and Keiran... he was just bad.

What kind of person did it take to form a bond with someone like Keiran? I thought about it before deciding I didn't want to know. Some things were better left unknown. "Keenan won't stop Keiran and you know it. He hates me just as much as Keiran because he thinks I framed him.

"Did you?"

I met and held her gaze before answering, "No."

"Good," she nodded and got up to leave.

I stared at her in disbelief. "You believe me?"

"If you say you didn't do it then I believe you unless you give me a reason, not to. It never added up, anyway. The boys were angry and beyond reason." She opened the door, but then immediately turned back to me. "You didn't frame Keiran, but I have a feeling you know who did..."

I sucked in a breath before nodding. "Yes."

"So if you didn't frame Keiran... who did?"

I hesitated and wondered if she would honestly believe me if I told her. "I can't tell you."

"Why not?"

"I don't trust you," I answered truthfully. "You can't help me anyway. No one can."

She didn't appear upset by my answer. Instead, she looked thoughtful. "Lake, remember in the sixth grade when Keiran broke Benny Wheeler's nose?"

I laughed, humorlessly. "How could I forget? That was the same day Benny tripped me and stole my music player because I told Mrs. Jensen he cheated off my test."

"Exactly." She winked and flounced away in her normal peppy fashion. I heard voices in the hallway and figured Keenan had come looking for her.

I thought back to the day Keiran punched Benny, but all I could remember was going home upset about my music player. I had found it lying on my steps. I never did find out who put it there.

\* \* \*

"BLAKE SAYS HE has our supply ready for pickup." Keenan whispered.

"Good. You put the word out?" I recognized Keiran's deep voice.

"Yeah, Dash and I are on it. He can't make this run with us, though. His dad has him tied up with something. So what are you going to do with her?" I tried not to panic at the possible meaning of his question as I eavesdropped. Sheldon must not have closed the door completely when she had left because I could hear everything they were saying.

"She comes with us. I can't risk letting her out of my sight, at least not right now."

"What are you doing with her anyway?"

"I'm getting my year back."

"She told me something today."

"Oh?"

"Yeah, when I was playing guard," he stated with sarcasm flooding his tone. "She told me she lost her cellphone the day the call was made. She asked me to believe her."

"Do you?" Keiran sounded disinterested, but I could also hear the bitterness in his tone.

"No—it's just... she sounded pretty convincing and looked scared as hell. Did you do something to her? Say anything? You left the other morning alone but showed up to school late *with her*."

"How do you know I showed up late?" he asked, ignoring his questions.

"Come on, man. When you show up to school with the one person everyone knows you hate, people talk. Not to mention she's the hottest piece of ass at Bainbridge."

"Watch it," he growled.

"See what I mean? That! What is that? You claiming her now?" Keenan's frustration increased the volume of his voice until he was yelling. I was curious to know myself why Keiran reacted so strongly.

"You don't want Sheldon to hear you say some shit like that. You are already on a tight leash as it is."

"Yeah, well, you let me worry about Sheldon. She's beautiful, no doubt about it, but Lake could give her a run for her money, that's all."

"Doesn't matter. I'm keeping an eye on her vindictive ass, nothing more."

"If you say so. Look, lets pick up the supply. Grab your girl. We have to drop Sheldon off at home. I don't want her involved with this. Her pops would have me wasted."

"He might just do it himself." Keiran laughed, and just like his smile, I wanted to see and hear more of it. It made him appear human.

I heard footsteps and quickly attempted to look as if I wasn't just straining to eavesdrop. The door opened, and then I heard him walk inside. I twisted my body and saw him with only a towel wrapped around his waist as he stood by his dresser. When his hand dropped to the knot in his towel, I quickly looked away. The sound of the material hitting the carpeted floor forged a visual of his naked body to the forefront of my mind. I desperately fought the urge and temptation to look.

Only when it was quiet, and the rustling of his clothing ceased, did I open my eyes. I didn't even realize I'd closed them. I turned again to see he had put on jeans and a dark hoodie. I could see the little beads of moisture from his shower glistening on the dark strands of hair covering his head. He was pulling on a boot as I watched the muscles of his broad back ripple with his movements.

"Are you taking me home now?" I asked hesitantly despite what I just clearly heard. When his boots were on his feet, he stood and finally glanced at me.

"I have shit to do, which means you're a part of it."

"I can't go anywhere with you. My aunt will want me to be home."

"Your aunt is thousands of miles away on her book tour and won't be back for six weeks. Besides... she trusts your judgment."

I gaped at his smug face. "How would you know if she trusts me?"

"I went through your text messages," he answered as if it were perfectly okay to invade someone's privacy. I wondered how much he might have gone through and if he'd seen the messages between Willow and me. Willow would check on me often throughout the day to make sure Keiran hadn't gotten to me. It was a failed attempt being that he always found me no matter where I was, but she was the best kind of friend.

"I don't feel comfortable going anywhere with you."

"And this is me not giving a fuck," he said. He walked over to where I was sitting and released me from the cuffs. "Let's go." He moved toward the door, dismissing me. Anger and frustration as I had never felt before flooded my senses. I wanted to argue.

I needed to fight back.

"No." I ground out the word and sat down on his bed again with my arms crossed. I didn't get a chance to rethink the danger of that move and the vulnerable state it placed me in, but he did. He froze with his hand above the knob. My heartbeat stuttered then slowed when he turned slowly to face me with a menacing expression plastered on his beautiful face.

"I told you, you didn't deserve my bed, but since you seem to want it now, I can accommodate you." Fear and confusion wound its way into my mind when he took threatening steps toward me while reaching for his hoodie and tossing it over his head. When he reached the foot of the bed, I panicked and scrambled for the head, only making it halfway before he grabbed onto my ankle and dragged me, kicking and screaming, back to him. I was relieved when he released me, but his next words made the panic come rushing back.

"Take off the dress. You can get fucked on the floor," he snarled. His gaze was stormy as he glared down at me. I watched his nostrils flare when I refused to obey his command.

"Why would I do that?" I fought to hold it together when all I wanted to do was run and hide.

"Because I said so."

"Just take me home!" Frustration rose inside me, and my tone reflected it.

"Take it off. You have three seconds."

"But—"

"One..."

"I really don't—"

"Two. Don't make me get to three."

"Or what?" I challenged as a last resort.

"I do it for you." He grabbed the hem of my dress and the sound of ripping material had me grabbing his hands to stop him.

"Okay!" I yelled in surrender and stood up. Our bodies were only a breath apart, and I could feel the simmering heat from his anger and his body penetrating my senses. My shaking hands rose to the straps of my dress, slipping them down slowly until my dress dropped to the floor with a whisper of sound. I kept my eyes lowered though I felt the weight of his gaze on my skin. I noticed his hands clench into fists, and I wished I had the courage to ask what he was thinking.

"Kill the fucking act. You don't have anything I won't see, feel, and taste. Again..." My knees shook, and my shoulders trembled at his harsh words. "...and again..."

"Stop," I pleaded.

"...and again," he continued. He looked me up and down before saying, "I've seen better. You don't have anything special." He picked up my dress and tossed it at me for it only to hit the floor again at my feet.

A sound of distress escaped my throat, and I rushed to pick up the pale yellow material and clutched it to my naked chest. With a look of disgust, he stormed out, the vibration of the door slamming echoed throughout the room.

* * *

"TURN HERE. HE said he'd be in the quad," Keenan directed. We'd just driven thirty minutes out to the local college. I wondered what the supply was that we came for. Keiran parked the car but kept the engine running. He watched me through the rearview mirror and held my stare. After he had destroyed me emotionally in his bedroom, I remained silent, wanting to lick my wounds in peace.

"There he is," Keenan exclaimed with excitement lacing his voice. He rubbed his hands together before jumping out of the car.

Keiran continued to watch me even after Keenan was gone. When my nervousness began to show through my fidgeting, he smirked. "Stay here," he ordered and then he was gone, breaking the connection he held me in.

I watched through the backseat car window as the three men slapped hands and pounded each other's backs in normal manly fashion. The guy who I assumed was Blake carried a small, black duffle bag. He handed the bag over, appearing casual when I was anything but. I stared at the black duffle bag, silently freaking out over the possibilities of its content.

When they turned back to the car, Keiran placed the bag on the backseat floor. I could hear the muffled movements of what sounded like glass knocking around. The temptation to open the bag was strong, and he must have known by the glare on his face.

"Don't touch it," he warned, and I realized Keiran was watching me along with Keenan and Blake.

"I wasn't going to," I lied but instead of leaving as I thought he would, he sat down in the backseat. The space became smaller, and suddenly there wasn't enough air to breathe. Why did I always feel the need to catch my breath when I was close to him?

He slid over the seat until he was sitting directly next to me and shut the car door with a resounding thud. He then reached over me to lock the door with a click that was soft but rang loud in my ears. I pressed my back against the car door, my breath releasing fast and uneven. He palmed the back of my head and then his fingers slipped over the strands until he wound my ponytail around his hand lightly.

"Say that again," he demanded. His voice was calm, but his eyes were not as he waited patiently for me to repeat myself. I reluctantly coughed back up the lie.

"That's what I thought you said," he whispered just before a sharp pain emerged from my scalp. My head was tilted back far enough to block my view of him. "Lie to me again, and I will hurt you, Monroe. I promise I will hurt you. There are worse pains than just the physical, and I won't hesitate to make you feel them. Do we understand each other?"

I nodded as best as I could with his grip on my hair. Just as fast as it happened, it was over. He was out of the car again and walking back over to Blake, who watched me curiously. Keiran must have said something to him because he abruptly turned his head back to him.

The campus was still occupied by a few students who were probably leaving a late class or studying in the library. The attention Keiran and Keenan were receiving from loads of girls, who appeared out of nowhere, didn't escape my attention. A few even stopped to talk and hand over a little slip of paper that I knew contained their number.

I quelled the disgust I felt and willed myself not to feel anything remotely close to jealousy. That wasn't possible. Instead, I focused on the scenery and the obvious signs that fall had arrived. I loved when the leaves would turn color. The various browns, golds, and reds painted a beautiful, colorful canvas of the world, shielding the reality that it was as dark as my beautiful tormentor. At least that was what he was intent on teaching me.

After a few minutes of ignoring the nauseous display of shameless girl's parading in front of the group with short skirts and low tops, they finally made for the car. I was willing to bet they never even exchanged names. Girls are stupid.

I pretended to pick my nails even after they got in the car, and we left the college campus behind. When we got to the highway, I still had not looked up from my nails, and by this time, I had nail polish shavings on my lap from picking at the paint. Full of spite, I cheerfully brushed the shavings all over the clean floor of his car.

You could call it immature. I call it revenge. It was my own little way to say 'fuck you.' I didn't realize I had laughed out loud until Keenan turned his head and looked at me funny. I quickly averted my gaze and stared out the window watching the day give way to night.

* * *

WHEN WE ARRIVED back in Six Forks, I fully expected to be driven home. Instead, I found myself once again at Keiran's house. I prayed for patience when he exited the car and opened the backdoor for what I assumed was the bag. Instead, he pulled me out of the car and Keenan retrieved the bag from the backseat.

With his hand on my arm, I wasn't brave enough to fight off his hold, so I let him drag me into his house. Keenan followed behind us to deposit the bag before retreating out the door. Moments later, I could hear the rumble of a bike drive away.

Realization dawned on me that I was now alone with Keiran. He had taken off for places unknown in the house, leaving me standing in the entryway. I eyed the bag left by the door, tempted to go against his warning. What if he was dealing and he just took me on some kind of drug run? Either way, I was screwed as either a witness or a participant. Depends on how the police would see it if we had been caught.

"What are you doing?" Keiran asked from behind me. I didn't hear him approach and jumped before whirling around to face him with a guilty flush spreading over my skin.

"What's in the bag? Are you selling drugs?" I answered with a question of my own.

When his jaw clenched, I thought he would lash out, but when all he said was, "Call your aunt, but make it quick and don't try anything," I was surprised. It was then I noticed he was holding my phone in his hand.

"Exactly what am I supposed to try? I love my aunt, and I will do anything to protect her. Just because you don't know the meaning of the word doesn't mean it isn't real."

Silence.

"So, you'd do anything to protect her?" His tone was too calm as he slowly stepped forward. "Is that right?"

"That's what I said."

"Give me a blowjob." I felt something quicken inside, and my entire body blushed.

"What?"

"You heard me the first time." My eyes widened when he began unbuckling his belt. The familiar feelings of panic began to set in as he continued to approach me. "On your knees. I want to feel those pretty pink lips on me."

"Don't do this."

"I'm not. You are. Prove yourself and save your precious aunt." His hand pushed me down until I was on my knees. My body became numb, and my ability to think fled. I could hear his harsh words replaying over and over in my head. Would he really spare my aunt if I did it? Could I even go through with it?

"Decide quickly. My offer won't last forever." His offer? Is that really how he saw it? *More like coercion and blackmail.*

"I—"

"It doesn't require you to talk." He lowered his jeans and boxers until they hung just around his hips. His cock had sprung out of the confines of his jeans, and a shiver of apprehension ran through my body while my eyes widened with shock and trepidation.

His erection was long and thick with angry veins

running the length. My attention was drawn to the pulsing head that had a bead of moisture shining on the tip. My belly had butterflies, and my mouth and lips suddenly felt too dry. I licked my lips to moisten them, and Keiran's gaze zeroed in on my lips as I did. A low, throaty sound erupted from his lips as he watched me.

He began a stroking motion, up and down while gazing down at me, daring me with his eyes. When I continued to hesitate, he grabbed the nape of my neck and brought my lips closer. The tip of his cock touched my lips, and he began rubbing it across slowly. I was shaking uncontrollably with an emotion and a feeling I couldn't explain. But I did recognize shame. Shame that I wanted to taste him even though he only wanted to degrade me.

"Okay, I'll do it, but please be gent—"

My words were lost when he plunged his cock into my mouth without warning. He continued to push forward with a groan, and I immediately felt pressure at the back of my throat, causing me to gag. I instinctively closed my mouth around the intruding length to relieve the pressure but soon realized my mistake. My body heat rose in response to his aggression, and I felt both fear and desire battle within me. Unfortunately, fear had won over, and I put all my strength into ripping away from him by pushing against his strong thighs. "I can't!" I cried out when my mouth was finally able to release him.

He pushed me away, and I fell to the floor, landing on my back and causing a loud smack to sound through the air. Rather than lashing out, he laughed. But it was full of anger and disgust as he looked down at me, nostrils flaring. "You can't because you won't. You're no better than the rest. You don't give a damn about your aunt."

I panicked at the thought that I might have screwed up my aunt's chances. "That's not true. You scared me. I can do it. I'm—"

"Nothing more than a fake. There isn't anything innocent about you, is there Monroe?" his lips curled as he spit his harsh words at me.

"Please, Keiran."

"Don't... say... my... name. Ever." I never understood why he forbid me to say his name. He was simply a mystery I may never solve. Before I could say anything further, the front door opened and I froze.

"What the hell?"

"Dude..."

"Shit."

I recognized the sound of Sheldon, Dash, and Keenan's voices behind me, in that order. We were still in the hall when he had forced me to my knees, so the door had opened up right on us.

Keiran continued to stare at me while righting his jeans and appearing unfazed by the intrusion. Embarrassment flooded my cheeks, and I was glued to the spot. Though Keiran was the only one exposed, it was apparent what had taken place. I was no longer lying on the floor when they arrived, but I was still on my knees.

Everyone had grown quiet. The humiliation of my situation was overwhelming, and then I was crying again. I was always crying. When would I fight back?

"That's enough. Lake, get up." Sheldon tugged on my arm until I was standing, but I kept my gaze lowered. She then turned on Keiran. "What the hell is wrong with you? She may be afraid of you, but I'm not. If I catch you doing some shit like this to her again, I will kick your ass. If I find out there was foul play, I will turn you in myself. Got it?"

"Foul play? You mean rape?" he asked in a sarcastic

tone. "I don't rape. But then, Monroe and I both know I wouldn't have to. She'd give it up, and I wouldn't hesitate to take anything she *offered*."

I hugged my waist and listened to him insinuate that I wanted him. I didn't want him. He was my enemy... or maybe it was just my body that desired him while my mind feared him. I just wished I knew what it was about him that made my body betray me in such a confusing way.

Sheldon hugged my shoulders and walked us away from the guys, and I felt a moment of self-loathing. I hated looking like the victim. I wasn't a victim. Right?

# CHAPTER NINE

SHELDON TOOK ME upstairs and locked us in the bathroom where she grilled me endlessly. I couldn't tell her the truth, but I didn't lie either. I told her Keiran had just been taunting me as usual. She had a few choices words to say about Keiran but let it go. I was cleaning my face with the warm cloth she'd given me when a hard knock on the door interrupted the silence. Sheldon opened the door to reveal Keiran standing on the other side and immediately moved to shield me from him.

"What do you want?"

"Leave," he said barely acknowledging her. His gaze was focused on me, and I stared back.

I wanted to look away but couldn't. I've never seen him look at me this way before. The memory of his cock in my mouth came rushing back. I blushed and finally looked away, breaking the connection.

"I'm taking her home." The relief I felt was short-lived by the look on his face. The cold calculation in his eyes told me that she would quickly become another victim of his wrath if I didn't interfere. I couldn't let her suffer the brunt of his anger. I'd had years to learn how to survive it.

"Sheldon, it's fine." She looked at me with surprise etched all over her face, and I wished I could take her help. "Really, it's okay." I had trouble holding her gaze.

"Sheldon, come here!" Keenan's voice boomed from somewhere out in the hallway.

She gave me one last look before leaving the bathroom with a terse 'fine.' Keiran motioned for me to follow him, so I tossed the cloth into the bin and followed him to his bedroom.

"Are you taking me home soon?" He ignored me and picked my phone up from the large black dresser and tossed it to me. I took turns looking from the device to him.

"Your aunt called. Call her back and let her know that everything is fine."

"Oh... right." I dialed her number.

"Put it on speaker," he ordered. I was careful not to show my aggravation for fear I would upset him. He could change his mind, and my aunt would worry if I didn't call.

Her anxious voice filtered through the phone after the third ring. "Hey, Aunt Carissa."

"Lake, thank God! How is everything?" She attempted to sound normal, but I could hear the stress and fatigue, which was weird because she usually had fun on her tours.

"Everything is great here. How are you?"

"Oh, you know, I've been signing books all day. Nothing major."

Her answer only increased my worry. Aunt Carissa was usually full of excitement and everything dealing with her books and readers. She loved being a writer. "Are you sure? You sound tired."

"Yes, I'm fine. Listen, I have to go, but how was

school?"

"School is school. I guess I will talk to you later," I stated slowly with a frown and a heavy heart.

"Great. And Lake? I love you, sweetie." The line went dead before I could respond in kind. I felt sick, despite her reassurance, remembering the last time I saw and spoke to my parents. *Would Aunt Carissa leave me, too?*

"I should go home. Can you take me now?"

"We're having a party. You should stick around." He plucked my phone out of my hand and pocketed it. I didn't like the sound of his *invitation*. It sounded more like the order I knew it to be.

"Thanks, but no thanks," I answered sarcastically. "I would really rather go home."

"I wasn't asking. Do I need to explain this to you again? I don't trust you. I'm keeping an eye on you. Simple as that."

"It isn't really about keeping an eye on me though, is it?" His body stiffened, and I could tell I struck a nerve. Rather than scare me away, it gave me the motivation I needed to push him. "What's the matter? You can't get it up unless you're angry?" I circled around him the way he did me that day in the cafeteria over a year ago. I taunted and tested how far I could go. "Is that what you hide? Some sick, twisted fantasy? Tell me... is it special for me or is it all women? Mommy didn't love you enough so you—"

The punishing hand around my jaw stopped me, and once again, my words were lost to me. He bent my body backward over his low dresser and leaned in close. The coldness in his eyes could not be mistaken for anything but deep hatred.

"It's only for you, never doubt that. No one else makes me feel this way. *No one*. It's always been you. It will *always be you.*"

The subtle threat in his words sent a cold chill through my body. Up this close, I could see the light stubble along his jaw, evidence that he hadn't shaved this morning, and I couldn't help to think how incredibly sexy and masculine he looked with it.

"Is that supposed to scare me?" I sounded tougher than I was feeling, but he didn't have to know that.

"It already does."

"Is that what you want to hear? That I am afraid of you? That I am *still* afraid of you? Yes, I am afraid, but that's all I will ever feel for you. It is the need to *survive.* You can't control me beyond that. Let me *go.*"

"I can't do that."

"Why not? I haven't done anything and don't plan to, whether or not you choose to believe it, but it's the damn truth." I searched his eyes for even a glimmer of belief, but they remained unyielding. My back was beginning to shake from the strain of nearly being bent in half, not to mention the effect his closeness was having on me.

"Because I still hate you, Monroe. Never forget that."

\* \* \*

SHELDON AND KEENAN were already downstairs by the time we finally emerged from his bedroom. His last words were still echoing in my head. While I had accepted long ago that Keiran would always hate me, it didn't make hearing it each time any easier.

We found them in the kitchen pre-gaming and setting up for the party that I was being forced to attend. Who knew my first invite to a party would be by the one person who has kept me from them... even if he was forcing me.

The first thing I noticed entering the kitchen was the mysterious, black duffle bag Keiran and Keenan was given now lay open and filled with bottles of alcohol.

Well, I'll be damned.

I couldn't believe that they actually bought alcohol in an illegal street sale. *At least it wasn't drugs.* The thought didn't make me feel better. Though, I always did wonder how high school kids found their supply of alcohol for parties. I just assumed they pilfered it from their parents, though it would be kind of hard to explain the missing alcohol.

I remember last year, the parents of Michael Hastings had divorced shortly after a huge party he had thrown. Apparently, his father was an alcoholic and swore to quit drinking, and one day, his mother found empty bottles of alcohol hidden, not thrown away, in the house. She immediately blamed his father and filed for divorce. He's been kind of a loner ever since. The guilt must be a bitch to deal with.

"Say, man, they are calling it a good year for snow this winter. I can't wait to hit the slopes this year," Keenan said as we entered the kitchen. He was practically bouncing with excitement.

"Why? You aren't tired of sucking back my snow, yet?"

"The only thing getting sucked is my dick tonight— aargh, damn it, girl! That hurt!"

"Don't look like that's happening either," Keiran snorted. Keenan was now bent over in the seat protecting his crotch. He looked as if he would faint. Sheldon winked at me, and I grinned.

"Anyway, Lake, it's really fun. We do it every winter over Christmas break. The slopes overlook Lake Tahoe, and it's gorgeous. Just like you, right, Keiran?" She grinned at him slyly.

Keiran grunted but said nothing. He grabbed a shot glass and poured an amber liquid into it, quickly tossing it back and reaching for more.

"Have you ever been skiing?" Sheldon asked.

"No, I, uh... don't know how."

"S'kay, we can teach you," she offered.

The guys had grown silent when Sheldon extended her invitation. Keiran stopped drinking, and Keenan was no longer moaning in pain as the awkward silence descended. "Um... no, that's okay. I usually just visit my grandmother at the nursing home in Red Rocks."

My maternal grandmother was stricken with Alzheimer's disease five years ago and was unable to stay with us despite my aunt's protests. "Is that where you're from? I remember you moving here in the second grade."

"Yeah, actually. It's about two hours east."

"Do you miss it?"

"No, I barely remember it," I lied.

Talking about Red Rocks meant thinking about my parents and how I ended up here in the first place. My grandmother's health was failing even then, and my mother never knew her father, so my aunt Carissa took me.

I felt eyes on me and looked up to see everyone's attention on me. Keiran was staring a hole through me, and I felt exposed, so I quickly averted my gaze.

"I swear if you boneheads make her cry, I'll castrate you both!"

I chuckled, grateful for Sheldon. We barely knew each other, but she was becoming a friend. Her fierce desire to stand up for me was winning me over. I can't handle Keiran. I was too afraid of him. He'd shown me who he really was on that playground, and I knew that boy was still inside—buried deep and waiting to come out.

* * *

THE DEAFENING BLARE of the speakers and Keiran's gaze always seemed to find me no matter where I hid. The party had been in full blast for over an hour. I watched the swing and sway of half-naked girls in short skirts and the raucous, hormonal males stumble and party, drunkenly from room to room.

Being a teen, I may not have found this so bad if I had a single friend here. I was isolated in a corner of the room, and directly across from me, I could see Keiran surrounded by other kids though he didn't seem to be paying much attention to them. Instead, his gaze would find its way back to me. I'm sure if he gave his group much attention, he would notice the hot brunette, who I was sure was one of the girls I saw on campus earlier, checking him out.

I looked around for Sheldon but didn't immediately see any sign of her anywhere. Anya had dragged her off somewhere, much to Sheldon's annoyance that she didn't try to hide. I didn't understand why she put up with Anya since she clearly didn't care for her or the rest of the cheerleaders. They all seemed to band together and didn't like outsiders. Oh, well. It was Sheldon's issue, not mine.

I began to brainstorm ways to sneak out of the party and go home without Keiran noticing. He didn't appear to be drinking beyond the two shots he had earlier. He didn't even look as if he was having fun, which was strange considering he threw the party.

My thoughts must have been transparent when a suspicious look passed over his face before he headed over to my corner. I tried burrowing deeper into the shadows thinking I could miraculously become invisible.

"Why aren't you partying?" he asked gruffly.

"I told you I wasn't interested. You are the one who wanted me here."

"You're here because I *told* you to be."

"Why are you so angry about this? I didn't want to be here," I stressed yet again.

"Get up and follow me," he ordered.

"I'm fine right here." I patted the seat. "The view is great, you know. I can see everyone make a fool of themselves and trash your uncle's place. He must be so proud," I said sarcastically.

I looked at him feeling smug as I watched his jaw clench and his nostrils flare. I was pissing him off and loving it. There were too many witnesses for me to be afraid.

"I can have everyone out of here in three seconds flat. Don't think for a second you are safe, Monroe. You will never be safe from me."

I slowly rose from my seat, not wanting to draw attention to myself. The smug look on his face was meant to provoke me further, and it was working. He led me over to the counter that was littered with the illegally purchased alcohol. He grabbed the same bottle of amber liquor I saw him drink earlier and poured a shot. I stared at the glass when he handed it to me.

"I don't drink."

"I didn't ask."

After a short staring contest of wills, I snatched the shot glass out of his hand, spilling some on my hand. He raised an eyebrow but otherwise said nothing. I sniffed the drink quickly and hated the strong, revolting smell. I fought not to gag as I brought the glass to my lips and took a tentative sip. My face tingled from the strong taste, and I reluctantly took another sip.

"That's not how to take a fucking shot. Toss it back," he instructed impatiently. I sent him a withering look and then opened my mouth to quickly swallow the liquid. The tingle from before erupted in full flames as my eyes watered and my cheeks flushed. I instantly felt the effects of the liquor to my head. I made a sound of distress and fought to get my bearings.

"Good. Now another."

"Please, I don't want to."

"I don't care. Drink." I looked at him in disbelief. It was bad enough that he made me do it the first time. How did people actually have fun drinking this stuff? I've had champagne before at one of my aunt's book functions but never anything this strong and disgusting.

"Do you have anything lighter?"

"Yes, but this is what you're getting." He poured another shot and this time a second. "I'll take this one with you."

Was that supposed to make me feel better?

This time I didn't wait to be prompted. I tossed the drink back and coughed as it burned down my throat. "Good girl," he praised. I didn't feel good at all. I felt sick. Six or seven shots later, my body felt loose and heavy at the same time. I was pretty sure my vision was blurry. Either that or I was hallucinating. I didn't know which because I'd never been drunk before. Or maybe I was just tipsy.

I was staring at the countertop willing my vision to focus, and I could feel Keiran watching me from the side. A guy who I don't think even goes to our school, had come in during my third shot as I was begging for Keiran to stop making me drink. He was watching me with too much interest in his eyes.

I didn't bother to beg Keiran to stop this time, but surprisingly, he did after we had been standing quietly for a few minutes. I found it seriously fucked up that I was drunk, but he was not.

"Hey, man, if you really want to get her going, you can have her pop a couple of these." The guy pulled out a Ziploc bag full of pills and waved them at me with a sly grin. "I'll even give them to you for free if I can get a turn."

My alcohol-riddled brain was slow to catch on, but when I saw the lust in the stoner's eyes, and Keiran take the bag from him, I looked on in astonishment. *He was not seriously considering drugging me, was he?*

"Can you walk?" Keiran asked.

"If it's to your car, then I can skip if you'd like." There was no way in hell I was letting him drug me.

"Go lie down in the guest room and lock the door."

"But—"

"Now, Lake." I didn't bother to argue anymore and headed in that direction, but just as I made it to the stairs, Trevor intercepted me. *I so did not need this right now.*

"Well, well, well. I never thought I'd see little Miss Prim at a party, much less Masters's party."

"Don't get your hopes up. I'm trying to find the nearest exit out of this cesspool."

"Looks to me like you were sneaking upstairs."

"No one would ever accuse you of having bad eyes. Excuse me." I tried to go around, but he linked his arm around my waist and leaned into me. I could smell the stench of alcohol on his breath.

"Have you been taking care of our little secret? You wouldn't want to make an enemy out of me too, would you?"

"It's not my secret, Trevor. It's yours. The only one

afraid of making enemies right now is you."

"Whether you like to admit it, Lake, you helped me bring Keiran down. You should be grateful. I even let you take the credit for all the work." He grinned and slithered away like the snake he was. As much as I hated Trevor's treachery, I think I was madder at myself. I should have seen it coming. I should have been more careful...

*"ENEMY? I DON'T have enemies. I'm no one," I stated, dumfounded.*

*What or who could Trevor and I possibly have in common? We didn't share the same social status and our circles—or rather, my circle of one—were different.*

*He looked at me impatiently when I stared up at him in confusion. Gosh, was everyone on the basketball team freakishly tall? He dwarfed my five-eight easily.*

*Trevor was blond and good looking, but Tiffany and her friends were right—Keiran was better looking with a hotter body. Trevor was bullish looking as his muscles strained and pulled against his skin while Keiran was lean with the right amount of muscle tone that made him look naturally powerful.*

*"Keiran Masters," he stated simply.*

*I stepped back, anxiety kicking in. It was my usual reaction to hearing his name. I also didn't understand what he was asking or what he wanted from me. I looked around thinking it was a setup, and Keiran was waiting to jump out to screw with me. He hasn't gone a day without a prank, condescending look, or taunt, in ten years. It was like my pain was an addiction, and he needed his fix. Sometimes I think he went out of his way to find me so he could hurt me.*

*"What about him?" I swallowed deeply wanting to be anywhere but here.*

"I know a way we can stop him so he'll no longer be a problem for either of us," he stated simply as if he was telling time.

"Why?"

He frowned down at me not expecting that answer I guessed. "Why what?"

"Why are you doing this?"

"Why not," he scoffed. "Keiran thinks he's untouchable. He runs this school, but he doesn't run me. Don't you want the bullying to stop?"

"Yes." It was true, I did, but how far was I really willing to go for peace?

"Good. I know the perfect way to teach him a lesson."

"How?"

"We frame him."

* * *

MY RUN-IN WITH Trevor and remembering the day he propositioned me sobered me up a little, but I still stumbled up the stairs one at a time. When I reached the landing I felt the urge to pee, so I stumbled further down the hall to the bathroom. Lucky for me, I found it on the first try and no one was in there. In fact, the second floor seemed deserted altogether. I thought people usually occupied the bedroom for... stuff.

After using the bathroom, I made it to one of the bedrooms and pushed the door open. I dropped face down on soft blankets that smelled familiar and quickly passed out. If I weren't so drunk, I would have realized what I'd done.

The sound of the door opening and closing, followed by heavy footsteps across the carpeted floor, jerked me out my sleep some time later. It was dark, and I couldn't make out much in the room, but I could feel eyes watching me while I remained as still as possible and tried not to panic.

It was the scent of the bed sheets beneath me that gave the first clue. The scent was familiar and undoubtedly masculine, and the sheets didn't feel like mine. *This isn't my room.*

"I know you're awake."

*Keiran.* Relief flooded my mind that it wasn't some creep from the party, and I released the breath I was holding... *Oh, God. It was Keiran.*

Panic returned full force and stronger than before when I remembered exactly where I was and exactly why I was there. I shot up from the bed and hovered by the headboard, pulling the blanket around me for protection.

His eyes flickered to the blanket and back up to meet my gaze, as a mocking grin spread across his lips. "What is that?"

I clutched the blankets—*his blankets,* tighter and closed my eyes, squeezing them tight. My knees were knocking together under the blanket, and I prayed he couldn't hear it.

"Is that supposed to protect you from me?" I could hear the sarcasm in his low voice coming from across the room but still, I remained silent. "Should I come over there and make you talk?"

"How did you get in here? I locked the door like you said." I thought I was safe from him with the door locked... at least for tonight.

"I have a key... and you didn't lock the door." I swallowed hard against the lump in my throat. My heart pounded too fast, and my breathing became short spurts of air. "Did you think you would be safe from me?"

"Yes."

"Do you feel safe now?" His voice sounded closer, and I realized he must have been standing next to me now, so my eyes popped back open.

"No."

"No, what?" he asked unnecessarily. I knew he wanted to taunt me. I could see it in his eyes and hear it in his voice.

"No, I don't feel safe."

"Yet you parked your ass in my bed anyway."

"I didn't mean to come in here," I said through clenched teeth. He leaned over his nightstand and turned on the lamp, creating a dim glow.

"I don't believe you," he said in a low voice.

"Look, why don't I just leave?" I offered, even though the look in his eyes told me he wasn't going to let me go anywhere.

"Uncover yourself," he said, confirming my fears. I clutched the blanket tighter to my chest, fighting the urge to obey him and let the blankets go. When he looked at me with angry lust, all I wanted to do was obey. The question being was it because of fear or desire?

His deep breath cut into my inner turmoil and was my only warning before his fist was closing around my right wrist. He pried my hand away from the blanket until it was pressed hard against the unyielding headboard. The corner of the blanket that I held fell to my waist, and I felt the heat of his breath and the smell of alcohol against my cheek when he leaned down. *He's drunk.*

"I gave you the chance to make this easy. Playtime is over." He yanked me down by my ankle until I was flat on my back, and then he ripped away the rest of the blanket. It was the only thing separating us. He stood up straight and slowly lifted his shirt until it was discarded in a heap on the floor. "I want that dress off."

It was becoming harder and harder to breathe. The force of his commands shook me to my core, but somehow, I managed to plead with him. He was the only one who held enough control to not let this happen. I couldn't say no. I didn't want to.

"Not like this, please."

"Why not?" he asked in a bored tone.

"Because you're drunk," I cried. My voice sounded desperate even to my own ears.

"Are you saying no?"

"You know I can't do that."

"Then I don't care. I'm done waiting." He reached for me so I scooted away from his reach and he laughed. "You're a walking contradiction, Monroe. Your eyes had been screaming 'fuck me' long before I told you I would, but yet you resist the temptation."

"Is that what you call it? Temptation? It's blackmail!"

He raised an eyebrow and cocked his head. "Which only means you have a choice, and you chose my dick because you want it."

"That's not true. You just confuse me," I said as I continued to scoot away.

"No more than you confuse me. The only difference is that I'm angry enough to make you pay for it." The look in his eyes held me captive as I watched him. I guess that's why I didn't notice when he made it to the other side of the bed just as I did. He didn't touch me when he stopped beside me. He just continued to stare down at me curiously.

"Please, you're scaring me."

"You should be scared because when I'm done with you, there will be nothing left for you to hold on to. I'll make sure of that. Now take off... the fucking... dress."

"Isn't there another way?" I asked even as the last of my resistance slipped away.

"No, Monroe, there isn't."

I took a deep breath, nodded, and then slipped the straps over my shoulders. As I did, I wondered if he would be gentle or care that it was my first time. As I rose from the bed in front of him to remove my dress, my eyes involuntarily wandered to his chest, and for the first time, I noticed what looked like a scar just under his heart. It was faint, which meant it must have been really old. I wanted to ask him about it, but the voice in my head told me it was a bad idea.

I quickly looked down before he noticed where my attention was held. His boots were touching the tips of my toes, and I felt small next to his large body.

*He never even kissed me.* The thought was unexpected, and I wondered if I wanted him to kiss me. I peeked up at his lips that looked kissable and perfect. I was so caught in a fantasy involving his lips and mine that I hadn't noticed when my dress slipped from my body and pooled around my feet.

His eyes perused my body, and just like downstairs, there was no emotion or reaction. He barely acknowledged my near naked state before he said, "On your knees."

"Don't you want me to finish?" The blush that stole over my cheeks hid my surprise, though I didn't know what I was more surprised over—my question or the fact that he didn't order me to continue. Then again, Keiran was never one to be considered predictable, and I already figured out my brain was pretty much useless when I'm around him.

"Did I tell you to?" The arrogance in his voice and his distant demeanor was increasing my nervousness.

"Th—this is my first time."

"So?"

"Shouldn't you kiss me?" Shit. My blush was blushing.

"Who said this is your first time?"

"Well, you said—"

"I said I wanted you on your knees."

"Yes, but—"

"So why aren't you on your knees?"

"Maybe because you didn't ask me nicely," I snapped. I had to admit, his mind games were getting to me.

"Nice or not, the result will be the same." At the look in his eyes, I finally sank to the floor and felt the plush carpet under my knees.

"I'm on my knees now so what do you want?"

"I want you to finish what you started."

I knew what he meant without having to be told. My eyes immediately lowered, and I eyed the thick leather belt with silver skull heads wrapped around his dark jeans. The way his jeans fits him was meant to tease. They always seemed to hang just around his hips bringing attention to the deep v carving into his waistline and disappearing into his jeans. His erection was straining against the rough material, waiting for me to let it out.

I can do this... should I do this?

"You're thinking too much..." Keiran barked interrupting my private thoughts, "...and I don't trust your thoughts."

I don't know what came over me when I asked, "Why?" I turned to look directly into his eyes. "Are you afraid of me?" I mocked him, grabbing at what little fight I had left in me. He was going to destroy me anyway. Why not give him a reason?

His stare, however, was overpowering in its intensity. His gaze pierced through my newfound resolve until I lowered my eyes in submission. I was soon kicking my own ass, realizing he just dominated me with a look. I also noticed his gaze was clear, and the realization that came to me had my heart pounding painfully against my chest.

He isn't drunk. He knows exactly what he is doing.

"The seconds are ticking away in my head, and if I get to one, you will regret it," he said menacingly. Without being told, I quickly began undressing him. I reached for the black strap and unbuckled it, but in my haste, I mistakenly slipped his belt completely off where it nestled in my hands. I looked up at him for reassurance, but only found his control was already gone.

The belt was snatched out of my hands, and I was flipped, face down on the floor. The thick carpet muffled any sounds I made. I could see in my peripheral, his booted feet planted on either side of me. My hands were then placed behind me and then something was wrapped around my wrists.

The belt.

The material of the makeshift restraint was tight, and a cry of fear escaped my lips before I could stop it, but I didn't fight back. I didn't tell him no. He would stop if I told him no, but he would go after my aunt. He would kill her because he was cruel and knew she was all I had left. I saw my parents again, and I cried for them. If they hadn't left me, I wouldn't be here, and I hated them for it.

I also hated Keiran's demons that constantly chased him. He lifted me by my hands until I was on my knees again in front of him. "I'm sorry," I cried, the words catching in my throat. I hadn't realized he had been walking out the door until I'd already blurted the words out. *Was he leaving?*

"For what?" He stopped and asked a second later. I could hear the suspicion in his voice.

"That someone hurt you and made you this way." I instantly regretted the words once they were out, but it was too late. His heavy footsteps were loud and hard against the floor as he walked back over to me. I knew he was angry before he even spoke, but I didn't know how much until he spoke.

"That's where you got it wrong," he gritted and slowly unzipped his jeans. He gripped my hair in his hands and tilted my head back slightly so he could look into my eyes. "I was the one doing the hurting."

My lips opened on their own accord, enveloping his hard cock, and I found myself once again gagging around him as he grabbed the back of my head and thrust slowly in and out of my mouth. His reluctant groan was animalistic as he gritted his teeth and tilted his head back. He seemed to catch himself quickly and lifted his head to peer down at me. I struggled to take all of him when the tip of him breached my throat.

"Don't pretend for a fucking second that you know anything about me." *Thrust.* "Or what I've done." *Thrust.* "Or who I am." *Thrust.* "The only thing you need to know is that I will destroy you."

When he finally drew back, I sucked in the much-needed air, but as soon as I managed to catch my breath, my lips greedily latched onto his cock again. I watched his eyes widen slightly in surprise before he narrowed them.

I kept my eyes on his and tried to take as much of him as I could, and then I pulled back until my lips were wrapped around only the head. I stared at the incredibly long length of his cock in amazement while I suckled on the tip and ran my tongue up and down his length. I had no clue what I was doing; I just knew I had to calm him somehow. His hand was still in my hair, but his grip wasn't as tight as few seconds ago.

For a moment, I thought I had succeeded. For a moment, I thought I had won. It was the growl erupting from his throat that should have warned me, but I was too caught in my own pleasure. I liked forcing a reaction from him, just as he'd done to me for ten years. It made me feel like I was the one in control. But that control, as imaginary as it was, was short-lived.

"If you're going to suck me, then suck me. Don't tease my dick, Monroe. You won't like the consequences."

It was amazing how he could make me feel shame for an act that he initiated. I started to remove my mouth from his cock and save some of my dignity while I still could, but he gripped the back of my head tight and pressed forward. I felt the tip of his cock touch the back of my throat again, so I opened up more for him, but when he started to slide down my throat, I gagged and sputtered.

"I want you to remember this moment," he said in a controlled tone while I struggled against him for air, "how I am now, how you are now." He took his cock out of my mouth and shoved me back. "I want you to remember there is *nothing* good about me, and there never will be."

I believed him. God help me, I believed him.

"You really enjoyed that, didn't you?" he snickered. "You thought you were pleasing me? Controlling me even?"

*He was playing me the whole time.* "Why are you doing this?" I could hear the bitterness in my own voice. He ignored my question and fixed his jeans. I swallowed nervously and tasted the remnants of him and felt a moment of disgust, keeping my gaze rooted to the floor. "You wanted this so why are you so angry?" I asked again.

"I'm not angry. That would mean I cared." He moved to the door, intending to leave me tied apparently, but he turned back and asked, "Did you really think you could manipulate me?"

"No."

"No?"

"That's not why you're angry." My gaze lifted to meet his dead on. "You're angry because it was working, and I did please you."

"Well, then that would be stupid of you."

"Why?" I asked curiously.

"Because then I would be forced to keep you. And you don't want that," he replied, ominously. A loud crash and the sound of running footsteps and screams filtered through the door, and then a guy's voice could be heard on the other side.

"Keiran, man, get out here. Dash and Keenan are fighting some guys who crashed the party. Shit is trashed."

He stalked toward the door, shirtless and left as quietly as he came. To someone who didn't recognize the signs he seemed calm, but I glimpsed the rage simmering in his eyes. I was left on the floor still bound by his belt and helpless. Moments later, the loud noise and screaming ended and the house grew eerily quiet, and then all at once, I could hear the sound of running footsteps again followed by screeching tires and cars departing.

I pushed myself up until I was standing. My legs were asleep from being stuck in one position. I licked my lips and immediately recognized the taste of him lingering on my lips, and curious, I licked them again before I realized what I was doing.

Some sick part of me liked the taste of him despite being manipulated. I tried to tell myself I had no choice and that I didn't enjoy being violated by him. But I didn't fight him either. If I fought Keiran, I would lose one way or the other.

# CHAPTER TEN

I THOUGHT ABOUT my journal. I *needed* my journal. It was where I kept all my pain and told all my secrets, and it spoke of only two things—my parents and him.

I hadn't thought about that journal since last year when he went away, and I no longer had anything to write about. The journal was old and something I kept to deal with the pain of losing my parents. I started it a year after they disappeared and when Keiran's bullying got worse.

The first entry about him was in the fourth grade after he got some girls to stick used gum in my hair and had everyone call me spit head at lunch. I locked myself inside the bathroom and immediately pulled out my journal to write. It was a mistake, but it soon became my salvation and way of coping.

Starting out, whenever a memory of my parents surfaced, I would write that memory down and how I felt about them. It was something my aunt suggested I do when she couldn't get me to talk about it. She said she would rather I tell a piece a paper than no one at all. I think that was the writer in her speaking.

Keiran had given me a new pain to focus on. So when I began to write only about Keiran, the journal became a vessel and now held every thought and emotion I ever had for Keiran inside of it. It even expressed the confusion I would often feel from being attracted to him as we got older. I finally admitted to my journal of having a crush on him a couple of days before I turned sixteen.

The school year had just begun, and I saw him for the first time in three months. He'd gone to some basketball camp that was sponsored by the NBA and NCAA for the best talent. The look he gave me as he swaggered down the hallway toward me was hot. I remember his gray eyes trailing slowly up and down my body as we grew closer from opposite ends of the hallway. Our gazes were locked the entire time, and I couldn't help but admire the light stubble he'd grown. It made him look older and sexier if that were even possible. Just as I was passing by him, thinking he would spare me his normal dose of public humiliation, he knocked my books out of my hand and sent them flying along with the few sheets of paper I had on top. I didn't react. I never did. I picked up my books and continued to my first class with my head held high and the anguish my heart felt buried in secret.

Keiran's torments came more frequently and grew crueler that year. For whatever reason, he seemed to despise me even more. I remember being confused about the strange looks he would give me followed by a vicious, verbal attack. But we were on an entirely different playing field now. Keiran was menacing enough when unprovoked, but now he actually had a reason to hate me.

I tried to look at it from his point of view. He lost a year of his life to the system. It was a year he would never get back while the drug conviction threatened his future because nothing stayed completely buried. Added to the humiliation of a public arrest it would be enough to piss off a nun. I understood why he wanted revenge, but threatening the life of my aunt was unforgivable. She was innocent in all this.

When his car stopped, it snapped me out of my thoughts, and I realized we were in my driveway. He didn't shut off the engine, and I was relieved. I couldn't handle anymore of Keiran today. After his party had come to a screeching, violent halt, he had come back upstairs and untied me. He then ordered me to "get the fuck out" and I would have gone running for the door, but I had to remind him that he drove me there, and I couldn't call Willow because he sabotaged our friendship. So here we were.

I touched the door handle to get out, but stopped and stared out the windshield instead. I took a deep breath and made a decision.

"It was wrong," I began. He turned to face me with his eyebrows raised. "You had a good thing going. You just made captain of the basketball team—rumor was scouts were already looking at you pretty heavy. It was the end of junior year, and you were supposed to graduate last year. You should be in college now surrounded by an endless supply of hot girls. You wanted a future. You *hoped* for a future."

I looked at him finally—he looked like he was contemplating something as he rubbed his bottom lip with his finger. I couldn't help but to track the motion, watching his finger sweep across. His lips were plump and kissable, and I was suddenly jealous of his finger.

"You were innocent. I know that, but not because you believe I framed you, but because if you had done it, then this—" I gestured between the two of us, "wouldn't be happening. You would have accepted the consequences even if someone did tip the police."

I felt the weight of his stare as silence filled the air in the close confines of the car. It became almost unbearable after a few minutes of waiting for him to say something, so I gave up and reached for the door handle again, having said my piece.

"What makes you so sure?"

I turned back to him confused. "Sure about what?" *Was he trying to say he was guilty?*

"That we wouldn't have happened."

His question immediately pissed me off. I knew it was just another tactic to get into my head. "Are you suggesting otherwise? The past ten years say different."

"You aren't as blind as you pretend to be, Monroe, so cut the bullshit. You come apart when I touch you without hesitation... naturally... as if the *past ten years say differently*." He emphasized the last part, and I flushed thinking about the classroom and the memory of his mouth devouring me.

"Exactly. Naturally. It's pure biology."

"You mean biology made you like me fucking your mouth like that?"

"No, but desire has nothing to do with hate."

"Doesn't it? You forget—I was there that day in the hallway when that limp dick kissed you." I remembered that day. Keiran had effectively ruined my first kiss and chance at a love interest.

"What does that have to do with anything? How do you know I didn't kiss him?"

"You didn't kiss him back."

I didn't say anything because he was right. I hated that. I didn't kiss Peter back. I consented to it but lost the desire to once his lips were on mine. I even remember counting the seconds until it was over and even feeling grateful that Keiran had found us and ran him off.

"So?"

"So you would have felt desire for him. Desire isn't based on biology, and I think you know that. It starts here," he tapped my temple before trailing his fingers down my body slowly, "before it reaches your sweet spot." I was sure I was flaming red by now.

"I don't hate you," I whispered rubbing my sore, red wrists. Bruising was already forming.

"Not even after what I did to you tonight?"

"I don't know how I feel about that."

"But you are afraid of me."

"And so you believe my fear sparked sexual desire for you?"

"Something tells me you came to this conclusion already." I shook my head in denial, not wanting to admit how right he was. "Monroe, you don't desire me because you fear me. You desired me long before I gave you a reason to be afraid."

I shook my head again abruptly. "Impossible—"

He blew out a breath in frustration. "How? You've been eye-fucking me since puberty. I've noticed you, Monroe—beyond the taunts and the rumors I spread, I've noticed you. You wanted me. You still do."

"It's impossible because I've been afraid of you since I was seven-years-old."

\* \* \*

It was just after midnight when I finally walked inside my house. I thought about the last thing I had said to him before he said good night, abruptly ending our talk. I must say I didn't expect his reaction. He all but kicked me out of his car and sped off before I even reached the door.

So much for chaste kisses on the doorstep. Not that I wanted to kiss him or anything.

After a hot shower, I was turning down my blankets for bed, cursing Keiran the whole time when I heard a noise. It sounded muffled and far away, so I quietly moved to the bedroom door and peeked around the frame.

My door was the closest to the stairs, so I saw a light that I didn't remember turning on. I crept down the stairs slowly, praying there wasn't a creepy burglar in the house. My aunt was too much of a pacifist to keep a gun in the house, not that I knew how to use one. How hard could it be, though? You just point, shoot, and hope the wrong end isn't facing you.

I was halfway down and finally convinced myself it was nothing when the light suddenly turned off. The only thing that could be heard after that was the wild beating of my heart as it dropped to the pit of my stomach. *Calm down, Lake. The power must have gone out.*

I looked back up the stairs to see the light still shining from my bedroom, and my body went cold. I'm talking Arctic cold. I knew I needed to call for help but was too afraid to move, fearing I would alert whoever was in the house by some small noise.

I knew Aunt Carissa wouldn't be back this soon without telling me first, so this had to be a break-in. I tried to recall if I had locked the door, but I couldn't remember a single thing past that light turning off. Finally, it came. The sound that confirmed someone was in the house with me. It sounded like footsteps, hard and heavy. There were only two and then it stopped.

The foyer? The kitchen?

They were the only two places in the house other than the bathroom that would produce the sound of footsteps that loud. I grabbed some balls by the skin and slowly began backing up the stairs, careful not to make a sound. I almost made it too, but the sudden sound of my cell phone ringing from my open bedroom door broke the silence. Keiran had given it back to me when he kicked me out of his car.

Shit.

I broke out into a run, not caring about keeping silent any longer. I made it to my bedroom and locked the door just as the ringing stopped. I ran over to my nightstand and snatched my cell phone up. It was a missed call from Willow. I hit the phone icon to dial the police, and a second later, there was a thump on my bedroom door. Followed by a series of thumps that became more forceful. Someone was trying to break down the door.

The operator finally came over the line. "Please, somebody is in my house," I cried. Suddenly, the thumping stopped, and I could hear the sound of footsteps again. I gave the operator my address and sunk to the floor in relief when the door rattled, and I felt my heart stop altogether.

"Go away, I called the police!"

"You did what? Open the door!" I heard a familiar angry voice boom from the other side of the door. I was too terrified to move so I sat there on my knees, clutching my phone, and wishing the police would hurry.

"Why are you doing this?" I asked in a gut-wrenching sob.

"Doing what? Open the door!" He continued pounding on the door until a crack split the wood. I jumped and began screaming at the top of my lungs.

"Leave me alone, please!" Keiran had almost succeeded breaking the door down when I heard additional footsteps running up the stairs.

"Police!" I heard the voices on the other side of the door instructing Keiran to place his hands up.

"Ma'am, it's Officer Reynolds and my partner, Officer Burkes. You can open the door now. We have him restrained."

I sat there numb for a minute before I finally stood to my feet and opened the door. An officer was standing on the other side. He looked familiar somehow, but I couldn't place him. The other officer was leading away a handcuffed Keiran, who was silent as he was taken downstairs.

"Are you okay, did he hurt you?" Officer Reynolds asked.

I found it hard to speak, so I shook my head. "We need you to come down to make a statement. Do you have someone you can call?"

"My aunt is out of town, but I can call my best friend. Can it wait until morning, Officer? I can't do this now."

He hesitated before asking, "How old are you?"

"Eighteen." He nodded before leaving. I sat back on the floor once they were gone and cried until I had nothing left.

* * *

PEPÉ WAS CURLED comfortably in my lap as I sat in Willow's bedroom staring out the window. He must have sensed something was wrong because he hadn't left my lap since I arrived. He was usually finding places to conquer and items to steal. I was pretty sure he already ran off with my keys as usual before he came back to cuddle with me. He was probably ensuring I wouldn't search for them, which was the reason for his unusual cuddling.

"Are you going to tell me what's wrong? You look like you've seen a ghost or something."

I took a deep breath before answering. "Keiran broke into my house and—"

"Oh, my gosh! What? Were you there? Are you okay? Say something!" Willow jumped off her bed and ran over to me, shaking my shoulders.

"Willow, I'm okay for now, but I won't be if you keep shaking me. You'll give me whiplash." She looked apologetic before releasing me.

"Sorry. I knew something was up between you two. It wasn't adding up, and by the way I didn't buy that, 'I don't want to be friends with you bullshit' for a second, but tell Keiran I said nice try."

"Willow, about that, I'm sorry I—"

"Don't worry about it. I figured the only way I could help you now was to play along until you talked to me. So, what happened?" I ran down the story ending with the police arresting Keiran. "Wait... you said you were on the stairs when you heard the phone ring?" She was frowning now, and I figured she was just upset.

"Yeah, what—"

"And you already saw the light cut off and footsteps downstairs *before* your phone rang?"

Yes. Willow—" She interrupted again holding up her hand to silence me.

"When you reached your room and grabbed the phone, I was the missed call?"

"Yes," I stated simply knowing she didn't expect more than that.

"The only missed call?" I nodded this time, not bothering to say anything.

"It couldn't have been him." I gave her a puzzled look, and she explained. "Lake, I passed Keiran coming home from work. I stayed late to help with inventory."

"Yeah, I told you, he dropped me off late after the party."

She shook her head before stating, "I saw him turning down your street, and *that's* when I called you. I figured he was coming to your house due to your recent 'relationship.' I wanted to know what he was doing coming by so late." She waggled her eyebrows suggestively, but I only gaped at her as dread gutpunched me and caused my head to swim. I leaned over placing my head between my knees, pissing Pepé off. He jumped off my lap and scurried out the room.

"Oh, God. Oh, no," I chanted, rocking back and forth.

"Lake, no worries. We just go to the police and clear him."

"No, you don't understand." I sat upright and looked at Willow with tears in my eyes. "He'll kill her."

* * *

MORNING CAME, AND I had little sleep. I tossed and turned all night keeping Willow awake as well since we shared her bed. I didn't rush off to the station knowing the damage was already done, but I didn't delay it too long either. I went home to shower and dress. Since I didn't know who the intruder was, I gratefully accepted Willow and Buddy's offer to come with me.

Thirty minutes later, I made my way to the station with Willow. She was still spooked over my confession last night. I regretted saying anything immediately, but I knew the damage was already done when she freaked. I blew off her questions and went to bed. She had been giving me the silent treatment since then.

We arrived and entered the station hearing loud voices. The scene that greeted me immediately made me want to turn and run.

"You pigs just haven't had enough. Where is he? You don't have shit—" He stopped when he saw me, his eyes narrowed as they pinned me to the spot. Willow and I instinctively took a step back.

Dash shook his head before running a hand down his face. "You didn't have to do this, Lake. He would never have—"

"We don't have to explain shit!" Keenan roared, interrupting Dash.

"Young man, I need you to contain yourself before I throw your ass in jail along with your cousin."

Sheldon burst through the door as the officer was reprimanding Keenan. "Keenan, stop being a douche. We don't know what happened," she scolded.

"She's right, son. Settle down," an older man stated.

"She won't get away with this, Mr. Chambers. Not again."

"Guy, you seriously need to chill. She's not after your precious cousin, so settle down so we can do what we came to do."

Willow had just laid down the law, and if this were any other situation, I would have found it amusing. Just then, an officer came through with Keiran, who looked tired in his rumpled clothing. He walked up to the desk to sign papers and collect his belongings. We immediately made eye contact and everything from last night came rushing back. I was so sure it was Keiran who broke into my house to scare me.

"You are free to go, Mr. Masters."

I frowned not understanding how he was already free to go. It was my understanding they could hold someone for forty-eight hours without charges. Keiran was only there for eight. Don't get me wrong. I wanted him released, but I hadn't even cleared him yet.

"Yes. We apologize for the misunderstanding, Mr. Chambers."

"Can you believe this? As far as they know, Keiran broke into your house, and they just released him because Dash's old man pulled some strings? Unbelievable," Willow whispered.

Mr. Chambers turned to me, sizing me up. "Think carefully about what you are about to do, Ms. Monroe. You won't succeed a second time." With that, they left the station, and I began to breathe easier.

"Officer, I would like to make a statement to clear Keiran Masters. He was not the one to break into my house. I brought a witness to testify to that."

The officer gave me a stern look before directing us to fill out the necessary paperwork. After heavy questioning, we were able to leave the precinct. Willow kept glancing at me during the ride to school, and I knew she was concerned.

"Lake, are you going to be okay?"

This turn of events definitely didn't look good for me. If I thought Keenan's reaction was bad then, I knew Keiran's would be ten times worse. "I don't know."

* * *

WE MADE IT to school in time for volleyball, so we headed straight there. I didn't see any sign of Keiran when I arrived, so I assumed he'd already gone to class. I still had to face him at lunch, so I wasn't out of the water yet. I used the physical demand of volleyball to distract me from the mental stress.

The class ended too quickly though, and before I knew it, I was dressed and biting my fingernails. I was expecting Keiran to pop up at any moment to terrorize me and hurl threats, but he never came. Lunch was halfway over when I gave up waiting. I headed to the cafeteria in search of him and found him seated at his normal table... with Anya in his lap.

The jealousy I felt was misplaced, and I reminded myself I wasn't his girlfriend and made my way over to his table. "Hey. I, uh... waited for you back at volley-ball."

Anya looked up at me and giggled, then whispered something behind her hand to Keiran. He smiled at her then kissed her on the neck to which she began to moan. He ignored me completely, so I looked around the table. Keenan was glaring at me while Sheldon looked at me apologetically.

"Look, about last night and this morning, I—"

"Monroe, you seem to think we have something to discuss. We don't. You seem to think we are in a rela-tionship. We aren't."

"It was a misunderstanding, but you won't get into trouble. I cleared things up."

He looked at me with his signature blank mask be-fore stating, "You're free to go."

"Bye, Lacy," Anya stated snidely. Everyone at the table erupted into laughter at her purposely mistaking my name. I ignored her cattiness and left the cafeteria.

I knew what he really meant by his last statement. He no longer wished to deal with me, but what did that mean for my aunt? I know I should be happy, but I wasn't. I felt empty as if I had just lost something. It was the same feeling I had when my parents disap-peared. I shook my head at my stupidity.

I can't lose something I never had.

\* \* \*

"LAKE, WAIT UP!" I heard Sheldon call out to me, but I kept walking. I didn't want to interact with anyone associated with Keiran right now. "Lake, stop. I swear I'll body slam you if you don't stop running from me!"

I stopped and turned around once I was on the other side of the school, far away from Keiran. "Sheldon, I can't do this. Not now."

"Why are you always running? You don't have to let him win, you know?"

"What am I supposed to do?" I yelled. I was frustrated beyond my limit.

"Fight back," she quipped.

"Why are you telling me this? He's your friend." I narrowed my eyes at her when she nodded.

"Yes, he is. They're all my best friends. And we could be friends too if you'd let me. I'm not your enemy."

"No, but you are in bed with my enemy. Besides, you have Anya and the other cheerleaders. Looks to me as if you have plenty of friends."

She snorted. "I could always use better, and I have a feeling you want more friends, too."

I shrugged. "Doesn't matter. Keiran would never let us be friends."

"Keiran doesn't run me. I decide who I am friends with."

"Keenan hates me, too."

"No, Keenan loves his cousin."

"How is that different?"

"His bond with his cousin makes him fight alongside Keiran and protect him if need be."

I looked at her suspiciously. This could be a trap Keiran set out to hurt me or get back at me. "Why are you so nice to me?"

"I don't know, Lake. Maybe because I like you, and

you've never done anything to me?"

"Still, wouldn't your friendship with them turn you against me? That's what friends do, right? Protect each other and fight their battles?"

"And I would if I thought you were a threat."

"Gee, thanks."

"No offense, babe. So, what do you say? Friends?" She held out her fist for a pound.

I studied her fist, thinking it over before finally giving her a pound. "Friends." *We'll see.*

# CHAPTER ELEVEN

I GOT THROUGH fourth period mostly unscathed thanks to Willow and Sheldon. I sat two rows ahead of Keiran, which was still too close, but it was the only row left that allowed Willow and me to sit together.

Not even ten minutes had passed after class started when I felt something light hit my shoulder. I thought nothing of it until it happened again, this time on my back. I looked down to see two paper balls on the floor and then another hit my head.

I heard, "Real mature, guys," before a chair scraped, and Sheldon came to sit with us. I'd looked back to see Keiran wearing a smug grin. Keenan looked pissed and was glaring at Sheldon. He'd mumbled, "Traitor," under his breath then rolled his eyes at me.

After school, Sheldon and Willow rode with me to my house. Keenan threw a temper tantrum in the parking lot. Sheldon was annoyed, but she just laughed when he yelled obscenities and kicked his car. We opted to watch a movie at my house instead of going out to the movies. We sat in the living room doing homework and having girl talk. It felt good. I had this with Willow, but it felt nice to have it with someone else, too. My friend count was now two.

*Gee, Lake, that has got to be a record.* I laughed out loud at my private joke.

"What's so funny?" Willow asked. I just shook my head and closed my textbook.

"I'm done," Sheldon announced. "So—the purple highlights? Did you do it yourself?" They had been discussing hair for the past ten minutes. Sheldon was in awe of Willow's freedom of self-expression. I wondered what or who was making her hold back who she really was.

"Yeah, I did. I'm actually going to add in highlights, too."

"Way cool. I wish I could try that. My mom would have a heart attack."

"I've been trying to get Lake over to the dark side, but she won't budge."

"I don't know, Willow, Lake's got the innocent, big, blue-eyed look going for her. The guys dig her... in secret, of course."

"Yeah, I call her the Barbie Ballerina."

"Guys, I'm sitting right here."

"Yeah, but you've been quiet. Thinking about a certain bad boy with a dark disposition?" Sheldon was still convinced Keiran and I were more than enemies.

"That's a ship that will never sail, Sheldon," Willow stated. "Lake is too accustomed to denying what she wants—out of fear... duty... protection."

"You actually think Keiran and I should date?" I asked incredulously. "Since when?"

"I don't, but you don't date at all is what I'm saying."

"I assure you it isn't by choice."

"So what is the deal between you and Keiran?"

Sheldon asked. "All these years I knew he liked you, but he also carried a grudge against you even before he went to juvie."

It was something I had wondered about for ten years. Why did he hate me so much? What did I do? How could I fix it? My mind drew a blank every time, and the tension between us became too thick to sever.

"I wish I knew," I finally answered.

Sheldon shrugged, "Too bad. I'm sure it would have made a great bedtime story." She rolled her eyes, making me laugh. "Did you hear about the random guy who crashed Keiran and Keenan's party the other night?"

"The guys Keenan and your brother fought?"

"No, some guy who was dealing at the party. Keiran must have caught him because Dash said he had to keep him from killing the guy."

"No way, what did he do?" Willow asked with a little too much excitement.

"He shoved some pills and alcohol down his throat and told him he might want to go get his stomach pumped."

"Jeez! The guy could have died!" Willow exclaimed.

"A couple of his buddies were there and drove him to the hospital. Keiran isn't in prison for murder so I guess he's okay. It's just strange because this isn't the first time Keiran has caught people dealing in his place, but it is the first time he's reacted this strongly. I can't believe you missed it, Lake."

"Oh, yeah. I, uh, went upstairs and kind of fell asleep." I acted nonchalant about it, but really I was freaking out in my head. It had to be the same guy that offered to drug me. The guy was a tool, but what Keiran did was dangerous and illegal. I mean, what if the guy had died? There was a party full of witnesses who could point their finger.

"I'm curious to know how you and Keenan got together," Willow stated, and I realized I'd missed part of the conversation. "He seems so... pushy."

"When he doesn't get his way. Then my baby acts like a two-year old whose favorite toy was stolen, but he is a sweetie pie at heart. He acts out, but I think it's to get his father's attention. His mother died in a car accident when he was seven and his father just checked out. Not a lot of emotional love shared in the Master's house."

"So where are Keiran's parents? I mean, how did his uncle become his guardian?" Willow was asking all the questions, but I would be damned if I wasn't listening.

"Keenan said his father refuses to talk about his brother, but apparently, Keiran's mother was one of the brother's two-bit one-night stands who left Keiran on John's doorstep when he was eight."

"So why Keenan's father and not the brother?"

"I guess she couldn't find him. Keenan said he'd never met his uncle, so I guess that also explains why John didn't hand him over to his brother. He probably can't find him either or didn't try if their relationship took a turn for the worse."

"What's the brother's name?" I asked.

"Can't remember, but I'm pretty sure it started with an 'M.' My parents did tell me that none of them are originally from Six Forks. John moved here a long time ago and lived alone until one day he brought home a woman and a baby. He was never even seen with a wife or girlfriend before, and then, seven years later, Keiran pops up."

She sat silent for a moment, thinking. "Crazy enough, but Keenan said his mother ran off around the same time Keiran was found. He didn't even know he had a cousin and that his father never mentioned a brother before. I guess they didn't get along. He told me about the day John brought him home. He said he knew Keiran wasn't normal... truth be told, I think Keenan was afraid of him. He never said it, but the way he would describe Keiran, and the look he would get in his eyes..." She looked thoughtful as her words trailed off.

*I can relate.* "What about her relatives? Maybe she went home," I said.

Sheldon's forehead wrinkled from her deep frown, and I found myself leaning forward in anticipation. "I guess she didn't go there either... or maybe she did. But Keenan has never met them."

"Wow... I never thought I would ever feel a twinge of sympathy for Keenan... or Keiran." Willow looked sad as she spoke.

"Uh huh, so what about you and my brother? He's got it bad for you," Sheldon asked.

"There is nothing to tell. Dash is chasing ass. He's too much of a playboy."

"So you're saying you want something serious with him?" Willow blushed as if she'd just been caught. *Did she have feelings for him?*

"No, I meant—" she paused as if thinking over her words, "I don't want to—I just can't."

"I know my brother. He is a charmer, but he is a manipulative son of a bitch when it comes to something he wants. He got that from our father. This is the first time I've actually witnessed him chase someone. So if you don't want to be a part of something with him, then I suggest you be sure because one thing Dash can detect is bullshit."

After Willow and Sheldon left, I called my aunt and spoke to her for a while. She reminded me that she was flying to her next tour stop in the morning before we said our goodnights. I quickly fixed something to eat and was channel surfing when the doorbell rang. I frowned, wondering who would be coming over when I saw Willow's notebook on the coffee table. I shook my head and grabbed her tablet. Willow was a forgetful person and would always leave stuff behind.

I opened the door with a smile. "Something here belong to you, Will—"

"Something here does belong to me, but I promise it isn't a tablet."

* * *

KEIRAN WAS THE last person I expected to see standing at my door considering last night and today. "What are you doing here?"

"You know why I'm here."

I tried to close the door, but his booted foot kept it from shutting as he shouldered his way in causing me to lose my grip on the door and stumble. He caught me before I could fall and hauled me close to his chest.

"You said we didn't—you didn't—" The purpose in his eyes as he held me was both provocative and scary.

"I said we had nothing to talk about. We don't. I said we weren't in a relationship. We aren't."

"Yes, but——"

"I never said you didn't owe me your body because you damn well do, and I'm here to collect."

"I don't owe you anything," I said through clenched teeth.

His lips crashed down on mine, and for a moment, I gave in to him and let my desires show before I snatched away. He grinned and said, "We'll see about that in the morning." He turned me around and pushed me toward the stairs. When we reached my bedroom, he dropped the bag I hadn't noticed he was carrying and locked the door.

"What happened last night?" he asked as he removed his hoodie.

"I told you it was a misunderstanding. Someone was here. They broke in and chased me up the stairs, but I locked myself in. I'm sorry, I never saw who it was and then you were here I just—"

"Did he hurt you?" His voice sounded neutral, but the tick in his jaw made me curious even when his question pissed me off.

"No more than you have for ten years. I've grown thick skin."

I don't know what made me snap at him, but I knew it was the wrong answer when his shoulders tensed and his hands balled into fists so hard the veins were bulging and straining against his skin. I didn't believe the tension in the air could grow any thicker.

Me and my mouth.

"Is that right?" My body and entire nervous system went on alert at the chilling way he asked the question. I carefully backed away, feeling sweat form around my face even as my body went cold and the hairs on my neck stood up. "I guess we are about to see just how *thick*... your skin has gotten."

I bolted for the door, but didn't so much as get my hand on the doorknob before I was snatched away, and then I was flying. I landed on the soft spread of my bed and shot upright. He was already standing at the foot of my bed, watching me as he lifted his shirt from his chest and dropped it on the floor.

"Wait! I'm not ready."

"Tough shit, Monroe. You had a year to get ready."
How could I have known this would happen? I knew he would be mad but this...

"Can we talk about this?"

"I'm done talking. It's time to fuck." I reared back, feeling both appalled and turned on by his crude behavior. I searched his eyes one last time, but didn't find any mercy in them.

"I'll fight you," I warned him, half-heartedly.

"You won't win if I fight back."

"Don't do this."

"I have every intention of doing this. I have since the first time you looked at me with the same need that I felt every damn day."

"What are you talking about? I never—"

"I read your journal," he interrupted with a smirk. My heart stopped in my chest. Or was it beating so loud that I couldn't hear it anymore?

He read my journal.

That meant he knew every single emotion or thought I ever felt or had about him. That also meant he knew about my parents.

"Have you ever thought about being a writer? You're very... descriptive. I particularly liked the entries dated, August 17th and May 27th. Those dates mean anything to you?" he grinned at me, but the smile didn't reach his eyes.

I dropped my head, knowing exactly what dates he was referring to. The day I realized I desired him and the day before he was arrested. They were both during the same school year.

"You're a monster."

"And you're a liar." He began removing his belt from his jeans. It was the same one from last night. My wrists still held the imprint of the skulls and were red and puffy.

"I didn't lie."

"Come here."

"No."

He sighed as if I was little more than a nuisance and then he was suddenly on the bed, dragging me to the edge of the bed and pulling me up. "Suit yourself," he whispered against my lips.

"Don't—" He gripped my waist tighter in warning.

My top was quickly unbuttoned and tossed away. The cold air hit my bare chest, hardening my nipples just before his head lowered and his mouth was on me, sucking. My back instinctively arched from the sensation, pressing my breasts into his mouth further. A sharp sting from his bite had me gasping and grabbing onto his head for balance as I felt my whole world shift from that little spice of pain.

The next moment, I was on my back and his hands at my shorts, pulling them off my hips and down my legs until they disappeared over the bed. The dark look of determination on his face scared me even as my body prepared to take him. I couldn't deny or hide the evidence of my arousal. I didn't understand all that what was happening or what was wrong with me. I tried reminding myself of all the horrible things he'd done and planned to do, but none of it worked.

When he reached for my panties, I finally got ahold of my senses and grabbed onto his hands to stop him, but he took those away from me, too. I was left bare and shaking on my bed. I should be screaming and yelling and cursing, but I wasn't. Instead, I watched him devour my body with his eyes, and I could see a hint of approval in them.

He pulled me up again and ordered me to finish undressing him. I reached for his jeans with nervous hands, unbuttoned them, and slid the zipper down. I grabbed onto the waist of his jeans with both hands and slid them down his legs all the while keeping my eyes on his, letting him see my disdain and praying I was shielding my hunger.

"You can keep fighting it, Monroe, but my dick will be deep inside you before the night is over. We have all night. There is no one here to save you. No one to hear you scream. No one to see you come." A slow, steady throb began between my legs from his threat. "Lie down and spread your legs for me."

I scooted back toward the headboard and slowly lowered my back to the mattress. I stared up at the ceiling while I spread my legs for him. I knew he could see my arousal.

"Look at me," he demanded. I let my gaze travel to his face and saw the anger there. "Don't hide from me," he growled.

"You should be used to it by now. I've hidden from you my entire life."

The deep hatred that flashed in his eyes, more than I've ever seen before, was my only warning. He covered my body with his and forced my thighs open wider to accommodate him. I could feel the head of his cock poised at my entrance as he grabbed a handful of my hair in his hand and leaned down to place his lips at my ear.

"I'm going to fuck you now, and when you've had more than you can take, I'm going to do it all over again, and I won't let up, no matter how much you beg me."

I looked into his eyes and couldn't see any hint of remorse, only angry lust. The past ten years rushed back to me all at once, and it felt like a punch to the gut. How could I ever think to desire him? He threatened my aunt; he tried to take away Willow. *I hated him.*

"When this is all over—" My voice caught in my throat as he began to enter me. I already felt so full.

"And you realize the mistake you're making, it will be me who makes you beg, and I won't stop until I bring you to your fucking knees."

He stopped and stared back at me, his eyes searching mine before he finally spoke, his voice chilling, "Thank you, Monroe. You almost made this hard for me."

It felt as if the loud cry I released came straight from my soul when he slammed into me. Shock and pain took over my body as he took my virginity. I clutched his shoulders and tried to push him away, but he seized my wrists in his fists and locked them against the mattress.

"Fuck," he groaned. Thankfully, he didn't move. His body was still on top of mine as he watched me closely.

I shook my head, feverishly. "I can't—"

"You can and you will. Take me, baby."

He continued to bury himself deeper and deeper inside me while staring into my eyes, and I knew he wanted me to feel his possession and I did. I felt him everywhere. When he began a slow, steady thrust into my body, it sent my senses shooting off into space. Pain began to fade, and pleasure took over.

When his pace increased, he wrapped my legs around his waist and bit into my neck. The little bite of pain caused me to flood his cock, and suddenly, his control seemed to snap and he began pounding me into the mattress, driving us both insane.

"Oh, God!" I moaned when it became unbearable.

"Do you feel that?" he asked as he destroyed me with deep strokes that took my breath away. "That's me owning your pussy, baby. Me. Not God," he growled.

He lifted his weight off my body, planting his fists by my head, and continued his long, deep, forceful thrusts with powerful hips that pushed me up the bed. The headboard began a steady beat against the wall, threatening to burst straight through it. I began thrashing and flailing around him, fighting not only him, but also the sensations he was creating within me.

"It's too much," I cried.

"No." He reared up, bringing me with him until he was sitting on his haunches, and I was in his lap. "It's not enough," he groaned against my neck.

Our new position buried his cock so much deeper inside my walls that I felt like I would suffocate. His lips took control of mine in a tangle of tongue and teeth and passion.

I was lost.

So lost in his potent kiss that I wasn't prepared for when he gripped my hips and rammed his cock up into me, stealing away my breath and inhibitions.

I screamed.

I screamed for so long that my screams were no longer that. They became hoarse whimpers that barely made a sound. The sweat and heat of his body mingled with mine, and I felt drunk.

"Please," I finally whispered. He continued to thrust into me with a grind that added a friction I couldn't get enough of.

"Tell me, Monroe. What do you need?"

"I need... I need to come."

"You think you deserve to come?" He kissed the top of my breasts, taking small bites into the heavy mounds pressed hard against his chest. He was back in control now that I had become unhinged. I knew what he wanted.

"Only if you want me to."

The lust and hunger that raged within the depth of his eyes frightened and turned me on. "Ask me properly," he ordered and deepened his thrusts.

"Please make me come."

"I'm going to do more than make you come, Monroe. I'm going to mark every sweet inch of your fucking body—inside and out, and when I'm done, you'll know who you owns you."

But instead of fucking me harder like my body seemed to need, he slowed his hips to a steady pace. "I've been picturing you like this for a long time, Monroe. Just like this. Hot and wet and open for me. Taking my cock, like a good girl."

His hand came around between us and began rubbing my clit just as his tempo increased, and he was once again pounding into me mercilessly. My cries for release were deafening as my body yielded to his. The need to come was there but for some reason, release evaded me.

"Come for me," he finally commanded and surged into me one last time, lifting my knees from the bed as he did. My screams went through the air, and I felt my walls suck at him, pulling his release from his body as he shuddered above me and gripped my hips tightly.

"You're mine now..." he warned.

\* \* \*

"WAKE UP." MY body shook from the heavy hand snatching me out of a deep sleep. All at once, before I could even open my eyes, the night before came rushing back along with the obvious signs of hard sex in my aching muscles. After we had sex, Keiran seemed almost human. He had been staring into my eyes for a long time after we finally caught our breath. The moment was gone when he blinked once and excused himself.

It all went downhill after that when I received two

phone calls. The first phone call was from Willow, looking for her tablet. The second was Jesse.

I answered the phone just as Keiran returned from the bathroom. He'd held a warm cloth in his hand, but tossed it away before taking the phone from my hands and hung up on him. He reached for me, and I foolishly went to him thinking it would be like before. But it wasn't. He was cold, hard, and merciless when he took me.

He didn't let up until a couple of hours later. If a girl ever imagined how her first night would be, I'm sure it was not in that way. I was partly to blame though... I never told him no.

I finally opened my eyes to see him staring down at me and looking dark, sinful, and unobtainable, with his mussed bed hair. He was shirtless but wearing jeans, and I could tell he'd already been up. *Or never went to sleep.* I'd passed out from exhaustion and the unfamiliar stress on my body, so I didn't know much of what had happened after he finally eased up on me.

Half asleep, I dragged myself off the bed and trudged into the bathroom with the sheets wrapped around me. However, once I dropped the sheet and took one look in the mirror, the sight that greeted me shocked me awake. There were red marks and bites all over my skin. I felt every last one of them, but that didn't make seeing them any less disturbing.

I touched one of the marks and winced from the dull pain. "What are you doing?" I jumped at the sudden sound of his voice directly behind me.

"Why are you sneaking up on me?"

"Hurry up. We're going to be late."

"I don't think I can go to school."

"Why not?" He sounded annoyed and disinterested, but I answered him anyway.

"Maybe because it looks like I've been beaten?" I didn't attempt to hide the disdain I felt.

"You came, didn't you? Many times as I recall."

"You do realize you blackmailed me into sex, right?"

"Keep telling yourself that." He smirked.

"You should have stayed away," I whispered, my eyes lowering.

"Maybe. But I didn't. This was always going to happen, Monroe. I told you that... I made breakfast, by the way." He changed the subject and gave me a warning look.

I couldn't conceal the look of surprise that crossed my face. "You did?"

He stared at me blankly. "I was hungry." He shrugged.

"Right." Silly me, thinking he would do something nice after the night we had. *But you enjoyed it, too.* I shook off the unwanted thoughts and turned the shower on. I stepped in and knew he was still there even though my back was turned. "Are you planning to watch me shower?"

"And if I do?" he leaned against the door and crossed his arms, watching me through the glass door. I didn't reply, knowing he was baiting me, looking for an excuse to strike, but then... he never needed one in the past.

"This isn't the first time I caught you in the shower, you know."

"What?" I turned around in surprise, forgetting my attempt to ignore him.

"I was the one who stole your clothes two years back."

"That was you? I mean... I knew you had something to do with it, but you actually went into the girls' locker room?"

He rolled his eyes and stuffed his hands in his pockets. "It wasn't the first time I've been in the girls' locker room, Monroe."

"Why else would you—oh." My cheeks turned red, and I felt a pang followed by anger, but I didn't understand why.

"You look jealous."

Jealous? I wasn't, was I?

"I'm not."

"Is that another lie?" His voice lowered to a level that screamed 'danger.'

I chose to remain silent and finished lathering my body. When his phone broke the silence, he finally left the bathroom to my relief. I quickly washed my hair before stepping out. I dressed and used some of my aunt's makeup to cover the visible marks and made my way downstairs. When I entered the kitchen, he ended his phone call and pushed a plate full of food toward me. I couldn't deny how good the food looked and smelled.

"You can cook?" He grunted and continued tapping the keyboard, ignoring me. "I want to talk to my aunt. How do I know you didn't have something done to her?"

"You don't," he replied tersely. "Do what the hell I say, and you won't have anything to worry about."

"That's bullshit!" I yelled.

He slowly looked up from his phone, and I snapped my mouth closed. He slid his phone over to me, and I picked it up cautiously. On the screen was a picture of my Aunt at an airport. "This doesn't prove anything," I stated.

"That's all you're getting. Let's go."

"But I didn't eat my food yet."

"Bring it with you."

\* \* \*

"YOU HAD AN orgasm today!"

I spit out the drink I had just taken a sip of and shot Charlie a murderous look.

"Now, now. Don't look at me like that with those magnificent blue-green eyes. There's no need to be a prude about it. Everyone has orgasms and the ones who don't… God bless their souls."

"Why would you say that?"

"Because it's all over your face. Who is he? I want details and don't forget the dirty ones."

I didn't quite know if it was a good idea to share my blossoming sex life with my boss, but I didn't think it would be fair to hold out. He cared so much about me finding love, or as he put it, '*A really good stick to ride.*' Charlie was as crass as he was flamboyant.

Lucky for me I was saved from answering by Mr. Martin coming through the door. "You know I think that man is up to something," Charlie whispered while eyeing the older man. "He only shows when you're here, and I never see him actually work out. I think you have a secret admirer, Lake."

"What? He is old enough to be my father and half a grandfather."

"So he's sugar daddy material."

"As if. Maybe he's here for you."

"Honey, he never even glances at me. What does he talk to you about anyway?"

"Nothing much. He is always polite and usually just asks me about school." I didn't want to tell him about the time he asked if I was dating anyone. It would only encourage Charlie. I made my way to the reception desk to check him in.

"Good evening, Mr. Martin."

"Ah, Lake. How are you today?" Well, I spent the night being fucked senseless for the first time, so peachy.

"Peachy. And yourself?"

"Oh, the usual. Just passing through." *Yeah, why is that?* "Any new developments?"

"Uh, no. Nothing new," I lied.

"As beautiful as you are, young lady, I find it hard to believe that you don't have someone special."

"Oh, um. Thank you." *I think.*

"Is there someone special? Someone you go to school with?"

"No..." His persistent questions started to make me nervous. *Please don't tell me this guy is a creep.*

"There is nothing to be ashamed of. You can tell me." His insistence on knowing about my love life was making me uncomfortable.

"Enjoy your visit, Mr. Martin." I handed him back his membership card and gave him a fake smile that he seemed to see right through.

"I suppose. I'll be seeing you, Lake." He started for the locker rooms, and I knew I wouldn't see him again until next time.

My phone vibrated in my back pocket, so I fished it out:

K: Where the fuck r u?

Lake: Working. A girl's gotta eat.

K: Monroe...

Lake: Yes?

K: Where. R. U?

Lake: The gym

He didn't text back after that so I went back to working. I ended up talking to one of the regulars that Charlie tried to hook me up with on numerous occasions, despite the fact that I just became legal two days ago. He was one of those guys whose muscles had muscles. It made me appreciate Keiran's body even more. He was lean and muscular and natural.

And not mine.

"Am I any closer to getting you to agree to go out with me? I can show you a really good time if you let me." I had the feeling he wasn't just talking about dinner and a movie.

"Thanks, Chad, but I'm—"

"Taken," a voice bit out behind me. I knew who it was without turning around. He always did have a knack for sneaking up on me.

"Somehow, I don't think that's what the lady was about to say. So why don't you run along, little boy."

"I'm saying it for her. She's mine. You want to try to take her from me?" He fists clenched as he stepped toe to toe with Chad.

Was he seriously trying to start a fight?

I looked around for Charlie, who seemed to have disappeared. There was no way I would be able to stop them if they fought, so I had to try to defuse the situation.

"She doesn't look like yours. Otherwise, she wouldn't have been over here flirting with my dick." The words had been barely out of Chad's mouth before he was flipped over the weight bench by a fierce right hook from Keiran. I was pretty sure I saw a couple of teeth fly, too.

"Stop! What the hell do you think you are doing?" I grabbed onto Keiran's arm to stop him from pursuing Chad, who was still laid out on the floor, motionless. He ripped his arm away and glared down at me, his face a mask of uncontrolled fury.

"Get your shit and let's go."

"What? No."

"Monroe!" he roared, and I nearly jumped out of my skin. His temple was throbbing again, and he looked ready to strangle me. Charlie had finally appeared and was attempting to revive Chad.

"I can't leave my job. Are you insane?"

As soon as the words were out, I was hauled over his shoulder and being carted out the door. A gym full of people and no one stepped forward to stop the un-stable teen. *Unbelievable.* His car was double-parked outside with the engine running. Something told me he was already planning to do this. It made me long for the Keiran who bullied me from a distance.

"Why did you come here? I told you I was work-ing," I said while he dumped me into the backseat. A second later, I heard the locks engage, and he was walk-ing back inside the gym. I unlocked the door and tried to open it, but it wouldn't budge so I tried the other, and it did the same. *Did he freaking child lock me in?*

I contemplated kicking the window in for payback but knew I wouldn't get far before he caught me so I climbed into the front seat, and by the time I was opening the door, he was walking back out. I hurried back into the backseat, but it was too late. He'd already caught me trying to escape.

"How long have you been working there?"

"A year. What gives you the right to jeopardize my job like that? I could be fired."

"I already took care of that."

"What?"

"I told them you quit. You aren't going back there."

* * *

I TOLD MY aunt I had really bad stomach pains and couldn't talk long when she called. It was partially true although the real reason was more because of Keiran. He watched me like a hawk when I talked to her, and I didn't want to risk my aunt detecting something wrong, so I kept the call short.

He immediately left when I ended the call. He said he had to go out of town, but took my car keys with a warning to stay and that he would be back. I didn't understand him. Why go through all that trouble to find me if he wasn't going to stick around? I thought for sure he would demand sex although I didn't think my body could handle another night like last night. I could feel the soreness between my thighs even now.

I thought about calling the gym and apologizing for what happened and maybe even begging to keep my job, but the humiliation was too fresh so I put it off for tomorrow and decided to do homework instead. I had to stay ahead so I wouldn't fall behind. I wished my parents could see me now. They were so devastated when I was diagnosed with dyslexia. It was one of my clearest memories. I learned it wasn't the end of the world when I realized the *disability* to learn normally didn't mean an *inability* to learn. One thing it did make me do was appreciate learning and education more. It was why I wanted to become a teacher. Dyslexia wasn't something I could outgrow, but it was something I could conquer.

I was in the living room searching for my favorite writing pen my aunt bought me on one of her trips when I noticed the corner of something black peeking out from underneath the couch near the side table. I bent to pick up the object, realizing it was an envelope addressed to me.

There was a birthday card inside so I flipped open the card. What I saw caused my heart to stop, and I felt gut-punched. Inside was a picture of a little girl.

A dead girl.

Her hair was blonde, and she looked to be no more than six or seven years old. The edges were ragged and worn from time or rough handling so the picture might have been a few years old. The bleeding hole in her head had me fighting back the need to vomit. I inspected the card but didn't see any sign of a signature or idea of who the card came from. My mind raced to figure out who the card was from and how it got here.

The break in!

It was the only thing that made sense. Since then, I have argued over the reasons why someone would break into an occupied house. They did it to leave this note. I searched the picture for a clue but came up empty. I was sure I'd never seen the girl before so why would someone leave me a picture of her corpse?

When a realization centered in my mind, the envelope fell from my hand and drifted to the floor. This would mean the break in wasn't random. *Oh, shit.* I picked up the card and flipped it over to inspect the back and to read the words that sealed my fate.

*This is your only warning.*

# CHAPTER TWELVE

REGRET AND NERVOUSNESS had me looking over my shoulder once again. "I shouldn't have come. Why did I let you talk me into this?"

"Calm down, Lake. It's Saturday, and it's just a football game. He probably won't even be here. But if he tries to bully you, we'll leave, okay?"

How do I tell her that it wasn't bullying I was worried about? That Keiran was using sex and death threats to torment me now? I agreed to come out here because I owed Willow, and I missed her. Besides, Keiran said he was going out of town. He didn't say when he'd be back, but I assumed it was for the weekend because I haven't heard from him since he left me stranded in my house.

The house that had been too quiet and the guilt that was weighing in on me, not to mention the creepy birthday card, all also caused me to break out of my cage. The house I shared with my aunt used to be my safe haven, but Keiran had managed to turn that against me as well.

I still haven't told my aunt about the break in after she called again to check in on me. With her tour, I didn't want her to worry or worse, cancel, so I put it off for now. Besides, I still believed, if she was gone, she was safer where Keiran couldn't get to her.

"Okay," I finally replied as we entered the gate. There was no going back now, I thought as I released a heavy breath. "But aren't you avoiding Dash?"

"Yes, but I refuse to let him keep me from living." Willow was right of course, but it wasn't that simple for me.

Keiran now controlled every aspect of my life. Actually, he always had. Every decision I had ever made for ten years began and ended with how best to avoid him, even though he always found me. Just like I knew that he would tonight. I came because I owed Willow. Despite her understanding, I know it hurt her.

The area around the football field was crowded with what seemed to be the entire town, as well as surrounding towns. Bainbridge usually had a great turnout because our school's athletics is the best in the state. I'd only ever been to one game before, and that was when Keiran was in juvie and Willow begged me to go with her.

"Do you see the crowd? Maybe you won't even run into him if he's even here." But what about the hundred or so other people in the past who would run to tell Keiran whenever I was in the vicinity? How did I dodge them all? "Sheldon wants us to meet her at the concession stand. She said it's urgent," Willow said looking at her phone with a frown.

It took us a while to maneuver through all the people, but we finally made it to the concession stand that was also crowded with people. The smell of popcorn and hot dogs greeted me as we approached. Sheldon was standing there in her green and white cheerleading uniform with a bottle of water in her hand.

"Hey, Sheldon."

She looked up and quickly walked over to us. "Kei-ran is here and much worse, he knows you're here. He's coming for you."

I stared at her, wordlessly. I wasn't surprised. I knew this would happen. I didn't understand it, but I wasn't surprised. "But we just walked in," Willow stated, looking at me apologetically.

"You know Keiran has his goons posted every-where. They probably spotted you and called him the moment you stepped foot in the parking lot."

"I should go," I finally replied.

"You shouldn't have come in the first place," his deep voice said somewhere behind me. Willow and Sheldon jumped in surprise, and I slowly turned around to face him. He was in the shadows, leaning against the back of the metal stands and dressed in a red, long-sleeve shirt and black jeans. He looked mouthwatering.

He swaggered over, grabbed my elbow, and walked away with me without another word. It took a second for me to realize it wasn't to the exit. I looked back help-lessly to see that Keenan and Dash had also appeared out of nowhere.

Keenan looked like he was chewing out Sheldon, and I knew it was because she was helping me. Dash had Willow pinned against the wall of the concession side. They were hidden in the shadows, but a little glimmer from the stadium lights allowed me to see that he had her hands pinned above her head, and he was saying something to her.

They quickly disappeared from sight as we rounded a corner, so I focused my attention back on Keiran. His face was set in a hard mask while his shoulders and back were tense as he walked. The sound of the game—*and the witnesses*—seemed far away when he led us a short distance away from the stands.

I immediately noticed his car parked near the back gates as we headed to it. *So that's why I didn't see his car.* We reached his car, and he walked to the driver's door, pulling his keys out.

"Where are we going?"

"I'm taking you home."

"What? Why?"

"What did I say to you when I left last night?" he asked instead.

"To stay put."

"And?"

"You would be back."

"And did I come back?"

"No."

"So what do you think you should have done?"

*Run far away from you.*

"I don't know. What should I have done?" I asked my voice dripping with bittersweet sarcasm. He gripped my upper arms and hemmed me up against the hood.

"You should have fucking listened," he whispered against my lips. His unexpected kiss was surprisingly soft yet it still took away all the breath and strength I had, as always. But the pleasure I felt at having his lips devour mine wasn't real. It was another mind game. One that had lingering effects on my mind and body.

I fought against it, forgetting the consequences of resisting him. A quick bite on my lip and his hand gripping my neck in warning caused me to soften against him with a needy moan. His touch put me on edge, but his aggressiveness was what pushed me over.

I liked his kisses and his taste far too much. I shouldn't like them at all, but that didn't keep me from standing on my toes so I could reach more of him. He groaned and pulled me closer, pressing his erection hard against my stomach. I'd forgotten he was angry with me. We didn't feel like enemies right now. We felt like lovers.

"You should have listened," he repeated absently, breaking our kiss just when I was ready to beg for more. "You should have stayed away..."

His voice sounded strained while his lips trailed down my chin to my neck, biting and sucking. My head fell back, exposing more of my neck in surrender as he continued to bite his way down. When his lips reached my breasts, he lifted his head and the cold look in his eyes caught me off guard.

"Give me one good reason why I shouldn't fuck you right here," he barked. Before I could respond, he flipped me around and pressed my upper body against the hood.

"Someone will see!" I blurted out in a panic, my voice a shriek in the night.

"Let them. I want them to see."

"Why?" He pulled my hair back from my face and braced his hand on the hood by face.

"Because then they'll know who owns you," he whispered in my ear, surprising me with the possessiveness evident in his voice. I almost asked him to repeat it so I could be sure. He was quiet now, but I knew he was watching me. "Why did you come here?" he asked while his other hand ran down my back.

"I wanted to see the game."

"You wanted to see the game," he repeated slowly. "Who is playing tonight?" His hand touched my lower back, and I could feel his thumb rubbing the dimples I had in my back.

"Piney."

"Wrong."

"Uh, Carver."

"Try again."

"I don't know!"

"Why did you just lie to me?"

"Why can't I be here? There is nothing I could do to you here."

"Did... you... just... lie to me?"

"I—Willow wanted me to come," I finally admitted.

"Willow."

"Yes, my best friend? My *only* friend. Do you remember her?" I knew I was defiant but didn't care at the moment.

"Yes, I'm starting to remember." The ice in his tone was unmistakable. "So, you disobeyed me because Willow asked you to?"

*Oh, shit.* I just remembered that I wasn't supposed to be friends with Willow anymore. "No, that's not what I meant. We—"

His hands gripped my ass, spreading my legs farther apart before his finger slid into my panties. I started to panic when his finger bypassed my pussy and lingered somewhere forbidden. *No freaking way.* Just when I felt a full panic attack emerging, he moved his finger back.

"So explain to me why you're bent over my car with your ass in the air, about to be fucked, if you didn't disobey me because Willow asked you to?"

"Because—" His fingers were now at my entrance, and the words I would have spoken gave way to a breathy moan.

"I'm waiting."

"I can't talk with you... doing that."

"Doing what? This?" A long finger entered me, followed by another until he was torturing me with the slow thrust of his thick fingers.

"Please," I heard the desperation in my own voice

as I began moving my hips against him. We both knew what I was begging for.

"Come here," he said, lifting me up until my back was against his hard chest, and I melted into him. The sounds of the game were drowned out by what he was doing to me, making me forget we were in a public place. *Or I just didn't care anymore.* "Do you remember what I said would happen if you lied or disobeyed me again?" The ominous threat in his voice was like a bucket of cold water, extinguishing the fire he had built up inside me.

"You said I would be sorry," I answered, reluctantly.

"That's right." He kissed my cheek, but it felt cruel. "And you *will* be sorry."

* * *

THE GAME WAS drawing to an end with both teams tied. Keiran was standing by the players on the bench talking to a few guys. I noticed they liked to look to him for playing advice and tips even though he wasn't a football player. It's amazing the type of admiration he gets around here. But then again... I was the only one he was ever cruel to. Sure, he'd been in many fights, but what guy hasn't? Still, Keiran was looked up to as some kind of role model, and I didn't understand it.

After he had promised to punish me, he walked me over to the stands with an order not to move. I looked around for Willow but didn't see her in the immediate area. I wasn't able to call her since Keiran had taken my phone, yet again. I did, however, see Dash standing by one of the cheerleaders with his hand on her ass. I shook my head in disgust at him, Keiran, and most of all, myself. I knew how they were using her for payback against me, yet I still didn't warn her away. I really felt as if I didn't have a choice. I just prayed Willow would forgive me in the end. It was the only way to protect them both.

"Lake?"

My name was called, and I instantly recognized the voice followed by a sense of dread. *This day couldn't get any worse.* I turned my head to the sound of the voice and saw a lanky form with a mop of brown curly hair, wearing a green and blue plaid button up and distressed jeans, standing at the end of the stands. A wide smile spread across his face when my eyes met his.

"Don't tell me you forgot about me already," he joked when I continued to stare at him. I knew who it was, but I was silently praying it wouldn't be him.

"Jesse?" I asked, and reluctantly thought I didn't have to.

"You are correct, but I'm hurt." He placed a hand to his heart and made his way up the bleachers toward me.

"Wh—what are you doing here?"

"You just keep digging the knife in deeper, sweetheart. Maybe you should give it a little twist. I missed you, too," he said sarcastically.

"I'm sorry, Jesse. You can't be here. This isn't a good time."

I looked around nervously, but Keiran's back was still turned. He was talking to one of the coaches. I didn't see any of his henchmen anywhere, but I couldn't take that risk, not after how he acted at my job... or rather, former job.

"Because of him? Where is he anyway? I'd like to meet him."

"You can't!"

"Jeez, Lake. You're fucking shaking. Did he hurt you?"

"No, Jesse. Just please go. You have to understand."

"I understand all right. What is he doing to you?"

"I can't answer that."

"What do you mean you can't answer that?" His
voice had risen, causing a few people to turn around. If
he got any louder, Keiran would hear him eventually.

"Lower your voice. I'm fine. He hasn't hurt me."

"Willow said it was a risk bringing you here, but I
didn't expect... I thought he was bullying you again.
There is something else, isn't there?"

I didn't answer him and instead, kept an eye on
Keiran. "I can help you, Lake."

I shook my head. "No, you can't. I have it under
control, just please go."

"No," he stated firmly.

"No? What do you *mean* no? Go!"

"Do you realize you're rhyming?" he chuckled.

"Jesse!"

"Lake, I'm not going anywhere. In fact, I'm going to
have a talk with him."

"You're what?" I shrieked. "Please don't do that."

"When are you going to stand up to him, Lake? You
can't be that weak!" he said, frustration lacing his voice.

"Excuse me?"

"What could he possibly do to you besides spread
rumors?"

Hurt my aunt. Hurt Willow. Hurt me.

"You don't know him. You don't—"

"You're right, I don't. But I can find out." With that,
he trudged down the bleachers toward the field, and
began walking across it while the game was playing!

"Jesse, stop!"

I wasn't as brave or as crazy as he was, but I quickly
ran around the track to try to intercept him. The crowd

in the stands was throwing a fit, and some of the players had a few choice words for Jesse. Some of them from school recognized him and greeted him, even though he basically interrupted the game and ruined the play. This, of course, caught Keiran's attention. If he was surprised, he didn't show it as he looked directly at Jesse. His eyebrow rose, and a smirk crossed his face. Damn it. He would know exactly who Jesse was by now.

"Masters," Jesse called, walking up to him. "I want to talk to you." *Oh shit, oh shit, oh shit.*

Keiran gave the football coach a look, and he walked away immediately, which was seriously ridiculous. "So talk," Keiran said, crossing his arms.

"Jesse, no. Let's go." He ignored me and squared up with Keiran.

"You need to leave her alone."

"Why would I do that?"

The air around us was charged with tension and people were beginning to notice the tension between Jesse and Keiran all but forgetting the game was happening. Even the players had stopped playing.

This was bad. I had to stop this... somehow. "Guys, that's enough. You're causing a scene," I scolded, stating the obvious. *Real genius, Lake.*

Jesse glared at me while Keiran watched me silently with no expression. That was the biggest sign that he was planning something bad, specifically to me.

"I'm taking her home," Jesse gritted turning back to Keiran. Keiran passed a fleeting look at Jesse, then me. He looked bored when he leaned back against the metal stands, casually.

"You do that." He stated, shocking us both. He nodded his head toward the field, and I could hear the beginnings of the game restarting, along with a lot of mumbling and hushed voices.

I didn't know what to say as I stared at him. His attention was already refocused on the game. Keiran wasn't one to be told what to do so I knew something was up. He moved in silence, never showing his hand. Jesse thought he had the upper hand now, but he didn't know how wrong he was.

Jesse walked over to me and grabbed my hand. Funny thing was I didn't want his hand on mine. I didn't want him to touch me at all. Not even in a friendly way. I wasn't mad at Jesse for helping me, but I didn't want to be touched by anyone else.

He turned us away but stopped long enough to say, "Stay away from her."

"Don't push it, Fitzgerald." Jesse stopped and turned to face Keiran again. "Take your hand off her. She's mine."

"She isn't property to be owned," Jesse argued. Keiran laughed, stood up and sauntered over to us, his eyes locked with mine the entire way.

"Well, then you've never had Monroe," he said cockily. My hand itched to slap him. I knew the meaning of his words, and I guess Jesse did too when his eyes flew to me accusingly. "Everything about her is meant to be owned. She makes you want to own her because she likes that type of control." He grinned at me, sneakily. "Don't you, Monroe?"

When he reached me, he grabbed my neck right there in front of the view of others and leaned down to whisper in my ear.

"Let go of his hand and maybe I'll let you come tonight when I fuck you." I immediately wrestled my hand from Jesse, cursing the fact that I wanted him. "Good girl," he praised. "I wouldn't want to have to fuck up your little friend and have a real reason to go to jail. No one touches you. Do you understand?"

"Yes," I whispered. I hated the eagerness apparent in my voice.

"I'll see you later," he said. His words were both threatening and lustful, as I had since learned they were one in the same with him and me.

\* \* \*

"I'M SORRY, LAKE. I thought he could help!" I sighed and shook my head.

"It's okay, Willow. At least there wasn't blood spilled," I said as I spoke into the phone.

It had been an hour since Jesse brought me home. I apologized to him and made him leave immediately. I wasn't dumb enough to rock the boat. I was just one incident shy of being sent to the crazy house. I tried to catch up on homework, but my nervousness wouldn't let me concentrate.

Willow had called me wanting to see how things went, and I tried not to let my frustration with her show. She was just being a friend, but Keiran now thinks I didn't obey him, and worse... he thinks I lied to him about breaking my friendship with Willow. How could he think a ten-year friendship like ours could be so easily broken anyway?

"Where did you disappear to anyway?" The other line became so quiet that I had to check to see if we were still connected. "Willow?"

"Oh, um, well, Dash, he…"

"Got it. Willow, are you sure about Dash?"

"What do you mean?"

"I just want to make sure you're careful."

"Well, we used protection every time—"

"Jeez, Willow! Not what I meant."

"Oh, sorry," she giggled.

"Willow, I don't want you to get hurt," I said being serious again.

"Lake, don't worry. I'm not falling for Dash. We're friends."

Despite her claim, I didn't miss the longing in her voice. It finally dawned on me that no matter the consequence, I couldn't let Willow be hurt. I'm sure my aunt wouldn't want that either. I had to find another way to protect them both.

"Willow, I have to tell you something. It's about Keiran and Dash. They plan to—"

"I plan to do what?" Keiran's sudden appearance caused me to drop my phone. I spun around to see him standing in my bedroom doorway.

"How did you get in here?"

"Answer me," he barked. I hesitated before answering.

"I was going to tell her." It probably wasn't wise to tell him the truth, but I wanted him to know I was stronger than he thought.

"Is that right?"

"I can't do this."

"Fine," he walked into the room. "Then I'll tell her."

He scooped up my phone before I could process what he planned to do. I tried to take my phone from him, but he pushed me against the wall and used a strong hand to cover my mouth. All that could be heard was the muffled sounds of my protests and Willow calling my name over the phone,

"Willow," Keiran's hypnotic voice spoke into the phone. "I would like to tell you something about your dear *friend*."

I was shaking my head as hard as I could to unlatch his hand from my mouth so I could stop him. This was not how I wanted her to find out, and he knew that. She would never forgive me hearing it from someone else.

"She is using you to—"

I didn't try to stop the tears that trailed down my face onto his hand. It caught his attention, and he dropped his gaze from me to his hand.

"It seems she has had a change of heart." He hung up my phone without saying goodbye and stepped closer to me pressing me against the wall. He planted his feet on the outside of mine and gripped my neck while keeping his hand over my mouth.

He pulled out his phone to dial a number and after a few seconds, began speaking. "Yeah, you still on her? Where is she now? Good. Her loving niece is no longer interested in our deal."

When it dawned on me what he was doing, I started to fight and scream against the hold he had on me but to no avail. I bit into his hand and clawed at his face, but he didn't flinch. As he watched me fight, a depraved smile spread across his face.

"Yes, I want you to kill her. Slit her throat, but before you do that... let her know her dear niece sends her regards." When he said the last, I managed to dislodge his hand from my throat, and as soon as I was free, a blood-curdling scream ripped from the depths of my soul for my aunt. Her death would be my entire fault, and if she died, I would die with her.

"Please," I croaked out when screaming was no longer possible.

"I gave you what you wanted."

"That's not what I want. Please... call him back. I'm sorry."

"What is it you are sorry for?"

"I'm sorry for disobeying you. It won't happen again."

"See, that's where you're wrong. It will happen

again because you think you can save them. You want to be a hero."

"No."

"Yeah, you do," he replied lazily.

"Please call him back. I'll do anything."

"Yes, you will, and I don't need to call him."

"What, why?"

"Because I never called him."

I narrowed my eyes when he smiled down at me. "You're an asshole."

"And you're a glutton for punishment. Maybe you really do like what I did to you last night." I shook my head, but he only grinned. "What did I say about lying, Monroe?" He turned me around so that my back was now facing him. "You have a few things to answer for, and I'd like to get started as soon as possible."

"What does that mean?" I was quickly becoming a nervous wreck at the sound of promise in his voice.

"You know what it means," he said while unzipping my dress.

"I won't allow her to get hurt so there must be some other way you can punish me. Just don't use Willow."

"And what way is that? Should I beat you? As much as I'd like to slap the fuck out of you, I won't. You don't have anything else," he sneered.

"So now you're a beacon of morality and goodwill?"

"No. It means there are better ways to hurt you."

"What are you going to do?" I asked when he peeled my dress off my shoulders and unsnapped my bra.

"Whatever I want."

"Are you going to hurt me?"

"Yes." The corner of his mouth lifted. "But you'll like it."

"I doubt that."

He was slipping my panties down my legs when I said that. He stood up straight, and the next second, he turned me back around, and his head lowered to bite down on my nipple. They were sensitive and always seemed to make me want to do things I knew I shouldn't. My legs shook, and I tried pressing them together to hide my reaction, but his hand was already there.

"Your body doesn't lie. Go stand by the side of the bed and bend over. Place your hands around your ankles and don't move. And, Monroe—don't make me have to tell you anything twice." I did what he commanded and walked over to the bed. I positioned my body to face him and bent over when he stopped me. "No. Turn around."

I felt my cheeks color as I thought about how the position would expose me to him completely. Still, I did what he said and turned around. "No matter what you hear or feel, keep your eyes on the ground and only speak when I tell you to."

His tone was all business. Despite his warnings, I wanted to turn around to see him. I was afraid of what he might do and wanted him to reassure me that he wouldn't really hurt me, but I knew he would never do that. He wanted me to be afraid of him.

His booted feet suddenly appeared between my legs and kicked my feet apart. I struggled to adjust without taking my hands from around my ankles. The sound of him removing his belt kicked my fear into high gear.

"Let's start with your first offense. What was it?"

"I went to the game."

"No."

A sharp pain spread across my ass as the sound of the hard lash on my skin resonated through the air. I let out a loud cry and nearly toppled over. When he caught me, I turned my head, but he quickly grabbed the back of my neck, holding me in place.

"That was one. It's up to you how many you get. What was your first offense?"

"I don't know," I cried. My ass was still throbbing when he delivered a second lash.

"Well, let me inform you," he said, talking over my crying. "Your first mistake was taking that fucking job. Your first offense was letting that clown near you.

"But he—" I felt the leather on my ass for a third time.

"Are you really going to make me repeat myself?" I shook my head quickly. My hair was falling in front of my face with a few strands sticking to my wet cheeks.

"Good, then we don't need this anymore." I heard the belt fall to the floor, and I felt a moment of gratitude until he pulled me over to the bed with him and laid me across his lap. He started massaging my butt and talking to me. "I want you to tell me everything you did wrong today. If you lie or leave anything out, I get the belt again. Begin."

"I talked to Willow." *Slap.*

"I left the house." *Slap.*

"I was going to lie to you." *Slap, slap.* I tried to ignore the burning pain the licks were causing me, but at last, my voice broke, and I clenched the sheets in front of me.

"Continue," he gritted.

"I talked to Jesse, but I swear I didn't know he was going to be there! I—" *Slap.*

"I didn't ask for your excuses. Continue."

"I let him touch me." *Slap!* "Ahhh!"

My scream ripped through the air when he delivered that blow. It was firmer than the rest. I was heavily sobbing into his pant leg and the sheets as I tried to get away, but a steel arm banded around my body, holding me in place. He sat still while I cried out my pain and continued to hold me down until I settled.

"Please. It hurts." All while I was moving, I could feel his erection through his jeans. I couldn't deny my own arousal, but I couldn't explain it either.

"What else did you do?" he whispered. His fingers were teasing my skin with a pinch every now and then.

"I was going to tell Willow everything. I wanted to stop you."

"And that, Monroe, is your *greatest* offense."

He proceeded to spank me with hard, unyielding hits across my bottom. He didn't stop. No matter how long or loud I screamed and begged—he wouldn't stop. I realized those licks from before were the prelude to what was to come. When he finally finished with me, he shoved me off his lap and onto the floor. My entire body was flushed red and throbbing in pain. I could see the bed through blurry eyes and the sheets that had been ripped off by me. He stood up from the bed and walked over to the closet and pulled out my small duffel bag and started to fill them with clothing.

"What are you doing?"

"What does it look like?"

"Like you've gone mad?"

"How does your ass feel, Monroe?" The threatening look he gave me told me to shut up and shut up fast, so I did. *It's cool. I can talk shit in my head.*

He went to my dresser and started stuffing the bag with my undergarments. "If there is anything you need, I suggest you get it now. You aren't coming back."

"Where are you taking me?"

"My place."

"What? I can't stay with you. My aunt will kill me!"

"Your aunt won't make it back if you keep talking."

I made a sound of frustration and hurried into the bathroom to redress and grab the essentials. When I returned to my bedroom, he had my backpack and duffel in hand waiting for me.

"Let's go," he commanded.

\* \* \*

WHEN WE WALKED into his house, I immediately looked around for his uncle and once again, found him absent. *What is it that keeps him gone all the time?* "Your uncle is gone a lot," I remarked aloud.

"So."

"Won't he be upset when he comes home and finds me moved in for the weekend?" His nonchalant attitude about everything, especially his uncle's absence, was unusual at best.

"My uncle only comes home when one of us is in trouble."

"Why?"

"Stop asking questions that you don't need to know the answers to." He led me into the kitchen where he dropped my bag on the floor and opened the refrigerator to peer inside.

"Why am I here?" I asked with extreme exasperation. Dealing with Keiran for long periods of time always made me weary, confused, and... horny. "What are you planning to do with me for the rest of the weekend?"

"You're here because you have a conscience. That's an inconvenience for me. But it is convenient for you to be available to service me immediately," he said matter-of-factly. He slammed the fridge door. Before I knew what he was going to do, my back was up against the fridge with his erection pressed into my stomach. "I want to fuck you hard and I want to fuck you often." He lifted my leg to wrap around his hip, bringing my center closer to his erection. "I'm not asking, Monroe. You want it just as bad as I do. I can feel your need... it's wet, hot, and all mine."

There was something annoying, but incredibly hot hearing him claiming my pussy as his, but I managed to shake off the urge to ask for exactly what he threatened to do, right here and now. "Why do you talk to me like that?" I asked instead.

"Like what?"

"Like I'm a slut."

"Because it makes you angry, and it also makes you hot. Slut, or not."

"But I'm not. You are the only one I've had sex with."

The sound he made low in his throat was angry. "Good, because if you have it with anyone else, I will kill him... slowly... and then you." His voice was unmistakably aroused and possessive.

"You can't just threaten to kill people!"

"It's not a threat."

"Normal teenagers don't threaten to kill people and mean it."

"Who said I was normal?"

"I know you're not." I just wish you were.

I looked into his gray eyes and wished I had the courage and ability to deny him. But I couldn't. I have always given him exactly what he wanted whether it was my tears, my fear or my body. "Why do you test me?" he asked.

I wasn't expecting his question, but the answer that followed was even more surprising. "It makes me feel like I'm trying."

"Trying what?"

"To not be afraid."

"Why, when you have so much to be afraid of?"

I looked at him carefully. "Why do you want me to be afraid of you? What do you gain?"

"What makes you think I gain something? Maybe it's just fun for me."

"You know some people think you have a thing for me?" I watched him carefully for a reaction or sign that I might be right, but, of course, he remained perfectly impassive.

"Some people are stupid. I don't have 'things.'" He dropped my leg from around his waist and walked away to sit in one of the kitchen chairs.

"So why fear? People are bullied in school all the time for shits and giggles, but you don't want laughs."

"You don't know what I want."

"Enlighten me then," I demanded with more force than necessary.

"No."

"No?"

"Don't ask questions you don't need the answers to," he said, repeating his statement from earlier. His tone was bored, but the muscles in his shoulders and back were tense.

"Why do you keep saying that?" My frustration was mounting, and when he smirked, I knew he wasn't done making me miserable.

"Because it's the best you're going to get so leave me the fuck alone." It was a warning I should have heeded, but I was never one to listen to my instincts.

"When you said you would make my aunt disappear... what did you mean? Would you really kill her?"

"Why would I do that? I would much rather you live with the agony of knowing she was somewhere suffering."

"Please, listen to me. I didn't frame you, but I know who did."

His eyes narrowed as he watched me. "Careful, Monroe. My goodwill is fading. Fast."

"No. You need to hear this. I knew about it only be-cause—" He was out of his seat with his arms around me, crushing my body to his. I cried out when he bit down into my neck. I screamed again, but he ignored my heated protests and bit down harder. He bent me over the kitchen table and pushed aside my panties.

"Because you're a conniving bitch?" he asked with unsuppressed scorn. I heard the distinct sound of a condom packet rip and soon after felt the force of his punishing thrust as he entered me. The table moved a few inches, so I grabbed onto it to keep from falling.

"No," I denied and pushed my hips into him. We both moaned at the feeling of him burying deeper. My pussy clenched at his cock in welcome.

"You did this. You." Each word he spoke was paired with a hard thrust until he let go completely and was pounding all of his frustration and anger into me. He was in my head and my body at the same time with no hope of escape. His hands were rough and hard on my hips as he pulled me into him. When his teeth sunk into my spine, I released a throaty moan. "Such a hot bitch, aren't you? I can feel you creaming all over my dick."

"Don't call me that." I squealed when he rammed his cock into me once and held it deep inside me while he growled in my ear.

"I'll call you whatever I want," he said, grabbing my ponytail and delivering a series of short, hard thrusts.

"Oh, God... Why does it feel so good?" I wailed as I tightened around him. He had me pinned to the table, completely immobile, and vulnerable to the demands of his cock.

"Good," he thrust deeper into me, stealing away my breath. "That means you feel all of me. You're mine, Monroe. You always will be, and I won't let you go. Do you hear that? I won't."

"You have to..."

The sound of the front door opening and Keenan's voice could barely be heard over the sound of our fucking. Keiran continued to pound me. I wasn't sure if he'd heard his cousin come in, but I knew Keenan would be able to hear us. The sound of our skin slapping, his groans, and my screams were echoing throughout the kitchen, and the kitchen door was wide open.

"Stop. He'll hear us," I moaned out weakly.

"I can see just fine too, sweetheart. Please don't stop on my account. You look like your enjoying it." I looked to the side to see Keenan leaning against the door watching us with a grin. I immediately swung my arm behind me to push Keiran away, but he caught it and held it at the small of my back.

"Let me go. He's watching!" Keiran's fingers being stuffed into my mouth silenced the rest of my protests. I bit down on his fingers, but he only chuckled and slapped my already sore ass. The need to come was strong, but my release was evading me. "Keiran, please," I begged.

"You've displeased me today, Monroe. You think you deserve to come?" His thrusts slowed down to a teasing rhythm.

"I want it... please." My body shook uncontrollably from the need to come.

He gripped the back of my neck and leaned down to whisper in my ear. "Then take what you need. Fuck me, Monroe."

His words were barely out before I pushed my hips

back against him again and again, desperately searching for what only he could give me. "Damn… she looks like a hot fuck," Keenan groaned. I'd forgotten he was watching us.

"Keiran, please!" I begged once more. His low groans and sinful promises told me he wasn't as immune to me as he pretended, but I needed him, so he wanted me to beg. I wasn't above begging. Not when his cock was buried deep. His fingers finally slid down, teasing and rubbing the tiny bundle of nerves. Once he touched me, a powerful orgasm ripped through me. My back curved and locked into place as I let my orgasm take over.

Keiran was still moving inside me, slowly, as he watched me come. I could feel his eyes on me even now. "Had enough?" he asked. I knew without turning around that the ever-present smirk was there.

*No.* My body couldn't take any more of his aggressive demands and the painful pleasure he subjected my body to, so I nodded my head.

"Stand up," he ordered.

"I can't." My legs were too weak to hold me up much less walk.

"Either stand up or get fucked again. Your choice."

He was still inside me, moving lightly. I could already feel the beginning of another orgasm rising. I stood up on wobbly legs and rested my back against his chest, and surprisingly, he let me. He slowly pulled out of me, and it felt as if he was still hard which meant he hadn't come. I discreetly fixed my dress and panties when I noticed Keenan still watching us silently.

"Go upstairs, clean up, and wait for me."

I did as he ordered without arguing. I knew where that usually got me.

\* \* \*

I WALKED INTO Keiran's room and couldn't help but admire the smell. He and everything he owned always smelled fresh and cool. I looked around curiously but didn't know what I was looking for, but like any person, the bedroom was a person's domain. It was the most likely place a person would hide their secrets to keep them close, and everyone had secrets... so what was Keiran's?

I walked over to his dresser first, forgetting about his order to clean up. There wasn't anything particularly telling or unusual on top, just as before, so I quickly opened the first dresser drawer while listening closely for the sound of Keiran coming. A quick inspection through his dresser revealed nothing. *What are you looking for, Lake?* It would probably help if I knew that much.

I opened his closet door and walked inside. Keiran's closet looked like every normal teenage boy's closet, but Keiran wasn't normal. Whatever it was had to be here. Dark clothing and various sneakers and boots littered the shelves and hung on the railing. I lightly touched his clothing being careful, not to disturb anything too much. The worst thing I could do was to be caught snooping. After a few minutes, I was looking through my third shoebox and had almost given up my search when I hit the jackpot. I wasn't expecting to find what I did. I swallowed and picked it up hesitantly, feeling the weight of it in my hands.

What is Keiran doing with a gun?

I inspected it further, turning it over in my hands. There was a button on the side near the handle and trigger so I pressed it. A slim case fell out the bottom, and inside, I could see it was loaded with bullets. I dropped the clip and hurriedly picked it back up to deposit it back into the gun. That's when I noticed the thin chain of a gold locket with a pearl wrapped around the handle. It was beautiful and... familiar. I searched my memory for where I might have seen the necklace. It wasn't new. It was... *the picture!*

I was almost sure the dead girl in the picture was wearing the same necklace when she died. I just needed to get my hands on the picture to confirm. I had hidden it in my desk and hadn't looked at it since I found it. At first glance, I didn't pay much attention to her jewelry or see it as a clue considering I wasn't ever expecting to come across it—much less in Keiran's closet.

Because Keiran wasn't the one to break in my house, I ruled out the possibility that he had left the picture to scare me. It wasn't his style to be vague. He was much more direct when delivering threats.

But if he had the necklace now, he must have known the girl. So how did he get it and who was she to him? The walls began to close in on me, and the closet suddenly felt too small as many questions flooded my mind. However, when I looked down at the gun in my hand, it was the only one that stood out and was the most dangerous to answer. *Did he kill her?*

I forgot to breathe as I stared down at the cold, hard steel of my reality. *I had to get out of here.* I needed to escape him before he took away everything I ever loved. I couldn't let him hurt my aunt. I knew what it was like to be hurt by Keiran. It dug deep and never let go.

Instinct was screaming at me to get out, and for once, I listened to it. I quickly slammed the clip back into the gun and carefully arranged it back in the box and threw it back on the top shelf. Just as I was sitting down, Keiran walked in. He immediately looked at me suspiciously. I probably looked as nervous as I was feeling.

"What were you doing?" he asked calmly.

"No—nothing. I was waiting for you like you told me."

"You didn't do what I told you to do." I stared at him confused, feeling sweat form on my brow. "I also told you to clean up, so what were you doing?"

*Think, think, think.* "I—I was, but... there wasn't any towels left to clean up with." *Shit! What a dumb lie.*

"Is that so?" I nodded dumbly and swallowed the saliva that was suddenly too thick and heavy for my throat. "Show me."

The room had begun to spin, and I could practically smell shit hitting the fan. I stood up and walked out to the hallway and headed toward what I hoped was the bathroom door. I was too distracted last time to remember where Sheldon had led me. I quickly played 'eenie meenie' with the doors and reached for one.

"That's Keenan's room." I rubbed my sweaty palm against my dress to hide my nervousness.

"Sorry. The thing about doors is that they all look the same."

"So do lies."

"I'm not lying."

"Then get your ass in the bathroom, Monroe. My favorite clock is ticking." He stood against a door further down the hall with his arms crossed over his chest, and the light bulb finally clicked in my head. I walked over to the door and stood in front of him trying to mask my nervousness. "Yes?"

"You're standing in front of the door," I whispered.

"Am I?"

*I hope so.* I stared up at him but didn't say anything. He smirked and pushed open the door all the while keeping his gaze on mine. I looked inside hesitantly and let out a slow, steady breath.

"Congratulations, you bought yourself a few seconds." He walked into the bathroom and leaned against the sink, waiting for me. I walked in and looked around the clean but plain bathroom. You could tell by looking that only men used this bathroom. There weren't any of the frou frou decorations that women liked.

"I didn't see where you keep the towels in here."

"That's because we don't."

"Then why did you—"

"I wanted to see if you were still lying to me."

You could hear a pen drop a mile away. I opened and closed my mouth, but no words came out. He stared at me for a few seconds longer before he walked over to the shower and cut the water on. When he walked back over to me, I took a step back, but he caught the front of my dress and pulled me to him. He spun me around and unzipped the back and when it was off, he nudged me into the shower. He left the bathroom and returned moments later with two cloths and two towels in his hand. He continued to ignore me while he slipped out of his jeans and shirt, and when he stepped into the shower, I moved over to put space between us.

He grabbed the bar of soap out of the dish and grabbed my neck next, pulling me to him again. "Wash me," he ordered, placing the cloth in my hand.

"Aren't you going to punish me?"

"Do you want me to punish you?" I faltered and realized I didn't know how to answer that question. *No, dumb ass!* I mentally screamed the answer to myself, but yet the words couldn't pass my lips. He smirked and said, "I know you better than you know yourself, Monroe. I'm not going to punish you... tonight. I'm fucking tired. Controlling you is exhausting."

"Am I supposed to feel sorry for you?" *Did I say that out loud?*

He eyed me and said, "Careful... I'm not that tired." I looked down and fingered the soapy cloth in my hand. He released a harsh breath and gripped my wrist bringing it up to his chest. "You can start here."

My hand automatically began moving in circles across his chest. He had an impressive build for an eighteen year old, but no one would ever have accused Keiran of being ordinary. He watched me as I washed him, and I almost dropped the cloth a few times. When I reached his lower stomach and the hard erection stretched against it, I paused. I slowly ran the cloth up and down, my nervousness making my grip firm, and I briefly hoped I was hurting him the way he does me when he takes me. *But you like the pain...*

The groan that erupted from his throat sounded pleasurable rather than painful, so I tightened my grip and continued the up and down motion. The hot water pounding over us was forgotten as I concentrated on making him hurt.

"Fuck," he groaned again. "Unless you want me to fuck you right now, I suggest you stop playing with my dick. I know what you were trying to do. It would be more efficient if you kneed me in the balls."

I kept my gaze down to hide the guilt and quickly finished washing him. When I finished, he soaped the other cloth and washed my body with surprisingly gentle, massaging strokes. Before I knew it, I was closing my eyes and enjoying the sensation.

When he finished washing me, he brusquely ordered me to get out, and I bit back a retort for his rudeness. I dried off slowly, hoping it pissed him off and then left to wait in his room. I could still hear the shower running as I rummaged through the bag he packed for me. After searching three times, I realized he forgot to pack pajamas for me. I huffed and sat on the edge of the bed. He finally came in moments later with a towel wrapped around his waist. This was my second time seeing him like that, and the effect was even stronger than the last.

"I don't have pajamas."

He unwrapped his towel and used a corner to dry off his chest. The urge to taste his skin was overwhelming. When he dropped his towel on the floor and switched off the light, plunging the room in darkness, my ire rose. He approached the bed and dropped down on the mattress.

"I sleep nude so you will, too."

"I really prefer not to so if you could loan me a shirt..."

"Sleep naked or sleep on the floor." He sounded as if he was already half asleep. I could only make out his shadow among the bed sheets.

"You're being unreasonable." Silence greeted me. After a few minutes, I stood up and dropped the towel. I pulled back the sheets while eyeing him carefully and quickly slipped inside using the sheet to cover my naked body. His breathing sounded even so I assumed he'd already fallen asleep. I shifted until I was as far away from him as I could get without falling off the bed.

"Keiran?"

"What?"

"Why did you have sex with me in front of your cousin?" I held my breath, waiting for an answer.

"He needed to see that you were only mine."

"Why did he need to see that?" I asked, confused.

"Because he wants to fuck you." He said it as casually as if we were discussing the weather.

I frowned. "What would make you think that?"

"My cousin will fuck anything that moves."

"And yet he hasn't fucked you."

"Monroe..."

"Sorry." I suppressed the sneaky laugh bubbling in my chest, but it quickly died when a disturbing thought occurred to me. "Would you let him have me?"

His arms were around my waist in a flash, pulling me across the bed toward him. He flipped me onto my back, tucked me into his side, and leaned over me to peer into my eyes.

"No one will ever have you but me."

"How can you be so sure?" I asked, feigning anger even as my heart skipped a beat.

"Because I'll kill you first. You're mine, Monroe. That will never change."

# CHAPTER THIRTEEN

"FUCK MONDAYS," I muttered to myself. The day was halfway over, and I kept thinking about the second I could escape this hell, but then I remembered you could never actually leave hell when you sold your soul to the devil himself.

I had been playing his shadow all day, and I was sick of it. Keiran was everywhere all the time, without actually being around. The stares and whispers I received were draining. Don't get me wrong, I was used to it, but for different reasons. There were so many rumors circulating about what I was doing with Keiran, none of them good. To make matters worse, Willow would barely talk or look at me in volleyball today. I had to find a way to talk to her later without Keiran knowing.

I pushed open the bathroom door and immediately caught sight of Anya primping in the mirror. What she needed to primp for in the middle of a class period, I had no clue. She was standing in her signature high heels and mini skirt. I evilly wished she would trip and fall at least once. Maybe then, she would get the clue that stilettos weren't meant for school.

"Well, if it isn't the whore of Bainbridge High," she sneered.

"Funny. I was going to say the same about you."

"I don't steal people's boyfriends."

"No. You just spread your legs for them. Do you at least ask for dinner first?"

Her eyes narrowed, and I noticed her fist ball at her side. "When Keiran is done with you, I will make you sorry."

"Too late. I'm already sorry."

"You think you're special but you're not. He just wants to fuck you for whatever reason. You're not even pretty."

"Gee, thanks. Maybe he wanted a change of scenery. Something less shallow."

She narrowed her eyes and placed a hand on her hip. "Did you just call me fat?" she huffed.

I choked back a laugh. *Wow, she really is an airhead.* "I'm sorry. What was I thinking?"

"Whatever. Stay away from Keiran. He's mine."

"That's kind of hard when he can't seem to stay away from me. But I'll tell you what... you can keep him, and when I'm through with him I'll toss him back."

"You'll never get the chance. Trevor has something planned for you, and Keiran will be all mine again."

I managed to maintain a bored expression. She was watching me closely for a reaction, but I refused to give her one. "You let me know how that works out for you, will you?"

"Bitch," she spat. She charged for the door and bumped my shoulder on the way out.

As I was walking back to class, I received a text message from Jesse saying that he wanted to talk. I chose not to respond. I had to distance myself from him and anyone else Keiran could use to hurt me. Besides, there was nothing Jesse could do to help me, and while we'd grown close, I didn't feel comfortable discussing Keiran with him.

When the last bell finally rang, I walked outside and found Keiran, Keenan, Dash, and Quentin all standing around Keiran's car. I had been wondering how I would get home when Keiran didn't show up for fifth period. Willow was there, but after what had happened Saturday night and with the phone call, I felt too guilty to look her in the eye, much less ask for a ride home. Keiran would also likely find out that I disobeyed him again. It all made me question once more if I was doing the right thing. The ending fate of the dead girl in the picture told me I was.

As I approached the car, the guys stared at me, but I didn't let my nervousness from their scrutiny show. I lifted my chin and walked up to Keiran. "Take me home," I ordered.

The guys chuckled as if I had just told a joke while Keiran watched me but didn't say anything. I tightened my hand on the strap of my bag and met his stare, but a few seconds later, I started to waver. He wanted me to squirm and, damn it, it was working. He managed to pick away my defenses and toss them away.

"Your girl doesn't have any manners," Dash commented. Keiran rubbed his chin where his stubble was growing thicker and grunted.

"I think she does it for attention," Keenan quipped.

"You would know all about begging for attention, wouldn't you?" Keenan was a walking advertiser for a kid with daddy issues. He played the rebel and the whore, but I saw right through his act.

"Yeah, but I don't beg as well as you do," he said smugly.

My face reddened at the reminder of Keiran and me in the kitchen the other day. I still couldn't believe Keiran allowed him to watch us, but then again, Keiran didn't have any warm feelings toward me. I was just another girl who would spread her legs for him. "You're a perverted—"

"Enough," Keiran commanded. "Get in the car." He opened his door and pushed the seat forward so I could climb in the back.

Once seated in the car, he slammed the door closed. I tapped my foot impatiently while he continued to talk to his friends. I pulled out my phone to text my aunt. My worry for her kept me checking in with her more frequently than was normally necessary.

The school parking lot was nearly empty by the time he decided to leave. He and Keenan climbed in the car, and we sped out of the parking lot. I watched the town pass by through the window and tried not to listen to their conversation. Keenan was yet again talking about some hot chick who wanted to bang him. I honestly didn't know what Sheldon saw in him. He was a pig.

My body wasn't accustomed to all the sex I had over the last twenty-four hours so I leaned my head back against the seat and closed my eyes. Before long, I had fallen asleep.

Somewhere between sleep and wake, I felt the car stop and heard a door open. I reluctantly opened my eyes, and when I noticed I was home, I sat up with excitement. I thought for sure Keiran would lock me away in his house again where I could *service* him at any time.

Keiran slid out of his car and lifted his seat. I eagerly stepped out and walked to the door without looking back or saying goodbye. As much as my body enjoyed what he did to me, I was exhausted. I unlocked the door and stepped inside, but when I tried to close it, he stopped it with a hand on the door. I turned around in surprise to see him walk inside.

"I thought you were leaving?" I asked, nervously.

"Take your clothes off," he ordered. His voice was husky and aroused as he slowly shut the door and shed his shirt.

\* \* \*

THE DISHEARTENING THUD of the door shutting after his departure echoed in my ears. I listened to him drive off from the couch where he left me naked, spent, and sore. Only when I couldn't hear the sound of his engine anymore did I pick myself up from the couch. Before heading upstairs for a soak, I picked my clothes up from the hallway where they were discarded.

I felt many emotions, but the one that was dominant was disappointment. He took me hard and then left without a word. It was pretty much the way he'd always treated me after he had me.

He'd fuck me and then ignore me. I may have been a virgin when we had sex, but I wasn't naive enough to think this was normal.

My inexperience was caused in part because Keiran made it his mission to run off any guy who showed an interest in me... even the unpopular ones. My first kiss ended in a disaster because of him.

I had decided to join the Math club because I was good with numbers and hoped to make friends. Willow was the love of my life as far as best friends go, but I couldn't smother her.

After two weeks in the club, Peter asked me out, and I immediately accepted. He was nice and pretty cute. He also wasn't popular either, so we understood each other, or so I thought. He asked to kiss me one afternoon as we were leaving a meeting, and I let him because I had never been kissed before. It was a simple, close-mouthed kiss that didn't get far. I just didn't realize that *he* had been watching us...

*"WHAT THE FUCK do you think you're doing?" I heard a gruff voice bark. He sounded more intimidating than usual. I looked up to find a furious Keiran, sweaty, in his practice uniform.*

*We were right outside the gym doors and because of my eagerness, I hadn't processed the danger of sticking around too long. But what threw me off was that he wasn't looking at me. He was glaring at Peter, who looked like he was trying to disappear into the wall. If looks could kill...*

*"Get the fuck out of here," he snarled at Peter making him run off instantly. I blinked not believing how fast he was gone. I turned to leave not wanting to dance with the devil.*

*"Where do you think you're going?"*

*I stopped in my tracks but didn't turn around, even when I heard him move closer.*

*"You"—he began but stopped. I heard a loud slam and I jumped, realizing he must have punched a locker. Oh, God. "Fucking look at me!" he roared. I slowly turned, terrified of what I might see. Keiran stood there—fists clenched, chest heaving. His jaw was clenched, and I could see a vein near his temple was throbbing.*

*He was furious.*

*Years of him bullying and taunting me, I'd never seen him this angry, not even when he pushed me off the monkey bars. I was used to cool indifference...*

*hatred even. But this... I didn't know, and I wasn't sure I could handle him like this.*

*"You let him touch you." He said 'touch' with disgust as if it was hard to imagine someone liking me or even wanting me. I hugged myself for comfort, fighting back tears. I couldn't let him tear me down like this.*

*"Keiran, plea—"*

*"Shut up," he ordered. The first tear felt like acid as it burned its way down my face.*

*"You don't get to say my name. Not now... not ever," he sneered.*

*I sucked in a breath at the cold hatred spilling from him in waves... I was drowning in it, my tears over-spilling now. He turned abruptly and headed for the exit. I stood frozen in the middle of the hallway when I heard tires squeal and knew it was Keiran taking off. I finally dropped to my knees sobbing as I felt a pain in my heart that I couldn't describe. I felt like I betrayed him somehow.*

The next morning I found out by some random girl in the hallway that I wasn't a part of the math club anymore. I tried going to the meeting that afternoon, but apparently, the meeting place moved. I didn't know what was going on, but always had a feeling Keiran was behind it.

# CHAPTER FOURTEEN

AFTER SOAKING IN a hot bath to ease my sore and overused muscles, I gave in and called Willow. I needed to know if we were okay.

The phone rang for a while, and I almost gave up when she finally picked up.

"Yeah?"

"Hey, Willow." I tried to sound normal despite the nervousness I felt.

"Hey," she replied in a dry tone.

"I'm sorry about Saturday night." I struggled with the right words to say in my mind, but the truth was I didn't know what else I could say.

"That's it?"

"What do you mean?"

"Cut the crap, Lake. You were getting ready to tell me something about Dash. What's going on?"

"I can't—I can't tell you." I knew it was lame, but while I couldn't tell her the truth, I couldn't lie to her either.

"You can't tell me?" she hissed. I could picture her standing with a hand on her hip and her eyes narrowed.

"It's complicated, Willow. But you know I would never do anything to hurt you."

"No, but apparently, you would lie to me."

"Willow..."

"Forget it."

She hung up the phone, and I sat there for a minute with my head in my hands. He'd done it. Keiran managed to break apart our friendship without doing much at all. I considered going over to her house and making her talk to me, but I decided it was best to let her cool off. Besides, what would I say to her anyway? My phone pinged a few minutes later with a message from Jesse again.

Jesse: Let me help

Lake: How would you do that?

Jesse: We could tell someone...

Lake: I can't do that and please don't say anything.

I silenced my phone and tossed it on the coffee table. Jesse was a good guy, but Keiran was out of his league. Keiran wouldn't see Jesse as a threat, but rather another pawn to use against me. I busied myself with chores and homework to pass the time and take my mind off my sorrows.

Normally, I would be at work, but Keiran had screwed that up for me as well. The day after the incident, I'd called Charlie, who assured we were good but also said I couldn't have my job back. The local owner apparently had gotten word of the fight and didn't want me back. It was yet another thing Keiran managed to steal from me.

* * *

Two weeks passed quickly, but nothing got better. In fact, everything just got worse. Willow wouldn't talk to me, Trevor was watching me, and random girls kept picking fights with me. Just yesterday, I was pushed against the lockers by one of Anya's friends.

Keiran also changed... sort of. He ignored me completely in school now, but every night, he came for me. As backward as it was, his nightly visits were the only time I didn't feel alone. I also felt like the dumbest girl in the world because, no matter how much he turned my world upside down, by body always welcomed him. Every time he touched me, he took without giving anything in return. Sometimes I cried after we had sex, but it wasn't from physical pain. It was the suffocating feeling of hopelessness. Keiran had succeeded in making me his prisoner.

# CHAPTER FIFTEEN

WHEN SHELDON WASN'T busy with cheerleading and Keenan, she made it a mission to break me out of my depression. My aunt was due back in three weeks, and I welcomed the chance to feel safe at home again and not just because of the recent burglary. I'd decided to wait until my aunt got back to tell her about it. I didn't want her to worry or cut her tour short.

There wasn't any way to explain the birthday card and photo to her since it was connected to Keiran somehow. Lucky for me, I haven't been dragged back to his house again since I found the gun and locket in his closet, but that also meant I had no way of figuring out his connection to the girl.

I decided to leave that part out when I told her. I knew that keeping it all from her was dangerous and irresponsible, but I needed her away from Six Forks as long as possible. I was sure Keiran would get tired of me soon. I'd never known him to be seen with one girl for long.

I was on my way to meet Sheldon at the local burger joint. I wanted to invite Willow, but she still wasn't talking to me. I felt a pain in my heart every time I saw or thought about her. When this was over, somehow I would make it all up to her.

The restaurant was jam-packed, and I expected no less, but Sheldon just had to pick here of all places to go. I walked in and scoured the place for her. The restaurant expanded a couple of years ago to accommodate the amount of occupancy the place experienced on Friday nights. It usually only lasted until someone decided to take the party to their house.

"Lake!" I looked behind me to see Sheldon pushing through the crowd looking extremely boho in a long, colorful maxi skirt with two splits in the front that made her legs peek out when she walked. She wore a dark green tank top and a long feather pendant. Her hair was in two braids with a thin headband to accessorize.

"You look like Willow," I said, surprised.

"Thanks! We were talking about fashion the other day, and Willow suggested this look when I told her I wanted to try something different."

"How is she?" I asked and tamped down the jealous feeling.

"She misses you."

"How do you know that?"

"She's your best friend. Why wouldn't she miss you?"

"I haven't been a very good friend."

"The thing about true friendships is that they are resilient as hell."

I was about to respond when someone passing through the crowd bumped me. "Seriously, of all the places, why here?"

"Come on, Lake. Don't be such a Debbie Downer. Where else would we go anyway?" I knew she was right. I just didn't like the possibilities of who I could run into.

"Are there any tables left?" I nearly had to scream to be heard over the music and people.

"Do you even have to ask? I was thinking, when they turn this into a house party, we should go."

I remembered the first and last time I went to a house party. Of course, Keiran was there, so it ended badly. Brian Lassiter, a senior in high school and the quarterback had struck up a conversation with me because his little brother was a fan of my aunt's books. He wanted to know if he could get a signed copy for his birthday when Becky Daniels came out of nowhere screeching and hollering about me flirting with her boyfriend. When she slapped, I swung and hit her back, and that's when Keiran hollered that I was starting fights. The kids whose house it was kicked me out, and I was never invited back to a house party.

"Not a good idea."

"Why not? Keiran hasn't been after you these past couple weeks so it should be safe, right?"

Except when he sneaks into my bedroom in the dead of the night. "I don't know. Last time I barely escaped with my life."

She rolled her eyes and said, "Now who's being dramatic?"

"I don't want that kind of trouble or *any* trouble. Have you noticed lately how I'm the target of so much hostility? The last thing I need is my aunt receiving a phone call saying I got into a fight or worse—ending up in jail."

"But how better to show the big bad wolf that he can't blow your house down no matter how much he huffs and puffs?"

I laughed at her comparison to Keiran. She was such a cornball sometimes.

"And I know you're calling me names in your

head," she said. She looked truly offended, which only made me laugh harder until she was laughing, too.

"What's so funny?" Trevor asked as he walked up and hooked his arm around my neck. "Please share."

My mood just committed suicide. "I'm sorry. It was a private joke in a private conversation shared between friends... privately."

"You've picked yourself up a smart mouth, but from what I hear, Keiran is done with you, so I would be careful about who you piss off," Trevor threatened.

"You see, you got the right idea about pissing people off. You should try it. Like now," Sheldon retorted.

I laughed, which only made Trevor angrier though it didn't faze me. An angry Keiran made me want to run and hide, but an angry Trevor just annoyed me.

"No one is talking to you. Why don't you worry about who your boyfriend is fucking besides you?" Sheldon's nostrils flared, and I knew his statement pissed her off.

"Sheldon..." I sniffed the air. "Do you smell that? It smells like... asshole." Sheldon and I sniffed the air until we both turned eyes on Trevor. "Trevor, I think it's coming from your direction. You should take care of that before it gets out of hand."

We began to walk away when I felt a sharp pain rip through my skull. Trevor had grabbed me by my ponytail and flung me to the floor in a fit of rage. I hit the floor, and the force of the impact dazed me.

"What did you say to me, bitch?" He charged toward me, his foot rising to kick me. I balled up to avoid the blow, but it never came.

"Oh, my gosh!" I heard Sheldon scream. When I looked up, Keiran was there and strangling Trevor, who was clawing at his hands to escape. He was turning blue and looked close to passing out.

He's going to kill him.

Keiran was finally torn away, but it took Dash, Keenan, and Quentin to stop him and hold him back. Trevor was fighting to regain his breath as Sheldon helped me up. Everyone in the restaurant was staring at Keiran as if he'd grown another head.

"What's your problem, man? You attacking me over her?" He spewed the words out with disgust as if I were the one with the problem. Keiran was still fighting to get loose, and Keenan's hold on him was slipping.

"He'd beat your ass for hitting any girl. I'd beat your ass. Half the guys in here would beat your ass," Dash growled.

"But there is only one girl he would kill you for hitting," Keenan added in a sinister tone.

"Why would you care? She set you up!"

Keiran went still instantly, his body tight with tension. I could see his jaw clenching and that infamous vein near his temple pounding a steady rhythm.

Keenan and Dash turned to Sheldon questioning her silently. She shook her head no, and I wondered what their silent communication was about. I figured now that Keiran was reminded he hated me, this situation would dissolve immediately, and they would all laugh at my expense. Instead, they turned back to Trevor, who Keiran never took his eyes off.

"Say, man, how would you know who framed Keiran? How would you even know Lake did it?" Dash asked.

"Once again... innocent." They looked at me with raised eyebrows, and I realized I must have said it out loud. *Oops.*

"Everyone knows she tipped them," Trevor said, nervously. His eyes were flickering back and forth but never making eye contact.

They watched him squirm, and then Keenan hopped to stand in one of the chairs. He didn't have to worry about getting anyone's attention because the entire restaurant was watching intently. "Does anyone know what this piece of shit is talking about?" he yelled over the restaurant.

All heads shook no.

"The thing about tips are they aren't released to the public," Dash sneered.

"My dad told me. You—you guys know he's a cop," he stuttered. I almost felt bad for him. Almost.

"Does your dad normally divulge confidential information? I'm pretty sure it's illegal," Sheldon asked.

He narrowed his eyes at Sheldon, and Keenan stepped up to him threateningly. "Watch where you point those motherfuckers like that before I rip them out of your head."

Trevor looked down at the floor immediately. I didn't get it because he was bigger than all of them. I guess bigger didn't always mean tougher.

"Come on, bro, you know how it is. There are perks to being the son of a cop. I know a lot of shit."

"Like when our random drug searches are scheduled?" Dash asked.

Trevor's face paled as his mouth opened and closed. He reminded me of a fish. "Are you trying to say I set Keiran up?"

The trio remained silent, his words resonating in the air. It felt like the truth. I looked over at Keiran, who was eerily quiet and still. Trevor still didn't look at him.

"That's bogus, man! Why would I do that?"

"Yeah, why would you?" Keenan asked just as the chime from the entrance door sounded diverting my attention to it. The quietness of the restaurant made the simple chime seem like a bullhorn was blown.

Anya was sliding out the door. I frowned, wondering why she was leaving so quickly. All the gossiping she does, and she volunteers to miss this?

"All right, folks, break it up." Officers appeared along with Officer Reynolds, who I now knew to be Trevor's dad. People were scattering to leave, but I was rooted to the spot.

"Son, what's going on here?" his dad questioned Trevor while glaring at Keiran. I wanted to take a page out of Keenan's book and rip the officer eyes out. *Gosh, Lake, could you be more of a dumbass? The guy is your enemy.*

"Nothing, Dad. We were just horse playing. It got out of hand."

"Good boy." Keenan mocked, earning Officer Reynolds glare now.

"You three, leave now. Son, I want you home. Don't talk to these boys anymore."

"Excuse me?" Dash asked.

Officer Reynolds frowned at Dash. "Look, boy, I don't care how much so-called power your *daddy* has," he sneered. "I am not afraid of some little boy barely off his momma's tit."

A slow grin spread across Dash's face. "We'll see about that—Dad or no."

Officer Reynolds opened his mouth to speak when Keiran finally spoke. "We'll go. We wouldn't want anyone getting hurt, would we, Officer?"

I had the feeling Keiran wasn't speaking about himself or his cousin and Dash. I saw fear flash within Officer Reynolds eyes before he narrowed them and said, "That's right."

Keiran and the guys left without another word spoken. He barely acknowledged me throughout the entire exchange. Sheldon and I left the restaurant soon after, and since Sheldon was parked closer than I was, she took off immediately with a promise to call. I walked around the building toward the extra spaces where my car was parked and stopped short.

Keiran was sitting on the trunk of my car, head bent with his hands clutching his hair. I'd never seen him look anything less than cool and confident, but now he looked stressed. I didn't make it too close to him before he lifted his head as if sensing me. He had a tortured look on his face while mine remained neutral.

"What are you doing?" I asked instead trying to appear indifferent.

"Waiting for you."

He jumped down gracefully considering his legs were freakishly long and was now standing in front of me. He brushed my hair, which was now loose and pushed back behind my ear, and gazed at me softly.

"Take me home with you." I flinched at his words, feeling confused.

"Why?" He dropped his hand the same time he dropped his mask, appearing cold and unobtainable again.

"Because I said so."

\* \* \*

"START TALKING."

We'd barely made it through the threshold when Keiran issued the command. He seated me across from him and stared me down. I felt like I was in an interrogation room instead of my living room. I didn't dare take him to my bedroom.

"Why should I?" I fidgeted under his scrutiny staring at the floor. I looked up at him, and he growled but said nothing. "Right." I looked down at the floor again, trying to count the stitches in the carpet. "You wouldn't listen before. Even that day in the cafeteria," I stated and peeked up at him.

I knew I was acting like a three-year-old and didn't care. I wouldn't let him intimidate me in my own home.

My safe haven.

He frowned, and I sighed. "The day before you were arrested." It pissed me off that he didn't remember because I remembered it all too well.

*I felt a chill run down my back and I wanted to run. This situation was making me uneasy, and I didn't know how to respond. I took a deep breath and let out a single word, sealing my fate.*

*"No."*

*His eyes narrowed as he grabbed my arm, squeezing hard. I cried out in pain as he brought his face down to mine. I turned my face away, unwilling to be so close to him. "You want to rethink that?" he asked threatening.*

*I shook my head vigorously.*

*"Listen, you bitch—" He was cut off as my knee connected with his balls, and he quickly released me, allowing me to run off before he could recover.*

*I ran out into the hallway quickly making my way to the cafeteria never stopping to think about the decision I'd made.*

*I had to warn him.*

*I burst through the cafeteria drawing the attention of everyone present as I headed to the table Keiran always sat at across the cafeteria, facing my usual table. When I reached his table, I was breathing hard. My hair was in disarray as I felt tendrils on my face and heavy strands around my shoulder escaping my* ponytail. He watched me with a blank look as if he was bored.

"I need to speak to you," I directed to him.

A few kids sitting at the table laughed at my request as I stared at him pleadingly. His cousin was there with his girlfriend, Sheldon, on his lap. Next to them was Keiran's best friend and right-hand, Dash Chambers, the school's richest playboy.

"Are you all ri—" Keenan started to say before Keiran flashed him a quick look, silencing him. He turned back to me with a distant look appearing unaffected by my disheveled state.

"Go... away," he simply said.

He was sprawled low in his chair, legs spread out, with both arms stretched across the empty chairs on each side of him. He looked as if he didn't have a care in the world as he gazed at me under his lashes.

"Please, Keiran, this is important."

"I told you before. You don't get to say my name. Last chance—leave."

I tried again, my heart beating fast. This wasn't going to end well.

"I need you—" He leaped out of his chair so fast it flew back. A split second later, he regained himself and casually sauntered over to me with a predatory swagger that made me feel hunted.

"You need me?" he chuckled darkly as he circled around me. Don't do this... please. I hung my head low, knowing what was coming.

"I thought I told you last time I didn't want your services. I can get fresh pussy for free." He sniffed the air as if he could smell something foul. He then leaned into my ear but stated loud enough for everyone to hear, "You stink."

The cafeteria had grown eerily quiet by now

*watching what was happening. The bell had already rung, signaling the end of the lunch period and the start of another, but no one moved.*

*He nodded toward my left arm where Trevor had grabbed me leaving a bruise. "Like it rough, do you? Your last customer must have given it to you good."*

*I'm not a whore. I'm not.*

*"I guess not good enough since you had to come running to me immediately after." He stopped circling me, coming to a stop in front of me. "You must be insane, Monroe. I wouldn't touch you with a 10-foot fake dick, but maybe Peter could help you out. It looked like he really enjoyed your skills last time."*

*I could hear laughter and a shocked gasp in the distance, as once again, I felt tears fall. Crying was a daily occurrence for me. Sometimes, I didn't even notice them. At that moment, I wanted to die thinking it would be the only way to escape.*

*"Lake!" I heard my name but didn't have the mental strength to lift my head. Light footsteps approached me, and I felt a gentle arm come around me guiding me to the exit.*

*"Lake, I'm so sorry. Why did you come here?" I finally recognized Willow's voice and lifted my head to find tears in her eyes.*

*"I had to try," I whispered.*

Recognition showed on his face, and I sat back, curling my legs underneath me, waiting for him to say something. "You said you needed to talk to me," he said.

"Yes."

He rolled his eyes. "What did you need to say?"

"I knew you were going to be set up." His jaw clenched, and his breathing quickened, and I wondered if he knew he was doing it. Being close to him, those few days, allowed me to see a lot. More than he was even aware.

"Is this a confession?"

"No." More jaw clenching. "It's chance."

"Enough with the games!" he roared suddenly and sprung to his feet pacing back and forth. "A chance for what?"

"A chance to tell my side! I've tried to talk to you—God—I tried to *warn* you! This would never have happened if you weren't... such... a... prick."

His eyes had flickered before he slipped his mask back into place. "So it's my fault? I didn't ask to be framed."

"It's not your fault, but you owe some responsibility to what happened."

"I won't apologize for what I've done to you. Any of it."

I felt as if my heart were ripped out of me and made a laughing stock. Knowing he wasn't sorry for the pain he caused me hurt more than all the pain combined over the years, but I refused to cry. I looked up at him and hardened my gaze.

I hated him.

"Then we have nothing to say to each other."

"Oh?" he asked dangerously low.

"You want an explanation. I want an apology."

"Not. Happening," he growled.

"I agree... bye." I flicked my hand to the door dismissively, but I guess that was a mistake because I found myself pinned against the cushions, his body keeping me prisoner, and his hand clutching my throat threateningly, before I could blink.

"You're going to fucking talk, and I'm not leaving here until you do."

* * *

HE WAS SERIOUS. I mean I guess I should have known that considering who he was, but it didn't take until Keenan and Dash furnished him with a duffel bag with what I assumed were clothes. They began to play a game that looked like military ops and ignored me.

There were boys at my house.

Three to be exact.

My aunt was going to kill me.

Then again, considering her concern over my lack of a love life, of the adolescent persuasion, she might be ecstatic, but I'm sure she would think three was pushing it.

"Leave. Now," I demanded for the hundredth time. Frustration had set in twenty minutes ago when Keenan asked me what was for dinner. I had gone for the butcher knife. I had never pulled a knife out on anybody before, but the situation called for desperate measures. I was sure they would see things my way if I threatened to dismember or separate certain appendages from their bodies. Of course, Keiran notified me he'd already hidden the knives.

Dash and Keenan looked at me as if I were crazy when I sat down. After an hour of being ignored, I temporarily gave up on kicking them out and headed upstairs to do homework. It's not like I could call for help. After his threat to seize my house, he took my cell phone again. *Such a prick.* After finishing my homework, I crept downstairs, hoping they were gone.

"You still think she did it?" I heard Dash ask. I knew they were talking about me so I stopped around the corner to eavesdrop.

"Hard to tell. She doesn't seem interested in clearing herself anymore."

"Why?" Keenan asked.

"She wants me to apologize," he stated. Dash and Keenan snorted.

"Yeah, that's not going to happen," Keenan said.

"Well, we at least know she had help if she did do it," Dash said.

"Or she *was* the help. That motherfucker Trevor is a done deal, the fuck," Keenan gritted.

"She said she knew I was going to be set up and tried to warn me the day before I was arrested."

"When you told the whole cafeteria she stunk?" Keenan asked.

"Man, how do you remember, but I don't?"

"Cause that's the first time Sheldon ever denied me my pussy. Not even when she caught me cheating the first time."

"One day my sister is going to leave you." Dash laughed.

"She doesn't have a say. It's us. It always will be us."

"I don't get her. Why is she siding with Lake, anyway?" Dash asked.

"She believes she's innocent, and you know she wants new friends. Rosalyn and Anya are a piece of work." *Who is Rosalyn?*

"Yeah. Anya seems to think I belong to her. She's an all right fuck, but really, she is just something to do when screwing with Monroe gets boring."

"Does it ever?" Dash asked. It was silent for a long moment, and I thought he wasn't going to answer.

"When she ignores me." His answer shocked me. *Why would he care?*

"Speaking of ignoring, what's up with you and the redhead?" Keenan asked.

"What about it?"

"You chasing pretty harder than needed."

He chuckled before answering, "She's fun. I'm having fun."

I pictured the shrug his broad shoulders most likely made, and I saw red. I wanted to go down and confront them but knew it would do no good. Willow still wouldn't talk to me.

"I bet. Her ass looks amazing." I heard the sound of flesh hit flesh followed by Keenan's cry of pain. Shit, if they started fighting and broke anything in the house, my aunt would kill me.

"She's mine."

"Damn, bro! You sure hit hard over *fun*. In fact, you usually share the *fun*." He kept emphasizing the word 'fun' while my blood continued to boil.

"Not this time. That goes for you too, Keiran."

"I don't want her," Keiran said nonchalantly. The way they were talking about her as if she was a piece of meat pissed me off.

"You know Keiran. He prefers sleeping with the enemy. He's kinky like that." They all laughed at Keenan's crack. *Hardy har har.* I didn't find anything funny.

"So what's the plan, man? I know you need to know if she's guilty and not just for payback."

"Wait around for her to crack. I've got three weeks."

"The aunt. She hot?"

"I see where she gets her looks from," Keiran stated, not directly answering the question.

"Fuck hot then." A slap resounded in the air, and Keenan cried in pain again. I couldn't feel sorry for him. I wasn't even flattered that he thinks I'm hot.

"What are you going to do if she's innocent?" Dash asked.

I held my breath waiting for his response until I was sure I was turning blue.

"Doesn't matter if she is or not," Keiran stated with disinterest. "It won't change anything."

# CHAPTER SIXTEEN

I GAVE UP on eavesdropping and headed back upstairs to shower. There was nothing I needed more at the moment than my bed. The house was quiet when I finished my shower and left the bathroom. I guess my guns were tougher than Keiran's, after all. I assumed he got bored and left, but was proven wrong when I pushed open my bedroom door and found him lounging on top of my bed.

"Ready to talk yet?" His smooth voice filtered through the room as he held my open journal in his hand.

"What are you doing?" I shrieked.

"Rereading my favorite bedtime story. There are new entries in here," he said without looking at me. The familiar feeling of dread returned as I watched him read my journal. Two weeks ago, I started writing again when the first strings of depression and loneliness began to take root. There was no one else I could tell, so I told my journal. I usually kept my entries short, but it was now almost full. It felt like I was running out of time.

"My journal is private. You have no right," I growled. I looked around my bedroom for something to throw at him, or better yet, gouge his eyes out with.

"I have every right considering most of it is about me." He looked way too comfortable lounging against my pillows and reading all my secret thoughts and feelings. They were *mine*.

"Why are you doing this?"

"You wouldn't talk so I had to find another way for you tell me what I need."

"And did you find anything?" I asked sarcastically.

"I found plenty." He closed the journal but continued to hold it, probably to drive me crazy. I wanted it out of his hands. It wouldn't erase what he now knew, but maybe it could relieve the humiliating pain.

"Good, then you can leave," I urged.

"I'm not going anywhere."

"Get out. I don't want you here," I said firmly.

"I think you want much more from me than you're willing to admit." He waved my journal pointedly before tossing it on the bed. *Finally.* "Come here," he beckoned.

"No." I braced my feet on the floor to ward off the power of the spell he wielded to make me obey.

"You're going to make me come get you then?"

"If you must." I clutched my towel tighter around me.

"Monroe?" he called quietly. His voice was soft, but the look he gave me was intense as his eyes swept my body with burning lust.

"Yes?"

"Are you sore?"

"No," I answered, feeling my pussy clench. It was eager for what was coming, and so was I, I admitted begrudgingly.

"When I get my hands on you," he said, rising from the bed, "I'm going to fuck you hard and make you come harder." He shed his shirt as he took slow steps toward me. "Are you ready for me?"

"If you hate me so much, why do you want me?" I blurted. If I weren't so focused on him, I would have missed the look of uncertainty that passed in his eyes before he hid it.

"I could ask you the same thing. Besides, I think it's a little too late to question it now," he retorted sarcastically.

I lifted my chin and backed up a step. "I don't think you want me. I think you do it to torment me."

"Then I'm torturing us both." He stole my lips with his and backed me up against the wall.

When I opened for him, he sucked on my tongue and unwrapped my towel. The material fell to the floor at our feet as he pressed harder against my naked body. He was well over six feet tall, which always made me feel so small. His bare chest was hot against my skin while his hardness teased my stomach through his jeans. I couldn't take the separation, so I unbuttoned his jeans, pushed them down his hips, and immediately gripped his cock.

He dug into his jeans and fished out a condom. Pushing it into my hand, he ordered me to put it on him. He wore a smug look as he watched me fumble with the condom. After a few deep breaths, I finally figured it out and sheathed it on him.

"Lift your leg," he ordered, tapping my thigh. I wrapped my leg around his waist and the movement opened me up to the feeling of his cock against my opening. "Put me in your pussy, baby. I need to feel you now."

My heart fluttered, hearing him call me baby, but I

knew it had to be the lust talking. Keiran always lost control when our bodies came together. With one hand on his cock, I used my other to grip his ass and as I led him inside my waiting pussy.

"Hold onto me," he grunted.

I wrapped my arms around his neck as he pressed his chest into my breasts and crowded me against the wall. Without warning, he slammed into me, forcing a shocked cry from lips. His eyes were glazed over as he stared down at the place we were joined.

"You're so deep," I said on a shaky moan. He grimaced, pulled back and rammed his cock into me again.

"Not deep enough," he groaned. We both seemed to lose control as his hard body rocked into me repeatedly. He did nothing to muffle my passionate screams, and I did nothing to stop them. His strokes were brutal and unyielding as his mouth latched onto my nipple, biting and sucking. I tossed my head back and pressed into him. He lifted my other leg around his waist while maintaining his rhythm and control over my body.

"I can feel your pussy clenching around my cock, Monroe. Do you like what I'm doing to you?"

"Yes."

"Say it," he growled and drove into me harder.

"I like it. Please don't stop."

"I won't stop. I'll never stop." He carried me over to the bed where he sat on the very edge. I wrapped my legs tighter around his waist as he pulled me deeper on his cock. "Your pussy is so hot and wet." He ground his hips into me, and I felt pressure in my lower stomach.

"Yes, right there. Fuck me there," I encouraged wildly. My inhibitions always fled once his cock was deep inside me.

"So... fucking... tight," he gritted, pounding me harder from below.

"Please... I need to come."

"Mmmh, but I think I'd like to make you beg a little more," he teased.

"No," I moaned. "Now." I gripped his shoulders and slammed myself down on him. The night he took my virginity, he made me learn how to ride him, and so it came in handy now as I rode him furiously, taking over the pace and rhythm. I fucked myself on his cock while he watched me with a smug look on his face. I was doing the fucking now, but I knew he still held all control. Just as I felt my orgasm rising, I found myself face down on the mattress.

"You're going to have to pay for that," he said with a hard slap against my cheek. I felt his hands caress my rear and then he was on top of me, sliding inside again. His hand came under to cup my pussy where we were joined, and he lifted my hips to him. His other hand came around my neck to grip me.

"Now let's get something clear between you and me," he said in my ear as he rammed into me again, causing me to cry out. "You don't run shit." He lifted his chest from my back and gripped my hair in his hand. "I told you before, Monroe. You will submit to *me*—not the other way around."

He used his cock to punish me as he rammed me repeatedly. My deafening scream mingled with his roar seemed to shake the house as we came simultaneously.

\* \* \*

IT WAS A TRADITION for Bainbridge to hold basketball games every Saturday morning before the start of the season for the community. It was also a way to scout out new players before tryouts and keep the players ready. The turnout was always huge as all of Six Forks attempted to crowd into the gym. Willow would drag me to these things once or twice in the past, but I was always too much on edge to enjoy the game knowing Keiran was there.

Now I was here *with* Keiran, and I was still very much on edge as I sat in the team section. Keiran had disappeared to the locker room with the other players after dumping me in the bleachers with a firm order to stay.

"Hey, you piece of shit, I've been calling you." I looked up to find an affronted Sheldon glaring down at me before she broke out into a grin and plopped into my lap. All the air whooshed out of me as her weight pinned me to my seat. She looked down at me mischievously as if she knew what she was doing.

"Sheldon, you're crushing me," I wheezed out.

She gasped in outrage before rearing back, "Are you calling me fat?"

"Sheldon!"

"I have a surprise for you," she said in a singsong voice. Before I could ask her what or toss her off, Keiran returned.

"Where is Monroe?" I heard Keiran's deep voice question. I raised my hand to signal I was there because Sheldon was still sitting on me. Raucous laughter erupted, and then her weight was lifted from me just as I began to see spots.

"You can sit on daddy's lap if you need a place to sit," Keenan drawled.

She rolled her eyes before pushing him away to sit next to me.

"So? Where have you been, and why were you screening my calls?" Sheldon questioned while blatantly ignoring Keenan, who then stomped off irritated.

I searched for a reasonable excuse to her but came

up short. Do I tell her that Keiran was keeping me hostage in my own home and isolating me from anyone who would help while fucking me to near unconsciousness to pass the time? I looked over at Keiran, who was busy lacing up his shoes, but I knew he was listening.

"Oh, um... I fell asleep. It was a long night, and I slept in this morning." She stared at me skeptically, and I knew she knew I was full of shit.

"Mhmm, so why are you here? You said you hated these things when I invited you."

I looked up when I felt Keiran watching me now. He shot me a warning glare before walking onto the court. The crowd erupted in an ear-splitting cacophony of cheers and whistles as they roared their welcome.

Keiran was back on the court.

The first string of players gathered on the court shaking hands. Keiran, Dash, and Keenan were on the same team, and I was surprised to see Buddy teamed with them. I didn't know he could play basketball much less want to join the team.

Trevor was there and on the opposing team with four other guys who I recognized from school. My assumption was he would be leading the team. He moved forward to shake Keiran's hand, but Keiran smoothly passed the ball to him and got into position to start the game.

"I can't believe he is just letting Trevor have the ball," Sheldon stated, bewildered.

I wasn't an expert in basketball, but even I knew that wasn't how the game began. Keiran's expression was flat giving the impression that he didn't care. He stared at Trevor, daring him to protest. I looked around and saw the confused expression among the crowd. The ref shrugged his shoulders and walked off while blowing the whistle signaling the game to begin.

Trevor dribbled the ball, but before he could pass the ball, Keiran stole it from him, passing it to Dash, who effortlessly took a shot, scoring the first two points. It all happened too quickly for anyone to comprehend and causing a delay in reaction, but soon, a deafening roar shook the gym.

Sheldon was worse. She nearly fell on top of me from her jumping and screaming. Trevor was furious. Keiran had basically humiliated him in front of everyone.

When Dash looked over and winked, Willow blushed and turned her head away. These two were hiding in plain sight, and Willow still wouldn't confide in me.

The game was intense as Keiran's team dominated the court and captivated the crowd. It was a no brainer who would win as Trevor's frustration grew, and he began to take it out on his team.

Keiran was like a general, commanding and cool. He easily read the opposing team's defense and exploited their tactics. I learned from Sheldon that he played point guard while Dash was shooting guard, and Keenan was the power forward.

Dash was the cockiest player, making shot after shot, and effectively handling the ball. He had no problem displaying his skill.

Keenan was the most aggressive player. He mostly stayed near the basket and went in for rebounds or assisted while dodging the player who was doing a poor job of guarding him.

I cheered mostly to encourage Buddy, who was playing the small forward. Dash looked out for him a lot on the court it seemed, encouraging him to go after the ball while he flanked Keiran to create openings for a shot.

The opposing team was too busy trying to ambush Keiran, especially Trevor, but he handled them with ease. The score was now an embarrassing 34-17, Trevor's team scoring half the points Keiran's did.

As it neared the end of the last quarter, Trevor grew more aggressive toward Keiran's team even though they had already pulled back. They were growing annoyed with Trevor's behavior it seemed if their expressions were anything to go by.

Keiran had the ball preparing for a shot but was blocked by Trevor, who looked close to assaulting him for the ball when he couldn't steal it. Keiran's face remained impassive, not giving anything away until his elbow connected with Trevor's nose causing him to fall. The ref blew the whistle signaling a foul awarding Trevor's team the ball.

The coach looked as if he wanted to pull Keiran out of the game but didn't. After all, there was less than a minute left. They had already won the game. Victory came for Keiran's team, and all the players from both teams gathered around the court to shake hands once again.

I sat there prepared to wait for Keiran, and I admitted I was happy to see him play for the first time. He was really good, and I wondered if he planned to make it a profession.

I saw Anya with a few of her minions from school and another unknown girl approaching, and I inwardly groaned. "Sheldon, why didn't you sit with us? Keiran and Dash told us to sit on the other side," Anya whined.

They noticed me sitting here and turned their noses up. "Really, Sheldon, you should've texted us so you wouldn't have to sit with a loser," Anya sneered.

"It appears to me that she is sitting on the side that just won," Willow snapped. I hadn't even noticed she had walked up. I laughed because she was never one to sit quietly. The girl who looked like one of those high society debutantes narrowed her eyes at Willow as she took in her hair and clothes with a disgusted look on her face. I wanted to wipe it off with the bottom of my shoe to her face.

"And who are you?" she asked snottily.

"Not the one." Willow rolled her neck, giving the girl her 'Don't fuck with me' look.

"Well, I am Rosalyn Cordell. Dash's fiancée and I believe you are in my seat."

*Say what now?* I quickly looked at Willow whose face had drained of color. I heard Sheldon mumble, "Oh, shit" and then Willow slowly got up and walked off leaving Rosalyn and Anya with smirks on their faces. Their cronies were cackling as my heart broke for Willow

"You should probably go with her, loser. Keiran doesn't want you, and you're sitting in *my* seat," Anya stated.

I didn't hesitate to move but not because of Anya. I moved because I had to check on my friend. I heard Sheldon arguing with them before I pushed through the doors. I checked the girls' locker room and immediately heard soft sobs coming from one of the stalls.

"Willow?" I called softly.

"It's okay, Lake. I'm not crying." She broke apart on the last word and cried harder, twisting my heart. I felt her pain and wanted to share it with her if only to take some of it away.

"Willow, please. Please open the door so that I can hold you. It's the only way because I don't know what to say. I don't know how to make this right. Talk to me."

She started coughing from the gut wrenching sobs and then I could hear the sound of her vomiting violently. I heard her whimper then the door suddenly flew open and Willow flew past me, running out of the locker room.

"Willow!" I yelled in vain.

I noticed something colorful sitting on top of the tank and moved forward to inspect it. It was a platinum charm bracelet with amethyst stones. The only charms were angel wings and the letters 'D' and 'W'. The right arm of the W was hooked around the curve of the D like lovers. It was beautiful.

I could tell it was expensive, and something neither Willow or her parents could afford. I'd never seen Willow with this bracelet before, and it looked too new to have been inherited.

Dash.

It had to come from him. The D and W made sense along with angel wings. He called her angel once before. I pocketed the bracelet intending to return it to her when I bumped into a hard body that blocked my exit.

"Where are you in a hurry to?" a familiar voice asked me. I was shoved back inside the stall as Trevor moved forward shutting the door behind him. I immediately called for help, but he clamped his sweaty hand over my mouth muffling my scream.

"I don't think so, sweetheart. We have things to discuss, and you aren't leaving here until we do." He pressed me against the side of the stall, trapping me. "You know, your friend is a dumb bitch. She never had a real chance with Dash—Oh, yes, I know," he stated noticing my shock.

"His family may be rich, but they are a bunch of lowlifes. They take what they want without regard for others or the law. I wonder how it feels to own that much power? Maybe one day I'll find out."

I fought not to roll my eyes at him and piss him off

further. The look in his eyes told me he was teetering on the brink of instability.

"So tell me. You giving it up to Keiran?" My eyes narrowed at him, disgusted, to which he simply shrugged.

"Of course you are. Either that or he's taking it. He isn't the guy everyone thinks he is, you know? But even he couldn't stop a drug conviction from tarnishing his image. And to think of all the hard work I put into setting him up."

I tried to talk, but it came out muffled so he lifted his hand. "What's that, sweetheart?" I instantly hated the word.

"I said you're a jealous, pathetic asshole."

He smiled. "Of course, I was jealous. The guy was stealing all the chicks and the fame. I figured if I got rid of him, Keenan and Dash wouldn't be much of a threat, and I could rule the school."

"So you framed him for status?" That had to be the dumbest crock of shit I had ever heard. *Dude has issues.*

"He also stuck his nose where it didn't belong. My mom left my dad because of him."

"Why would Keiran have anything to do with your mom leaving your dad?"

"Because he convinced her to divorce him and abandon her own family." I had heard rumors some time ago before Keiran was arrested that Trevor's parents were getting divorced, but how would Keiran be involved?

"So, why frame me?"

"I needed a fall guy. You were always going to be it even if you did help me. I have to tell you, sweetheart, I did not count on you denying me. It would have made my task a lot easier, too. I mean, who knew you would be in love with the guy after all he did to you."

"I'm not in love with him."

"Oh, yes, you are. After you said no, you could have just walked away, but no, you even tried to warn the guy, and he crushed your poor little heart right there in the cafeteria. Tsk. Tsk."

"That doesn't mean anything."

"The whole school knows that Keiran wants you. Damn near craves you. Everyone except you, that is. But instead of just having you, he fucked with you. Made your life a living hell. That's got to be the most fucked up foreplay I ever heard of."

"You don't know what you're talking about," I continued to deny. In truth, I was blown away by what Trevor was revealing, and a part of me knew it was true.

"Come on. Even Anya knows Keiran wants you. She thinks you're a threat, and I have to say, you are way hotter than she is. That is why she helped me."

"Anya helped you? But she is Keiran's girlfriend."

"Yeah, in her head she is."

"So what? You wanted her, too?"

He shrugged. "I told her sending Keiran away for a little while was a small price to pay to make him get over you. She stole your phone and called the tip in as you. Simple. My father and I handled the rest." He grinned.

"You're fucked in the head, you know that?" I wanted out of that stall and away from his craziness. *Keiran should be looking for me by now.*

"Careful now. You don't want to make this worse on yourself." Cold dread invaded my body at the look in his eyes.

"Make what worse?" I asked in a shaky breath.

"Keiran humiliated me on the court today, and in front of the town, the school, and my father," he said through clenched teeth. "What better way to make him pay than to take what he wants most? I really should have done this instead of framing him." Without warning, his lips slammed into mine causing me to gag as I fought his grip in the confines of the stall.

"No!" I screamed when I felt his hand slide up my skirt. The other gripped my left breast roughly. I tried to bring my knee up to his balls, but his legs made me immobile.

Just as I started to panic, and desperation set in as I fought for what felt like my life, it was over. I was left gasping for breath when Trevor was ripped away, and I was gently lifted out of the stall. I looked over just in time to see a formidable looking Keiran snap Trevor's right arm in half with a sickening crunch of broken muscle and bone. The last thing I heard was his blood-curdling scream of pain.

# CHAPTER SEVENTEEN

A MALE VOICE was speaking somewhere close as I began to wake up in a room that smelled like antiseptic and fresh paint. "She doesn't seem to have suffered any injuries so, when she wakes up, she is free to go home. Have her parents been notified?"

"Her aunt is her guardian and is currently out of town, but she has been notified and is expected back tomorrow morning."

My eyes flew up at the mention of my aunt returning home and why. This could not be happening.

"Lake, honey, are you awake?" The voice sounded like Willow's mother.

"Mrs. Waters?" My voice sounded groggy, and my throat was dry. I looked to my right and saw her standing near the doctor. I wasn't surprised she was there. My aunt listed her as an emergency contact because she was frequently on the road for book tours and research.

"It's me. How do you feel?"

"Fine. Wha—what happened?" I was confused as to how I ended up in the hospital for the second time in my life...

Keiran.

"Keiran, did he –"

"Oh, that devilishly handsome young man in the waiting room? He saved you from the guy who attacked you. Don't you remember?"

It all came flooding back to me at once, and I found myself nodding.

Willow.

Trevor.

The locker room.

I felt sick and wished I didn't remember at all when I thought about how his hands groped and pulled at me. I also felt guilty for assuming Keiran had done something to me. *Wait. He's here?*

"Hi, Lake. I'm Dr. Landing. You suffered a pretty traumatic situation. Are you feeling any pain?"

Dr. Landing, a middle-aged man with salt and pepper hair, checked me over and asked me some routine questions He then informed me that police were waiting outside to ask me questions about the attack, and he would send them in if I were ready.

I didn't want to talk to anyone, but I knew it was better just to get this over with. They came in, and I answered their questions and repeated the confession Trevor had told me before he attacked me. After they had left, the doctor told me I was free to go. Immediately after they departed, the door to my room pushed open and in walked Keiran. I took in his appearance and instantly noticed the bloody, broken skin of his knuckles. He looked as broken as I felt.

"Hi," he greeted in a grim tone. He watched me with hard eyes from his place by the door.

"Hi," I whispered. We continued to gaze at each other silently.

"I sent everyone home. Willow and her mom are

still waiting. I want to take you home. Will you let me?"

"I don't think—"

"Please," he cut me off. His plea was nothing less than surprising. Keiran was a 'take all and fuck all' type of person. He did what he wanted without permission or worry. It may have been guilt eating away at him that changed his attitude... at least for the moment, so I decided to give him something he never gave me. Mercy.

I nodded my assent, and we entered the waiting room together. Willow was there as Keiran said. A flurry of emotions crossed her face when she saw me, and I knew she was on the verge of breaking down. She ran up to me and embraced me with tears streaming down her face.

"I'm so sorry. I shouldn't have left you." Her small body shook with tears, and I hated that she blamed herself. She was in the midst of her own emotional turmoil. She didn't need the burden of mine as well.

"Don't do that. No one is to blame but Trevor and his own fuckedupness. Not you and not me." I kissed her forehead before releasing her to face her mom. "Mrs. Waters, I appreciate you coming, but I'm going to ride home with him if it's okay with you."

"Oh, um... are you sure? It's really no problem."

"I'm sure." She looked like she wanted to protest further, but Willow grabbed her hand to lead her out, but not before glaring at Keiran in warning.

"Call me when you're home. Your aunt will be flying in tomorrow morning." She finally departed, leaving me alone with Keiran in the waiting room. He was standing directly behind me, and I could feel the heat of his body radiating into me.

*Not the time, Lake.* I looked over my shoulder at him to find him studying me intensely.

"I'm ready," I stated.

\* \* \*

MONDAY MORNING FINALLY came, and I was happy for
the distraction of school. Aunt Carissa arrived Sunday
morning, and I had been under her watchful eye ever
since. As far as she knew, I was randomly attacked in a
locker room at school. She wanted to home school me
for the rest of the year, and I almost let her, but I didn't
want to hide anymore.

After many arguments, she finally agreed to continue her tour and was set to fly back out the next day,
but she made me promise to let Mrs. Waters keep an
eye on me. That meant regular check-ins.

I left for school early that morning, not wanting to
run into Keiran. After we had left the hospital, Keiran
drove me home, but once we pulled into the driveway,
he received a phone call. He argued on the phone with
someone before hanging up with a furious expression.
He had turned to me with regret in his eyes and told me
he had to leave. I hadn't heard or seen him since.

I picked up Willow on the way to school. Willow
and I were able to hash everything out last night though
I still didn't tell her about Dash using her to set me up. I
just didn't think now was the time to add to her plate
considering she just found out he had a fiancée'.

We disappeared into the library once we arrived to
wait for first period to begin. I had the feeling Willow
wanted to hide just as much as I did.

"Oh, Willow, I almost forgot," I said, reaching into
my bag. "You left this in the locker room."

I pulled out the lavender and platinum bracelet I
found Saturday and handed it over. She just stared at it
longingly before a look of disgust passed over her face.
She shook her head before saying, "I don't want it. It's

meaningless."

"Don't ever let me hear you say that shit again, angel."

We both looked up in surprise to see Dash and Keiran standing in front of our table wearing fierce expressions. I didn't understand how they found us so quickly. I was more surprised that they bothered to look.

"Go away, Dash, and you may take that thing with you. I'm sure your *fiancée'* would appreciate it. But then her name doesn't start with a W does it?"

Willow lowered her gaze to her textbook so she didn't see the look in his eyes before he yanked her out of her seat and quickly disappeared with her in the bookcases. I could hear her reading him his rights with a few of her favorite choice words. She sounded as if she had it under control, so I turned back to my textbooks.

I was prepared to ignore Keiran, but it seemed he had other plans when he lifted me from my seat and sat me on his lap. I struggled against him, but he wrapped his arms around me and buried his face in my hair. "Fuck, I missed this," he muttered, shocking me completely before I realized he said 'this' and not 'me.' All he wanted from me was my body and my pain. I was annoyed with myself for how quickly I could forget.

"Don't—" The sound of books falling from the shelves and a steady thump, interrupted what I was going to say. I shot out of his lap, intending to make sure Willow was okay when I felt Keiran's hand clamp around my wrist, stopping me.

"I wouldn't do that a second time," Keiran cautioned.

"What are you—*Oh!*" Understanding dawned on me, and I could feel my cheeks blush. "He wouldn't—" Keiran raised an eyebrow. "She wouldn't—"

I was interrupted by what sounded like a feminine

moan coming from their direction. I couldn't believe they were having sex in the school library! We couldn't be more than a few feet away from them. I didn't know who my best friend was anymore, and the thought made me sick.

"You don't look so good. Sit," he ordered, pulling me back down onto his lap. I could still hear the muffled sounds of sex, and I desperately tried to tune them out.

"You need to keep Dash away from Willow. He's corrupting her." I narrowed my eyes at Keiran in a pitiful attempt to intimidate him. The corner of his mouth lifted in a half grin.

"She wants it."

"You don't know her. You don't know what she wants."

"Apparently, you don't either, and her moans say different," he said matter-of-factly.

He didn't sound cocky about it, but it still pissed me off because I knew he was right. Despite Willow's wish to stay away, she seemed to always give into him. I snuck a peek at Keiran and admitted I could understand how it felt to be that confused.

"She's confused." I didn't know if I was trying to convince him or me. He looked at me as if I was dense before his eyes softened, and he held my gaze.

"If it makes you feel better, he's just as confused as she is, and maybe just a little bit addicted." Something told me he wasn't speaking only of Dash and Willow—if at all.

"Why would he be addicted?"

"Because she's so goddamn beautiful. In every way that counts." I drew in a breath at the raw emotion evident in his voice. He *wasn't* talking about them. He was talking about us. "Why did you run away from me this morning?"

"I didn't run," I lied.

"Don't lie to me. Don't ever do that." His gray eyes hardened into steel.

"You ran Saturday. You got a phone call and just left without a word."

He blew out a breath before answering. "I didn't run. My uncle got word of what happened, so I had to split and go home."

I still got chills thinking about Trevor and what he tried to do. "How did you find me that day?" Keiran was still on the court when I left to chase after Willow and didn't think he saw me leave.

"I saw Anya and Rosalyn approaching you and was watching for trouble when I saw Willow run off and you run off behind her."

"I saw Willow run out of the locker room and went back to the gym to get Sheldon to drag you out. That must have been when Trevor slipped in," he gritted. I could see the self-blame in his eyes and once again wanted to comfort him, but I held back.

"Sheldon went in and came back out moments later for help."

"So you still think I set you up?"

He shook his head. "No. Sheldon heard most of his confession. I heard enough."

"So what happens now? What are we doing?" I was confused as to why he tracked me down if he knew the truth. "We are still enemies... aren't we?"

"I—I don't know," he frowned in confusion. *Huh?* I wasn't expecting that answer. "Trevor was right." He swallowed heavily before continuing. "Last night, I thought about you and about this thing between us that I have kept alive for ten years. It was fucked up, but it was the only way because I hated you. That part was real."

"So what, you think we can just pick up where we left off? You want to continue to bully and humiliate me because it gets your rocks off?" I stood up to leave, way beyond pissed. "Screw you." I flipped him off for kicks and turned to leave.

Of course, he didn't let me leave. I found myself flat on top of the table with his hard body hovering above me before I could take a step. I looked around for help, but it was still too early for other students to be around, and the librarian wasn't leaving her solitaire game any-time soon.

"Shh." He tried to soothe me. "I can't say I will nev-er hurt you again or that I won't even want to."

"No? And you would hurt my aunt too, won't you?" He closed his eyes as if in pain and took a deep breath.

"I thought you framed me. It was never about going to jail. I've done more than enough shit to deserve that sentence, and I'm not talking about to you. Anyway, I thought you were fighting back. I thought you weren't afraid of me anymore. I had to make you afraid again because I couldn't lose that control. I needed it."

"So am I just supposed to forgive you?" I narrowed my eyes at him.

"I'm trying to be honest with you. I don't have the right words to say to make this right. I just know I would have done anything to control you. I still would."

*Is he serious?* The look in his eyes told me he was. "What if someone tried to hurt your uncle? How would you feel?"

Nothing. Not a flicker or emotion or regret. His eyes and face were as still as death.

"Don't you care about your uncle?" I tried again.

"No." His tone was flat and unapologetic.

*Well, shit.* I stared up at him dumbfounded not

knowing what to say. "How? I mean... why not?" He shrugged his shoulders and got off the table, pulling me up with him to a seated position and then he was standing between my legs. "Well, what about my aunt? Are you still having her followed?"

"No," he said as he stared down at me. His hands started rubbing up and down my jean-clad thighs slowly. I wanted to pull the hood off his head so I could see all of his features and maybe run my hands through his hair. I started to relax when he confirmed my aunt was now safe until something occurred to me.

"Are you trying to distract me?"

The corner of his mouth lifted in that half-grin I was growing to love. It made him look boyish and not so scary. "Is it working?" he asked.

"No," I lied, but he didn't have to know that. He gave me a skeptical look before removing his hands and balling them into his sweatshirt pockets. I wanted to snatch them back, and he must have known that from the cocky look on his face.

"Look," I took a deep breath, willing the courage for what I had to say, "I can't stop you from hating me, so we have nothing more to say to each other."

"No, we have so much more than words we owe each other. I'm done hating you for something that isn't your fault."

"But you hated me before then."

"I'm not talking about the set-up." His mesmerizing eyes stared back into mine, willing me to understand.

I didn't.

"I don't understand and I don't care. We're through here."

"Then let me make it clear for you." His eyes had turned cold at my dismissal and belied everything he'd just said. "You messed up when you let me near you.

You messed up when you let me touch you. But you *fucked up* when you let me have you."

"I didn't have a choice!" His hand shot up to my neck to hold me lightly. His thumb swept my lips, and I unconsciously licked my lips, tasting his skin. His eyes were now also dark with lust. He was hot and cold at that moment. I shivered wanting to run away and yet get closer.

"I decided the first time you let me in between your sweet thighs, guilty or not, you were mine. I'm done denying myself what I want. You want me just as bad."

"Newsflash, I had you," I retorted, "and I'm over you." I crossed my arms over my chest and stared at him defiantly.

"These bitches are seriously fucked!" Dash gritted, bursting from the bookcases and interrupting whatever Keiran would have said. I was so wrapped up in Keiran I'd forgotten about Willow and Dash.

I took in his appearance and felt my eyes widen. His hair was tousled, sweat dripped from his skin, and his belt was now unbuckled. There was no question as to what they had been doing.

"What did you do to Willow?" I jumped off the table to confront Dash but ended up trapped between Keiran and the table when he refused to move. I looked up to glare at him, and he glared right back.

"Nothing yet," Dash stated ominously and looked at Keiran. "You ready, bro?"

Keiran ignored him and gripped my ponytail lightly in his fist. "Go take care of your friend." He kissed the tip of my nose, and I felt my body soften against my will. "But remember what I said," he ordered.

He had to go and ruin it.

\* \* \*

THEY FINALLY LEFT, and I rushed to find Willow in the bookcases. I found her crying quietly and immediately, wrapped her in my arms. "Willow, look at me." She shook her head no and kept her face buried in my shoulder.

"What happened? Please, let me help you."

"Fate must have a sick sense of humor. We were the only two people from our school in the summer program, so we gravitated toward each other. He was always so sweet. And charming. Half the time, I knew he was full of shit, but it didn't matter because he was funny and down-to earth. I always thought he was just some spoiled rich kid with his nose stuck up in the air. But he wasn't. He wasn't fake or phony. He was real—all the time, about everything. Or so I thought."

"He's breaking your heart," I guessed. I was tempted to track him down and kick him in the nuts.

"It's silly really and my fault. He never promised me anything. He just always made me feel special. And for the first time, I wanted to be special for someone other than me. I wanted to be special for him. I cared about what he thought."

I tried to hide my surprise, but I knew my face said it all. For her, that was big. Willow was a 'take me or leave me' kind of girl.

"One day, I even tried to be normal. I dressed like a square to please or impress him—I don't know. We were going to hang out, and he showed up dressed like I would dress." She let out a small laugh, her cries finally subsiding. "He looked ridiculously beautiful and proud, and I *loved* him for it. That was the day I gave myself to him."

"Why were you crying just now?"

"I threatened to get a restraining order if he didn't

stay away from me." I raised my eyebrows in surprise. "He got upset. *Really* upset. He said it wasn't fair to try to force him to stay away just because I couldn't."

"I get that he is supposed to be engaged to Rosalyn, but why were you fighting him before you found out?"

"You know Charles is my adopted father and Buddy's real father?" I nodded. "My mom doesn't like to talk about it, but my birth father is some rich guy she fell in love with. Well, they were supposed to get married, but his family didn't approve of her. Apparently, he was already engaged to someone else. My mom didn't say much about her—just that she came from a rich family, too."

"This is sounding familiar," I stated dryly.

"Yeah. That's why I freaked out Saturday—for once, I had to admit my mother was right, and it hurt like hell to hear here say he'd been playing me."

Guilt ate at me the more I listened to her because I knew of Keiran and Dash's plan, and in a way, I took part in it by saying nothing. At the time, I thought it was the right thing to do, but now...

I took a deep breath and steeled myself for what I had to do. "Willow, Keiran set Dash up with you so he could use you to blackmail me. I knew about it, but I couldn't tell you because, if I did, he would tell Dash to break your heart." The words rushed out of my mouth before I could think it over.

She shook her head and released a humorless laugh. "He succeeded. My heart is broken."

"I am so sorry, Willow. I should have told you sooner. Please forgive me."

"Yes, you should have," she affirmed. "But I don't blame you." I hugged her to me, and surprisingly, she hugged me back.

"So why get involved with him?"

"I actually didn't find out until I got back. He came over to my house the second day back. He said he missed me, and it was weird not seeing me, so I let him in. I introduced him to my mom, and she just grew so cold toward him. It was awkward, so I apologized and asked him to leave. My mom and I had a huge fight and then she forbid me to see him. I demanded to know why and that's when she told me about my father. I felt so bad for her, and it seemed really important to her, so I gave in. It was the hardest thing I ever had to do. Just when I was becoming something with Dash, I had to let go, and it hurt. After a while, Dash began to remind me of who he really was. He was the popular playboy. He's different now—not my Dash. But then again... he never was mine. He refuses to understand why I have to let him go and why he has to let me go." Her voice broke at the last.

"So what are you going to do now?" I asked with a heavy heart. It seemed they were doomed to fail from the very start.

"I'm going to stay away. Even if it kills me."

Seeing her so broken and lost filled me with a burning anger, and I finally felt what Keiran must have felt these past few weeks. "Willow?"

"Yes?" she sniffled and looked up at me with fresh tears in her eyes, reinforcing my decision.

"I want to make them pay."

P a g e | **260**

# CHAPTER EIGHTEEN

I WALKED WILLOW to her first class with enough time to make it to English. I was expecting to see Keiran in class, but he wasn't there. I assumed he was running late, but he never showed up. He wasn't at lunch or fifth period either. I was tempted to ask Dash or Keenan where Keiran was, but we weren't exactly friends. I wasn't supposed to care anyway.

The tables have now turned, and it was I who was out for revenge. It was insulting to me for him to think that after everything he'd done and tried to take away, we could just start over and be friends. Fuck that. I was out for blood. I was surprised at how fast Willow agreed. I didn't have a plan yet, but it was all that was on my mind. He had a lesson to learn, and I was going to teach it to him.

I went straight home after school with Willow tagging along. By the time I made it home, I knew exactly what I had needed to do when I had remembered the girl in the photo. But in order for my plan to work, I had to tell Willow everything. Starting with the day at t¹ pharmacy. By the time I finished, Willow had v·

every sort of harm there was on Keiran. Needless to say, our friendship was completely restored after that. She started to blame herself for not seeing it sooner, but I told her it was a load of crap. Keiran was a master at manipulation. No one was to blame but him.

"So, what do we do?"

I pulled out the photo and handed it to her. "We find out who she is and how Keiran knows her."

"Okay, but why?"

I hesitated before answering. "I think he killed this girl."

"What!" she shrieked.

"Willow, calm down."

"I can't calm down. Why do you think he murdered that little girl?"

"I found the locket the girl is wearing in this photo in his closet with a gun."

"Oh my God."

"We just have to—"

"Lake, are you seriously thinking about crossing him *again* knowing that he *murdered* someone?"

"Yes," I said without hesitation. "I don't have a choice. He threatened my aunt and tried to ruin our friendship. He can't get away with this."

"Lake..."

"Dash hurt you, too. Don't you want closure?"

"How does Dash fit into all this?"

"He's his best friend. For all we know, he may have something to do with it too, or at least know about it. You know what they say—birds of a feather and all that. If not, then we find another way. Either way, they are going to pay for what they did."

She put her head in her hands and muttered, "This is crazy."

"We aren't doing anything wrong or illegal. If Kei-

looked around as if searching for someone.

"Fuck. Let's go," he stated throwing money on the table.

"Keiran?" She stepped over to our table just as we were rising to leave. "I thought that was your car I saw outside. How are you, darling?" She moved to hug him, but he sidestepped her bringing me with him and headed for the door.

"Take care of yourself, Joan," he said not bothering to answer her question.

"Tell your uncle to call me!" she called out. I so wanted to know who she was and why Keiran was rude to her. Then again, Keiran was rude to everyone.

\* \* \*

I WATCHED HIS fingers clench and unclench the steering wheel as we drove. His mood had shifted from playful to dark, and I didn't know if it was my refusal to have anything to do with him or his run-in with Joan. I was curious what kind of relationship she had with the uncle I have yet to meet.

"Does your uncle have work that keeps him away? I've never seen him around." I decided to start off asking unassuming questions.

"Why do you want to know?"

"Think of it as an interview of sorts."

"An interview? For what?" He briefly took his eyes off the road and regarded me with narrowed eyes.

"You said you wanted to be friends." He grunted.

"You are something else you know that?"

I stared at him wide-eyed, projecting innocence. "What do you mean?"

He shook his head and licked those luscious lips, and I instantly remembered the way they tasted. Like mint and sin. "Tell you what—we play for your answer."

"Play?" I watched him warily.

"Basketball. One on One."

"But you'll beat me. It won't be a fair fight."

"I'll make it easy. If you can get two shots before I get ten, I will answer your question."

"It's just a simple question that needs a simple answer."

"I'll sweeten the deal. I'll answer one question for each additional shot you can make. Two shots get you your first answer. Every shot after that gets you an additional answer to any question you want to ask."

This could work for me. "Any question?"

He nodded and waited for my answer.

"What do you get out of it?" There had to be a catch, I thought as we pulled into his driveway.

"If I win, then you give us a shot."

He didn't hesitate to answer, and it was then I knew I'd been setup. My heart pounded in anticipation, but it wasn't for the game. "To be friends?" I clarified.

He looked into my eyes, and I knew they were exposing my deepest desires and showing him exactly how much I wanted him. The forbidden was always the hardest to fight. I just hope he couldn't also see how much I hated him.

"You know it will be much more than that, but if that's what you need to tell yourself, fine. Friends." He sneered as he spoke the word, mocking me.

"I could say no," I stated.

"But you won't." His jaw clenched, and I could tell he was on edge. He was right. I couldn't say no. I wanted answers.

"Let's do it."

\* \* \*

I WAS GROWING frustrated, but I refused to quit. Quitting would only mean he would win by default, and I wasn't about to just hand my sanity over to him. I managed to score one shot so far, but Keiran had already scored seven. At this rate, he would surely win, but the fat lady hadn't sung yet. No way.

I figured, if I stopped staring at his biceps long enough, I could score a few more shots. He had changed into a muscle shirt before we started playing, and I'd been drooling ever since. After seeing the fierce way that he played with Keenan, and the skilled way he played the game, I knew he was taking it easy on me, but I still couldn't deliver.

"Foul!" I called after he slapped my ass and took a shot. Eight. He grinned and dribbled the ball between his legs watching me.

"Doesn't that mean I get a free shot?"

"Nope. That just means you get the ball. He passed it to me, and I quickly took a shot before he could try to steal it from me. It bounced off the rim, and he was there to catch it, dunking the ball and scoring his ninth shot.

So much for taking it easy.

"Why are you toying with me?" I heard the whine in my voice and cursed. I sounded like the numerous bimbos at school. I always thought they were born like that, but maybe it was just male attention that made them act that way.

"I'm not. You're giving up."

"And you're cheating."

"I'm fighting for what I want. Are you?" He raised an eyebrow and wiped the sweat from his forehead with his shirt.

I got a peek at his glistening abs and felt my own

tummy flutter. I touched my stomach, feeling the soft skin. He was hard where I was soft. Sculpted where I was smooth. I longed to rub against him to compare the difference.

"I can always show you more. Just say the word." Shit. He caught me staring. I dropped my hand and got my head back in the game.

I was dribbling the ball fighting to keep the ball as he kept guard on me. We were close. Real close. Our breath mingled, and our bodies touched. I grew hotter from a different kind of heat when my hip lodged into his groin.

"You know what I think? I think what you really want is to give in, but you want the decision to be taken away from you so you won't feel so guilty."

I faltered and lost the ball to him as he effortlessly took a shot. I heard the telltale swish of the net signaling he'd just won our match. The world seemed to stop until it was only us as we stared at each other. He was gauging my reaction, and I knew he saw my need when his eyes darkened with lust.

"I win," he gloated. The only sound that could be heard was the basketball bouncing in the background until that, too, had stopped.

# CHAPTER NINETEEN

HE DROVE ME home to shower and change with a promise that we could return to school for third period. I was upset that I'd already missed Volleyball. Willow had texted me, wondering where I was, and I sent her the condensed version of what happened in English.

I left Keiran downstairs and peeled off my sweaty clothes, checking the temperature of the water before stepping in. Our match was stuck in my head along with everything he'd said. Did I want him to take the decision away? I still hadn't accepted the reality of losing our deal and what it meant.

I closed my eyes and tilted my head back to run water through my hair when I heard the curtain slide back. I opened my eyes and found Keiran in the shower with me.

"I—what—you..." I lost the ability to talk when I noticed he was naked.

The shower suddenly seemed tiny as he crowded my space and pushed up against me. My back was against the wall, and his erection was pressing against my stomach.

"You got something you want to say?" He was daring me to protest even though he won the bet fair. I shook my head but thought seriously about kneeing him. "Good girl."

He reached above my head to grab the shampoo and squirted some into his hands before lathering it into my hair. I tried to keep my eyes off the erection that moved with him, slapping my skin.

His fingers felt wonderful massaging my scalp. I reluctantly closed my eyes to enjoy it. I swayed toward him, feeling like I was floating on a cloud and mistakenly grabbed his waist. I immediately withdrew my hand, but he caught it, bringing it back.

"You can touch me anywhere you want." His eyes were half-closed when he whispered those words.

His rod was thick, swollen, and ready. Even though he had been inside me many times already, it wasn't any less intimidating.

I chewed on my lip nervously as I reached to touch him. His fingers paused in my hair a split second before he resumed massaging my scalp and relaxing me at the same time.

A drop of clear fluid leaked from the tip running down the length. I swallowed and blushed when I realized where my thoughts had wanted to take me. I wanted to be on my knees taking him in my mouth.

"Does it hurt?" I looked up at him while wrapping my hand around his length, squeezing lightly to see if more would escape.

"Yes," he answered his voice deep and low.

"Show me how to make it better."

He watched me closely as he wrapped his hand around mine covering it completely. Together we massaged his length with a pumping motion. Our breathing grew heavier as we stared into each other's eyes, lost in the moment.

Our speed quickened, and soon his body was jerking, and his low moans turned into deep groans. I stood on my toes to bring our mouths closer, wanting our lips to touch. We breathed each other in, his scent driving me wild.

"Baby... fuck."

I felt his hot release on my stomach as he gripped me, pulling me closer to his body. We stood there silently, the water cascading over our bodies as we used each other for strength. Once our breathing was under control, we quickly showered and dressed before heading back to school.

* * *

I WAS PANICKING. The entire ride back to school and throughout the rest of the day, I constantly thought about what it could mean for Keiran and I to actually be *friends. Fucking hell.*

"Dude, you've been staring at her with stars in your eyes or some shit. Spill. Was she good?" I heard Keenan's pitiful excuse for a whisper and began humming to myself.

We were in fifth period now. I still sat with Willow and Sheldon although we were now in the row directly in front of the guys. It was the only way Keiran would allow me to sit elsewhere. Already his possessiveness was getting out of hand. I don't think possessive is the correct word for him. Maybe crazy or psychotic.

Earlier today, a guy made the mistake of telling me my ass looked nice in my jeans. Luckily, Dash was with us and pulled Keiran off the guy before any real damage was done. I didn't know how to handle the look in his eyes, so I remained silent while he led me to class before leaving for his.

Keiran saving me from Trevor's assault was one thing. But the Keiran from a couple hours ago was an entirely different animal. I hoped I didn't make a mistake by accepting his friendship even if it was for revenge. I was beginning to think Willow might be right about it not being worth the risk.

"Shut up, Keenan," he barked.

"Lake. Hey, Lake," Keenan called, clearly ignoring the warning in his tone.

I warily turned in my seat to face him. "Yes?"

"What did you do to my cousin? He looks love struck, girl." His grin threw me off since he was supposed to hate me.

"Um, I don't know, but he gives a great shampoo." I winked at Keiran and turned back around. Dash and Keenan taunted Keiran endlessly to my delight. My phone vibrated after a few minutes, and I checked it:

K: You're going to pay for that.

Lake: Moi? What did I do?

K: I can't wait to make you CUM again

Lake: We never agreed to any of that

K: Too late. That was the hottest shower I've ever had.

I squeezed my thighs together to assuage the need.

K: You're squirming again...

Lake: Maybe I'll make you wait...

K: Maybe I'll make you beg 4 it...

Lake: Oh, yeah?

K: Yeah...

I made a big show of tossing my phone in my backpack and heard his chuckle behind me. Willow and Sheldon looked at me curiously. I shrugged absently and focused on taking notes.

When class ended, I walked with Willow and Sheldon to the door, ready to go home. Just as I was walking out, I felt a tug on my bag. Keiran turned me around, and immediately, planted a deep kiss on my lips, shocking everyone around us. When he finally came up for air, he glared down at me. "Where are you going?"

"I rode with Willow."

"So?"

"So... I'm going home with her."

"Are you asking me or telling me?"

"I'm telling you." The look that passed over his face would have scared me before, but I held my ground. His jaw clenched and then he released me.

"I'll be over later." With that, he walked off and left me standing there with Willow, whose bottom lip was touching the ground.

"Lake, what the hell just happened?" she shrieked. I looked around and noticed the many eyes that were still on me.

"Not here. I grabbed her and rushed for the exit, wanting away from prying eyes. I saw Keiran in the parking lot next to his car, surrounded by a ton of people. He spotted me as soon as we cleared the door and watched as we headed for Willow's car. Just as I opened her car door, he mouthed 'behave' and turned back around.

\* \* \*

WILLOW SHOT ME accusing looks the entire ride home and continued to glare at me once we got to her house. I felt like a bad child who got caught stealing cookies out of the jar. "So can I say my piece or are you going to continue accusing me?"

"I didn't say anything," she pouted. I rolled my eyes. I then started cleaning up her room when I got tired of having a staring contest. I picked up a pair of her jeans and found Pepé sleeping under them.

"Willow, why is Pepé out of his house?" We called it a house because she was convinced Pepé disliked the word cage. *Yeah, that was all Willow.*

"I don't know... he escaped?"

"Willow, your mom will have a fit if she knew he was left out."

"He has a soul! He doesn't belong in a cage!" *Here we go.* I turned on her speakers to avoid another animal rights speech. "I've got a date with Derek Ryan tonight," she blurted.

"Dash still not talking to you?"

"No. Who cares anyway?"

"Willow—"

"Nope. Not going there. He has a fiancée, remember?"

"Do you even know if that's really true? You know how girls like that are. They're self-serving. They think the world belongs to them."

"He didn't deny it either."

"You asked him? When?"

"He snuck in Sunday night when my parents were asleep."

"What did he say?"

"What do guys like that always say?" He told me his *relationship* with Rosalyn had nothing to do with our *thing*." She let out a humorless laugh. "I asked him if I was supposed to be his mistress or something, and he just shrugged and said we were friends who fuck, and there was nothing to talk about."

"Oh, Willow." I sat down on the bed next to her and hugged her.

"You know what the worst part is about this fuckery?"

"What?"

"I let Dash throw away my favorite vibrator! It was special." I laughed at her silliness. I was happy she didn't let Dash break her because her spirit was amazing. "So you still plan to go after Keiran and Dash, huh?"

The way she asked instantly had me turning around to face her. "I won't go after Dash if you don't want me to..." She shrugged and stared down at the floor.

"Willow?"

"I don't want you to go after either of them."

"Look, I don't even know what I'm going to do. I just know I need to find out if he killed that girl."

"Why?" She finally met my gaze again, but she looked truly angry now. "You don't even know her."

"But she's an innocent little girl."

"How do you know that? Really, Lake. How? All you have is a picture. So you found a locket in his closet that looks like hers. That doesn't mean he did it."

"Willow..."

"I know how it sounds, damn it! I just don't want you to get hurt."

"I promise, I'll be careful," I reassured her.

"Yeah, well... promises are made to be broken."

Sheldon came over an hour later with news that Anya had a bounty on my head. Apparently, word spread that Keiran and I were a couple now and that I stole her man. "I wouldn't worry about Anya. She's all talk. Keiran won't let anyone touch you anyway."

"I'm not worried about her. Keiran and I are just friends anyway."

"Sure, babe."

"Lake, I have to agree," Willow chimed. "That kiss earlier didn't look friendly. It was hot."

"We just have an agreement. A truce of sorts." A truce that was a half lie, but it would get me what I needed. There was no way Keiran was getting away with this.

"Uh huh, and how did this agreement come about?" Sheldon asked.

"We played basketball." They gave me a weird look, and I ran down everything that happened starting with English. I didn't however tell them about our impromptu shower.

"He totally hustled you, Lake."

"What do you mean? It was a fair game."

"Come on. You saw Keiran play. He used your curiosity and made the odds sound good enough that you couldn't resist."

"You got played," Willow added.

"And if I know Keiran, he is after more than friendship."

"I know. He made it pretty clear he wants sex."

"Are you sure you know what giving it up to Keiran will lead to?" Sheldon asked.

"An orgasm?" I laughed.

"Lake, Keiran is playing for keeps."

"He has had to have fucked almost every girl at Bainbridge and then some. Does he *keep* all of them?"

"Of course not. And he isn't as big of a man whore as you may think. He's too calculating. Most of what he does has a purpose."

"Like his sudden interest in me?"

"Have you been listening? It's always been there."

I didn't understand why everyone was so convinced that Keiran has always wanted me. He has done everything in his power to convince everyone that I was an undesirable waste of space. I've never once been on a date because of him. I didn't go to parties. I didn't hang out. Up until now, I had one friend. No matter how much I hid in the past, he found me. I ran, and he chased. I couldn't escape him. It was as if my pain fueled him.

This year was supposed to be about getting through and breaking away with the hope that I would never see him again. Now I was being told the past was a lie. It felt very real to me because I still carried the scars. After his last play on my sanity, the scars ran deeper than ever before.

I guess I still haven't gotten away from wearing my emotions on my face because Sheldon quickly changed the subject. "Willow, what are you doing to my brother? He's been snapping and growling at everyone. My dad put him in a chokehold when he snapped at Mom. It was awesome."

"I took your advice. I showed him I was serious."

"I never doubted you were serious. I'm wondering though if you're sure."

"What do you mean?"

"You want him, so what's the deal?"

"He's engaged."

"Oh, that." She shrugged and answered, "He's not engaged."

"Sheldon, don't lie for him."

"He's not. There was talk between our fathers about Rosalyn and Dash marrying, but it was more like matchmaker bullshit. At least for my dad it was. He called the idea off when Dash told him he wasn't interested. Rosalyn's dad, however, has it in his head that they made an agreement. We all know he's just after money. His finances are failing, and our family is richer, so they want to marry into the family. "

"Are you talking about an arranged marriage? Who does that?" I interrupted. I couldn't believe what I was hearing.

"Our families are old money, so they follow a lot of old traditions and customs. My dad is more realistic and believes in marrying for love. Besides, he would never make us do what we wouldn't want to—to a point anyway."

"What point is that?" Willow asked.

"Dash and Dad got into an argument Sunday night about what school Dash would attend. He wants Dash at a more promising school so he can take over the family business."

"Dash doesn't want to take over?"

"He wants to. He just wants to do it his own way. Anyway, the argument escalated and he disappeared for a few hours."

"He came here Sunday night around nine, but he was only here for a few minutes. I asked him about Rosalyn, and he took off." Willow repeated the conversation to Sheldon, who wasn't surprised.

"He didn't mean it, Willow. He was already pissed and looking for someone to take it out on. Dash is crazy about you. He told me there was no one like you."

"Great. I'm his favorite toy. I'm honored."

Sheldon shook her head, exasperated. "You two are going to get caught in the worst way. Don't say I didn't warn you. Dash may be mad now, but he isn't letting you go, and Keiran won't let you run, Lake."

"How are you so sure?" I asked.

"Because you let them in."

# CHAPTER TWENTY

RUMORS WERE SPREADING hard and fast. To everyone at school, I was Keiran's girlfriend, and we were the topic of everyone's conversation. What really threw me for a loop was the birdie by the name of Angela, who said that Keiran started the rumor.

Willow had stopped her in the hallway one day to ask about where it came from. Angela's exact words were, "How could it be a rumor if it came straight from the horse's mouth?" I knew then it had to be Keiran because I didn't say that shit.

When I confronted Keiran, he'd only shrugged and said, *"You're mine. Now they know it."*

To make matters worse, Anya was doing everything in her power to tarnish my reputation, which was really a pathetic attempt after being bullied by Keiran for years. I was immune to anyone else.

Basketball season was coming, so I haven't seen much of Keiran outside of school. He still used every opportunity to feel me up and violate me in school though. I was becoming pretty familiar with inappropriate places to do inappropriate acts.

Keiran's possessiveness wasn't the only contributor to my growing frustration. Time was ticking. My aunt was due back in a few weeks, and I wasn't any closer to finding answers about the girl in the picture. A few times, I came close to just asking Keiran about it but knew that would be dangerous and stupid. We may be 'friends' now, but he could quickly become my enemy again if I weren't careful.

After many failed attempts to find anything on him, I gave in and called Jesse. He was a criminal mastermind with computers and finding things that weren't meant to be found. I even thought about asking him to find my parents, but in the end, decided I didn't want to know. It would be too painful to learn they abandoned me. Maybe one day I would have the courage to find the truth.

The doorbell rang, and I rushed to answer it. We didn't have much time before Keiran's practice was over, and I couldn't risk Keiran finding Jesse here or worse, to find out what we were doing.

I opened the door to find an annoyed Jesse on the other side. "Tell me what this is about and it better be good. I did ninety all the way here."

"Well, you said you wanted to help me. This is it. Help me."

"So how and why does it involve my computer?" he asked as he set up his computer in the kitchen.

"I need you to find everything you know about Keiran, especially who and where his parents are."

"Okay... Why?"

"I can't explain it to you... not yet."

"Here we go. Why not, Lake?"

"Jesse, we don't have a lot of time. Are you going to help me or not?"

"Fine," he mumbled something about bossy girls

and harebrained schemes while he booted up his computer. I kissed his cheek in thanks, but he batted me away.

"When did you get so grouchy?" I teased.

"Right around the time you started keeping secrets."

"Whatever. I'm going to do homework."

"Great, you can do mine, too," he said good-naturedly as if he had just offered to do my homework instead.

"What?"

"I brought Calc and Chemistry," he said without taking his eyes off the computer.

"You can't be serious..."

"I don't joke about getting out of homework." He took out his books and shoved them across the table.

"This will take me all night!"

"Thanks, babe," he grinned at me cheekily.

"Gosh, you can be such a bitch." I folded my arms and glared at him across the table.

"My, my. When did you grow claws?"

"Sorry, Jesse. I'm just stressed."

"The bags under your eyes tell it all and is that a hickey?" When I got home, I had changed into a tank top that I was just now realizing was a little revealing. The hickey Keiran had placed at the top of my breasts this morning was partially peeking out of my top. The flush I couldn't hide heated my skin, and I jumped up from the table.

"I'll be back, scrub." I ran upstairs to grab my homework. When I picked up my books from my desk, I saw the picture lying underneath it. *Who are you?*

I rejoined Jesse downstairs and settled in for a long night of homework. Jesse had his ear buds in, so I knew he was in the zone. After what felt like hours, I finally finished Jesse's homework because he really wasn't kidding about that.

"Lake?" he called my name with a sense of urgency even though we were sitting at the same table. "You might want to see this." I jumped up from my seat and practically ran around the table.

"Did you find something?" I peered down over his shoulder at the headlines he had pulled up:

*A New Heir for the Masters Fortune?*

*The Masters family celebrates a new addition, but it's not the arrival of a newborn baby.*

*Sources say, John Masters, oldest son of Charles and Victoria Masters, now has care of an eight-year-old boy by the name of Keiran Masters. But where did he come from? Who fathered this mysterious child?*

And:

*Is Mitch Masters the Father?*

*Sources reveal that the mysterious eight-year-old child is rumored to be the son of the youngest Masters heir, Mitch Masters.*

*Could little Keiran Masters be the result of a secret love affair?*

The articles were spaced months apart, which meant there had to be more, so where were they? The articles he found held little to no information... maybe that was why they weren't buried with the others.

"These were all I found, and I had to do some heavy digging. Someone paid a lot of money to keep this a secret with little questioning," he said, voicing my thoughts. "I can't even find any medical records on Keiran. Or any information about the mother."

"What about a marriage certificate for his father?"

"Nada. He was never married. Mitch was only twenty-five when Keiran was born."

"All this publicity and no hint or word of his mother?"

"I'd thought the same, so I searched court records for any history of a paternity suit or child support hearing, but there was nothing at all. Without as much as a birth certificate for Keiran, his mother would be pretty hard to trace."

"What about school records? He was eight when he came into John's care so he must have been in school."

"Blank, babe."

"So he just appeared out of thin air?"

"The only way you can keep someone a secret is if they want to be kept a secret or if they aren't alive to tell you otherwise."

"You think the mother's dead?"

"Why not? Ten years and no trace of her?"

"So there would be a record of her death."

"Without a name, how would we find it?"

"Someone has to know something about who Mitch was dating."

"Not necessarily..."

"What do you mean?"

"Rich guys like that change women more than they change their underwear. She could have been just another notch on his belt—used and invisible."

"The only person who would know is John, but I've never even seen the guy. He's never around." I had thought long and hard before a thought occurred to me. "Where are they from? If they were from a place like Six Forks, it wouldn't be nearly impossible to figure out. People gossip."

"Beauty and brains. My hero." He chuckled.

"Some days I don't feel so smart..."

"That's because you let your vagina do the talking, babe." He quickly tapped his keyboards and only after a few minutes, he came across something. "He's from

Camden. That's only a two-hour drive."

"So it's close."

"You aren't seriously thinking about going there are you?"

"Why not?"

"Maybe because this whole family seems shady as fuck? You can't just show up on someone's doorstep and start asking questions about something they've obviously tried so hard to bury. Think about it, beautiful... Keiran was a child when he was found... he didn't hide all this himself."

I thought hard about what he said but knew I didn't have a choice. This was becoming more than just a need for revenge. I wanted answers. I *needed* answers. "What else can I do?"

Instead of replying he went back to typing. "It looks like he had a housekeeper."

"How do you know that?"

"Her resume was uploaded on this social website for professionals who use it to make connections." He studied the resume and then turned to look up at me. "What month is Keiran's birthday?"

"February, I think." I shrugged nonchalantly when he grinned at me with a cheeky expression.

"You think?"

"Okay, I know."

"Well, it looks like Mrs. Jenkins was dismissed."

"When?"

"Nine months before he was born," he answered dryly.

"Shit! Well, maybe we can find out where his father disappeared? No one just leaves all that wealth behind."

"On it. But I got to head back. My parents are going to kill me if I stay for much longer," he said as he packed up his computer.

"Thanks, for everything, Jesse. I know you want to do more, but I can't let anyone fight my battle—not anymore."

"Just promise you'll be careful."

"I'm not so good with promises, Jesse." Not after the two most important people in my life broke theirs...

"Right. Catch you later." He gave me one last hug and was gone.

\* \* \*

THUNDER ROLLED AND lightning flashed, lighting up my bedroom. The setting was so cliché and one straight out of a horror movie, especially when it illuminated the tall figure standing across the room. I came fully awake and jumped when I realized I wasn't dreaming and someone was actually in my room. His back was turned, and I guess I made a sound because he suddenly turned.

It was Keiran. He was standing there, drenched and soaking from the rain. His shirt was plastered to his skin outlining his chest and abs. His breathing was deep and uneven.

"What are you doing here?"

"Was it here?"

"What?" I asked, confused.

"Did you fuck him on your bed?" he growled. His voice penetrated my senses making by body quake with awareness.

"What the hell are you talking about, Keiran? Get out of my house!" He moved too fast. I was trapped between the mattress and his hard body and my trembling doubled.

"Why was Jesse here and think twice before you let a lie pass between those beautiful, pouty lips of yours. I'm not keen on being nice to you right now." We stared at each other, letting his words and the meaning settle around us. The only sound that could be heard was our deep, erratic breathing. "I'll ask you again, Monroe. Did you fuck him?"

"I didn't do anything with anybody, and if I did, it's none of your business. I don't belong to you. I. Never. Did!"

His bright gray eyes blackened as the brewing storm finally broke and raged harsher than the one outside. "No. But you will."

That was the only warning before his lips slammed into mine. The sound of surprise I made opened me up to his passions as his tongue penetrated my lips. I couldn't help but welcome the taste of him. I craved it more each time.

Before I could rethink it, I was wrapping my arms around his neck and surrendering to the need. My clothes were torn away until I was left naked under his dark gaze. His gaze remained locked with mine as he lowered his head between my shaking thighs. He finally looked away to stare at the wet heat between my legs. I shifted, fighting the urge to beg for his mouth on me as his lips lifted in a predatory grin. Suddenly, I remembered the fear I had kept close all these years as it returned. I didn't think I could handle him like this.

"Don't look at me like that, baby. I'm not stopping. Now, say you want it."

*Please, don't stop,* I thought. "I want you," I uttered without hesitation. I immediately felt his hot mouth and tongue on me. I moaned and writhed as he devoured me. However, the buildup of desire was much more powerful than the pleasure I felt from his tongue. I needed more.

I gripped his hair in desperation, searching for what was missing until I was drowning in tears. Suddenly, I was turning, and then I was upright. I looked down at Keiran underneath me as I straddled his face.

"Ride my face, baby. Take what you need."

So I did. Hard and fast. I felt his hands grip my ass and pull me deeper onto his tongue. It caressed me until I shattered. I was still shaking when I was flipped onto my back. I opened my eyes to find Keiran kneeling before me, watching me with an intense look in his eyes.

His hand reached for his shirt and then it was gone. I was staring at his chest, following the thin line of hair that trailed from his belly button and disappeared into his shorts. I licked my lips in anticipation. He lowered his shorts slowly, and my breath caught in my throat when his erection finally escaped. It strained toward me, begging for me to touch. He quickly slipped on protection while staring at me with a dark look in his eyes.

I reached out for him, but his hardened gaze froze my movement. "Put your hand down," he ordered then wrapped his hand around his length. "Give me what I want and all this is yours."

"Maybe I don't want it," I teased.

"Maybe the fact that you just came all over my face says differently."

"I can always call someone else."

I was eating the bed sheets with my ass in the air before I could blink. "Don't fuck with me when my dick is out, Monroe. Give me what I want."

I felt him rest his pulsing cock against my entrance, teasing me with light thrusts that slid his hardness against my folds.

"I don't know what you want!" I cried.

"You do," he answered simply continuing his torture on my senses.

"Please... I can't."

"Not even for this?" He gripped my hips tighter and slid the head inside. My pussy immediately gripped and sucked him in.

"I want it," I moaned hoping it would appease him.

"I know you want it," he whispered seductively. "I want it, too... I want all of it." It was then I knew what he was asking for.

My complete surrender.

I had to be his.

I wanted to be his.

"I'm yours," I whispered, a feeling of lightness taking over as if a weight had been lifted. I felt complete even though I knew it was a lie.

"Say it again," he growled. His body poised to take mine.

"I'm yours. *Only* yours." I turned my head around to look deep into his eyes. "Fuck me," I whispered desperately, holding his gaze with mine.

The force of his thrust shattered my senses as he slammed into me without warning and my scream ripped through the air. His head was buried in my neck, pressing soothing kisses against my skin. I locked his lips with mine as our hunger took over and our kiss became deeper.

"Fuck, baby," he groaned when my walls contracted around his cock. His hips shifted, and he began thrusting, slowly inside me. I could tell he was holding back for some reason. "Does that feel good?"

"Yes," I moaned. "More." I knew I sounded like a bitch in heat, but I was too drunk off him to care.

"More?" he repeated. "Like this?" His thrusts picked up speed until he was pounding into me. He seemed to always know just what I needed even when I didn't know myself. "Lake..." I screamed at the sound of my name on his lips.

"Yes."

"Say my name, Lake. I want to fucking hear it."

"Keiran." His name was caught on a scream when he nearly lifted my knees off the bed with a single hard thrust.

"You're mine," he growled. I felt my orgasm approaching and grew desperate for the end and the pleasure that came with it. Keiran was driving me insane under his possession. His groans became louder, and I knew he was about to come and I craved it. "Come with me, baby." His finger found my clit and worked the bundle of nerves until I felt my body seize and my belly quiver. My long, guttural scream and his roar echoed throughout the room as the powerful orgasm took over us both.

Keiran had taken me once more before he left the bedroom, leaving me tired and overworked on the bed. I thought about the love we just made and shivered. It was fierce, and it was brutal, but it was us. I *loved* it.

He came back after a few minutes and cleaned me up but didn't rejoin me on the bed. I watched him dress in silence as I listened to the storm still rage outside, lost in my own thoughts. Once the sex fog cleared from my mind, I remembered sleeping with him again wasn't part of the plan. Just like the shower, I got caught in the moment. I was also pissed he was once again doing a hit and run.

What did you expect, Lake? Cuddling under the covers? Pillow talk?

"I'm going to ask you something, and I'm only going to ask you once," he said as he walked across the room. The tone of his voice was sharp, and I instantly knew why when he picked up the only thing lying on top of my desk. My heart stopped, when he asked, "Where the fuck did you get this?"

"I can explain," I said lamely. I was kicking my own ass for leaving the picture on the desk. After Jesse had left, I passed out from mental exhaustion. Digging into Keiran's past was more complicated than I originally thought it would be.

"I'm counting on it."

"I don't know."

"Lake," he growled.

"I'm serious! I don't know. I think whoever broke into my house that night left the picture. It was in a birthday card that was addressed to me."

"Bullshit. That was a month ago. Why didn't you say something?"

"Because... I—"

"Because you wanted to use it against me," he said all too calmly. It immediately made me wary. Where was the shouting? Where was the anger?

"You're being ridiculous." I sat up and pulled the covers around my naked body, no longer feeling as comfortable being in the nude.

I felt vulnerable enough with his threatening stare bearing down on me.

"Am I?" he asked.

"How would I even know the picture involved you?" Keeping his eyes locked with mine, he shoved his fist in his pocket and pulled it back out immediately. I thought it was odd that he did it until he opened his fist and let the gold locket dangle between his fingers.

"This look familiar?"

"It's starting to," I said petulantly. I knew I was caught, and truth be told, I was scared, but I wouldn't let him see it.

"How about if I wrap this around your neck and strangle the fuck out of you?"

I jumped from the bed, forgetting about my naked

state, and the words were spewing out of my mouth before I even knew what I was going to say.

"Go ahead and do it! You've been threatening to kill me since we were kids! Sometimes I wish you would have just put me out of the misery you caused me!" My chest was heaving up and down while he watched on silently. "Yes, I was going to find out the story behind that picture, the story behind you, and the story behind the past ten damn years, and I was going to use it to make you pay for what you've done to me."

His eyes narrowed, and his voice filled with venom as he asked, "What I've done to *you*?"

"I never did anything to you. I didn't deserve your hatred."

"That may be so," he said nonchalantly and shrugged, "but that doesn't mean you didn't affect me—because you did."

"Affect you how?"

"You made me realize how fucked up I was or... am."

"Why is that a reason to hate me? I was seven, Keiran. I didn't even know you!"

"It didn't matter. I blamed you for making me realize it, so hurting you became a way for me to accept who I was. Ten years ago, I was serious when I said I was going to kill you, but then hurting you became an addiction, and I couldn't stop."

"If it was fear you wanted, why only target me? There are so many people who are afraid of you."

"None like you."

"Keiran, you're sick." Instead of anger, I was filled with pity and empathy for him. It couldn't be easy being that type of person.

"I'm not sick, Lake. I was just doing all I've ever known." I still couldn't imagine what could turn an innocent child into someone so dark.

"J—Jesse found these articles today. I know your mother abandoned you when you were eight."

"How did he find that? It's supposed to be gone—all of it."

"He's good at finding things."

"I see."

"So help *me* see. What happened to you?"

"What did the article say?" I frowned at his question. He didn't look angry or sad about me finding out his history. Instead, he looked curious.

"Not much. It said John took you in and Mitch Masters is your father. It said nothing about your mother. Who is she?"

"My mother was a prostitute and a drug addict. She left me with my uncle so she could go off and die." He tried to mask it, but I heard the contempt in his voice when he spoke about his mother, but he still held no emotion.

"What about the girl in the photo?" His eyes clouded over as he looked back down at the picture.

"She's no one," he replied. I could hear the bitterness in his voice. "She was weak." The contempt in his voice spurred my next question.

"So what happened to her?" He had to know something considering he had her locket. Could he have been there when she died?

"I killed her." As much as I was hoping for honesty, I didn't actually expect him to be so honest. He just admitted to murdering someone yet he was so casual about it.

"Why?" I asked reluctantly. My voice shook, but I managed to hide most of it.

"Because I couldn't save her." His eyes had glossed over with some unnamed emotion when he spoke. It was a look I'd never seen on Keiran's face before. It was regret.

"Save her from what?" His beeping phone interrupted whatever he would or wouldn't have said. When he spit out a harsh curse, and his face transformed into a savage mask, my attention shifted to whatever held his attention now.

"What is it?" I couldn't help asking.

"Reynolds made bail."

"When?"

"Yesterday."

# CHAPTER TWENTY-ONE

THE SUNLIGHT ON my skin woke me up, and I swear I could hear the birds chirping outside, and I felt like singing. *I'm such a dork.* I stretched, and my body felt sore in all the right places and remembering how it got like that brought a smile to my face.

"Good morning, baby."

I was surprised to hear his voice even though I knew he stayed the night. After we had found out that Trevor was out—probably thanks to his dad—I'd wordlessly gotten back in bed and closed my eyes, wishing for sleep to come quickly. I told myself I didn't care what Keiran did or where he went, but when he climbed into bed and spooned me from behind, my heart did jumping jacks all over my chest.

I finally opened my eyes and found him sitting on the floor next to the bed. His knees were bent with his arms draped over them. He wore an intense expression on his face, and I wondered what he'd been thinking.

"Why are you on the floor?"

"You kept kicking me. I nearly fell off the bed... and you snore."

"I do not!" I threw a pillow at him and then realized I had no way to hide my flushed cheeks. He laughed when he caught the pillow.

"You're pretty wild."

"Well, I'm awake now. So come on." I patted the bed and looked at him with a look that I prayed was seductive. He smiled sheepishly and shook his head.

"I've created a monster. We don't have time for the bed." He stood up and headed for the door, and I pouted. "But if you come get your sexy ass in the shower with me, I'll give you your first quickie," he tossed over his shoulder before leaving.

I wasted no time hopping out of the bed and running after him. I had already decided sometime between him pounding me against the shower wall and my screaming orgasm that it was my favorite place to have sex.

Not long after, we were downstairs making breakfast when he said, "I want you to stop digging into my past."

"I can't do that," I said without looking at him. I heard him slam his cup down and felt his eyes burning into me.

"Why the fuck not?"

"Because I want answers you won't give me."

"And for a damn good reason. Damn it, Lake. This goes beyond you and me. You're going to uncover some shit you'll wish you hadn't, and I won't be able to save you."

"So what happens then? You'll kill me, too?" Instead of answering, he shot up from his seat and was around the table before my brain caught up with common sense. His hand was in my hair, pulling my head back, and my eyes met his stormy gaze.

"It won't come to that because you're going to do

what I say. I don't want to have to hurt you again. Don't push me that far. Are we clear?"

I peered into his eyes and saw something I never thought I would see ever. I saw fear. "What are you afraid of?" His gaze had shifted from my face before he met my stare again.

"I'm not afraid of anything," he answered, shortly. He let go of my hair and left the kitchen before I could respond.

"Everyone has something to be afraid of," I whispered to an empty house.

***

I DON'T REMEMBER the ride to school. After the breakfast I had eaten alone, I looked around for Keiran even though I knew he was gone. I purposely made it to school with only a few minutes to spare. Even though Keiran was no longer terrorizing me within these walls, his attention put me on the receiving end of glares and snide comments from his ex-cum buckets—Anya especially.

I was surprised she was walking around unscathed and even still claiming Keiran after Trevor's confession that she was a part of the setup. The irony of the situation did not escape me. Maybe he really did have feelings for her...

I entered art class and found my seat was taken. I didn't think it was a big deal until I noticed the only seats left were one beside Keenan and the other next to a member of Anya's twat squad.

Keenan didn't seem to hate me anymore, but I wouldn't exactly call us buds. I tossed my head back annoyingly before marching over to his table. He looked up and grinned when he saw me. It was still uncanny how much they looked alike. I reluctantly sat down next to him.

"Sup, sis-in-law. You still mad at me?" I tried not to react to his nickname for me. People were getting ideas about Keiran and me that I wasn't particularly fond of.

"Not mad. Aware."

He frowned before saying, "I didn't make the best impression..."

It was more a statement than a question. I shrugged and left to retrieve my project. I returned to my seat and looked at him curiously. He was glaring at his poster as if it offended him. I took a peek and saw he was drawing a picture of Sheldon doing one of her routines at a game. I was impressed at how good he was and with how he seemed to capture so much detail. His art really seemed to come to life.

"You're pretty good. Is art something you want to do?" Making conversation was my way of a truce... sort of. I didn't owe Keenan anything, but I wasn't going to be a bitch either.

"Huh?" He jerked his head up and looked at me. "Oh... maybe. Hey, uh... can we be friends?"

"Why?" He definitely threw me off guard with that one, and I didn't try to hide my surprise or suspicion.

"Because I was a dick to you. I'm sorry for how I treated you."

"I get it. You were protecting him." I didn't get it, but that didn't mean I had to be the dick.

"Keiran hasn't had the best experience with having a family, so I try to have his back."

"I know. Last night, he told me about his mother being a prostitute and a drug addict after I dug up some things from his past." Keenan's expression was mixed with surprise and confusion.

"He told you that?" he asked as his brow furrowed

from his deep frown.

"Yes." I studied the expression on his face and then asked, "Did he not tell you?"

"Uh, yeah. Yeah, he told me. I'm just surprised he was so... forthcoming about it to you."

"Yeah, no kidding," I said absently. Keenan's look was more than just surprise. "Anyway, do you think he would have done the same for you if he doesn't believe in family?" He hesitated, and I could tell he was thinking his words over.

"He would have done much worse." I studied his face and saw something odd hiding in his eyes. I recognized that look.

"Are you afraid of him?"

"No. I'm afraid for him."

"Why?" He hesitated again, and I could tell he didn't want to answer my question, but I wasn't letting this go.

"We can't be friends if I can't trust you." I knew it was manipulative to use that against him, but these two have done much worse. He looked amused before shaking his head.

"Keiran is going to have his hands full with you," he chuckled.

"No more than I will with him. Tell me."

"I'm afraid for him because every day, he has to fight the person he is in order to be the person he wants to be."

"What happens if he loses?" I asked while the hairs at the back of my neck stood up.

"People get hurt." I didn't miss the sad look that passed over his face before he focused on his poster and began working on the picture.

"Something tells me you aren't going to elaborate." I knew Keenan knew more than he was letting on to

Sheldon or anyone else. I can't imagine living with someone like Keiran and not seeing more than the rest.

"Not unless you have something else to offer." He waggled his eyebrows suggestively, and I laughed.

"Yeah. You, me, and Sheldon could all have a good time," I quipped sarcastically.

He turned to me with wide eyes that were glazed over with what looked like hope. "Don't say that unless you mean it because if Keiran fucks up, I got dibs." He winked and turned back to his project.

* * *

"I WANT YOU at practice with me." It was just after fifth period when Keiran delivered his latest demand. We were leaving the classroom when I had turned to kiss Keiran goodbye because he wouldn't let me go otherwise.

"I'll pass." I turned to leave, irritated but not wanting it to show. *So much for the honeymoon phase.* Then again, I didn't know what this was between us. Keiran had made it known he wasn't going to leave me alone, so either we are friends or we are... I don't know. I chose to be friends, but he was taking so much more.

"I'm not asking," he gritted while tugging on my arm and pulling me in the opposite direction. I looked back at Willow for help, but she was distracted and looking uneasy from Dash's scrutiny. Yeah, he still had it bad for her.

"Keiran, this is ridiculous. What am I supposed to do at your practice? I'll look like one of those clingy, hoe bag groupies. No thanks."

He continued to pull me until he got tired of fighting and threw me over his shoulder. I couldn't fight, but I cursed him almost the entire way until he gave me a sharp slap on my rear that had me seeing stars. We got to the gym where he finally released me, and I saw Buddy sitting on the sideline, lacing up his sneakers. Willow told me he made the team this year. Everyone was impressed with his skill at Saturday's game.

I unconsciously looked around for Trevor. Even though he was out on bail, he was suspended from school until trial. When I didn't see any sign of him, I walked over to Buddy and felt Keiran's stare penetrating my back as I walked away. I rolled my eyes because I knew he couldn't see, and I sat next to Buddy.

"You've become a hot commodity for Bainbridge. To what do you owe your success?" I held out an imaginary microphone for him.

"The endless supply of hot chicks they promised me."

"Well, there you have it, folks. Another brain-dead athlete. When will the cycle end?"

"Hi, Mom!" He spoke into the fake camera. I hit his shoulder and laughed at him. Buddy was so adorable. "Speaking of hot chicks, when will you quit breaking my heart and run away with me?"

"Never, shit stick, and quit hitting on my girl." We looked up at Keiran standing over us looking aggravated.

"That's my cue to leave." He slapped hands with Keiran before sauntering away. "She wanted me first anyway!" He yelled when he was a safe distance away. I was laughing hysterically at the look on Keiran's face from Buddy's comment. He looked torn between wanting to laugh or kill him.

Buddy had a crush on me for as long as I could remember, but it would never go anywhere. Don't get me wrong—Buddy was insanely hot. He could even give

Keiran a run for his money. Even though he was only a freshman, it was obvious Buddy would take over the reins once Keiran left.

By the time I quit laughing, Keiran had turned his menacing look on me, and for the first time ever, I wasn't afraid. "Hey, don't look at me. You are the one who insisted I come here. Now all your teammates get to ogle me."

"Yeah?" Before I could answer, he stalked off in the direction of the locker room. Twenty minutes later, the team emerged from the locker room and began to warm up. I pulled out my books to pass the time.

Every once in a while, I would watch the team practice, or more specifically, Keiran. There was a lot of shit talking between the guys as they practiced, and I found myself cracking a smile or two at the crap that came out of Keiran's mouth. I've never seen this easygoing nature from him. It almost made him appear human.

After some intense drills, they had a brief break to grab water, but Keiran stayed on the court to make sure everyone got water. I heard him tell the new players that his number one rule was to stay hydrated at all times, and he would be watching. Keenan grabbed his water bottle and ran up to me as I was closing my Lit book.

"Say, what is up with our boy?" he asked grinning.

"What do you mean?"

"He came in the locker room and threatened to break the balls of anyone who looked at you during practice." He began cracking up when my jaw dropped in shock.

"Tell me you're joking."

"I cannot make this up."

That must have been why number eight wouldn't look at me when I handed him the ball that rolled over here. I just thought he was really shy. I had seen Keiran watching us with an intense look on his face. His jaw was clenching in anger, and he looked pissed. *Was he jealous of Keenan talking to me?*

I met his stare and beckoned him with my finger. He didn't hesitate and made his made way toward us from the other side of the gym. When he reached us, he took my hand pulling me up and sitting in my place before seating me in his lap. I breathed in his sweaty scent and couldn't think of anything that ever smelled better.

He was glaring at Keenan with a possessive and cocky expression. Keenan was staring back at him challengingly before he rolled his eyes and grinned. "Relax, bro, I got my own."

Keiran grunted his response before kissing me on my neck and sending chills down my spine. My throat emitted a little moan before I could stop it. "You are two seconds from getting fucked hard on these bleachers if you don't stop moving your ass all over my dick." His voice was harsh in my ear making my eyes pop open.

Keenan was still standing in front of us watching through lowered lids and biting his lip with a curious expression on his face.

"Fuck off," Keiran barked when he noticed Keenan staring.

"Pussy whipped motherfucker," Keenan muttered walking off.

"That is the second guy you ran off in less than an hour. You won't have any friends if you keep it up. What's your deal anyway?"

"You."

"Me?"

"You're too fucking sexy."

"You're crazy, numb nuts. No one has ever been interested in me before."

"That you know of. I made sure of that."

"Come again?" I looked at him as if he'd grown two heads. Sometimes, I thought Keiran really did have two heads with two completely different minds. One sane and one not so sane.

"Breaks over. Behave," he ordered before walking away.

I sat there dumbfounded. I always knew Keiran's bullying was the cause of my dateless, boyless life, but I didn't think he had a direct hand in it. *He has some explaining to do.*

My phone vibrated with a message from Willow. She sent me a cute picture of Pepé in a sailor uniform. Willow was great at designing and making clothes and wanted to get a degree in textile.

I haven't told her yet about my night with Keiran. I still thought I would wake up and find it was all a dream. Did Keiran being sent to juvie bring us together or delay the inevitable? A year ago, no one could pay me to believe sex between us would even be possible.

The team stopped for another water break, and this time, Dash approached me and sat down. He stared at me for a moment before taking a deep breath.

"Hey." He sounded sad.

I raised an eyebrow at him. "Hi." He rubbed the back of his neck and ran a hand through his dark blonde hair roughly.

"So you and Keiran, huh?"

"We're friends." *Jeez, what is with everyone?* I wondered what his motive for talking to me was. He sat there for another minute, staring off into the distance, and I could tell he was thinking.

"How is Willow doing?" he finally asked.

*And there it is.* "You see her every day. Why don't you ask her yourself?"

"She won't talk to me." His nostrils flared in aggravation.

"And that bothers you?" I tilted my head and studied him. He was a rich playboy and a major hottie who could have any girl he wanted yet he sat here looking almost lovesick over one... *My girl got game.*

"More than it should."

"Willow is phenomenal," I stated harshly.

"I know."

"Smart."

"I know."

"Loving."

He nodded.

"Crazy as hell."

He laughed.

"Beautiful with a *banging* body."

"I know," he growled, his eyes clouded over with lust.

"She's too good for you," I stated bluntly.

"I know." Determination spread over his features making him appear ruthless.

"You don't care, do you?"

"I tried but... I'd rather have her than do the right thing."

"That's selfish."

"That's life," he retorted.

"She has feelings for you. Did you know that?" He swallowed deeply before shrugging. "I doubt she even knows it... or doesn't want to admit it.

"I won't hurt her."

"So setting her up to fall for you to get back at me—you think that didn't hurt her?" It was a rhetorical question, and he knew it because he didn't answer. "You won't give her what she needs either. That will hurt her so let someone else give her what she needs."

"She's mine." Primal emotion took over his features, and I grinned at him. He shook his head as he realized the trap I had led him to—getting him to admit he had feelings for her, too.

"Keiran is going to have his hands full with you," he said, standing up.

"So I've heard."

He held out his hand to me. "Friends?"

I stared at him for a minute, gauging his sincerity. "Why the hell not? Friends." I shook his hand, and he pulled me up into a bear hug, swinging me around. I shrieked and was taken aback before I laughed.

"You better put her down before Keiran gets back in here and kills us all," Coach Lyons reprimanded while walking past.

Great. The coach was afraid of him, too.

\* \* \*

WHEN PRACTICE ENDED, Keiran drove us to his house where he told me he was taking me on a date. I didn't know what to say, and apparently, he didn't either because we just stood there staring at each other before I shrugged and answered with a terse, "Sure."

So tonight was my first date... our first date. Keenan and Sheldon decided to come so I guess you could call it my first double date, too. Dash was going to come along when Keenan suggested a girl to take—until I gave him the stink eye. That would be the wrong move, and he knew it. Everyone knew the way to a girl's heart was through her best friend.

We climb into Keiran's car with plans to catch a movie and to go to the local bowling alley after. We were both out of our element, but I couldn't tell if he was as nervous as I was. He held my hand the entire way, rubbing his thumb in the center of my palm. Keenan and Sheldon were too busy swapping DNA in the backseat, so we were left in our own world.

We got to the theater, and the guys let us decide on a movie. The first movie we picked earned us endless groans and complaints about chicks and their flicks, so we chose a comedy instead. We had twenty minutes to spare until the movie started so we played in the attached arcade. Keiran led me over to the basketball game. There was a divider between the lanes with balls sitting inside. He picked two up and handed me one.

"Want to make a bet?"

I looked at him sideways and caught his sneaky grin. "No?"

"Please? I'll be a good."

"Basketball is your thing. You're going to beat me." He rolled his eyes before leading me over to the whack-a-mole table.

"This better, baby?"

I shrugged and picked up a whacker—*whacker?* "So what's the bet?"

"What would you like to win?"

"Answers," I answered without hesitation. He didn't look surprised. In fact, I suddenly got the feeling I had been led into a trap when he grinned down at me.

"What do you want?" I asked while keeping a wary eye on his face. The predatory look on his face made me suspicious.

"I get to fuck you senseless. All night. For as long as I need to." He stepped closer bending his head down until his breath fanned over my neck. "And you can't tap out—no matter how good it feels."

My breath shuddered out unevenly as my body succumbed to the heat of the underlying threat in his tone. "What happens if it's a tie?

"Then you get your answers, and I get you under me again."

I shuddered again in anticipation. Eye of the tiger, Lake. Don't wimp out now. "Deal."

"It's not a deal unless you seal it with a kiss…"

I immediately closed the remaining space between us, challenge shining in my eyes. I slowly wrapped a leg around his hip while sliding my hands up his muscular chest. I traced his incredibly sexy lips with my tongue and then nipped his bottom lip, hearing him emit a low, throaty growl. I winked at him before pecking his lips and moving away.

"Oh, hell no." He grabbed me and pulled me back to him before devouring my lips hungrily. My lips opened for him eagerly, and he conquered me with a kiss. I melted, handing the control back over to him as he fed from me.

He finally let me go with a slap on the ass and turned to start the game. I looked around and blushed at the number of eyes that watched our display including Keenan and Sheldon, who wore goofy expressions.

I shook my head. Day two and he was already turning me inside out. We started whack-a-mole, and we did everything in our power to distract each other. Keenan and Sheldon came over to cheer each of us on separately and to make jibes. Keiran was currently ahead of me by one point with only a few seconds left, and I was becoming desperate when I had an idea.

"Sheldon, did you see the guy who just came in? Crazy hot." Keiran swung around with a scowl on his face, and I quickly made my move, ending the game in a tie. Keiran figured out my trick and beamed at me with what looked like pride in his eyes. "You aren't mad?" I asked him.

"Nope. I still get what I want." He licked his lips

and grabbed my hand, leading us into the theater room. It was pretty empty considering it was a weekday. There were two couples seated in the front, so we took the back row. Keiran and Keenan seated Sheldon and I then disappeared back out into the lobby.

"Okay, spill, bitch, and quick before they come back."

"What?" I asked innocently. Sheldon had a knowing look in her eye and a grin of approval on her lips.

"Keiran has been looking at you like you hold the key to the promise land all day."

I snorted. "I doubt that's it."

She gave a dramatic gasp, her eyes widening with excitement. "You totally gave it up!" she yelled.

"Shhh! Sheldon, jeez!"

"Did you?"

"Well, he came over last night and one thing led to another..."

"Ahh, no wonder you've been glowing all day. You're dick dizzy."

"Dick what?" I swear I could not keep up with Sheldon's vocabulary. Every day she had a new word to describe something. It was usually sex.

She grinned. "Don't worry. It has nothing on the power of the pussy. You just have to know how to use it. So you guys official?"

"No."

"That means yes. Keiran doesn't do dates."

I rolled my eyes. "That doesn't mean we are dating."

"Oh, it means. Trust me, Lake. You're dealing with a special kind of male here. You're dating."

"My aunt is going to kill me. She wants me to date, but I know she didn't expect this. I feel so guilty, not to mention scared."

"Losing your v-card?" I nodded. "At least you're eighteen. You're an adult. Anyway, parents are never ready for their kids to cross that line. I was sixteen when I first did it."

"Was it with Keenan?"

"Yeah," she sighed with a dreamy look in her eyes.

"Were you scared?"

"Absolutely. It was unexpected and was after our first breakup when I found out he made out with Jessica Stanton at a party. Dash was actually the one to tell me about it. They beat the brakes off each other over it."

"How are they still friends?"

"Hell if I know. Men don't hold grudges like women do, I guess.

Dash stayed out of it after I took Keenan back the third time." Her voice lowered and she sounded sad, so I let her have a moment. I thought about what Keiran had planned for me later tonight when we were alone and felt a shiver run through my body.

"Do you still get scared?"

"Yeah, but I never tell him no because I know he wouldn't hurt me. He can be an animal," she grinned. "And sometimes I guess the need just overtakes him. He gets in these moods..." She trailed off and looked lost in thought.

Before I could find out more, the guys had come back, each with popcorn and drinks. I was curious about what Sheldon meant and knew there was a story there. Keiran sat on my left while Keenan sat on Sheldon's right, leaving us in the middle. The lights dimmed, and the previews started to roll so I settled into my seat for the movie.

"I got it loaded with butter." He sat the popcorn in my lap before slumping down in his seat and spreading his legs apart in a lazy yet sexy pose. He let his head rest against the back of the seat and looked me up and down.

"Thanks," I smiled at him, but he didn't return my smile. Instead, he turned to the screen and stared broodingly at it.

I frowned but hesitated only a second before deciding to say something. I gave my body to him—I wasn't allowed to be afraid of him anymore.

"Something wrong?" He continued to stare at the screen, ignoring me. He didn't look angry, but his body language screamed 'disinterested.' I leaned forward and waved my hand in front of his face. Still nothing. I then snapped my fingers twice to get his attention. "Hey... I'm talking to you. That means you say something back."

"Atta girl." I heard Sheldon say and snicker quietly.

He finally turned to me, a frown marring his features. "What?" he asked coldly. I drew back in surprise for a moment before regaining my composure.

"If you're going to act like an ass for no reason, then you can just take me home. Now."

"That's all I want to do is get you home."

"Then why did you bring me here?" I felt tears burning the back of my eyelids, but I refused to let them fall. Not this time.

He let out an aggravated breath. "Hell if I know."

"Then, by all means let's end this *date* now." I bit out the word date and felt the sneer transform my face. "I wouldn't want you to feel obligated."

"Are you this stupid on purpose or can you really not help it?"

"Don't call me stupid. I'm not stupid. Or maybe I am because I'm sitting here with you right now." I stood up before he could say anything else and left for the lobby, almost tripping over Sheldon and Keenan.

I heard him spit out a harsh curse, and Sheldon call him a 'dumb dickhead' before I burst through the doors. The bright lights of the lobby almost blinded me, or maybe it was the hot liquid spilling down my cheeks.

Fuck. I said I wouldn't do that.

I contemplated walking home before I realized I wasn't that stupid and headed for the restroom. I pushed inside and pulled out my cell phone to call Willow for a ride.

"Aren't you supposed to be on a date with Mr. Tall, Dark, and Evil right now?"

"He's being a jerk. Can you pick—" That was all I was able to say before the phone was plucked from my hands. Keiran ended the call and stuck my phone in his pocket. *Big surprise there.*

"What are you doing in the girls' bathroom?" I hurriedly tried to wipe my cheeks before he could see I had been crying. He took my hands away and used his own to gently clean my face.

"I came to apologize and this is the men's bathroom." My eyes widened, and I looked around and noticed the urinals before squeezing my eyes shut in embarrassment. Could I be any more of a dork?

"Go. Away." I backed up until my back touched the wall, needing space between us, but he only followed.

"No."

"You're not my favorite person right now."

"That's okay because I can guarantee you'll change your mind the next time I get my dick in you."

"If you say so," I returned flippantly while shifting against the ache between legs.

"Want to test that theory now?" he challenged. I shrugged and turned my head away, giving him the cold shoulder. He gently grasped my chin and turned my face up to him. My lips opened instinctively for his. He eyed my mouth before grinning down at me. "I'm talking to you. That means you say something back."

He threw my words back at which pissed me off, so I drew my knee up to hit his balls. He caught my leg under my thigh and wrapped it around his waist and pressed me harder into the wall.

"Are you trying to get round one started right here?" His eyes were heated with sexual intent, and despite the way my body responded, I shook my head no. "Then behave."

"Why are you always telling me to behave?"

"Because you want it."

"Do explain..." I stated sarcastically and rolled my eyes. He grasped my chin again, this time in a tight, unyielding grip. I watched the flash in his eyes and quaked all the way down to my toes.

"I don't have to. You and I both know how wet your pussy gets every time I issue a command. You love it." I started to protest as he transferred his grip to my throat. "You *need* it," he growled.

God help me—I do.

"Don't make me prove it to you right here. You aren't ready for the type of fucking I'd give you right now. But you will be... after tonight."

I drew in a deep breath almost begging him to carry out his threat. "I don't know what to say." It was a stupid response to the hot promises he had just made to me, but it was all I had, dammit.

"All I need is for you to say yes when I need you. That's it."

"Why should I say yes? You were being *him* again. I don't like it."

His hand dropped from my throat as he frowned and searched my eyes with what looked like panic. "Him?" he asked.

"Yeah... the Keiran before now." I didn't miss the look of relief that crossed his features.

"I won't apologize again since it seems you aren't listening so I'll explain instead. I am happy to spend this time with you. I just wish we could spend it alone. I can't help but want you all to myself all the time. I missed ten years with you because I couldn't wake up from a nightmare that played over and again. But even more selfishly, I wish we were locked away in my bedroom instead of a smelly theater. Believe me, baby, I would do anything not to be *him* again."

His arms had come around me sometime during his speech and held me tight as if to keep me from running away. His possessive demeanor told me I was dead on. The sincerity shone through his gaze, but I couldn't forgive him just yet.

"Anything?" I stressed.

His hands dropped to my butt and lifted me up and into him. "Yes."

"Then you should know this is my first date. Don't ruin it, okay?"

"Not even if it meant my life," he agreed.

# Chapter Twenty-Two

"Lake, how good do you play with balls? Aaargh! The bowling balls, babe!" Sheldon had driven her elbow into Keenan's stomach. I laughed at his pained expression because he never seemed to learn his lesson.

"I'm telling Keiran," Sheldon stated.

"Snitch," Keenan returned.

"Slut."

"That's it. I'm choosing Lake as my partner."

"You can't choose Lake."

"Why not?"

"Maybe I want Lake."

"Too bad. I called dibs."

"You can't have dibs. She's *my* friend. She doesn't even like you."

Ouch.

"Lake, tell her we are friends now. Remember? BFFs? Art?"

"Lake, is this true?" Sheldon asked, accusingly, with her hands on her hips.

"Uh—"

"Obviously not," Sheldon sniffed.

"Obviously, she likes me better and just doesn't want to hurt your feelings."

Keiran approached with our shoes, but they continued to bicker over me so they hadn't noticed. I eyed him for help, but he merely smirked and sat down to change out shoes. I watched him pull off his hoodie, revealing the plain grey shirt that molded to his skin and instantly salivated. No one should be that hot.

"My body's hotter. And I have better hair. Your hair is stringy."

"Stringy? You mean like your dick?"

"You weren't saying that last night when you came all over it."

That was my cue to leave.

I walked over to where Keiran was and sat next to him. "Do they always argue like that?"

"They aren't arguing. That's just what they do. When they argue, they break up."

"Just like that?"

He shrugged. "It's normal for them. They once broke up for an hour before they were back under each other."

"Some would say it's unhealthy."

"Probably. But their relationship is theirs, not someone else's."

"Is that how you feel about us?" *What are you saying, Lake? Not. A. Relationship!*

"Yes," he said without hesitation and grinned, catching my slip. "No one else's opinion will never matter to me about us. Only yours." He turned his head to stare at me until I nodded my understanding and then began setting up the game.

I looked over at Keenan and Sheldon, who were for sure making out now. He practically had her laid across the tabletop as he groped her. I would never understand those two, but then it wasn't for me to understand.

We stood up to start playing the first round when I heard my name called.

"Lake?" I swiveled to face the sound of the familiar voice at my back.

"Hey, Willow. What are you doing here?"

"Oh, uh—" she gestured to a guy with dull brown hair and square-framed glasses standing behind her. He was of average height and wearing khaki pants with a dark brown collared shirt. He was cute but shockingly plain and so not Willow.

"Hi, I'm Thomas." He moved forward to shake my hand, but when I reached out to grab his, I was moved away. Keiran placed me behind him with a scowl on his face before I could shake his hand. I glared at his back and then peeked around him to mouth sorry to Willow and her date.

"Who's the square?" I heard Keenan ask as he released Sheldon and moved forward. He blatantly looked the guy up and down challengingly with a sneer on his face.

"Really, Wills? You couldn't do better?" he directed at Willow.

"It's not your business, Keenan."

"You're right. You're Dash's business. I'll let him handle that." He nodded once and stepped back to perch himself on a nearby table. Everyone turned their focus back on Willow and Thomas. However, I watched Keenan pull out his cellphone. I immediately became suspicious at the sneaky look on his face.

"Hi, Thomas. I'm Sheldon. Do you—"

"Don't get that ass spanked, babe," Keenan warned, never taking his eyes off his phone. His fingers moved over his keyboard swiftly. When he finished, he pocketed his phone and made eye contact with Keiran and nodded. Keiran nodded back and ended their silent communication.

They were up to something.

It became really awkward, the air filling with tension since the guys wouldn't let us speak to Thomas, and they continued to glare at him. She finally pulled him away with a promise to talk to Sheldon and me later.

"Don't go too far, Wills. I have something on the way for you," Keenan called. I saw Willow's back stiffen as she continued to walk away. There was a gleam in Keiran and Keenan's eyes.

I poked Keiran in the back, and he finally pulled me back around in front of him. "What was that?" I demanded while sending Keenan a displeased look.

"You got the first roll," he said, gesturing toward the lane and ignoring my question. I was pretty sure there was steam coming from my ears as I walked to the lane. I took one last look at Willow, who was at the counter getting shoes with Thomas before picking up a ball.

Two strikes later, I was admitting that I sucked at bowling, but didn't have time to pout about it because in came a pissed off Dash. Right now, he was a far cry from the easygoing playboy who could charm the panties off any girl he chose.

He headed straight for Willow where she was two lanes away looking bored. Willow had yet to see him when he came up behind her. He snatched Thomas's arm from her shoulder before gripping the back of her neck, picking up her purse and shoes, and guiding her toward the door.

He gave a brief nod to Keiran and Keenan as he passed us with Willow, who never said a word. She was either in shock or just happy to be ending her date. Just like that, he was out the door with her. It ended as fast as it had begun.

I turned accusing eyes on the culprits who shrugged and feigned innocent looks. I wasn't buying it. They called him here. I looked over two lanes at Thomas, who was red-faced and confused. *Poor guy.* He seemed nice enough, but he unknowingly entered a battle he had no hope of winning. Ever.

"Are you going to let me call her?"

"Why?" He picked up his ball for his turn.

"To make sure she's okay?" Guys could be so dense.

"She's okay."

"You don't know that."

"I know Dash."

"And I know Willow." I held out my hand, indicating that I wanted my phone. He held my gaze and reached into his pocket.

"You're a handful, you know that?"

"So they keep telling me." I turned away and immediately dialed Willow. I had to phone her twice before she answered.

"Aren't you on a date?" I heard Dash's smooth voice filter through the line.

"Why are you answering her phone? Put her on."

"No." That was all I heard before the line went dead. I looked over at Keiran, who was trying his best not to look amused.

"Satisfied?" he asked with a smirk. I made a face and pocketed my phone.

"Whatever. Is it my turn? Where did Keenan and Sheldon go anyway?" I was more than annoyed and didn't do anything to hide it.

He shrugged and picked up my ball then handed it to me. "You suck at this."

"Thanks. I hadn't noticed," I quipped.

He ignored my sarcasm and wrapped his arms around me, duck walking us to the lane. "You got a good ball, but you need to adjust your stance. Your legs are spread too wide." He kicked my left foot forward slightly and adjusted my stance.

"Now, when you aim, aim for the right since you are right handed. You're aiming for the middle, which is causing a split when you actually do hit the pins. It makes it hard to get the rest. I want you to release the ball in front of you. Don't swing back so much because, if you hurt yourself, and hit those pretty, long legs and can't wrap them around me, I'll be mad as fuck at you. Bend at the knees, not at your back. The only thing allowed to break your back is me, and I promise you will love it, but this way, not so much. Pay attention to your aim. You're not aiming at the pins. You're aiming at the arrow you want the ball to follow. The pins just happen to be in the way."

I'll be honest here. I wasn't sure if we were talking about bowling or sex. Maybe Sheldon was right, and I am dick dizzy.

"Let's see you try." *Oh, bowling. Right.*

I tried to remember what he had said once he released me, and his scent wasn't driving me nuts. I kept my stance like he told me and aimed for the arrows and released. The ball smoothly rolled forward and hit the pins.

All except one fell, but I released a victory shout, which was probably more like a screech. I turned around and jumped on Keiran wrapping my legs around his waist and kissing him. When I finally came up for air, I looked down at him.

"Good job. Let's see if we can get a strike."

"Or you can take me home now and do what you promised..."

* * *

SHELDON TOLD HER parents she would be sleeping over with a friend, so we headed straight to Keiran and Keenan's house. I didn't know how comfortable I was yet sleeping over at Keiran's house, but he didn't give me much choice after I gave him the green light to take me home.

Thinking about how Keiran hunted down Sheldon and Keenan from their dark corner and practically threw our shoes at the poor cashier before hauling ass out of the alley brought a smile to my face.

We entered the house, and I noticed once again that their uncle wasn't home. I tried not to judge, thinking about how often Aunt Carissa was on the road because of her career. I didn't know their story, so it wasn't my place to form an opinion.

Keiran seemed indifferent to his uncle's absence, but I noticed how Keenan would discreetly look around before disappointment shadowed his features. He never let it show for long, though. As quickly as it would come, it was gone again.

I knew how it felt to wonder if your parents loved you or not. At least he knew where his was... and he knew they were alive and hadn't abandoned him. I shook off the thought and turned to Keiran, who was watching me.

"What are you thinking about?"

"Why do you always want to know what I'm thinking?"

"Because you're still hiding."

Was that what I was doing? A part of me still believed this was a cruel joke and he still hated me. Ten years of fear doesn't just fade away, does it?

"So are you." It was the only thing I could think of to take the heat off me.

"Maybe. But not because I don't trust you." His tone was accusatory. "But because I think it will keep you safe."

"From what?"

"Me." His expression was pained. I definitely needed answers.

"Did I ask you to protect me?"

"It kind of comes with the package." His lips curled in a sneer, and I could tell he was pissed.

"Well, I did pretty well when you were the threat. Maybe you still are..."

"You'll find out if I'm still a threat as soon as you get your ass in my bed."

"Is that all you care about?" I asked, feigning anger.

"At the moment."

"You can be such an asshole." I moved to sit on the couch and got comfortable. I wanted to remain in the living room for as long as possible to keep us on equal grounds. As soon as he would get me into his bedroom, I knew all bets would be off.

"What the fuck do you want from me, Lake? I'm trying."

"I never asked you to!" I screamed the words before I could catch them. When had we started to argue?

"And I'll never give you a choice!" he roared back. He was standing on the other side of the room, but I felt his anger as if he were standing right in front of me. "You keep fighting this. Fighting me. Why?"

His voice was guttural and pained. I wanted nothing more than to give him what he wanted, but I couldn't. I was still holding on.

"Because I don't believe in happily-ever-after, Keiran. You took that away from me a long time ago. How am I supposed to forgive you if I don't even know *why*?" My voice broke at the last.

I lifted my head and saw him turn away from me to face the wall. His hands gripped the built-in bookcase as his back tightened with tension.

"Keiran, please—"

"I went to the court to play basketball, just like every day. I didn't intend to like the game. I just wanted to embrace the one thing I was good at besides what I was taught to do. I would even sneak out in the middle of the night to play so I wouldn't have to sleep. John finally caught me one night, so he put up the hoop in the back. It didn't stop me from leaving though because I wasn't willing to accept anything from him. I didn't want to have to say thank you because what the hell would I have to be thankful for? Eventually, the nightmares stopped, and I could sleep again... until you came along."

He gripped the mantle once more before letting go to face me. His eyes were burning bright with silent fury.

"You looked so innocent that day. So sweet and nurtured like you never had a bad day or did a bad thing. You reminded me of everything I was and what I wasn't. That night, I had nightmares again for the first time in weeks. But this time was different. It was you in my nightmare now, not *her or any of them*. I told myself that none of it was real anymore and that I wouldn't hurt you or anyone. I didn't want to be a bad person." He released a dry laugh and rubbed the back of his neck. "I knew then that she got to me."

I desperately wanted to ask about this mystery 'her.' Had she been a girl or a woman?

"I wasn't prepared to see you again. I thought—I hoped maybe you were just passing through, but then I saw you again on the playground. You were going to save Buddy when no one else would. Not even his sister would try." He swallowed hard and took a deep breath, averting his eyes.

"There is nothing more in this world I hate than heroes..." his gaze caught mine once more as he said, "not even you."

"Is that why you pushed me?"

"When I tried to stop, and you wouldn't listen, I wanted to punish you. After I pushed you, I realized I could hurt you and that I would never be good, and I hated you for it. I didn't expect you to stay. I thought again you would go away, but you never did, and I was stuck with the constant reminder of who I was every time I saw you. No one could make me feel that way but you so I tried to break you. I guess it backfired because, as we grew older, I began to want something different from you, and suddenly, making you cry wasn't nearly enough. I knew I couldn't have you because you weren't meant for someone like me, and it pissed me off."

My mind raced with questions. I didn't know whether to be mad at him or sad for him. No child should have those types of thoughts or think of themselves that way, especially at that age when your childhood is crucial to your future as an adult.

"Say something," he demanded.

"Who was she?"

'What?" His eyes shifted away, and his face paled.

"You said you had nightmares again but about me and not her. Who was she?"

He took a deep breath and ran his hand down his face. "She was someone who didn't deserve what happened to her."

"Was?"

"She's dead."

"The girl in the picture," I said. He nodded as I stood up and walked over to him, but he took a step back, retreating from me until his back hit the book-case. I took his face into my hands and kissed his lips softly before gazing into his eyes. I saw heat and emotion flash in his eyes and felt his body shift toward me.

*That's good, baby. Stay with me.*

I wanted to ask him about his nightmares but decided against it. I didn't want to risk it. His moods shifted around like a ticking clock—except no one knew what would come next.

"When did you first see me?"

"At Pies, Shakes, and Things, two days before the playground. I was riding by on my bike and saw you on the other side of the sidewalk with your Aunt. It was your voice that caught my attention. You were singing along to Sweetest Thing by U2. I sat there on my bike and listened to you try to hit every high note. It was the first time I could remember smiling ever. I didn't see you for long because you went into the shop. I wanted to follow you in. I almost did."

I remembered that day clearer than I'd remembered any day. I was feeling sad over being separated from my parents for the first time, so my aunt took us out to get ice cream to cheer me up. I heard the song come over the radio when we arrived. It had been my favorite song, so my aunt turned up the radio, and I hopped out of the car to dance along to the song. I was so caught up in forgetting I was sad I hadn't realized I was being watched.

"What was her name?" I asked. He swallowed hard and shook his head, but I gripped his face tighter. "It's okay, Keiran. Tell me. Please, I need to know."

"Why?" His voice was laced with emotion.

"Because she's the real reason you hate me, isn't

she?" He stared into my eyes for so long I thought he wouldn't answer.

"Yes."

"You don't have to tell me why, at least not now. Just tell me her na—"

"Lily," he blurted out before I could finish.

"Lily," I repeated, testing her name on my lips. Strangely, I felt a connection to her. Maybe it was because she was the bond that tied Keiran and me together.

"I can't talk about her, Lake." Keiran pleaded with me through his eyes. I kissed his lips softly which seemed to relax him and tried an easier question

"Earlier, you said you made sure I wasn't asked out by anyone. Why?" His eyes darkened with obsession, and then his hands were on my hips, yanking me into him.

"I'm not a good guy so I didn't mind being selfish. If I can't have you, no one will."

"You mean would?"

"No, I mean will."

"You can't decide that for me." He shrugged and shot me a look that said, "*Wanna bet?*"

"I already did. It wasn't just guys anyway. I didn't want anyone near you. Sometimes, it felt like I was trying to protect you. Or rather who you are. Ironic, isn't it? I wanted to protect the very thing I hated," he said bitterly.

"I had Willow," I argued.

"She wasn't a threat. To be honest, she is much like you are but weird."

"Willow isn't weird. She's special."

"That's the same as saying she is weird."

"It is not."

"Okay," he smirked.

"If you felt that strongly about me, what will you do when school is over? We all go our separate ways once we graduate. Some people never see each other again."

"Do you really believe that?" He shook his head and continued on instead of waiting for my answer. "I don't think you will go far."

"Why?"

"I won't let you. I know that now."

"That doesn't make sense."

"It isn't meant to make sense, Lake. It just is."

"You realize what you are saying isn't normal?"

"It's how I feel. Fuck normal."

"Keiran, you—"

"Enough questions. Let's go." Without warning, he grabbed my neck and began walking me backward to the stairs.

"I'm not done!"

"I don't care. I need to be inside of you now" he whispered. I relaxed against his hold and let him cart me off upstairs. We reached the landing, and I could swear I heard moaning and a distinct thumping sound coming from Keenan's bedroom across the hall.

Just as Keiran opened his bedroom door, Sheldon's voice shrieked out, "Quit playing Marco Polo with my ass, Christopher Columbus. This isn't an exploration, so you aren't putting your ding dong in this donut hole!"

I was laughing hysterically as Keiran forced me into his bedroom and shut the door.

\* \* \*

WHEN KEIRAN FINALLY released me, I backed toward the bed but stopped when he didn't follow. He remained by the door wearing an uncomfortable expression. I stood there, motionless as I watched him watch me. He didn't pounce on me as I expected. His demeanor was different from all the other times we'd had sex. The angry lust that was normally present in his eyes was missing. I moved toward him, thinking he was playing another one of his mind games and wanted me to make the first move. During the weeks when he had made me his personal sex slave, Keiran would often fuck my mind harder than he fucked my body.

"Lake?" he asked, stopping me in my tracks.

"Yes, Keiran?"

"I want," he swallowed deeply as a look of uncertainty passed over his eyes, and I realized this was what Keiran looked like vulnerable. "I can't explain what I want to do with you right now, but will you just... let me?"

I didn't answer immediately. In just a few words, he managed to make me feel like a virgin all over again, and not the girl who secretly craved his hard, rough, angry sex and mind games. This could very well be another mind game... in fact, I knew it was, but I didn't seem to care. I also didn't realize I was nodding my head until he pushed off the door and stalked toward me. The look is his eyes although softer, still made me feel very much like the prey he'd always made me feel.

When he finally reached me, he wrapped his arms around me and pulled me close. "Fuck," he groaned and unexpectedly wrapped his hand around my neck again, nipping my cheek and then throat. "Are you going to make me explain myself?" he asked gruffly.

I wrapped my arms around his neck and stood up on the tips of my toes to reach his lips. "No. Whatever it is, I... I want it." I shouldn't have wanted it, but I did, and somehow, I knew his behavior was because of what had happened downstairs. Did I push him too far?

He undressed me slowly and then laid me down on his bed before undressing himself. All the while, he kept his eyes on me as he stared at my body hungrily. When he was fully naked, he stood above me, stroking his cock, preparing it for whatever punishment he needed to inflict on me. "I don't know where to start first," he said and bit his lip. His eyes lowered, and I couldn't help but admire how sexy he looked.

"You can start by kissing me," I whispered nervously. "I always love that." With a smirk, he leaned down to kiss my lips. It quickly turned into a kissing frenzy as we devoured each other's mouths. When the need became too strong, I started to pull on his body. I needed to feel his hard body molding to mine and to feel his weight on me. There was something highly erotic about that to me.

"You're so fucking sweet," he groaned. Being who he was, I didn't know whether to take that as I compliment or not. His hand trailed my leg and around my thigh inching up where I needed him most. "But you taste so much sweeter here," he whispered, slowly slipping two fingers inside of me. I whimpered against his mouth and lifted my hips into his plunging fingers. He crooked his fingers and increased the pressure while keeping his rhythm until I came around his thick fingers, soaking the bed beneath me. "Turn around," he demanded before I could catch my breath.

I was taken aback by the strong tone of his voice and didn't immediately obey. I searched his eyes, now burning with intensity, with the need to give in to his urges. There was none of the cold distance I was used to in his eyes, so I turned around despite my nervousness and settled myself on my knees. I braced myself for the hard thrust of his cock, but it never came. Instead, I felt him plant soft kisses across the back of my thighs and his hands rubbing my bottom with soothing strokes.

Just as I was on the verge of begging, his tongue

swept across my swollen lips, and I let out a small cry as my pussy welcomed the pleasure his mouth created. By the time he was satisfied, I'd come twice and was left a writhing mess on his bed.

The bed dipped under his weight while I was still catching my breath. He turned me until I was settled on my side and then spooned me from behind and wrapped his arm around my waist. "Keiran?" I turned my head around to face him wondering if *he* had changed his mind.

"Lift your leg for me."

I did what he asked without a second thought. The look in his eyes told me he still wanted me. He pulled me closer to him until every inch of our skin was touching. We'd never been this intimate before. He'd always held some part of himself away from me whenever he took me, but now I felt surrounded by him.

He brought his top leg in between mine and began entering me slowly. The sensation alone stirred my need to come, and when he gritted his teeth, I knew he felt the same. It felt like forever had come and gone when he was finally fully seated inside me. He rested his head on top of mine and took a deep, shuddering breath.

"This is killing me," he groaned. He lifted his head and peered into my eyes. He was so close I could see the sweat on his brow. I shifted a little to see more of his face, and when he groaned again, his eyes fluttered and his gaze lost focus. "Don't—ah shit, don't –," he grunted as my walls clenched and pulled at his cock. I grinned up at him and portrayed innocence.

"Don't do what?" I asked sweetly. A part of me wanted him to lose control and take me harder than he'd ever taken me before.

He narrowed his eyes at me and then flexed his

hips once, driving his cock hard into me where he breached my cervix. I released a sharp cry and whimpered against his lips. "That was your only warning," he gritted before kissing me softly.

He thrust into me again, but this time, he was surprisingly gentle as he continued to rock against me. The new position let me feel him in places I'd never felt him before, so when he rolled me onto my back and reentered me swiftly, I almost protested, but the sheer wonder in his eyes as he gazed down at me stopped me.

The raw emotion in his eyes overwhelmed my own. I gripped his hair in my hands feeling the dark, silky strands slip through them and bit his lip. His lips parted, and he deepened his strokes, moving us further up the mattress. *He was letting go.*

"Keiran?" I shuddered out.

"Yeah, baby?"

"I love the way you make love... but I *need* the way you *fuck* me." His body stiffened, and his eyes hardened when I said *make love,* but I didn't get the chance to take it back or realize my mistake. He spit out a harsh curse, sat up on his haunches and yanked my hips off the bed leaving my lower half suspended in the air as he delivered short, brutal strokes that left me gasping for breath and clawing at the sheets.

"Keiran, wait," I whimpered.

"Shut up." His hand closed around my throat, squeezing and cutting off my air supply. The panic and the feeling of him moving inside me was a dangerous combination, and after the fifth or sixth drive of his cock, I came on a piercing scream. He watched me come, seemingly mesmerized while keeping a hard rhythm inside my trembling body.

"There is nothing sexier than watching you come around my cock," he growled and then tossed his head back. I felt his fingers digging into my hips and saw the veins in his neck stretch and knew he was coming.

We each then lay in silence, trying to catch our breaths and our thoughts. I wanted to run and hide, but that would be admitting my feelings for him.

"I should take you home," he said absently.

*Too late, you dumb twat... you already did.*

# CHAPTER TWENTY-THREE

EVER HEARD OF the walk of shame? It's when a one-night stand has to endure embarrassment after getting fucked, literally and figuratively. Despite what people may think, I have some respect for myself. It's ironic really because after a knockdown, drag-out fight, I stayed. Why? Because he didn't get to sex me the way he did and then kick me out. But I had been too busy celebrating my victory to realize I may have won the battle but not the war... Well, the war was multiple orgasms.

Since I stayed, Keiran didn't leave me alone the entire night. In the middle of our fight, he shoved me onto his naked lap and made me ride him until I was spent and even then, continued to take me throughout the night. I knew he regretted our one true spark of intimacy so he tried erasing it by being the same cold bastard he'd always been.

In the morning, he'd barely spoken two words to me except to tell me he was taking me home to shower and change clothes for school. "Can I make you breakfast?" I heard Keiran ask behind me when we walked into my house.

I turned wide eyes on him. "You want to make me breakfast?"

He shrugged before shedding his black, leather bomber jacket. "It's the least I could do after last night."

I paused in surprise. "Are you apologizing?"

"No." He turned away, quickly disappearing into the kitchen. I walked upstairs to shower, and when I looked in the mirror, I immediately noticed the numerous large, red hickeys and bite marks all over my neck and trailing beneath my shirt to my breasts.

I panicked, wondering how I could cover them up. I hurried to text Sheldon and Willow, who both told me to use makeup and assured me it would be gone in a couple of days. I stepped into the shower and ran the shower gel over my aching muscles, hoping to soothe them. To say Keiran worked me over was an understatement.

After showering, I quickly blow dried my hair and then unceremoniously threw on jeans and a button up and left my hair to hang in soft waves down my back and finger-combed my overlong bangs, also making a mental note to have it recut.

The smell of food greeted me as I made my way downstairs. *He really did make breakfast.* I found Keiran in the kitchen spooning our food onto plates. I guess my stomach liked what it saw when it growled... loudly. *Way to go, you. Very sexy.*

He grinned at me and pushed my plate toward me. "Help yourself," he stated, deepening my embarrassment.

"Don't mind if I do," I admitted grudgingly.

I picked up a fork and began digging into the delicious looking eggs when his phone rang, and he left the kitchen to take the phone call. I was a little glad he did because my table manners are atrocious when I was hungry. I finished my food and considered seconds, but he hadn't come back yet to eat. I mean, it would probably be absolutely shitty of me to eat his food and mine. I canned the idea but then thought about how he tried to kick me out of his house. *Maybe not.*

I devoured his food, and when he still hadn't returned, curiosity took over, so I hopped off the bar stool to search for him. He wasn't anywhere downstairs, so I headed upstairs next and heard his low voice drifting from my bedroom. Lucky for me the door was cracked, so I peeked.

He was standing by my desk holding a picture of me that was taken last year while he was in juvie. Willow and Aunt Carissa had convinced me to take an extremely long road trip to the beach when I started to become depressed for some unknown reason. Aunt Carissa had taken the picture of me standing barefoot in the water, wearing the first smile I'd had in a long time. He was staring down hard at the picture with a tight grip on the frame as he spoke on the phone.

"No, I want you to keep a tail on her. Find out why she lied." His voice was menacing, and I felt sorry for whoever it was he was referring to. "Oh, and tell your boss he'll be receiving a new package soon and to do as he pleases."

He dismissed the caller, and I panicked, thinking I would be caught, but he continued to stare down at my photo intensely. I took a deep breath and headed back downstairs as quietly as I could before I was caught. I didn't have time to think about all that I heard before he was back in the kitchen. He had looked around for his plate of food before he raised his eyebrow at me. I merely shrugged and took the plates to the sink. When my back was turned, I found the courage to ask the question that had been on my mind since the game.

"Keiran?"

"Yeah?" I could feel his eyes watching me, amping up my nervousness.

"What are you going to do about Trevor and Anya now that you know they set you up?"

"You didn't get enough information eavesdropping at the door?"

Busted.

"I, uh..."

"Don't do it again," he ordered with a flat tone. I spun around, holding a soapy dish in my hand and felt the urge to hurl it at his head.

"Why can't you tell me, and who were you talking to on the phone?"

"Why do you need to know?" he asked with heavy disinterest.

"Because he tried to rape me in a locker room or because he framed me, too. I'll let you pick." Sarcasm was laced throughout my voice and hard to miss.

His eyes narrowed menacingly, but I didn't flinch away. *I was getting good at that.* Instead, I held his stare until he rolled his eyes and pushed me out of the way to take over washing the dishes.

"Keiran, I need to know. I—"

"I'm well aware of what he did to you and what he tried to do to you," he said, emotionlessly, as he made meticulous circles on the plate. He rinsed off the dish and moved on to the other.

"You don't care, do you?" I fought back the misplaced hurt I felt and grabbed onto the counter for strength to hold in my emotions. He continued to wash the dishes with a shrug of his shoulders.

"Caring doesn't make a difference. It just gets people killed."

"Maybe you're just incapable of feeling anything."

"I feel many things—anger, hatred, pain, lust. I don't need to feel anything else."

"What about love, compassion, and happiness?" He finally looked at me and smirked as if he was amused by my question. "I don't believe in it."

"Then I feel sorry for you."

"I'll live. Those emotions you carry on your sleeve are what makes you weak... but you also feel anger and hatred too, don't you?"

"Who exactly would I have to hate?"

"Your parents. You think they abandoned you and left you here to suffer. You think if they weren't gone, then the past ten years wouldn't have happened. You hate your aunt, too. If she hadn't taken you in, if she didn't love you, then you wouldn't be here. You don't believe in love—you are a hypocrite."

"Get out," I barked. He leaned against the sink, crossed his legs, and continued to watch me with a knowing look in his eyes and his ever-present smirk. Anger like I'd never felt before passed over me so I grabbed the motherfucker by the horns and held on.

A knife was in my hands with no recollection of how it got there. I charged toward him, ready to hurt him just as he'd hurt me. When I was close enough, I raised my arm higher. His foot shot out, kicking my feet from under me, and I was falling, the knife snatched out of my hands. He was on me before I could move. He spread my legs open as he pressed the knife against my throat.

"You want to hurt me?" he said, unbuttoning my jeans and shoving them down my legs. "You wouldn't even know where to begin because first I'd have to give a fuck," he growled. His fist was in my hair as he pulled my head back and thrust savagely into me. My screams were just as wild and wanton as I pushed my hips back to take more of him. He pressed the knife deeper against my throat and leaned down to whisper in my ear, "I should kill you right now and put you out of the fucking misery you claim to live in every day, but I can't let you go. Fuck me, I can't let you go," he repeated with a single hard thrust and then he was coming, spilling his seed into my unprotected body.

\* \* \*

"HEY, THE FAIR tonight. Are we going?" Sheldon drawled as she appeared, leaning against the lockers with a leg propped up behind her. I'd been distracted by the many thoughts racing through my head.

"Uh, I'm not sure..."

"Come on, Lake. This is my only night off this week!" Willow exclaimed as she walked into our conversation. She never could resist the Ferris wheel. "Besides, you owe me a prize," she pouted.

"All right, all right. Don't lose your panties," I snapped. Willow looked at me in shock, mirroring my own surprise. I never talked to Willow like that. I mumbled a quick sorry and opened my locker to store my books for lunch, but it was slammed back by a small hand with red fingertips.

"I don't know what you told my man, but you better stay away from him or you'll be sorry. Keiran is mine."

"Funny, I've heard that before." I mentally gagged at the stench of pure evil coming from the she-witch named Anya. "You better move that hand," I warned. I was still angry from this morning and the disaster that happened after the argument. To say I was scared shitless was an understatement, and it wasn't because he threatened to kill me with a knife digging into my throat.

"Or what, loser? You need to stop whoring—"

She didn't get to finish her statement because she was eating metal. I subdued her with a strong hand against her skull, pushing her face into the locker. I swear I could hear her teeth scraping against it. *Note to self: disinfect it later.*

A crowd quickly gathered at the chance to witness a fight.

"Listen carefully, please. I don't want to have to re-peat myself. Keiran... isn't... yours. He never was. So back off. And I would be *very* careful in the near future. I won't be so forgiving. M'kay, pumpkin?" I smiled evil-ly at the back of her head. I realized it was totally out of character at the moment, but I didn't care. I needed an outlet, and Anya elected herself as a tribute.

When she nodded, I let the pressure off the back of her head and patted her once. "Atta girl. Now, get." She flounced off in her high heels. *Seriously, what was with the pumps in high school?*

"I am so hot for you right now," Willow dead-panned.

"Raaawr! Who knew goody two-shoes had it in her?" Sheldon included.

"What the fuck was that?" I heard a voice growl. The crowd had nearly doubled, so I hadn't realized one of the spectators was Keiran.

"I don't know. What did it look like?" I thought at any moment his face would crack under the pressure he was placing on his jawbone.

"Tell me," he demanded.

I sighed in exasperation and turned back to face my locker. I pulled out one of the sanitary wipes I kept on hand and wiped the front of my locker.

"Lake," he called warningly.

"I was keeping your ex-cum buckets in line since you seem to be incapable."

"Ooohh! Burn! Damn!" A volley of jeers sounded from the crowd.

"Leave," he commanded, and when the other kids scurried, he turned his attention back to me. "You want to explain what your problem is?"

"Is that a serious question?" Maybe it had something to do with the fact that he might have impregnated me while he threatened to slice my throat open, but I could be wrong. I couldn't tell him that anyway. Not with Willow and Sheldon watching us closely. We'd always been careful before, but I admitted I was just as mad at myself for giving into him once again.

"I'll see you later," he stated simply, but it sounded threatening at the same time. With that, he turned on his heel and walked away. It didn't have to be said. I knew I messed up, but if he could do what he wanted, then so could I.

"He looked pissed," Willow commented. "What is up with them anyway? They are so hypocritical and bossy. It's always *'do what I say', 'now,' 'no,' 'mine.' 'Me Tarzan, you Jane. Now bend over!'*"

"Don't forget the grunting and growling," Sheldon added.

"I keep expecting to be dragged off to a cave or something."

We shared a long laugh over the guys' expense but were interrupted by a throat clearing. We whipped around at the same time to find Dash and Keenan leaning against the lockers watching us and looking irate. I guess they'd heard what we had said. *Oops.*

"Oh, shit, um... I love you, honey bun?" Sheldon jokingly attempted to soothe Keenan's feelings. He rolled his eyes and walked away in the same direction

Keiran had retreated.

Dash remained a beat, and I could see the struggle in his eyes before he mumbled, "Fuck it," and walked off after Keiran and Keenan.

Willow, Sheldon, and I were left standing alone in the empty hallway. We each shared a look before shrugging and heading to the cafeteria. Lunch was one big social gathering that I still haven't become accustomed to after many years of avoiding the area and people in general.

Willow still refused to sit at Keiran's table because of her drama with Dash, so we headed for an empty table to sit, and I automatically looked around for Keiran but didn't spot him. I was sure this was the direction he had walked in and assumed he would come here. I looked around more and didn't spot Keenan or Dash either.

"Hello, ladies and Thing." Buddy straddled a chair next to me wearing a toothy grin.

"Get lost, kid," Willow huffed.

"Since when do I do what you say?"

"Since I know where you keep the dirty magazines and stash of pornos, and I'll tell Mom and Dad."

"Ha! Who do you think I got them from? Dad needed to get rid of the evidence," he said secretly as his grin stretched wider.

"Ew."

"Indeed," he mimicked in a smarmy tone, then turned to Sheldon and me. "Hey, lover. Hey, Sheldon."

"Don't 'Hey Sheldon' me. Next time you use the bathroom, put the seat back down. I fell in and got an ass full of toilet water!" She threw a green bean at him, which he caught with his mouth.

"Don't get mad at me because you don't watch where you park your ass."

"Wait, when were you at her house and why?" Willow grilled.

"Call of Duty. Duh. What's your issue?"

"You're fraternizing with the enemy? My own brother!"

"No one told you to give it up and get the guy sprung." He had a disturbed look in his eyes as he snatched a fry out of Willow's tray.

"You don't know what you are talking about, Buddy. Don't start rumors."

"I don't have to. It's already out there. Dash put the order out that you were off limits weeks ago. The poor schmuck from the other night was the only one to try, but that was only because he's new. Don't worry. Dash already spoke with him, too." He shot Willow a devilish grin, and her face paled before turning red.

"He had no right—"

"Tell him that, Sis. I'm just an innocent bystander."

"As his twin, I can tell you Dash is up to something. He's sneaky. He may be quiet now, but I assure you he's plotting, so I hope you're ready to give in."

"That's not going to happen," Willow scoffed, but it sounded forced.

"Willow, maybe talking to him instead of ignoring will work better. Tell him how you feel," I suggested. Keiran may have been right. I was a hypocrite.

"My brother doesn't care about how Willow feels, or what she wants. He is acting on his own feelings now, and what he wants is you. Right now, he's looking for a weakness and the right moment to pounce."

"This isn't a war, Sheldon."

"No, this is a Chambers. You're screwed."

"Thanks," Willow replied dryly.

"Anytime, babe."

"That's why I stay single," Buddy included smugly.

"Because you're ugly?" Willow asked.

"Just for that, I'm inviting Dash over tonight."

"You better not!"

"Already happening," he taunted, pulling out his phone and sending a quick text.

"That's it. I've disowned you." Buddy scoffed and rolled his eyes before locking them with mine.

"So Lake, what did you do to my boy?"

"And who would that be?"

"The muffin man," he replied impatiently. "You know who."

"What's it to you?" I asked rather than answer his question.

"Because he's snapping and snarling at anyone who even walks past. He's got some serious Lake fever going on."

"What?"

"Yeah. I swear you guys are better than my stories." I shook my head at Buddy. He really did watch soap operas faithfully.

"I can handle Keiran."

"Can you?" His tone was laced with seriousness, and his eyes bore into mine with concern, the complete opposite of his normal playful self.

"Yes, Buddy. I promise." And apparently, I'm a liar too...

* * *

"I'm going to the fair tonight with Willow and Sheldon."

"Oh?"

"Yes." Silence. "So?"

"So, what?"

"Nothing." More silence. "Are you mad at me?"

"Should I be?"

"No."

"Then I guess I'm not."

I was growing sick of his short answers. Keiran had been giving me the cold shoulder since I made Anya eat my locker at school. It didn't seem like the situation with Anya was enough to walk around with a stick up the ass.

We haven't exchanged words since then.

It was after school, and we were lying in his bed, having just finished a few sweaty rounds of sex. He'd tricked me into my car by telling me he'd take me home, but I ended up here instead.

"I think you are, though." Silence again. "You won't talk to me," I tried again.

He released a breath. "You're pissing me off."

"Ditto."

"I want you to stay away from Anya," he ordered. *Bingo! We have communication!*

"Believe me, I don't approach her willingly. Besides, she started it." He stared me down until I shrunk back in my seat. "Fine," I huffed.

"What time are you going to the fair?"

"Six."

"Don't do anything stupid tonight."

"Yes, Dad."

"Lake..."

"Lighten up. You can't control me, Keiran, so stop trying."

"I can and I will," he answered unapologetically. I don't know why I bothered to tell him otherwise. Keiran would always do what he wanted, but he wasn't God, no matter how much he pretended to be.

"I won't let you."

"You can't stop me. Do you even really want to or

are you trying to save face?"

"I—I don't know." It was the truth. I really didn't know.

"Listen. Trevor may be there. Don't approach him and don't provoke him. If he gets near you, then you call me. Immediately. Do you understand?"

"Keiran, he can't come within a thousand feet of me. I will be fine."

"Do you need me to repeat myself again?"

The look in his eyes told me to drop it, which I did reluctantly. His body tensed when he mentioned Trevor, which was weird for someone who claimed not to care.

"Are we ever going to talk about it?" I looked up at him from my place on his chest, but his eyes were closed. A deep frown line marred his features.

"There's nothing to talk about."

"How can you say that?" I stared at him incredulously. "What if I get pregnant?"

Being pregnant at my age would be the biggest threat to my future but being pregnant with Keiran's baby would be the biggest threat to my sanity.

"No more questions. Get dressed," he said, lifting from the bed and displaying his nakedness shamelessly. It took everything in me not to drool watching his butt flex as he pulled on his discarded jeans.

"Why aren't you coming to the fair?"

"Not my thing."

"Oh... well..."

"What?"

How do you tell the guy who is supposed to be your enemy that you wanted to do all the corny things couples usually do like win prizes for each other and ride the Ferris wheel while holding hands without sounding like a lunatic?

I wasn't supposed to want these things with him. We were two people who hated each other and got lost in each other's bodies. He'd said he didn't hate me anymore, but I knew that wasn't true. He still carried hate in his eyes for me, but it was clouded by lust.

"Nothing," I answered dejectedly.

# CHAPTER TWENTY-FOUR

THE SOUND OF children's laughter and the smell of fried food greeted me as we entered the fair. It was a fairly warm, clear night.

We ended up arriving over an hour late because Pepé decided to hide Willow's keys keeping her from leaving. It took us a while to find them, and in the end, we brought him along with us even though I wasn't too sure pets were allowed.

"First things first. I need a smoked turkey leg and funnel cake in that order, and you bitches better get your own because I'm not sharing," Sheldon announced. The girl could really put it away.

We headed for the nearest food stand, weaving our way through the thick crowd. "So Lake, does your aunt know about Keiran?" Willow asked. I wasn't expecting her to ask me that considering she shied away from questioning our 'relationship.'

"Uh, somewhat. He came over once and met her, but she doesn't know anything. I feel guilty actually. She trusts me to keep my head, but I've been keeping secrets."

"Yeah, and so has every other teenager to ever live. She knows what it was like to be eighteen."

"Yeah, but—"

"Talk to her when she gets home. Lay it all out on the table. She still has no idea the house was broken into?" Sheldon asked.

"No. I didn't want to ruin her tour by stressing her out. I'm worried she may not trust me again."

"Disappointing parents is a part of the circle of life. You could have done much worse if you ask me."

"It's just new territory. With sex in the equation, I'm no longer sure of the rules and boundaries. The law says I'm of legal age, but the circumstances make everything skewed."

"And isn't it ironic that the very person who kept your love life non-existent now consumes it?" Willow let out a wry chuckle before purchasing a turkey leg and soda.

We grabbed our food and quickly found seats to eat. "Is Keenan talking to you yet?" I asked Sheldon.

"No. Strangely enough, I haven't heard from him this afternoon. I think he mentioned his dad coming home earlier this morning."

"What does his dad do that keeps him away all the time?"

"He does construction work for his company and takes jobs all over the country for the right price, but I think it has more to do with him *wanting* to be away. I've been with Keenan for over two years and have only seen him a handful of times. He makes sure Keiran and Keenan are taken care of but mostly, he stays away. I know it hurts Keenan, but he ignores it. I actually heard that John used to be a very outgoing man long ago, but after Keenan's mother ran off, he shut down."

"But there has to be more. Keiran doesn't care for

his uncle, and I don't think it's just because he's an absentee parent."

"You may be right, but neither of them is willing to talk. Keenan doesn't seem to know much anyway."

"But Keiran does. I know he does."

"And his parents are dead, right?" She shrugged and bit into her turkey. "You don't think so?"

"There was never any proof. They both just vanished."

"Vanished?" Willow asked. I thought about the articles Jesse found a couple of days ago. He was still searching for any trace of his father with no luck so far.

"Yeah. Keenan once told me Keiran's father was disowned by their family and had ran off years ago. He's probably never even met Keiran if his mother was a one-night stand. He's been with his uncle for years with no sign of his father."

A disturbing thought popped into my head when she'd said that last part. "Wait, so he'd just moved here when I came to Six Forks?"

"Yeah, about three or four months before, I think."

"Talk about Lifetime," Willow interjected.

"I wish I could get Keiran to tell me about his past. I feel like it has everything to do with why he's the way he is."

"You ever think he might just have a really dominant personality?" Sheldon asked.

"You mean he's an asshole?" Willow asked. "People's parents split all the time. Your parents are gone, and you're just fine."

I ignored the pain I felt at the reminder that my parents were gone, and I had no idea why. Besides... was I really okay?

"Guys, he told me he was a bad person because he did bad things. That *people* made him do bad things.

He never once mentioned his mother, but he did tell me she was a prostitute and drug addict."

"So what are you thinking?" Willow asked.

"I don't know for sure, but what if—what if he wasn't with his mother?"

"Where else would he have been?" Sheldon asked.

"Maybe her family took care of him until they couldn't anymore? People are plural. Wherever he was for eight years, his mother wasn't the only person around him, and whatever bad things they made him do had followed him. It still follows him, and I don't know what to do. I don't know how to help him."

"You mean fix him?" Sheldon asked.

"I think what you are doing is what works. He seems a lot less... broody... these days. Maybe that's enough," Willow offered.

"Besides, he may not like the idea of you trying to fix him. He could take it the wrong way."

"Guys, he told me I made him have nightmares! What am I supposed to do?" Sheldon coughed and spit out soda at my outburst.

"Wow," she stated still coughing.

"That's romantic," Willow finished sarcastically.

"Nightmares of what?" Sheldon asked once her coughing fit was over. I ran down everything he had told me the night before, and when I finished, they looked more than a little disturbed, and it wasn't even a complete story.

"Do you think Dash and Keenan know?"

"Dash, maybe. Keenan, no." Sheldon answered.

"Why Dash and not Keenan?"

"Because he has Dash's back, but he protects Keenan. Keenan looks up to him. He cares more than he lets on so he wouldn't want to taint that."

"I know what you are thinking, Lake. Dash won't

say a word, though. He's loyal to a fault," Willow stated.

"I think someone else cares more than they let on, too. You should give my brother a chance then." Sheldon smirked at Willow, who scoffed and looked away.

"Look, I came for rides and prizes. Let's go, Pepé. We got shit to do." She grabbed Pepé and stomped off with him.

"Why did you have to say that?" I fussed at Sheldon.

"What? You know it's true. They are dying for each other, and I'm sick of his ass walking around the house with pissy panties stuck up his ass."

"Let them figure it out."

"It isn't me you need to tell that to. I'm telling you—Dash won't wait forever."

"So? He'll move on."

"No, he'll force her hand. The men in my family don't play fair. Consider that a warning. Now let's go get her. I can't have my future sister-in-law mad at me."

\* \* \*

"I CAN'T EAT any more cotton candy. I'll puke," Sheldon whined.

We were on the Ferris wheel after inhaling ample amounts of cotton candy. Sheldon, of course, wanted to outdo us all and turned it into a competition.

"Eww. Puke that way," Willow fussed, her voice filled with disgust.

"Stop pushing me."

"Get away, yuck mouth."

"Ugh, tell her to stop pushing me, Lake."

"Settle down, children... Hey, slide over, will you? I'm being crushed."

"I'm going to murder you," Willow threatened Sheldon, ignoring me.

"Not if I puke on you first."

"What are you, three?"

"You're hurting my feelings."

"Toss the candy, already."

"We're on top of the wheel!"

"Maybe a kid will catch it."

"Mmm," Sheldon moaned as she took another bite. "Good cotton candy... Oh, god," she slapped a hand over her mouth. "No more."

"Sheldon!" Willow shrieked.

I tried not to listen to my two friends bicker and even harder tried not to think about pushing them both off. *That was bad, right?*

"Quit licking me!" Willow screamed.

"There was cotton candy on your face!"

Maybe not.

The ride started again, and once it stopped for us to get off, I was tempted to fall to my knees and kiss the ground. Willow had to hide Pepé in her bag so he could get on the ride with us, and she quickly took him out. He rolled his eyes at her before settling on her shoulders and looking around.

"Hey, look. Eleven o'clock."

I looked over near the stage of acrobats and saw Trevor... with Anya. Kissing. Seeing the two of them together without a care in the world made me sick, and suddenly, I wanted Keiran here with fierceness. "We need to move. I don't want him to see me."

"Too late. He's already looking at you."

Sure enough, Trevor and Anya were both regarding us with hateful looks on their faces. I sincerely hoped Trevor wasn't stupid enough to try anything. I took Sheldon and Willow's hands and hurried away in the opposite direction.

"Hey, Lake!" I heard my name called out in a gruff

voice.

"Well, no one ever accused him of being smart." Willow's voice dripped with sarcasm.

"Keep walking," I urged, rushing for the exit.

"He's mighty ballsy," Sheldon stated. She let go of my hand but kept up as I made my way to the car. A moment later, she was on the phone telling someone that he was here. I had a good idea who.

We'd just cleared the gates when Trevor grabbed my arm, yanking me away from Willow and Sheldon. "Not so fast, sweetheart. Didn't you miss me?"

"Take your hands off me."

"Why?" Anya snarled. "You think because you have Keiran, no one else is good enough for you? You couldn't even get a boyfriend before."

"Anya, please get over yourself. Keiran never wanted you. You threw yourself at him."

I almost had my arm out of his grip when he tightened it and began walking off with me in tow. "You're coming with me. There is someone who wants to meet you."

Before I could respond or scream for help, I fell to the ground. Willow had jumped on Trevor's back. She was hurling insults and pulling his hair while Sheldon hit and kicked him from every angle. Luckily, with Trevor's arm broken, he couldn't get the upper hand, or so I thought.

"Get off me, you crazy bitches!" he roared just before Willow went airborne and Sheldon hit the ground.

I saw red at seeing him manhandle my friends, and before I could rethink it, I delivered a two-piece to his face and a swift kick to his groin bringing him to his knees.

I turned to help Sheldon and Willow, who weren't moving from the ground. Pepé was sniffing at Willow's face and making small sounds for his mother.

"Lake, watch out!"

I turned in time to see Trevor lunge for me with a murderous expression, but before he could grab me, he was thrown a few feet away by Dash and grabbed up by Keenan, who delivered powerful blows to his face. They proceeded to tag team and beat the shit out of him. I winced at the beating he was taking. What surprised me most was the absence of Keiran and how they had gotten here so fast.

Sheldon was screaming for them to stop, and as much as I hated Trevor, I had to agree. They were quickly moving from assault to attempted murder if they carried on.

After a few more blows, Keenan grabbed Trevor by the arms and dragged him to Dash's waiting car and threw him inside while Dash hurried over to Willow. He gathered her up into his arms and scooped up a scared Pepé.

"Where is her car?" His voice was rough and harsh, and his face was a mask of unconfined fury. His whole body was shaking with barely controlled rage.

"Over—over there." I pointed to her purple eclipse a few aisles over with a shaking hand.

Willow seemed a little dazed from the fall, but she was conscious and didn't appear to have any injuries. He placed her in the passenger seat along with Pepé and turned to me.

"Go to her house and stay there. Keiran will come for you." He jogged back over to his car. He and Keenan hopped in and drove off... with an unconscious Trevor.

I looked around the empty parking lot and sighed in relief that no one was there to see Trevor assaulted and basically kidnapped. Then again, that could have been a bad thing. If Sheldon hadn't called her brother, who knows what Trevor would have done or where he would have taken me? What did he mean someone wanted to meet me?

I looked around again and noticed Anya was gone as well. "Where did Anya go? Did she run off?"

"Unfortunately, no. Keenan grabbed her, too."

"What!"

"Yup."

"Why?"

"I don't think I want to know."

"We can't just ignore the fact that just happened, Sheldon."

"Do you really want to go against all three of them?"

"But Keiran wasn't here."

She looked at me as if I were dense. "Where do you think they are taking them? Look, let's get Willow home and worry about that later."

I reluctantly got into the car and dropped Sheldon off before driving us over to Willow's house. Willow was silent the entire ride home, and I kept checking to make sure she was still conscious. It didn't look as if she hit her head from the fall.

"Are you okay?"

"Yeah," she croaked.

"It doesn't sound like it."

"I'm fine."

"What did Dash say to you?"

"What makes you think he said something?" she asked.

I shot her an impatient look but didn't say anything more. I knew Willow sometimes better than I knew myself and vice versa.

She released an aggravated breath before stating, "He said he would be over to deal with my stupidity later."

"He's not making this easy for you, is he?"

She snorted. "Nothing about Dash is easy. He's always so determined to have his way. He doesn't even really want me. He just thinks the world is supposed to change to fit him."

Willow sounded so sad and heartbroken, and I cursed my inexperience with boys because I had absolutely no idea what to tell her.

"So what are you going to do?"

"Wait for college to start and run away?"

"Aren't you and Dash interested in the same school?"

"No. He only went to piss his father off. He will end up at some Ivy League school. If luck is on my side, it will be on the other side of the country."

"I don't know, Willow..."

"What don't you know?"

"I don't know if it will be enough."

"It has to be."

"I don't know him very well, but I know a man slut when I see one. He seems different with you. He looks at you differently."

"Because I have meat on my skin?"

I laughed at her comment. Willow had curves but fat she was not. "No, simpleton. Because you're beautiful in a way he has never known and will never know again. Guys like him only have this opportunity once, and he is smart enough to seize it."

"Can I ask you something?" She asked.

"Sure."

"How could you forgive Keiran so easily?"

"You think I forgave him?" She shrugged, and I sighed. "I don't know what I'm doing with him. I've been hurt by him, Willow. I was hurt too many times, and I still feel something for him, and it confuses me."

"You're still afraid of him," she stated.

I nodded and felt a pang of guilt admitting it. In truth, I was his proverbial punching bag. He took the frustration of his past out on me, and I was afraid that any moment he could slip back because no one knew just how buried his past really was but him. I knew I couldn't survive that again after knowing him so intimately. There was more between us than attraction, but I wasn't brave enough to say it out loud.

"You're right, Lake. Something is haunting him. It's there in his eyes. Guilt. Shame. Anger. It's all there. I don't want you to get hurt."

"I don't know what else to do, Willow."

"You survive, Lake. That's all you can do. If he loves you, he will do what it takes to make sure you do."

\* \* \*

*IF HE LOVES you...* She'd said love. I was sure she had. I was numbed into silence and haven't spoken a word since Willow's last statement. She took my silence as an opportunity to retreat back into her own thoughts.

Keiran and I had never discussed love. I was still coming to terms with the fact we had even had sex with each other. There wasn't any space for love, was there? Our relationship was on shaky ground already without adding love into the equation.

I couldn't help but think of what it could be like to have someone as sinful and dangerous as Keiran love me. The powerful feeling that swept through my body made me shiver with delight.

*Oh, God.*

I shook off the feeling and checked the time. It was after ten and getting later. Willow's parents had taken a trip for their honeymoon. Willow said it took them forever to save for it. I knew they wouldn't mind me being here so late since I had slept over many times. Buddy was nowhere to be found as usual on a Friday night so we were there alone. I was beyond tired, but I knew what I was waiting for. Dash had told me Keiran would come for me. Two hours passed, but he still hadn't arrived.

I briefly wondered what they had done with Trevor and Anya. Trevor was dangerous, but Anya was little more than a simple bitch. She didn't have the mental capacity to be anything more. *Maybe that was a little harsh.*

I got comfortable on the couch, prepared to fall asleep. Willow had long turned on a movie, but her attention was currently directed at the ceiling as she glared at the smooth cream surface above. I really wished I could help her overcome this love triangle between her, Dash, and her mom's past. I checked my cell phone once more before giving in to sleep and dozing off.

The doorbell woke me some time later, and a quick check of the time told me it was just after midnight. I had a good idea of who might be on the other side of the door. Willow began stirring from her place on the couch with a grumble. I hated being around Willow when she first awakens. That girl was a straight up grouch when sleepy.

"Who is it?" she asked with her eyes still closed.

"I don't know. It's your door." The doorbell rang again at the same time Willow's cell began ringing. She picked it up and answered without looking. "Hell— What are you doing here? I am not answering the door. I don't care. No! Do you know how late it is? Go away!"

Willow was fully awake now and pacing the living

room floor as she argued with the person on the other end of the line. I got up to peek out the window and saw Dash and Keiran standing on the porch.

Keiran was leaning against the pillar, dressed in a black, long-sleeve Henley and black jeans that hung low on his hips. His arms were bulging as they rested against his chest, crossed. His stance was casual, but his face was hard.

His head slowly turned to the window, and his eyes connected with mine, holding my gaze. "Open the door," he mouthed.

I bit my lip and moved away from the window, not knowing what to do. I knew Keiran would be mad about what happened at the fair, but that didn't make the reality any less intimidating.

"Willow, we have to open the door," I whispered to her across the room.

"No, we don't. They will go away."

"And when they catch us later?"

We had a stare down, and Dash proceeded to pound on the door. Any minute now, the neighbors would wake up and maybe call the police. The last thing I needed was for Keiran to think I called the police on him... again.

"Fuck! Fine."

She moved to unlock the door and as soon as the lock was switched, the door flew open letting in an enraged Dash. Willow backed away before turning to flee up the stairs with Dash hot on her heels. I heard a door slam, then a squeal and a second door slam. I instantly regretted making Willow open the door and moved to help her.

"I wouldn't worry about what he is going to do to her. I would worry about what I am going to do to you."

I stood with my back facing him, listening to the furious pounding of my heart. He was so still and quiet behind me, and it made my nervousness increase.

"Come here."

"Keiran," I cried still facing away from him.

"Don't!" he yelled. "Don't fucking do that. Come here," he ordered slowly. "Don't make me come get you."

I slowly turned, my mind racing for a way to placate him. My heart skipped a beat at the sight of Keiran without a door separating us.

"Why are you here?" I asked, stalling for time.

"Time's up," he stated, moving for me.

Before I could react, he hoisted me over his shoulder and carted me out the door. I watched his ass flex the entire way to Dash's car, which, unfortunately, was a short distance away. He drove off, and we were parked in my driveway minutes later.

He came around to open my door and held out his hand to me. The gesture said more than what the eye could see. He could have easily had lifted me out of the car without me being able to do anything to stop him, but instead, he was asking for my consent. To accept what was about to happen.

I did what any girl would do when faced with a seriously hot male that wanted her. I took his hand. He led me to the door, took my keys, unlocking it.

Here goes everything.

"Tell me what happened before Dash and Keenan got there."

We were sitting in the kitchen while he checked over my body. I wasn't expecting this once we had walked through the door. I was able to relax but not much.

"Not much. We spotted Trevor and Anya inside together." I paused and looked for a reaction, but there wasn't even a flicker, so I continued on. "He spotted us, and I left the area and even the fairgrounds, but he followed us out to the parking lot and grabbed me."

There it was. He reacted to my last statement. Anger flashed in his eyes and his fists balled. I pretended I didn't see and told him the rest of what had happened. His expression was murderous by the time I finished.

"What do you think he meant by someone wanted to meet me?" I still couldn't believe Trevor had stooped to kidnapping.

"Doesn't matter. It will never happen."

*Wait. What?* "You know who he was talking about? Who could Trevor and I have in common?"

"It's not someone you have in common. It's someone I have in common."

"I don't understand…"

"You don't need to. I'll handle it."

"The hell I don't. He was going to kidnap me, Keiran, or don't you get that?" My voice level rose with my frustration.

"Leave it alone."

"No," I stated, crossing my arms.

"No?" His eyes were nearly black now, and that rebellious vein near his temple was throbbing.

"I'm going to find out what you are hiding, Keiran. I deserve to know. Your past is the reason why you screwed up mine, and I want to know why. I want to know all of it. Not the half-truths you gave me."

"Do I ask you about your parents, Lake?" he yelled. The vibration of his voice shook me as it thundered through the kitchen.

"It's your parents?" I asked surprised. I could see the moment of realization as it dawned on him. He cursed and stormed out of the kitchen, his footsteps pounding the floor until the front door slammed.

I hopped off the counter top and raced to the door. I didn't know if I wanted to stop him or make sure he was gone. I opened the door just as Dash's car raced down the street, recklessly. I stared at the receding tail-lights until they disappeared around the corner.

Way to go, Lake. You pissed him off and still don't have any answers.

Once his car had disappeared, I noticed a dark car with the headlights turned off sitting across the street. It pulled off in the direction Keiran had just gone, and I frowned. I closed the door against the cold air and made sure to lock it before rushing for my cell phone in my jacket. I tried Keiran's phone multiple times before giving up and heading for my own car.

I didn't have a clue as to where he might go besides home so I headed over there. I continued to call him and cursed when I realized I didn't have Keenan's number, so I tried Sheldon.

"Hello," she mumbled sleepily on the third ring.

"Hey, is Keenan with you? It's important."

"Sure. Hold on." I heard shifting and muffled voices before Keenan's voice came over the line.

"Great. Now she knows about our secret love affair, Lake. Way to go." I heard a slap ring through the line.

"Keiran took off after we had an argument. I'm heading over to your house. If he isn't there, I need to know where he would go."

Silence filled the line, and I could sense his hesitance. Chances were Keiran would be home, and chances were he could be in danger.

"Keenan, please."

He released a loud breath into the phone before answering. "The court. He would go there," he stated before hanging up.

I came to a stop at one of the town's forks. The left

led to Keiran's house while the right would take me to the playground. I hadn't stepped foot on that play-ground in ten years. I had seen it riding past, and it hadn't changed much, but the memories all began there.

I made my decision and sped the rest of the way there.

# CHAPTER TWENTY-FIVE

I STEPPED ONTO the lawn looking around for signs of Dash's vehicle. I spotted the gleam of the sleek silver car and hurried in that direction. I didn't see signs of the tailing vehicle as I looked for Keiran. I had a good idea of where he might be.

I heard the sound of the ball hitting the concrete a split second before the swish of the net. I broke through the trees and spotted Keiran moving swiftly across the court. Even from there, I could see him covered in sweat and his shirt clinging to his chest and arms.

He played as if in a trance, and I realized this was his way of hiding from the present and the past. He was using basketball as a defense mechanism to escape from himself. *But who was the real Keiran?*

"Keiran, stop!" He kept playing though I was close and loud enough for him to hear me. His moves were aggressive as if there was an opponent playing against him. He was in danger of injury at any moment if he kept it up.

I ran onto the court and ripped the basketball out of his hands just as he was going for a jump shot. Desperate hands grabbed me up just before his lips descended on mine. I inhaled his sweaty, masculine scent that intoxicated my senses. The basketball fell listlessly from my hands in favor of his sculpted abdomen that heaved under my touch.

His hands cupped me under my butt, lifting me, and I wrapped my legs around his hips and let him carry me... somewhere. His lips never left mine, and air became inconsequential to the need to feel him take me.

My back was pressed against a hard surface and only then did he let me stand on my own, but when he started to rip away at my clothing, I got an uneasy feeling so I began to push against his shoulders. However, that wasn't enough when he continued to kiss me passionately. He seized my hands above my head and pressed them into the wall behind me.

"Keiran," I managed to say around his plunging tongue. "Keiran, wait." As much as I wanted him, I needed to stop him. He continued to ignore my protests and pressed his body harder against me. "Keiran, stop!" I bit down on his lip before ripping my mouth away.

He shoved away from me and glared at me through narrowed eyes. "Are you fucking telling me no?" I nodded and kept a wary eye on him. He looked as if he would pounce at any moment.

"I can't let you hide behind sex anymore."

"Let me?" he scoffed. "You think I need you to let me?"

"It'd be pretty hard to do without my consent, don't you think?"

"I don't hide," he said, ignoring my question. He fixed his clothes and sat down on a nearby bench with his head lowered. "Why did you come here?" he asked, but his voice was disinterested.

"I wanted to make sure you were okay. You were

pretty mad and driving recklessly. There was a car, too... I thought it was following you but I guess I was wrong."

He shrugged and looked off into the distance. "I can take care of myself."

"So can I," I countered.

He turned his head and studied my face. "No, you can't. You're too sheltered. You don't have a clue, girl."

"And you do?"

"More than you would think. I am the monster you would hide under the covers from as a kid."

"You were a kid then, too."

"I was never a kid, Lake. I didn't have a childhood. I didn't have parents or a family. I was a body used for selfish gains that hurt people."

"What about your mom?" I asked with a frown.

"She wasn't much of a mom. I hardly knew her."

"And now? Who are you now?"

"I'm a hopeless fuck who is obsessed with a girl he still wants to hurt." I didn't react to his confession. In truth, I didn't know what to say or do. Obsession was a pretty powerful thing. How deep did his run?

A wind broke through the air, and I shivered from the cold temperature, which he seemed to notice. "Let's get you home," he stated grimly.

\* \* \*

I WOKE UP the next morning to find Keiran gone. His side of the bed was warm, which meant he hadn't been gone long. Resigned to an early start, I let my feet sink into the plush carpet and made my way to the bathroom deciding that a hot soak was needed to relax my tired muscles.

While the tub filled with hot water, I reached for

my bath salts and coconut oil and poured it into the rising water. Knowing it would take a while to fill up the large garden tub, I left the bathroom to call Willow. Whoever woke up first usually called the other. We liked to torture each other that way.

"I'm going to visit grandma today. You up for it?" Willow sometimes came with me to Red Rock to visit my grandma. I figured she might need an escape after dealing with Dash last night. Speaking of...

"Yes! When are we leaving?" Her voice sounded desperate, and I frowned at the phone.

"Are you okay?"

"Tell you all about it on the ride. So... the time?"

"Oh, uh. An hour or so?"

"Can't you make it faster?"

"Willow—"

"Fine. An hour it is then. But make it a quick one!" The line went dead before I could say anything else. This just when I thought Willow couldn't get any crazier. I figured Buddy was home and driving her crazy, but when she answered, her voice sounded as if she had just woken up.

I walked back into the bathroom and looked over at the separate shower. I contemplated foregoing a soak to save time, but my strained muscles protested when I lifted my shirt over my head.

I'll just have to make it a quick soak.

I stepped into the steaming water and resisted the urge to jump back out when the heat pricked my skin. Goose bumps covered my skin as I sunk into the water. I quickly wrapped my hair into a messy, high bun and relaxed. Before long, my eyes were closing in content, and I forgot about my time constraints.

Minutes later, I realized I had dozed when a sound jarred me awake. My eyes flew open, and I saw Keiran sitting on the edge of the bathtub watching me. He was fully dressed in fresh clothing and looked well rested.

"Sore?" His voice sounded like liquid velvet melting over me. It felt better than the hot water and soothing salts.

"How did you get in here?" I asked instead.

"I swiped your key when you were sleeping, and you didn't answer my question." I nodded my answer while his eyes raked over my nude body. "That's too bad," he muttered.

"Why did you come back?"

He shrugged and ran a hand through his dark hair, causing it to spike. "I wanted to be with you."

"So why did you leave? You were afraid I would pry?"

"Are you going to?" He held my stare until I broke it. I released a slow breath and rested my head against the back of the tub.

"Not at the moment," I stated and picked up my sponge. "I need to bathe..."

"Then allow me." He sunk to his knees beside the tub and took the sponge from my hands. I sat there unsure while he soaped up the sponge leisurely. I watched his large hands grip the sponge that looked as helpless as I usually felt under their strength.

He reached for me, and I sucked in a breath when he began washing me starting at my neck and methodically moving across my body, barely skimming my hot spots. My breasts began to tingle with anticipation from his neglect, and I felt an ache spike from the hard points. His hand ran down the taut planes of my stomach and then shifted around slowly to my lower back before moving up and lifting me. I was now arching into his chest as he rubbed circles across my back before dipping below the water to my waist and coming back around to my lower stomach. I moaned and gripped the sides when a finger began teasing my belly button lightly.

"Easy," he commanded softly.

My right leg was then being lifted out of the water, and he hooked it over the tub side, resting my foot against his chest, leaving me open and exposed. The water instantly soaked through his dark blue shirt as he ran the sponge over my leg, starting at my foot and working down my thigh.

Unexpectedly, he tickled the back of my knee with his other hand, diverting my attention away from the hand with the sponge until it finally reached my throbbing center causing pleasure to explode the length of my body leaving me quaking in its wake.

I vaguely noticed his head lowering, and then his tongue swiped over the peaks of my breasts teasingly before he closed his lips over one and suckled. My hands clutched at his head desperately, needing to keep him there. I heard the low keening sound made deep in my throat, and suddenly, his hand was there, where I needed him most. He skimmed it briefly over my clit before plunging two fingers inside my waiting walls.

My hand followed him down, directing his movements where I needed it, and together, we worked to fuck me with his invading fingers while he latched onto my other nipple with his hot tongue, giving it the same treatment.

My orgasm came swift and was over as quick as it had come. In the background, I could hear the trilling of my phone ringing. *Shit. Willow.*

I jumped up from the tub quickly, causing Keiran to lose his balance and fall on his ass. He shot me a bewildered look, and if I weren't in a rush, I would have found it funny.

"Sorry. I have to go. Willow is waiting for me." I rushed from the bathroom for my bedroom to get dressed.

"Where are you going?" I heard his deep voice across the room and turned to find him standing in my bedroom doorway with annoyance plastered all over his face.

"I'm going to see my grandma in Red Rock." He remained quiet, and I continued getting dressed, and then ran a brush through my hair before letting it fall in long waves down my back. When I was ready, I brushed past him to leave, but he caught my arm.

"I'm going with you."

"What? No, you aren't. Why?"

Instead of answering me, he led me to the front door and used my key to lock up. The chill of the morning air greeted me, and I suddenly wished for Keiran's body heat. I noticed he'd switched cars as he opened his car door and all but threw me inside. I watched him saunter to the driver's side through the windshield until he seated himself and was grateful when he blasted the heat. I hated how cold it got in the North, but Keiran never seemed to mind, even forgoing a coat sometimes. It made me wonder where he grew up if he was so comfortable in this weather.

Minutes later, we were pulling into Willow's driveway, so I hopped out barely letting him stop the car and rushed for the door. I rang the doorbell and waited. After a few heartbeats, I heard footsteps moving to the door, then it opened, and a half naked male body greeted me.

My mouth opened and closed when words failed me. I was pretty sure I resembled a brain dead fish. I was not expecting him to answer the door. He was shirtless, and his jeans were left opened, revealing tanned skin and the hard planes of his upper body. I looked up into his smug face, noticing his ruffled bed hair. My shock turned into anger, and I glared at him, but he only smirked and moved aside to let me in.

I bound up the stairs for Willow's bedroom where I found her wrapped in bed sheets in the middle of the room, and I took in her disheveled appearance. Her wide, sensual mouth was kiss-swollen, and passion marks decorated her neck and the top of her ample breasts, and I was sure there were more under the sheets. She looked frustrated and close to tears, and I immediately embraced her.

"I'm a failure to women around the world," she cried out. Even in her stressed state, Willow still managed to find a joke in the situation.

"Why didn't you tell me he was here? I would have come sooner." I ignored the guilty feeling over what held me up.

"What would be the point? The damage was already done. Your phone call woke me up, and when I saw him lying there beside me, last night came rushing back, and then he woke up and we— we... Oh, God," she groaned.

That explains her not being dressed yet.

"What do I do, Lake? He will never let me go now."

"Is that really what you want?"

"It doesn't matter what I want. We can't do this. We are from two different worlds."

"It doesn't seem to bother him."

"But he's using me. What happens when he gets tired of me?"

"Then he would be a fool."

"I would get Buddy to kick his ass, but the little shit has a man crush on him. They're 'the bestest buds' now." She rolled her eyes, and I laughed. We both knew

Buddy would never let anyone seriously hurt his sister. He adored her although he gave her a lot of shit. He may be younger, but Buddy was fiercely protective.

"Where is he anyway?"

She shrugged. "I honestly don't know. He isn't around much anymore. My little Buddy bean is growing up," she stated using her nickname for him that he hated.

"Well, let's get you dressed. Grandma is waiting."

"Yeah, we don't want to keep that firecracker waiting too long. She will curse us both out."

"Uh, more like all of us. Keiran is coming."

She lifted an eyebrow curiously. "Oh, wow. Grandma Lane will eat him alive. I can't wait!" She rushed out of the room, and moments later, I heard the shower turn on.

I looked over at Pepé, who was in the corner curled up on his pillow sleeping. I hoped the little guy slept through whatever occurred in this room. I remembered the depth of her screams when I walked in on them weeks ago. Poor guy was probably traumatized.

I left the room and headed back downstairs where I heard two male voices speaking low. I cleared the living room doorway where they were sitting, and their talking immediately stopped as they looked at me.

I shot Dash a withering glance before plopping down on the recliner. I felt their stares on me, but they remained quiet.

"Are you two done man-bashing already?" Dash joked. I snorted and pulled out my phone to text my aunt rather than answer him.

However, when he stood up and headed for the stairs, my attention diverted back to him. "Where are you going?" I questioned, hostility dripping from my voice.

"Bro, get your woman out of my business," he laughed. I ignored his insinuation that Keiran could control me even though we both knew he did.

"Leave her alone."

"I'll never leave her alone. You of all people should know that." His eyes flicked to Keiran and back to me, suggestively.

"She doesn't want you, Dash."

"And yet she hasn't told me no," he grinned, and I hated his cocky attitude.

"You could be the man you claim to be and give her what she wants."

His entire demeanor changed in a flash. I watched his eyes harden, and his jaw clenched leaving behind traces of the easy-going guy. "I'm not interested in what she thinks she wants. But I do know what she needs, and I'll be the one to give it to her. The rest doesn't matter."

# CHAPTER TWENTY-SIX

"I STILL DON'T understand why you needed to come," Willow griped from the backseat. Willow and I were finally on the road, heading to Red Rock—plus two.

"Because it upsets you so much. You know... we were friends for a short time, but when did you get so bitchy?"

"Right around the time your dick started showing... and I don't mean the one between your legs."

"Ssss, ouch. You burn me, baby. You burn me."

If they kept up the bickering, then I was in for a long ride. Keiran had yet to say a word to me since we left my house. I could tell he was pissed, but I didn't know what about and told myself I didn't care. I peeked at him in the driver's seat, but his face was unreadable.

It was at least an hour and a half drive ahead of me with a bickering couple and a brooding lover for company. I pulled out my iPod and played the first song in the cue.

My favorite song, *The Sweetest Thing,* flowed through the tiny buds of my headphones. *Nice.*

* * *

WE PULLED ONTO the flowery estate of Whispering Pines an hour later, and only then did I remove my ear buds. Sometimes I begrudged my grandmother the peaceful hideaway, although I could do without the smell of Bengay and antiseptic.

On these visits, I made sure to keep my appearance as close to the pictures my grandmother had in her room as possible. I was really young when she was diagnosed with Alzheimer's, so she still associated me with the image of the younger me. During each visit, I brought her a new picture of me to make it easier. She also kept pictures of Willow since she often came with me.

"I need you two to stay away for a moment. She doesn't know you, so I don't want to alarm her. She likes to take walks so I'll bring her out so she can feel more comfortable out in the open."

"Sure thing. I can't wait to meet you in sixty years. I bet she's hotter." Dash grinned.

"You can't seriously be considering flirting with a seventy-year-old woman?" Willow's voice dripped with disgust and a hint of jealousy.

"That depends on if you are seriously going to be jealous of a seventy-year-old woman," he countered.

And the bickering began again.

I looked at Keiran, who nodded his head once and headed over to a chess table currently occupied by an elderly man with a thick mane of snow-white hair.

I grabbed Willow and pulled her to the entrance to avoid another nauseating session of foreplay with words.

"Ugh, he just bothers me so much." Willow groaned while I signed into the front desk before making my way to grandmother's room.

"He doesn't bother you, Willow. He affects you."

"The difference, O' Wise One?"

"His effect on you is only possible because of your feelings for him." I pushed open the door while she sputtered and huffed. My grandmother was sitting by the window gazing out onto the front lawn, and I wondered if she saw when I arrived or more importantly, whom I arrived with.

"Who are those strapping young men you two gals rode in with?" she asked without turning her attention away from the window. I had no doubt of who had her so transfixed.

"Strapping? Gals? Grandma Lane, you get older every time we see you," Willow jokingly stated.

"Ha! I may be old, but I still got it and don't you forget it. If I was just a few years younger..." She ran a hand through her hair suggestively, and I couldn't hold in the bouts of laughter any longer. I didn't get two steps inside, but she had already managed to make me smile and laugh all in one.

"Just a few, huh?"

"You girls come in here and let me look at you." She turned away from the window to face us finally and gave us a stern look.

We moved forward to the bay window where she was seated and each hugged her before taking a seat. "So why are they out there in the cold and not in here with you?"

"I didn't want to alarm you because—"

"Yes, it would be most displeasing not to remember such fine looking men. I'd never thought I'd see the day when you two would give in and *get a man*. I thought... spinsters for sure."

"Is that so?" I laughed deeply.

"I'll have you know—"

"Willow, Pepé does not count as a male friend. Though handsome, I meant someone of your own species." She gave her an admonishing look that shut Willow down.

"Yes, ma'am." She hung her head low, and I tried not to laugh at her expense. Willow and Grandma Lane together was a trial.

"Now. Tell me all your news and make it quick. I want to meet those two."

We spent the next twenty minutes catching her up on school and college plans. You know... the safe topics that people always stick to when dealing with a relative.

After catching up, Willow excused herself to get Keiran and Dash from outside leaving me alone with my grandmother for a few moments.

"So how is my daughter?"

"Good. She should be returning from her book tour on Monday and plans to come visit you by the end of the week."

"Good, good. I need to get ahold of that wayward child of mine. Leaving a seventeen year old alone for so long."

"I'm fine. Aunt Carissa trusts me."

"Yeah, well, she shouldn't. You're a fine young woman, Lake. You are incredibly beautiful and smart. I may not remember much these days, but I do remember what it was like to be seventeen and so should she."

She looked at me knowingly with a mix of disapproval and empathy, and I wondered just how much I was giving away.

"I can see it in your eyes, dear. When you walked in here, you weren't the same Lake. I assume it's because of him?" She nodded toward the guys who were still sitting at the chess table engrossed in a game with the elderly man.

"Who?"

She shot me an impatient look for playing dumb. "Mr. Tall, Dark, and Brooding."

"Yes, but not in the way you think."

"And what way is that?"

"We... weren't always friends. Even now..." I didn't know how to explain to my grandmother that Keiran used to hate me as much as he hated himself or that I was sleeping with him.

"I see," she sighed. "Why does love always feel like a battlefield?"

I blinked twice to clear my head and replay what she just said. "Grandma, did you just quote Jordin Sparks?"

She looked at me indignantly. "What? I'm hip."

"No one says hip anymore."

"It's cool. I'm cool." She threw up the peace out sign, and I was done.

My stomach felt like it had caved in, and I couldn't seem to bring air into my lungs. I was curled into a ball at my grandmother's feet, clutching my stomach, and that is how they found me when the three walked in.

"Someone please get my foolish grandchild off the floor, please."

Dash reached for me but stopped at the look Keiran gave him. He picked me up and placed me back in my seat.

"Oh, my..." My grandmother whispered softly. She was watching Keiran and Dash closely. No doubt taken aback at the possessiveness Keiran had just displayed. Her hand fluttered up to her neck before discreetly smoothing her hair. "Such fine young men indeed."

I briefly wondered if she might have been a cougar in her younger years.

"How old are you, young man?" She directed the

FEAR ME

question at Keiran.

Yup. Definitely a cougar.

"Eighteen," he answered before kneeling down on one knee and taking her frail hand within his much larger hands. "It is nice to meet you." It was a smooth move made to charm, both surprising and annoying me. I was so going to disown her if she fell for it.

"Likewise." Her smile was bashful and lit up her face clearly enjoying the attention.

"Give me a break," Willow muttered.

"Hush and you might learn something," she berated and shot her a scathing look. "Tell me, what are your intentions with my granddaughter. She's never had a boyfriend, you know."

"Yes, ma'am. I am aware."

"And did you have anything to do with that?"

The corner of his mouth lifted in a half grin. "I might have."

"Why?"

"Because she's mine." Any moment now, the ground would disappear from beneath my feet, and I could escape this nightmare.

"Is that so?" She regarded him curiously before seemingly deciding something. "They say there is a thin line between love and hate. Do you know what that means?"

"No."

"It means two people are too dumb and too blind to know the difference."

He cocked his head to the side. "So what should we do?"

"Get your shit together, man. And take care of my Lake or leave her alone." *Well, I'll be damned.* She didn't fail me after all. She turned at the sound of Dash snickering and lifted an eyebrow. "Same goes for you,

P a g e | **380**

pretty boy. I see the way you look at Willow and the way she tries to avoid you. I'm pretty sure your mother told you at least once that there would one day be a special woman who wouldn't be fooled by your bullshit."

"I'm, uh, sure there was a time or two."

"Smart woman. Are your parents still together?"

"Yes, ma'am, though she threatens to divorce him often."

"I'm sure. You come from money, don't you? I can smell it on you."

"My dad does okay." Dash shrugged nonchalantly, but I could see the question bugged him.

"But not you?"

"It's his empire. I'm just a freeloader until I can earn my keep."

"So there is something to you other than your looks."

"I like to think so."

"Yet she still won't give you a chance..." she whispered knowingly. He averted his gazed at Willow with longing heavy in his eyes before his jaw hardened in anger.

"No. She won't," he stated while his gaze remained on Willow.

"So you're going to force her, is that right?" Her blunt question threw us all for surprise. Dash's eyes flew back to Grandma Lane while Willow shifted uncomfortably. He met her stare, but rather than deny it, he remained silent. "I should hope if we meet again, I will have a better impression of the two of you. Don't let me down."

I noticed the fatigue setting in and figured it was time to end our visit so she could rest. "Guys, I'll meet you at the car. I just want to say goodbye to her."

The three of them left the room after saying goodbye, and I helped my grandmother over to her bed. She must have really been tired because she didn't fuss over the help as usual.

"Thank you, dear. There is nothing like old age for the muscles."

"It seems to make you feistier, too."

"Now don't go getting your knickers in a bunch. Those boys needed to be brought to heel. If only your father was here to meet that man of yours."

"Why is that?"

"Because those two couldn't be more opposite. Your father was a gentle soul, both he and your mother. They would probably faint if they knew their baby girl was in love with a guy like him."

"We never said—"

"Just because you haven't spoken it doesn't mean you don't feel it."

"I don't understand much of what I feel or think these days."

"Honey... that is just your heart holding onto what your brain is saying you can't have."

"So which should I listen to?"

"Whichever feels right—you don't need to understand it. Trust in yourself. That's all you can do." She closed her eyes, fatigue taking over, so I tucked her in and rose from my chair.

I was placing the picture I brought with me on her nightstand when I noticed a photo of my mother that wasn't there before resting on the wooden top. She was dressed in a pretty sundress, her blonde hair falling around her shoulders, and I could tell it was a summer picture.

She was standing in front of the beautiful brick house I once called home... and holding a baby I knew to be myself. Her smile alone gave the picture life as she looked down at me clutching the top of her dress and looking back up at her, a grin expanding my chubby cheeks.

By the age of eight, I had plenty of memories of my parents and in none of them could I ever remember not feeling loved. I remember my mother crying the day they left. My father almost canceled the entire trip.

"Did my parents leave me?" I asked before I could rethink or stop myself.

"They will never leave you, Lake." The pain in her voice was evident. She was fighting to hold onto to her memory while I had long since let them both go. Though she never talked about my mom either, I knew she missed her. I never thought about how hard it must be to lose a child and not know why.

"So where are they?" Everyone was so sure my parents hadn't bailed, but there was never any sign of foul play. How could they just vanish?

"I wish I knew."

* * *

ONCE WE WERE through the door of my house after returning from Whispering Pines, I turned on Keiran, who stopped just inside the door and looked at me curiously. "Stay away from her," I said simply.

The entire ride back, I battled feelings of regret. I had exposed my grandmother to Keiran. Now he had one more person to use against me if he chose. He now knew who she was and where she was—and worse...she wouldn't remember who *he* was.

He wore an indifferent look on his face when he shut the door. "Are you going to give me a reason not to?"

His lack of reassurance was unexpected and dangerous to my peace of mind. "Keiran, this is my grand-mother! She's old and helpless. How can you even think to—?"

"I wasn't. But that doesn't mean I wouldn't, so I won't tell you otherwise."

"But what reason could you possibly have to go after her?" Out of the two people in this room, Keiran was the dangerous one, yet all the hostility and anger radiated off me.

His nonchalance for human life was chilling.

"I want you to stay away from my past. I know you're still digging, but it ends now."

"Where is this coming from?"

"I've asked you before. I'm telling you now."

"Just tell me whatever it is you don't want me to find!" I yelled, losing patience, but he was gone before I had finished, and the sound of the front door slamming was my only answer. I slid to the floor in defeat when I realized Keiran would never open up to me.

# CHAPTER TWENTY-SEVEN

"WHY DIDN'T YOU answer your phone last night? I called you a hundred times." I listened to Sheldon fuss as we walked down the hallway. It was lunch period, and I'd just got out of volleyball, which wasn't as fun without Willow. She texted this morning to say she was sick and skipping school.

"Sorry, I just had a lot on my mind and needed time to think."

"Bummers. I wanted to talk to you about my audition. Felix is looking for a face for his new clothing line."

"I'm really sorry, Sheldon. How did you do?" I asked, feeling like shit because I forgot about her audition.

"Canceled. I was too nervous. Dash had offered to go with me, but he disappeared, too."

"Are you sure modeling is what you want to do?"

"It's been my dream since I saw my first show. Dad says I have to go to college first, but after that, my dreams are my own."

"Are you okay with that?"

"I guess so. Going to college isn't so bad." I shook my head and started putting my bags in my locker.

"Sheldon you have to think—"

"Is that a bite mark?" she asked, interrupting what I was about to say.

*Shit.* I'd become so used to Keiran leaving bite marks on me, I had stopped noticing. I looked down to see my oversized sweater had fallen off my shoulder exposing the red patch and indentations where my neck met my shoulders. I quickly pulled it back over my shoulders and finished stuffing my books into my locker. I avoided her gaze as I heard her laugh.

"Kinky. I like it." She chuckled. "Dash told me you guys went to see your grandmother. I'm shocked."

"Why are you shocked?"

"Because of Keiran's obvious disdain for anything that resembles a parent."

"Why?"

"I don't know. Maybe because he didn't know his father and his mother dropped him off on a stranger's doorstep?"

But bad parents don't cause someone to become this troubled without something much worse happening. There were so many holes only he could fill. "I wish I could get him to talk to me."

"If anyone can get him to open up, it would be you."

"Why do you say that?"

"You're the only one who affects Keiran in any way. He would talk... for you. You just need to know the right words to say."

"S'up beautiful ladies?" Keenan came and hooked his arms around our shoulders with a cute grin on his face. "Do you know just by standing there together you've already fulfilled one of my fantasies? Now I just have to figure out how to get you two naked... with me in between."

"Before or after Keiran and I take turns killing you?" Sheldon quipped.

"Semantics. What are you two whispering about?" He cast suspicious glances between us and attempted to look intimidating. I'm pretty sure he could if he wasn't such a goof.

"Our periods," Sheldon answered gleefully.

"Eww, babe."

"You asked."

"But you didn't have to tell me that!"

*Aaaaand they're arguing again.* I listened to them bicker back and forth. Sometimes I think they argued on purpose. Sheldon told me makeup sex was out of this world, but I've had Keiran's angry sex so I don't think it would be wise to pick fights with him.

"Guys, I'm hungry," I said interrupting their argument. "Anyone know where Keiran is?"

"He's with the coach. He told me to take you to lunch if he's running late."

"So I guess that means you're still my bodyguard?" I asked, slightly annoyed. *Did he still not trust me?*

"In a way," he smirked.

"Because I can't be trusted. I get it." *I really don't.*

"No, because Keiran doesn't trust anyone. Especially with you."

"What happened to his parents?" I blurted. I wasn't planning to ask that question in a crowded hallway during the middle of the school day but, hey, shit happens. I was done skating around the issue.

Keenan froze and then glared at Sheldon, who actually looked contrite for once. "What makes you think something happened?"

"Keenan..."

"I don't know, okay? He doesn't talk about it. He probably doesn't even remember." He looked away, and I could tell he was either lying or holding something back. Just then, Dash walked up to our circle with a scowl on his face.

"Where's your girl?"

"You tell me... you were with her last."

He thumbed his chin and eyed me before rolling his eyes and fishing out his phone. He punched in some numbers, mumbling. After dialing into his phone three times, he muttered, "This is bullshit" and walked off.

"Willow still won't talk to him?" Sheldon asked.

"Would you?" I asked.

"I'd cut his dick off and hang it over my mantle."

Keenan gave Sheldon a crazy look. "So you'd touch your brother's dick?"

"Of course not. I'd make you do it, pumpkin." She planted a loud kiss on his cheek.

"Oh, no. I'm not doing that again."

"Again?" We both asked at the same time.

Keenan scratched the back of his neck. "I, uhh... lost a bet last year so I had to hold his dick for two minutes."

My mouth fell open, and Sheldon was bent over laughing. "Oh, honey, you're such a pussy," she chortled.

"Hey, he had pants on!" Keenan said defensively. He looked at me pleadingly and said, "Don't tell Keiran, all right?"

"Why?"

"Because then he'd make me hold *his* dick."

We burst out laughing, and I fell to me knees clutching my stomach. Keenan's face was surely a Kodak moment. "What's so funny?" Keiran's voice suddenly came from behind us. I was still on the floor laughing as he approached. "Why is she on the floor?" he asked, mean-mugging Keenan.

"Whatever, you guys are lame," Keenan muttered walking off. Sheldon followed after him, still laughing.

"Lake, get off the floor, baby." *Oh, so now I'm 'baby' again?* I rolled my eyes and ignored the butterflies that erupted in my stomach each time he said it. It always sounded so sexy and sensual and intimate. Now, he only used my last name when he was a dick, or I was being punished. He scooped me up when I took too long to move but kept his hands on my hips, tugging me into him.

"How was volleyball?" he asked pecking me on my lips. I stared at him in surprise considering what had happened the last time we talked. It was becoming really hard to keep up with his moods. Or maybe I was the only one who carried grudges over an entire weekend.

"Oh, you know... someone hits the ball over the net, so I hit the ball back over. It's sort of like playing hot potato, but with a volleyball that's not hot." He ignored my sarcasm and used the opportunity to feel me up instead. Thankfully, everyone had gone either to lunch or to class so no one was left in the hallway but us. "What did you have to see Coach about?" It wasn't important for me to know, but I needed a distraction from the feeling of his hands on me.

"He wanted to talk to me about our next win." I smiled at his assumption that the team would win their first game.

"Cocky much?" He gave me a lopsided grin that I thought made him look adorably human, and then he started kissing me on my neck. "Are you trying to go pro?"

"That's the plan," he mumbled against my neck.

"Are scouts still considering you for college ball?"

"Coach said they're eager to see me perform this year." He lifted his head from my neck and looked down at me with a serious expression. "Actually, I wanted to talk to you about that."

"Okay."

"I need to bring my game stronger than I have before considering the year I missed and the circumstances. I'm not blaming you so fix your face," he added when I sent him a withering look. "That year was justified for the shit I had done." *Like murder a little girl?* I masked the nauseous feeling that overcame me, but realized I missed part of what he was saying. "...I'm going to be practicing a lot and won't have a lot of spare time."

The bell rang just as I caught on to what he was telling me. "I understand."

"Do you?"

"We aren't dating, Keiran. No worries." He had narrowed his eyes before he took my lips with his in a possessive kiss that said otherwise.

We ended up spending the entire lunch period making out against the lockers.

Thankfully, we weren't caught. I had to end it when he tried to stick his hand down my pants. He didn't put up too much of a stink, even though his face said he wanted to, but the bell rang.

He wordlessly led me to class and when we arrived, he slapped me on the ass and walked off.

I watched him swagger down the hall and couldn't help but admit how much I loved his walk... and every other girl in the vicinity watched, too. Some even stopped to stare or reach out to touch him.

Horny hoebags.

I wanted to yell that he was mine even though he never would be.

I still took evil pleasure in how he ignored and

shook them off, and before he turned the corner, he looked back at me as if sensing I was still there. He winked and disappeared around the corner.

* * *

IT WASN'T EVEN five minutes into class when a couple of uniforms walked in flashing badges. For some reason, my heart dropped to the pit of my stomach. I didn't know why until I looked over a few rows and noticed an empty seat.

Anya's empty seat.

The fair and everything that happened rushed back. Dash and Keenan drove off with them, and Keiran hasn't said a word, but I knew they had to have taken them to him. Whatever I was expecting them to do in retaliation didn't include Anya not showing up to school.

*Maybe she's out sick.*

The other students started to get riled as the two officers spoke to our teacher.

"Class, settle down. The police are looking for Anya Risdell and Trevor Reynolds and are asking for our full cooperation. Every student will be scheduled for an individual interview with your parents over the next few days. They ask if you have any information on their disappearance for you to come forth with it as soon as possible."

Just then, one of the officer's eyes connected with mine, and I recognized him as the partner of Trevor's dad and the one who cuffed Keiran the night of the break-in.

*Shit.*

He was grilling me with his eyes, and I fidgeted in my seat nervously. My phone buzzed in my pocket so I pulled it out, thankful for the distraction from the officer:

K: R u ok?

Lake: No...

K: I'll take care of it.

Lake: Like you took care of them?

K: Jeez, Lake. Don't say that shit over the phone.

Lake: Sorry. I don't know what to do.

K: Be there in two.

No matter how much I tried, I couldn't tamp down the nervous feelings or the bile that steadily rose. Keiran appeared in the doorway and walked right in.

He ignored the officers who were talking to the class and my teacher, who looked pretty pissed off, but didn't say anything. He walked up to my desk, grabbed my hand, and pulled me up from the seat. I hurriedly grabbed my bag just in case I didn't or couldn't come back.

"You are quickly putting me on every teacher's shit list, you know."

"At least we'll be together," he smirked.

"Keiran, what did you do?" I asked once we were out of earshot. He backed me into the lockers and rested his forearm above my head.

"I was *caring*," he answered sarcastically. "The less you know, the better. This is my shit."

"Someone could have seen them being taken."

"Let me worry about that. You don't know anything. That's what you tell them when they ask."

"But I do know something!" He narrowed his eyes, and I felt that familiar chill I mistakenly thought was long gone.

"So what do you plan to tell them?"

"Don't do that. You don't get to look at me as if I already betrayed you. I don't owe you anything."

Instead of responding, he took my lips with his, opening me up with his tongue, which I took greedily. The stress and fear of our current situation had me needy and trying to climb his body right there in the hallway.

"Do you want to get out of here?" he asked, lifting his lips from mine.

"I would like that very much, but I can't. I have a test coming up and a project due in art next period. Are you leaving?"

He shook his head. "I'm not leaving you here alone."

"My hero," I whispered, smiling teasingly up at him. When he flinched, and his gaze became murderous, I remembered his feelings about heroes. His reaction made me think it was more than just an opinion.

The police officers came out of the room and cast us hard glances. I looked back at them nervously. I was probably giving everything away with my face.

Keiran's back was turned so he didn't see them come out. I was distracted from their scrutiny when Keiran used his thumb to rub small circles over my lower stomach, just as I was about to warn him.

"I should get back," I whispered.

"You should. The pervs are watching," he said indicating the cops at the other end of the hall. I looked back at the cops and noticed them saying something to each other, but they were too far away for us to hear.

"You're way too calm about this," I remarked. It was actually making me nervous rather than assuring me. The cops were watching us too hard and standing around as they were waiting for something. He shrugged, dropped his arm from over my head and backed away from me.

I missed the safety his closeness created. It felt like

my personal hideaway from the world. Funny since he used to be the only thing I needed to hide from not so long ago. Maybe he still was, I thought, thinking about Anya, Trevor, and what he said about my grandmother.

He nudged me to the door, but this time, he waited for me to go inside before heading in the direction of the officers.

I couldn't resist so I peeked my head out the door, fully aware that the entire class along with my teacher's attention was on me.

When Keiran was in hearing distance, the officer said something to him, and I tensed even though I couldn't hear. Keiran didn't stop to talk to them, though.

His only acknowledgment was to flip them off. I watched him climb the stairs, taking two at time until he disappeared.

"Ms. Monroe, if it's all right with you, please take your seat so that I may resume class," Mrs. Bisette, barked.

*Definitely on her shit list.*

# CHAPTER TWENTY-EIGHT

I LEANED MY head against the wall and closed my eyes drawing out the sound of Keiran's practice. My head felt like it was spinning, and all I wanted to do was go home and hide under my covers. I'd fully expected to go straight home after school, but like always, Keiran had different ideas, and like always, I followed.

"Is it Friday yet?" Sheldon griped from her seat next to me.

"Nope."

"Fuck. I don't think I can tolerate going to practice today. I'm too stressed."

"Can you skip that now? With Anya missing, aren't you the captain now?"

"Oh, my gosh. What if people think I did it?"

"Why would they think that?"

"So I could take her spot as Captain?"

"You watch too much TV."

"Trevor did it to Keiran," she pointed out.

"Point taken."

"Ugh, what do you think they are going to do about the investigation?" she asked.

"What makes you think they are going to do anything?" I asked while keeping my eyes shut.

"Because they are too calm and quiet about it."

"What do you think they did to them? You know them better than I do. What would they do?" She paused from tying up her sneakers and hesitated before answering. "If Keiran is behind it, I don't think I want to know. Dash says he has connections that money *can't* buy." I watched her carefully for any sign that she was holding back, but her answers sounded genuine.

I remembered the conversation I had overheard him having last Friday, but none of it put me closer to figuring out what may have happened to Trevor and Anya. Keiran was dead set on making me leave his past alone, but his past didn't seem to be much of a past at all.

"They don't say much around me anyway," Sheldon continued, breaking me out of my thoughts. "Keiran said I had a big mouth. Can you believe that?" she yelled drawing the attention of a few players and cheerleaders.

I raised my eyebrows and pursed my lips. "No... I can't imagine," I said sarcastically. She gave me an indignant look and went back to fixing her shoes. "Are you guys practicing in here today?"

She nodded. "It's raining outside. You hadn't noticed?" she gestured to the double doors leading outside. She left with a quick "see you later" and headed to the other part of the gym. Our gym was unique in that it had multiple sections so it wouldn't impede on basketball practice and other events.

I looked over to the court in time to catch Keiran make an effortless shot at the halfway line.

Keenan began to gloat as if he had just taken the shot, and I shook my head. Keiran made eye contact with me and called for a break.

"What's wrong?" he asked approaching me.

"Besides my raging headache and impending jail sentence?"

"Sure," he said rolling his eyes.

"Then nothing. I think I'm going to head home." I stood up on my tiptoes and pecked his lips. He wore a scowl and looked as if he were going to protest as I picked up my messenger bag.

"Go to my place."

"I'll be fine at home."

"What did I say?"

"You're not my father, Keiran." He gripped my chin hard and stared down at me without saying anything. "How am I supposed to get in?" I rolled my eyes at him. He bent and dug into his gym bag and produced his key ring. He popped one of the three keys and handed it to me. "Straight there."

"Well, I'm kind of hungry, so I was thinking about grabbing a burger on the way," I said just to piss him off.

"Monroe," he warned over his shoulder as he walked away. Mission accomplished.

* * *

I PULLED INTO Keiran's place and noticed a large black pickup truck parked in the driveway. Keiran didn't mention anyone being at his house, and I contemplated calling him before going inside, but I knew he wouldn't get my call until practice was over.

I got out with my bag... and my burger and entered with the key he gave me. I didn't hear anything or anyone when I walked in. I walked deeper into the house with slow steps. Just as I reached the edge of the stairs, the backdoor opened down the hall, and a tall, imposing man entered. We both froze as we stared at each other in surprise.

After a couple of minutes of staring each other down, he closed the door and moved closer. I gripped the banister and battled between the choice to fight or flight.

"Who are you?" he finally asked. His voice was smooth and husky, and as I looked closer, I decided he was quite handsome in his faded jeans and white, collared shirt. He also looked amazingly like my enigmatic boyfriend and his volatile cousin. I suddenly realized this must be their uncle. John Masters. I continued to gape at him, his question hanging between us.

"You must be here for Keenan. I assume he is cheating again." He sounded more resigned than angry.

"Actually, I'm a friend of Keiran's," I said, finding my voice. I caught the look of surprise as his eyebrows rose.

"Is that so?" I nodded, and he continued to stare. "Where is Keiran?"

"He has practice."

"Ah, yes. Basketball. So why are you here?"

"He asked me to meet him here."

"What is your name, girl?"

"Lake Mo—Monroe."

He rubbed his chin and continued to stare me down. "Why is it I've never heard of you before?" *Maybe because you're never around?* "I've never known Keiran to bring girls home. Much less entrust them with a key."

"I—I should go."

"But then Keiran wouldn't like that, would he?" My feet were rooted to the spot, and I mentally shook off my nervousness. "Don't worry, girl. I'm not going to hurt you. I am never home, and my nephew barely spares me a glance." He had looked at me curiously before he asked, "How old are you?"

"Eighteen," I answered while wondering why my age mattered.

"I don't believe I know your parents," he said, but it was more of a question.

*You wouldn't. I don't know them either. I thought I did.* "Carissa Anderson is my aunt and guardian." A look of pity crossed his faced, and I hated that. I hated when someone pitied my parents or me. They didn't deserve it, and neither did I because sometimes I did hate them.

"I see. Well, that's something you and Keiran have in common." He walked off toward the kitchen, leaving me confused.

The encounter was strange, making me feel nervous and awkward. I practically ran up the stairs and quickly locked myself in Keiran's room. Pulling out my phone, I sent a quick text to Keiran letting him know his uncle was here. My headache had only worsened since leaving the gym, so I slipped under Keiran's covers and let sleep overcome me. I'd worry about the rest later.

\* \* \*

I HEARD THE first light thud followed by a second, and I automatically wiggled my now free toes still covered by socks. My eyes refused to open as I came awake, but when I felt the familiar scent I had come to love, my eyes finally flew open. Keiran was standing over me, still dressed in his practice uniform. He usually showered before he left practice, so I figured he had rushed here. Most likely to see if I really obeyed him.

"What did he say to you?" I blinked a few times before I fully comprehended what he was asking me. John was here earlier, and our conversation rushed back to me

"Well, he was a lot more pleasant than you were when we first met."

"Lake..."

"No, Keiran. He didn't. We talked for a little while, but that was it."

"What did he say?" he gritted.

"Nothing much. He just wanted to know who the strange girl was walking into his house with a key. Why didn't you tell me he was here?"

He ran a hand over his head. "I didn't know. Apparently, they called him to schedule an interview since Keenan is still seventeen."

"Oh. Right." Sometimes I would forget I was a few months older than Keenan. I sat up in his bed and ran a self-conscious hand over my hair. I didn't get the sexy bed hair that Keiran did. I was thankful my voice wasn't as croaky as usual when I woke up. "Is he still here?"

He nodded and opened a dresser drawer. His back was turned to me so I didn't see his face when I asked him, but I did notice his back muscles tense. "He is talking with Keenan right now about school and all the other fatherly shit I have no interest in." The bitterness in his tone didn't escape me.

"Why aren't you and John close?"

"Why would we be?"

"He's your uncle."

He shrugged and lifted a fresh shirt out of the drawer. "Not my problem."

"I don't think it's good for you to be so distant."

"Why do you care?"

"Because I care about you." My voice was now raised from the frustration I felt.

He blew out an annoyed breath. "You shouldn't. Why would you?"

"You have to let people care about you. You can't just keep your emotions bottled up and ignore them. Sooner or later they will come out."

"I told you I do feel emotion. I feel anger and I feel hatred. Isn't that enough?"

"No. You have to stop punishing yourself."

He shook his head. "You wouldn't say that if you knew *why* I *punished myself*, as you put it."

"Try me," I challenged. Sheldon thought I could get him to talk. I wanted to test that theory.

"I'll pass." He picked up my forgotten burger and walked to the door. *I was totally busted.*

"Keiran?" He stopped at the door but kept his back turned, his head turned to the side. "How is anyone supposed to love you if you can't even love yourself?"

His jaw clenched, and his hand fisted around the knob before he answered. "I don't want anyone to love me," he said coldly. He walked out and slammed the bedroom door, and I felt like he had just slammed the door keeping my heart as well.

For once, his words didn't make me cry, but it didn't mean it didn't piss me off. I sulked on his bed with my arms crossed, tapping my foot on the mattress. That's how he found me when he returned from his shower wearing only a towel. I could see his bulge pressing against the material. *Oh, God, stay focused.*

"What do you mean you don't want anyone to love you?" I asked as soon as he cleared the doorway.

"Do you?" he asked dryly.

"I—what?"

"Are you planning to fall in love with me?" His voice was harsh as he glared at me from across the bedroom.

FEAR ME

"I'm not sure that's possible for us," I answered truthfully.

"Then what are we talking about?" he asked and turned away, letting me know he wasn't interested in an answer. Nonetheless, I struggled over what to say and most importantly, why I cared so much that he didn't believe in love. Keiran wasn't a forever person and neither was I because neither of us believed in happily ever after.

When he dropped his towel, my attention shifted at the sight of his strong body still damp from his shower out on display. Suddenly, I wanted him in the worst way despite the danger of it all. He must have felt the same because, when he turned back to face me, his erection was prominent, and the look in his eyes was dark and promising.

"We may not have love, but we have this. This is all it will ever be," he said as he undressed me.

"Do I have a say?" I asked with bitterness heavy in my mind and making its way down to my heart. Soon it could very well take over my soul—and then it would be too late.

"No, baby. It's already done," he said as he laid his body over mine and entered me slowly. He closed his eyes briefly before opening them again. "I'm addicted to you."

# CHAPTER TWENTY-NINE

I HADN'T REALIZED I'd fallen asleep until I woke up in a dark room again, but this time there wasn't any feeling of fear. I reluctantly rolled over to my back with a low groan. I thought about the homework I needed to do. Keiran was distracting me way too much. I had to keep a head start on my homework for good grades.

I rubbed the spot next to me where he'd been and found it cold.

*How long was I out?*

I quickly left his room and heard the television downstairs, so I followed the sound. When I reached the living room, I saw only his uncle sitting on the leather sofa. He looked up at me seemingly sensing my presence. I couldn't meet his eyes after what Keiran and I had done upstairs. I'd forgotten he was home. Sexual desire had once again clouded my judgment, and I prayed he hadn't heard us.

"They're in the basement," he offered. I would have said thanks, but he'd already turned back to the television, so I left.

When I opened the door, I could hear a buzzing

sound drift up from the bottom of the stairs and the low rumble of Keiran's voice. I walked down and found Keiran sitting in a chair with a bottle of alcohol in his hands and Keenan sitting behind him holding a needle gun. They looked up and noticed me as I walked closer.

"What are you guys doing?"

"He finally let me work on him." Keenan grinned and dipped the needle in ink and brought it to his back. I instinctively stretched my neck to see but couldn't see what he was drawing from where I stood.

"Keiran?"

"I forgive myself," he said with sarcasm, holding my gaze and bringing the bottle to his lips again. I hadn't known Keiran to drink heavily, but then again, I still didn't know much about him.

"By getting a tattoo?"

"By confessing my sins the only way I can."

That took me by surprise. "Oh."

"Come here." He patted his lap and Keenan scowled at his back.

"Be still, man." Keenan looked up at me with a sly smile. "Hey, Lake, what's with all the claw marks? You ruined my canvas." I ignored Keiran's offer and Keenan's comment and pulled up a chair in front of him. As badly as I wanted to see what he was doing, I ignored the temptation and rested my hands on my knees.

"Don't you need a license to do that?" They both snorted, and Keenan continued to work. "Is it because of what I said?" I went on, changing questions.

"No," he answered without hesitation.

"Oh." I wondered again what sins could an eight-year-old possibly commit, and I once again thought about the girl in the photo. I didn't know if it was wise to bring it up to him. It would open up a can of worms for sure, and I still may not get any answers.

"How bad does it hurt?"

"I've felt worse."

"I should get one—"

"No," he said vehemently. "I want your body just the way it is. And there is no way in hell anyone is getting their hands on you."

"Be real, Keiran."

"I am. I said no."

"Shel's got one," Keenan piped in, interrupting our silent stare-down.

"Where?" I asked. I hadn't seen one, and she never mentioned getting one.

"On her ass. I put my name there a few months ago," he said cockily. Sheldon was still seventeen, so I was sure her parents hadn't allowed it.

"Let me guess... her parents don't know?"

"Nope. Her dad would kill me."

"So why do it?"

"We were drinking and—"

"Wait, you tattooed her while you guys were drunk?"

He shrugged. "It came out pretty good."

"That's not the point and you know it."

"Ha, all four of us have been drinking since we were thirteen. We can handle our liquor." I shook my head but didn't say anything else. They were all crazy. "I promise not to tattoo your ass while I'm drunk."

"You won't go anywhere near her ass," Keiran barked.

Keenan snorted and rolled his eyes. "Guy gets his first girlfriend, and suddenly, he thinks he's the boss of everyone."

"Keenan—" Keiran began.

As much screwing as he did, I was sure there had to have been a girlfriend or two—or six, so I asked, "What about Anya?"

"That crazy nut? No way! She isn't even that good of a lay," Keenan said before Keiran could respond.

"And how would you know? She was Keiran's girl-friend. You already have a girlfriend."

"She wasn't my girlfriend," Keiran finally answered cutting Keenan off.

"That's not what she said." I crossed my arms over my chest and sat back in my seat.

"Are we really going to do this right now? I fucked her twice. The second time only happened because I was drunk, and she hopped on my dick uninvited."

"Whatever," I rolled my eyes again. I seemed to do that a lot around him. He narrowed his eyes at me and breathed through his nose, and I could tell he was getting pissed.

"Why do girls always ask questions they don't want to know the answer to?" Keenan asked. Keiran ignored him and continued to stare at me.

"They're hardwired that way," Dash said appearing from the stairs with Sheldon right behind him. "Aw, man, you're getting tatted? Me next."

"I haven't finished your design yet. Why do you have to be so complicated anyway?"

"I'm a deep man. What can I say? This one is special." He then turned his gaze on me. "Hey, Lake. You talk to your girl yet?"

*Shit, Willow!* I'd forgotten about her because I was so wrapped up in Keiran. *I am such a shitty friend.* "No, actually, I haven't. Excuse me," I said standing up and heading for the stairs.

"Hey, I'll come with," Sheldon said. I shrugged and made my way up the stairs. When I got to Keiran's room, I pulled my cell phone out of my bag and saw a missed call from her. I dialed Willow and waited for her to pick up.

"Thank God. I thought you had abandoned me," she sniffled.

"Do you have a cold?"

"No. My mom is home." Willow and her mom didn't usually get along well. She hated how independent and free Willow was. It only got worse when she found out about Dash. Now all they did was argue. Her mom was always pushing her past hang-ups on her. "Are you home? I want to come over."

"I'm at Keiran's, but I'll come now."

She let out a dry laugh. "We both know that isn't about to happen. When was the last time you slept in your own bed?"

"His uncle is home."

"Oh, snap. You met him? What's he like?"

"Intense."

"Maybe it runs in the family."

"Yeah, maybe. Anyway, I don't think I'll be staying over tonight. That would be too weird." We had talked for a few more minutes before I passed the phone to Sheldon, who wanted to talk to her. I left the bedroom and went back to the basement. Their low voices instantly put me on alert, and I paused on the stairs.

"Arizona, Kentucky, and Wisconsin are battling right now. They're at the top of my list. I haven't made a decision."

"Because of Lake, right? Where is she going?"

"I don't know. She hasn't said."

"So ask her."

"I'm getting to it, moron. I had to take care of those other two."

"What did Mario do with them?"

"He's keeping them on ice for me."

"He's a scary motherfucker. How do you know that

guy?"

"He used to be a partner with the people who owned me."

"Shit."

"Fuck."

*Owned him? Someone owned him? Oh, hell no.* I needed him to talk. "Who owned you?" I asked, walking the rest of the way down the stairs.

"Lake…"

"No, Keiran. You just said someone owned you."

"Let it go," he said through clenched teeth.

"I can't just let it go. I have a right to know."

He stomped over to me and pushed me against the wall by the staircase. "You don't have the right to shit except what I tell you. My past is my own."

"But you said—"

"I know what I said. It's none of your business."

"Why do Dash and Keenan get to know?"

"For fuck sake, girl—"

"Um, guys? As much as this turns me on to watch you fight, we need to go." Keenan deadpanned.

"Go? Where are you going?"

"*We* are going to play laser tag," Keiran emphasized.

"Yeah, it's Monday Madness. All the food you can eat and my boy Teddy is working tonight, so we get drinks, too. Let's roll!" He and Dash ran up the stairs tripping and shoving each other to get to the top first.

"I've never played laser tag."

"No? Well then, you can't be on my team. I don't lose," he gloated. I hit him on the shoulder, and his eyes danced with mischief.

"Can I see your tat?"

"It's not finished."

"Oh… later then?" As he stared down at me, I could

see the turmoil behind his eyes. He stepped away from me and jammed his fingers into his hair. *Did he already regret getting the tattoo?*

"We need to go," he said, taking my hand and pulling me up the stairs. I heard Keenan creating a ruckus as soon as we reached the first floor.

"What are you pigs doing here? This isn't the time we scheduled."

"We'd just thought we'd come ask a few questions and maybe have a look around. We hope you don't mind," one of the suits said, but his tone suggested he didn't care otherwise.

"You can ask your questions from the doorstep because you aren't stepping foot inside this house without a warrant."

"Do we need one, Mr. Masters?" the second detective asked in a gruff tone. "Is your father home by any chance? We'd really like to speak with him, as well."

"Don't you guys have some donuts you need to suck back or was that just my cock?"

"Keenan, watch your mouth and stop being a pain in my ass," his father ordered from somewhere in the house. Keenan sucked his teeth but didn't budge. I was surprised John hadn't come to the door, but considering the many times he'd bailed them out of trouble, it wasn't all that surprising he would ignore the law standing just outside his door.

Keiran went straight to the door, and I followed behind. I don't know why, but I felt the need to stand between Keiran and trouble. Someone had to be the voice of reason.

"We aren't interested in whatever the fuck you think you know," he said without preamble.

"You know why we're here, son. We just want to ask some questions about the disappearance of Ms.

Risdell and Officer Reynolds's son."

"So ask them." He crossed his arm over his chest and stood next to Keenan, who now wore a cocky expression on his face.

"This is hardly the way to conduct an interview." The officer appeared flustered and angry, and I tried to stifle my laugh, but they must have heard when their gazes landed on me.

"Ah, Ms. Monroe. How convenient. We were planning to pay you a visit next. Do invite us in."

"Not my house," I said and walked up to Keiran, molding myself against his back. My touch seemed to relax him as I felt the tension in his back fade.

"How cute," the officer mocked, noticing our embrace.

"We'll be back," his partner warned as they retreated to their car.

"Dude, you sound like a Terminator reject."

"I loved that movie," Keiran commented.

*Ha! A fact about Keiran. I was getting somewhere.* "Me three," I piped. They turned to grin at me.

"Thanks for sending those pigs squealing," Keenan grinned. "One for all..."

"And all for one." I bumped fists with him when he held his out.

"I hated that movie," Keiran added.

"Only because it had a happy ending."

"I hated that movie too, actually."

"You two lovebirds make me sick."

"Jealous?"

He snorted. "No. Dating Sheldon is like dating a guy and a girl at the same time. It's awesome. Although I do wonder sometimes..."

"Where is Sheldon," I asked, looking around.

"She and Dash went ahead. I hung back for you

guys. Took long enough."

"Shut up." Keiran cuffed Keenan on the back of his head. Just then, their uncle came out of the living room.

"Where are you boys going?"

"Laser tag," Keenan answered shortly. Keiran barely spared him a glance.

"Well, stay out of trouble and get this girl home at a decent hour. Don't make me come looking for you," he warned.

"Sure thing pops," Keenan agreed, halfheartedly. John grunted and went back into the living room.

Keiran pulled me by the hand, and we left out of the house. "Oh, wait. My phone." I turned to go back inside for it when Keenan stopped me.

"Shelly gave it to me to give to you." Keenan handed me my phone.

"Hey, do you think Willow could come?"

"I don't mind, but you do know Dash will be there, right?"

"Yes, I know. It won't hurt to ask." Once we got into Keiran's car, I dialed Willow, who answered on the first ring.

"Please tell me you're home," she breathed into the phone.

"No, but I have something better. Come play laser tag with us."

"Us?"

"Yeah. Keiran, Keenan, Sheldon, and..."

"And Dash?" she guessed.

"Yeah, but—"

"I'll come," she cut in. "But I'm bringing Buddy as reinforcement."

\* \* \*

"You can't wear bright colors to laser tag! Dude," Keenan looked at Dash, "tell her she can't wear bright clothes to laser tag." Willow had just met us outside of the arena appearing as flamboyant as usual despite her earlier mood. She'd dressed in only jeans and a T-shirt that showed off her figure, but her jeans were pink and her shirt was purple.

"I tried to tell her," Buddy said walking up to slap hands with the guys.

"Suck it, morons. I'll wear what I want."

"She's on your team," Keenan whined to Dash.

Dash ignored him and continued to stare at Willow while Willow looked everywhere but at him. After a few moments of tense silence, he smirked and walked over to Keiran and began whispering low to him. I knew they were up to something.

"All right," Keiran spoke up. "We aren't pairing up. This is a free for all."

Willow then flipped off Keenan, who smiled and blew kisses at her. Sheldon caught them and hit his arm, growling, "She's mine." I laughed at the little competition they seemed to have over her. Sometimes I think Sheldon really did have a crush on Willow.

"Thank fuck! I love you, sis, but you'll get me killed." Buddy had his war face on as if this was real. *Boys.*

"You guys are ridiculous." She snatched the gear he offered to her and huffed.

Dash explained the rules, and we activated our sensors. Just before we started, I noticed Dash lean in behind Willow and whisper something in her ear with an evil look on his face. Her face paled, and her eyes widened and suddenly she took off in the darkness of the arena. He chuckled and followed after her, but it didn't seem as if he was in a hurry. Sheldon, Buddy, and Keenan all ran into the arena, and I could immediately hear the sound of lasers firing.

"Standing there is a good way to lose," Keiran said. "It's okay. I always save the best for last." He disappeared inside the arena, the dark swallowing him up.

I clutched my weapon and slowly walked in. As soon as I did, my sensor beeped, and I looked over to see Keenan bouncing up and down in victory. On his second bounce, he was tagged in mid-air by Keiran, who turned and winked in at me. Another series of shots were fired, so I ducked for cover behind a low wall near the entrance. My blood was already pumping with excitement. Keeping low, I moved cautiously around the arena, which had grown quiet, so I knew the guys were on the hunt. I wondered how Sheldon and Willow were fairing.

"Ah, babe, you got me! How could you?" I heard Keenan yell somewhere in the distance.

I looked over the wall and saw a flash of blonde hair a few feet in front of me. It was Buddy with his back turned, but he looked like he was concentrating on something, and that's when I noticed Keiran. He was about to catch him unaware. I knew we technically weren't on the same team, but the fierce need to protect him even in a silly game overrode my common sense. I shot up and tagged Buddy from behind just as Keiran turned and tagged Buddy from the front. *He knew he was there all along!*

Buddy spun around and looked at us both in shock before running off, leaving Keiran and me to face off. He stared at me, and I stared back while he seemed to be praising and challenging me with his eyes. I quickly fired a shot but missed, and as I ran off, I could hear him say, "I'm hurt, baby, but you still have to actually aim the gun at me."

*Cocky bastard.* As I maneuvered through the arena, I realized it was built like a maze with a few good hiding spots, but I was now too into the game to hide as I searched for my next target.

I quickly rounded the corner and bumped into a hard chest that knocked me down on my ass. "Well, well, well. Look who I have here. Tell you what, sweetheart. Say you'll leave my cousin for me, and I might consider letting you live."

I plastered a thoughtful look on my face while he stared down at me. "Not a chance," I said and fired off two shots at his chest. I rolled away like they did in the movies and ducked behind another wall, escaping his return fire.

I stalked around the arena looking for my next victim. *Jeez, Lake, you're having way too much fun with this.* "Pssst." I looked around for the source of the sound but didn't see anyone. "Up here, girl." I looked up and saw Sheldon sitting on one the walls.

"How did you get up there?"

"Being a cheerleader has its perks." She jumped down in front of me with a wily grin on her face. "Want to form a secret alliance and take these douchebags down?"

I didn't even have to think about it. "Sure."

"Sweet."

"Wait, where is Willow?"

She shrugged and said, "Don't know—haven't seen her." *Dash probably got his paws on her.*

"Where is your brother?"

"I don't know that either." She smirked, and I knew she was thinking the same thing I was. "We got to move. I'll take right, you take left." She was gone again before I could respond.

"Consorting with the enemy?" I whirled around

and found Keiran lounging against the wall.

"Are you following me?"

"Yes," he answered shamelessly.

"Why?"

"It's laser tag, babe."

"Well, stop it anyway." He didn't respond but continued to watch me. "Are you going to shoot me?"

"You mean like you tried to shoot me?"

"Well, do it already."

He shook his head and stood up straight. "I told you I was saving the best for last."

"I could shoot you."

"You could. But you won't."

I aimed the laser gun at him. "I won't?" *Oh shit, will I?* Keiran was watching me intensely so he didn't see the dot on his chest until it was too late. He'd been tagged.

"Score for the Dream Team. Yeah, baby!" Sheldon burst around the corner and shuffled her feet around. "I got the big bad Keiran!" She blew imaginary smoke from her weapon.

Keiran watched me with a small smile on his face. "You're going to pay for that later," he promised me even though Sheldon had been the one to tag him. A shiver of anticipation ran through me.

"Don't make promises you probably shouldn't keep." His smile spread wider at my challenge.

"Will you two stop eye-fucking each other? We have a war to finish!" Sheldon dragged me off, and Keiran had once again disappeared from sight, but I knew he was still stalking me around the arena.

We played non-stop after that. Buddy, Keenan, and Sheldon were tagged out, ending our secret alliance, and leaving only Keiran and me. Oh, and Dash and Willow—if anyone could find them.

FEAR ME

The arena was silent as I moved through it. Keiran and I seemed to be evading each other pretty well... unless he already knew where I was. I quickly looked behind me but didn't see any sign of him. I was hunting him just as much as he was hunting me, but that didn't stop me from feeling like the prey. I stopped by one of the high walls and took out the map the officials gave us. *Where the hell was he?*

"You never were good at hiding from me." I heard him behind me and spun around to find him moving out of the shadows. I tried to run, but he was too fast as he hit me twice in the chest. I was tagged out. "I win."

\* \* \*

WE LEFT THE arena with my hand swallowed up by his larger one. I lost, but it wasn't surprising. Buddy, Sheldon, and Keenan were waiting nearby, their gear already shed.

"Where are Dash and Willow?" They all shrugged, and I immediately looked up at Keiran. When he quickly averted his gaze, I narrowed my eyes.

"Buddy, could you please go see where you sister is?" Keiran's hand squeezed mine in warning, but I ignored him.

"Why?" he asked and stayed seated.

"Remember that time in the fifth grade..."

"I'm going." He shot up from his seat and disappeared back inside the arena.

"What happened in the fifth grade?" Keenan asked.

"A lady never tells," Sheldon answered for me.

He looked at her with his eyebrows raised. "You're a lady?" She slapped his arm, and he stole a deep kiss from her. In no time, she was in his lap, and they were making out.

Keiran and I were shedding our gear when Buddy came out of the arena with a disturbed look on his face. "Buddy?" I asked concerned.

"There are just some things a brother should never see." He shook his head and walked past us and into the main lobby.

"Come on. I want to feed you," Keiran said and took my hand.

"But we have to wait for Dash and Willow." He ignored me and continued pulling me into the dining area. Buddy was already seated at a large booth, so we slid in with him.

"Buddy, what did you see?" Instead of answering me, he looked at Keiran and then back at me, and shook his head.

"I'd rather not relive that, thank you very much."

"Hey, did you order already?" Dash asked as he sat down and pulled Willow in after him. I stared at Willow, willing her to look at me, but she avoided my gaze and looked down at her hands so I kicked her under the table.

"Oww!" She finally looked at me, and I gave her a pointed look, which she ignored.

"Dude, what the fuck?" Buddy asked Dash.

He grinned at him. "You'll thank me later, youngin."

"But that's my sister! Besides... I've been dancing that dance since I was thirteen."

"Ewww, Buddy!"

He cut his eye at her. "Do you really want to go there after what I just saw?" Her cheeks colored, and she looked back down.

"Keiran, let me out. I have to pee," I huffed when he didn't budge. When he finally moved, I raced to the bathroom. I hadn't realized I'd been holding it, but

FEAR ME

when the excitement of the game died, I felt the need to pee. I used the bathroom and looked in the mirror. For some reason, I found myself freeing my hair from the band and letting it fall around my shoulders and down my back.

*For fuck sake! When did I start caring about how my hair looked?* I left the bathroom, annoyed with myself. Next, I would be wearing five-inch pumps to school. I once again thought about Anya and Trevor's disappearance. *I have to get Keiran to talk.*

"You should be more careful of the company you keep."

"Mr. Martin?" I couldn't hide the surprise from seeing him standing near the back exit. I'd only ever seen him come to the gym. *What was he doing here?*

"Yes, dear."

"Sorry. I didn't think this would be your type of place."

"There is a lot you don't know about me, young lady."

*Whoa. Because that didn't sound creepy...* "Well, it was nice seeing you," I replied feeling awkward and creeped out.

He quickly approached me with his hand reached out as if he would grab me. "Before you go—"

"Come here, Lake." Dash appeared behind me and was standing near the men's bathroom. The look he gave Mr. Martin was chilling. I walked over to him, and he grabbed my hand. I was secretly grateful for his sudden appearance. I didn't like the vibes I was getting from him.

"I was only talking to her, young man."

"Yeah? Well, you're done talking."

The hard look that appeared on Mr. Martin's face scared me. I'd never seen him be anything other than

Page | **418**

charming and polite. But as soon as the look appeared, it was gone again. He gave us a polite smile and excused himself, leaving out the back door.

"Who was that guy?" Dash asked while frowning at the door Mr. Martin disappeared through.

"Mr. Martin. He comes by my job—excuse me—my old job, a lot. Why?"

"I've never seen him before."

I shrugged his suspicion off. "Six Forks isn't all that small."

"Still, you should stay away from him."

"He's harmless, Dash. Charlie thinks he has a crush on me. He's actually very polite and a gentleman," I argued.

"Would you rather hear this from me or Keiran?" He raised an eyebrow and looked down at me.

"Good point," I grumbled then thought better of it. "Despite what you or anyone else thinks, Keiran isn't my father. I had a father and he left."

"Keiran wants to control you, but he also wants to keep you safe. I can understand that need."

"You know... you may have a shot again if you stop trying to manipulate her."

"Oh, yeah? How?" He raised an eyebrow and looked at me skeptically.

"Be the guy she fell in love with."

\* \* \*

A COUPLE OF hours later, Keiran was parking his car in my driveway, and I finally admitted I had a fun night. My aunt would be pissed if she found out I stayed out this late on a Monday night. I leaned over to kiss him goodnight and couldn't deny how natural it felt, but when he leaned away from me and shut off his engine,

FEAR ME

the feeling faded fast.

"Who is Mr. Martin?"

"No need to be jealous, babe. He's like fifty." I smiled at him, but he didn't reciprocate. When he continued to stare me down, I sighed and sat back in the seat. "I don't know really. He's some guy who came to the gym. I met him about a year ago."

He shook his head and took his gaze off me to stare out through the windshield. "You continue to test my patience," he whispered, and I got the feeling he wasn't really talking to me.

"How am I testing you?"

"Stay away from him."

"He's harmless."

"Lake!"

"Don't raise your voice at me, Keiran. I can hear you just fine."

"You're a pain in my ass," he gritted.

"Ditto." We sat in silence for a moment, each in our own thoughts. "What did you do with Anya and Trevor?"

"What makes you think I did something to them?"

"Maybe because I saw Dash and Keenan take off with them and maybe because I overheard you tell them that Mario has them. Tell me the truth."

He sat for so long not saying anything that I almost gave up on it. "I'm setting them up to be given to the same people who kept me for seven years."

"Kept you?"

He looked reluctant to go on before he answered. "Yes. Before I came here, I worked for some bad people at a very young age."

"But I thought you were with your mother?" Keiran's past was puzzling. I struggled to put the pieces together with the little I had. Nothing made sense.

"She's the reason I had to work for those people."

"Don't you know who they are?"

"No."

"So how will you know who to give Trevor and Anya to?"

"Mario will handle that. I don't know because I don't want to know. The less connecting me to them, the less chance I have of getting caught."

"So what will he do with them?"

"They'll disappear. They won't be killed... as long as they do what they are told." Keiran's explanation was sketchy at best, and it all sounded horrible. As much as I hated Anya and Trevor for what they had done and all that they had planned, I didn't think I could live with it on my conscience.

"Get them back," I stated, holding my voice firm.

His head whipped around, his gaze burning hot over me. "What?"

"I want you to bring them back."

"No." His jaw hardened, and I could see the muscles of his cheekbone clench.

"We can't do this to them. Look at what it did to you."

He shrugged. "I survived."

"Did you?"

"Doesn't matter. They don't come back. Ever."

"Then I want nothing to do with you. Stay away from me." I threw open the passenger door and slammed it shut. Keiran was out and around to my side before I could move two steps. He grabbed me up by my upper arms and forced me up against the side of the car.

"If you have any idea of what they were planning for you, you wouldn't be spouting this bullshit out of your mouth. I don't give a fuck if you like how I protect you, but *I will* protect you. It's my burden to bear."

"And mine!" I cried.

He released a ragged breath and looked as if he wanted to strangle me. "Lake..."

"I'm serious. Get them back or stay away from me. I won't let you make my soul as ugly as yours." When he flinched, my hand flew to my mouth, muffling my horrified gasp. I realized what I had just said at the same time my heart crashed and shattered at my feet. The look on his face broke my heart. I did that. I knew I hurt him worse than he'd ever hurt me.

"Keiran, I—" I was cut off when he shoved away from me and looked down at me with a deeper hatred than I had ever seen in his eyes before. It was suddenly over as abruptly as it had started, and then he was gone.

I could only assume he would walk out of my life now.

# CHAPTER THIRTY

I NEVER MEANT to call his soul ugly. It was beyond mean. It was downright cruel. Some might say it was justified or even true. After all, his cruelty and manipulations were far more hurtful than anything I could ever say to him.

So why did I still feel so damn guilty?

I thought I wanted Anya and Trevor to pay for what they had done, but the truth was I just needed this whole nightmare to go away. I needed to be seven years old again and with my parents.

After ten years, I still felt a strong connection with them—one that hurt more than helped, though.

I made it to the front door with a heavy heart. I failed to think of just one way to make this right outside of begging for forgiveness. But it was also because of what I knew I had to do if Keiran didn't bring them back.

I wasn't afraid anymore. I was tired.

As I opened the door and stepped inside, I felt the familiar need to run. It wasn't so much what I saw or heard but what I felt. I looked around the empty house.

All was quiet, and nothing seemed disturbed, but I couldn't shake the feeling that something wasn't right.

"I've been waiting for you." The eerie sound of a voice that should not have been in my home startled me. The scream that would have torn through my lungs was silenced by the sudden press of cold steel against my cheek. "Don't scream. I don't have to hurt you, but I will."

"What are you doing here?" The shriek of my voice did nothing to show the terror I felt.

"I tried to warn you away. I tried to help you."

"Warn me about what?"

"I thought you were smart. You're just like every other dumb slut."

His enraged and almost psychopathic voice was the last thing I had heard before I felt the butt of the gun slam down on my skull.

* * *

SHE WAS BACK. She was smiling down at me, but her smile didn't reach her eyes. In her eyes, there was fear. I knew because they were like my own in so many ways.

She looked sad too, but I could tell she was happy to see me, and for the first time since they had disappeared, I was happy to see her, too.

I didn't fear the anger or hatred feeling of being abandoned. I felt relieved because they'd finally come back for me. I was going home.

A strong hand appeared on her shoulder. It was him—my dad. But he didn't smile at me.

He wouldn't even look at me. He was looking at Mom. He was saying something to her. She shook her head and reached out for me, and I felt my hand reaching for her. A drop of moisture dropped onto her shoulder. He was crying when he finally looked at me.

He was so handsome and tall. I remembered moments spent on his shoulders when he would play with me.

I remembered now.

He loved me, and I loved him, too. I loved them both. I missed them.

*"Why?"* I tried to ask, but no sound came out. I tried again but stopped when I realized he was pulling her away. *"No! Don't go. Don't leave me. Not again."* I screamed and I screamed, but nothing happened.

He looked back at me once more while my mother cried and cried as he led her away.

*"We can't help her now," he said.*

My mother turned around almost desperately. She was pointing. Pointing at something behind me.

I turned my head, and suddenly, I was on the playground. I saw a little boy a few feet away from me.

Keiran.

He was as I knew him first—eight again with the sun shining, but this time, the world was quiet.

Quiet like death.

It was then I noticed he was holding a gun in his hand and dangling from his fingers was the gold locket.

His eyes were sad when he looked at me, but they were also full of anger.

He looked down at his hand, and I noticed the discoloring on the locket.

It was... blood.

"Keiran?"

"I killed them," he said.

"Who? Who did you kill?" He visibly shook as he took deep, ragged breaths. "You have to tell me who they are!" I yelled desperately.

His hand rose slowly and pointed the gun at me. I

shook my head, but instead of trying to get away, I moved closer. "I kill," he cried and fired the gun.

\* \* \*

I WAS RIPPED away from my nightmare and left drenched in sweat and gasping for breath. I would have thought my nightmare was over, but my throbbing headache said otherwise.

I opened my eyes and looked out of a window. I could see the unkempt lawn but nothing else.

"It's good to see you awake. I was beginning to think I might have hit you too hard. How is your head, by the way?"

"It *was* fine," I said sarcastically. He smiled wide, and for the first time, I didn't find anything charming about it.

"I'm sorry I had to do that, but I didn't think you would come with me willingly." I stared back into the cold eyes of Mr. Martin as he sat in the corner of the room.

"Why are you doing this? You were behind the break-in, weren't you?"

"Why does anyone ever do anything? For money, dear girl, and yes, I did leave the photo. Sad what happened to that little girl."

"But my aunt isn't here and she isn't rich." He laughed as if I'd just told a joke or said something witty. Or maybe the man was just nuts. The latter explanation fit better.

"I don't want money from your aunt or you. In fact, this has little to do with you at all."

"What? Then why—"

"You are merely bait, Lake."

"Bait for who?"

"Are you really this blind or is it by choice?"

"I'm sorry, Mr. Martin. It must have been the blow to my head I recently received. You'll have to help me with this one."

"Well, for starters, my name isn't Martin. It's Masters, and I'm here for my son."

# CHAPTER THIRTY-ONE

THE TIME IT took for me to process what he'd just said was two and a half seconds. No shit—I counted. "But everyone thinks you're dead."

"No, I'm very much alive." He crossed his leg over the other and appeared way too casual for my liking.

"If you've been alive all this time, then why are you just now coming around?"

"Because my son would have put a bullet in my head the moment he saw me," he answered, full of disdain. I frowned because, like everyone else, I was under the impression Keiran had never met his father.

"If Keiran is your son... why would he want to kill you?"

"I haven't been the best father." He shrugged, noncommittally. "I've told a lot of lies, Miss Monroe and have done many ugly things. Things that were necessary to get what is rightfully mine."

"Are you even sorry for it? Why should I believe you now?" There wasn't a hint of compassion in the way he talked about his estranged son and his dead mother.

"I really don't care if you believe or not. You serve

one purpose, and that is to bring Keiran to me. I've watched you both for some time now. Long before I ever made myself known to you. I must say it was intriguing to see the way my son treated the girl he loves."

"What makes you so sure he's in love with me?"

"For your sake, I hope he is."

"I'm sure a man such as yourself wouldn't be willing to risk so much off hope... that's if you really even believe in it."

His eyebrow lifted, and he pursed his lips. "My son lets you get away with a mouth like that?" His eyes darkened much like the way Keiran's often did, and I was smart enough to know when I was out of my league.

"What amount of money is worth all this?"

"Millions." His eyes shone with greed. "Millions that should have been mine years ago."

"How do you expect your eighteen-year-old son to pay you that kind of money?"

"You and I both know Keiran is far from being helpless and more than capable of doing many illegal acts. Oh, yes, I know all about Anya Risdell and Trevor Reynolds. I have connections, too," he said in a conspiratorial tone. "Keiran is part heir to a vast fortune that he will inherit once he turns twenty-one."

"Where have I heard this before?"

"I realize the situation is extremely cliché and yet extremely real."

"You said part..."

"Yes, the other boy—Keenan." I didn't miss the contempt in his voice as he spoke his name. "And my brother as well... if he ever marries."

"So won't you get part of the fortune, too?"

"Unfortunately, I've already received the first portion of my inheritance. The same portion that Keiran is set to inherit in three years."

"I don't understand."

"Our family has always been determined to contin-ue the Masters lineage for many generations to come. For the past fifty or sixty years, the rate at which we have been known to marry respectfully and reproduce has declined so much so, there are now stipulations in place to ensure our name does not die. In order for any of us to receive our full inheritance, we must marry and produce children. We receive our initial and much smaller portion when we become of age and the rest once we have completed our duties."

Talk about blackmail. Rich people were grade-A crazy. "So you have money—"

"I *had* money, Miss Monroe. I have expensive tastes and owe a great deal of debt that could cost me my life if it remains unpaid. I've got by the past ten years on a lucky gambling streak that has since run out."

"Ever heard of bargain shopping?" He regarded me with narrowed eyes that mirrored his son. How had I not seen this before?

"Please do try not to test my patience. I assure you I won't hesitate to hurt you—although I can't kill you... not yet anyway."

I nodded once and held my tongue. "Understood."

"Good." He uncrossed his legs and stood, heading to the dresser where a bottle of brown liquid that I knew to be alcohol waited. He poured a glass and quickly tossed it back before pouring another. "Where was I?"

"You're broke." He sent me a sharp look, and I shrunk back against the headboard. "Sorry... old habits. So if Keiran hates you, and he doesn't inherit for anoth-er three years, why are you doing this now?"

"Those debts I previously mentioned aren't willing to wait three years."

"But I seriously doubt he will help you."

"No... he won't."

"Then how..." Realization dawned on me at the look in his eyes. "No!" I yelled, jumping from the bed. My feet were planted wide as I faced him. "I won't let you hurt him," I growled. If Keiran died, then his money would undoubtedly forfeit to his father as his next of kin.

He laughed, which pissed me off further. "You know it astounds me that you are so ready to protect him even if it means harm to yourself—"

"If that's what it takes," I interrupted with steel in my voice.

"That is truly remarkable, Miss Monroe. My son has done nothing but hurt you for years." He must have noticed the surprised look on my face, so then he said, "Yes, I know all about that. The Reynolds boy filled me in. He was all too willing to bring my son down. It's a shame Keiran got to him first because I would have eventually killed him myself. I could have had the money I needed a year ago if it weren't for him."

I couldn't believe it, but he was right. If Trevor hadn't framed, Keiran... he would be dead. "You were the person Trevor said wanted to meet me the night of the fair."

"Yes, I was, Miss Monroe."

"You're insane."

"Call it what you want. I knew then you were just the pawn I needed to reel Keiran in. I need an advantage when I face him."

"What makes you so sure Keiran would kill you? That's a little extreme for being an absentee father."

"No, I was much worse than that."

"I'm not buying."

"Keiran has killed before. Many times. Do you believe that?"

"No," I lied but my voice wavered as I thought about the girl in the photo.

"You're a terrible liar, Miss Monroe. One thing my son and I have in common is a lack of mercy or remorse. He'd harm his own mother if it suited him. He's already proven that."

"What do you mean? What happened to his mother?"

"She'd dead," he answered. His face and voice were void of any emotion.

"Did she overdose? Keiran said she was a prostitute and a drug addict."

He regarded me with an impatient look and a twist of his lips. "No wonder my son has such an easy time manipulating you. Your propensity for being gullible is astounding or is it my son's cock that makes you so trusting?"

"What happened to her?" I bit out. Mitch was treating this whole situation like a puzzle that he wanted me to piece together with half-truths.

"She was murdered." All the moisture in my mouth disappeared instantly.

"Who murdered her?" I managed to ask around my nervousness.

He watched me with an amused look. "I can tell by the look in your eyes that you already know who."

"You're lying!" I cried. My emotions were spilling over and overwhelming me. I was unwilling to believe that Keiran would murder his own mother in cold blood.

"Yes, he most certainly did." he said, answering my silent question.

"How do you know that?"

"Because I was there when he put the bullet in her

head. My son is a cold piece of work. I see he worked you over pretty well. Got you to fall for him, did he?"

"I don't know what you're talking about. Why would he kill his own mother?"

"Because he's a cold-blooded killer. He was trained that way. While most kids were being tucked in at night and being read bedtime stories, my son was out running with the most deadly of criminals and committing un-speakable acts."

"But why would she let him do that? She was sup-posed to protect him."

"She hardly had a say in anything he did. I was re-sponsible for that. His mother was weak. We had some... disagreements, and so she left me just after he was born without a word or trace." His voice lowered, and his eyes darkened as he spoke. "Naturally, I searched for them but came up short for a while. Her father had been her only family but had died when she was six months pregnant, so it was difficult to find her. I'd almost given up until a month before his first birth-day. By then I was filled with nothing but contempt for the bitch and the need for revenge, so I took my son."

"Why wasn't there any record of his birth or a cus-tody suit?" He looked at me in surprise as a smile spread across his face.

"I see you've been doing some digging. She had a home birth, and there wasn't a custody case because I wasn't going to let a judge decide if my son belonged to me or not."

"Oh, God... you kidnapped him."

"Yes, I did." He watched me closely for a reaction as he took a sip of his drink.

"So there would have been a missing person's re-port..."

"Not if his mother didn't file one."

"Why wouldn't she file a missing person's report for her child?"

"Why indeed. I think it might have had something to do with the fact that she was running from me. She never even had him registered after she left me, so there was no record that he was even born—so who would believe her?"

"Why would she hide from you?"

"Because she's a selfish bitch. I offered her the chance to have money and status, but it wasn't enough," he bit out angrily.

"So what did you do with Keiran for seven years and how did you keep quiet for so long that you had a son?" I just had to keep him talking, and then maybe I could figure my way out of this and get some answers.

"I was in debt to a man who ran a very lucrative crime organization that was slightly unorthodox."

"In what way?"

"Let's just say they put a new meaning to the term 'child slavery' because these kids weren't thrown in a sweat shop and working for less than minimum wage. These kids were working for their lives."

"So you gave him to them?" My heart felt like it stopped as I pictured Keiran suffering along with God knows how many other faceless children.

"No, I sold him to them." The gasp that left my chest was heavy and full of pain and sorrow. *He used to be a partner with the people who owned me.* I recalled Keiran's words from earlier today. My heart broke for him all over again.

"You sold your own son?" I wanted to punch some-thing—preferably Mitch fucking Masters.

"My son," he sneered, "was created to make me money, nothing more. If he couldn't get it for me the way I planned, then I had to make adjustments."

"He's your son!"

"He was a means to an end!" Mitch roared. His face was now contorted with barely controlled rage. I fell silent as I pieced together what he was telling me. A moment later, he was the cool, unassuming man I was fooled to think he was. "I left him with a family who worked under their organization until he was old enough to work. I kept tabs on him because he was still valuable to me."

"What is this organization called?"

"Come now," he reproached. "You're going to get me killed." *I wish.* "Not even Keiran knows who they really are." *Could that be true?* It was believable considering his age at the time.

"So how did he end up with his uncle? Did you suddenly grow a conscience?" I asked in disbelief.

"Just after he turned eight, my money ran dry again, so I realized I needed to resume my old plan and marry. I coerced his bitch mother with a chance to save her son if she came away to marry me."

"But how would you explain your eight-year-old son?"

"I would have explained to my family that she was a long lost love and had gotten pregnant before we lost touch. My family had never met her before, nor had any of my friends."

"But Keiran ruined your plan when he killed her."

"Not quite." Just then, his phone rang, and he sent me an apologetic smile. "Excuse me. I really must take this call." Once he stepped out of the room, I rushed for the door but heard the sound of a key turning. I tried the doorknob anyway and found it locked. I banged furiously against the door, but he never returned for some time.

I sat in that room running through everything he

had revealed. It felt like hours later when I heard any semblance of sound outside the door. I could hear heavy thuds and grunts that sounded strangely as if someone was being beaten. I hoped, by some miracle, Keiran or someone had found me, so I began screaming for help.

Not long after, Mitch reappeared in the bedroom where I was being held. The scrape of the key in the lock alerted me of his return. "I want you to behave now. We have company."

"Who?"

"In due time. I've just learned that my son has left Six Forks unexpectedly. This will certainly put a delay in my plans that I cannot afford. I need a favor."

"You're joking, right?"

"Afraid not."

"Well, that's too bad because the only thing I'm willing to do for you is to show you where to fuck off." The hard feeling of his palm on my face sent me flying to the floor and burning pain followed.

"Now that was your first and only warning." He pulled out his cell phone and handed it to me. I cautiously looked up at him from the floor. "Call my son."

Despite his warning, I wasn't willing to put Keiran in danger. *Yeah, I don't get that either.* "No."

"Excuse me?"

"I said no. You're just going to have to kill me."

The temperature in the room seemed to drop a few hundred degrees that could freeze over hell. He watched me for a moment with unmistakable rage simmering within his eyes before he swiftly turned and headed back out the door. He was back before I could make a dash for the door and freedom. It sounded like he was dragging something or rather someone as I soon found out. I first noticed a familiar head, full of dark spiked hair. "It may not be you that I start with..." he warned.

"Keenan!" I was horrified at the sight of his still body bleeding in various places. I immediately crawled over to him to see if he was breathing. When I felt the shallow rise and fall of his breathing, I sent a silent prayer. How did he get Keenan and why?

"What did you do to him?" I screamed.

"My nephew wasn't exactly cooperative with the men I hired. Took three of them to bring him down. They roughed him up pretty good." He shrugged as if it didn't matter either way to him.

"Why Keenan?"

"I've decided to go after all of it. We are essentially the last of a dying breed, and I could give two shits about continuing the line. If I kill them all, then all the monies are mine."

"No." I shielded Keenan with my body. I had to do whatever it took to keep him safe.

"Oh, don't worry. I won't kill him just yet. He is an extra incentive to get Keiran here."

"What about his father, your brother?"

"I'm saving him for last. I want his death to be slow and painful." As he spoke about his brother, I couldn't miss the deep hatred lacing his tone.

"You would take your brother's life, too?"

"My brother has taken much more from me." He looked in Keenan's direction briefly before shooting his eyes back to me. "Now make the call." He dropped the phone in my lap, but I let it lay there untouched until he suddenly pulled out a gun and aimed it at Keenan.

"Okay!" I held out my hands in surrender before picking up the phone.

"Good girl. Keiran trained you well."

I dialed Keiran's number and prayed he didn't answer. But when he finally did, I realized how much I loved and missed the sound of his voice even though now it sounded gruff and full of impatience.

"Who the fuck is this?" he barked.

"Keiran..."

"Lake? Where the fuck are you?" he asked. I could hear the rage, but I could also hear the desperation in his voice.

"I don't know." I instantly broke down crying. Mitch snatched the phone out of my hands.

"Hello, son. You haven't forgotten about your father all these years, have you?" I didn't hear the rest of the conversation. Mitch had walked out, locking me in the room with an unconscious Keenan.

I was afraid for him with not knowing the extent of his injuries. Not to mention being unable to form a clue as to how to get us out of all this safely. I wasn't dumb enough to believe Mitch would let me walk away from this. Not after all he had revealed.

"Keenan," I whispered. "If you can hear me, you need to wake up... please wake up." I nudged him, and amazingly, he began to stir and groan in pain. When his eyes finally opened, he instantly squeezed them closed again.

"Shit," he grumbled.

"It's worse than shit," I half joked.

"Lake?" he groaned out.

"Yes, it's me. Can you sit up?" He exhaled and slowly moved until he was sitting on the floor next to me. "How bad did they hurt you?"

"They?" he asked with a confused look.

"You don't remember?" He was quiet, but the moment he remembered what had happened, his expression changed to anger.

"You mind telling me who the fuck that guy was?"

he growled.

I blanched and stared at him. This time I was the one confused. "You mean you don't know?" He shot me an impatient look, and my frown deepened.

"No, I don't."

"He's—he's your uncle." The silence stretched between us, but a look of incredulity was plastered all over his face.

"My uncle? I don't have an uncle. The only uncle I would have is Keiran's father, and he's dead."

"Well, the dead have risen from the grave because that is him."

"Are you shitting me?"

"I'm afraid not." He blew out a breath and shook his head. "Not to rock the boat or anything, but the guy is whacked."

"Yeah, thanks, I hadn't noticed," he said sarcastically.

"Did he say anything to you at all?"

He frowned. "Only that it was time I paid what was owed to him. Who says shit like that?"

"How much do you know about your inheritance?"

"Inheritance? I have a college fund my dad said was set up for me, but that's about it."

"Well, apparently you're worth millions and he wants it."

"No way."

"It's true."

"Son of a bitch," he groaned. "We need to find a way to call Keiran."

"Already did."

"How?" he asked with his eyebrows raised.

"He made me. He wants to kill you both."

"Well, fuck..."

* * *

KEENAN AND I were thinking up an escape plan when Mitch burst into the room along with two other men. He looked between Keenan and me before motioning the men toward us. However, his little henchman both grabbed Keenan up. Keenan managed to elbow the bald one in the face before he was knocked down with a hard kick to the back of his knee for his trouble.

Once they managed to wrestle him out of the room, I was left with Mitch. He stared at me with a smug look. "Are you going to come more peacefully or do I need to force you?"

"I think I can manage."

"Good to hear. That nephew of mine could be taught a few manners. It's show time, my dear."

"Do I get any last requests?"

"What makes you so sure I will kill you?"

"You told me too much... and your eyes give away everything. You're evil and empty. Incapable of goodwill or remorse."

"You have a wonderful mind. It is such a shame that it must be eradicated. Shall we?"

He gestured to the door, and I walked through it but stopped once I was in the hallway. The house from what I could see looked ordinary but large. He led us outside where two cars with heavily tinted windows were waiting. I slid into the car he directed me to and waited for him to finish talking with his men. Once he climbed into the car, he pulled out a black scrap of material

"This is for your eyes. Can't be too careful." He wrapped and tied the blindfold around my face, and once complete, the car drove off.

"Where is Keenan?"

"Don't worry about it. Your part is all that should matter to you. The pieces will fall where I tell them to."

\* \* \*

I KNEW THE moment we were no longer on the main road. It must have been a dirt path or a gravel road we turned on when the ride turned bumpy. We finally stopped with a screech of tires as the driver slammed on the brakes and cursed.

"Leave it to my boy to take me by surprise." I heard his amused chuckle come from my right.

"Boss, what do we do?"

"We get out."

Mitch had tied my hands minutes ago, so when I heard the sound of the car doors opening, I was dragged out of the car and thrown to the ground. "Careful with her," Mitch said, his voice sounding annoyed. "She's precious cargo, and by the look on my son's face, he looks ready to kill us all right now."

"It sounds as if you are afraid of your own son," I mocked.

"Lake," I heard the familiar call of my name from a short distance in front of me. *Keiran.* He must be closer than I thought. I unconsciously took a step toward the sound of his voice but was snatched back by a rough hand on my hair. My cry of pain pierced the cold night air, and I was brought back against a man's chest. "You're going to lose that when I kill you," I heard Keiran say. The stench of the man's breath spread across my cheek when he laughed and pulled on my hair more.

"Son—" Mitch began.

"I'm not your son." I could hear the anger in Keiran's voice and wished I could see his face.

"Keiran, they have Keenan!"

"Ah, yes. Bring the bastard out," Mitch coldly stated. I heard footsteps, and then the sound of doors opening and slamming. Keenan began yelling obscenities as soon as he was out of the car. My blindfold was suddenly ripped away, and when my eyes adjusted to the darkness, I could see Keiran standing about thirty feet away. He was dressed in all black with a duffel bag on the hood of his car.

"Why the fuck are you here?" Keiran asked. He didn't at all seem surprised to find that his father was very much alive or else he hid it well.

"I would think you would be happy to see me since you have been looking for me."

"I made no secret of it."

"No... you didn't, did you? Well, here I am."

"And all this?"

"The only reason you didn't kill me as soon as I arrived." Keiran stared at him and then grabbed the duffle bag, tossing it to Mitch's feet. Mitch's gaze flicked to the black bag and then back to Keiran. "What's this?"

"Twenty grand in cash. Leave."

Mitch smiled at Keiran. "She must be a special girl," he remarked. "That's romantic of you, son, but I'm afraid that isn't enough. You see... you and Keenan," he sneered at his name, "are worth so much more than that."

"Take the money, bitch." Keenan spit at the ground near Mitch.

His gaze was cold as he took in Keenan. "You are every bit of your father."

"You mean your brother, pussy?"

"Keenan!" Keiran yelled, catching Keenan's attention. The cousins appeared to be having a silent battle, and then Keenan sucked his teeth and glared at Mitch.

"Why wait ten years?" When everyone's heads

shifted to me, I realized I had spoken the question aloud.

"Believe it or not, Miss Monroe, I did not come to the decision to kill my only child so easily. There was still hope of marrying someone as naive as his mother had been. After all, I was pretty young myself. And there was this other little hiccup that says I'm supposed to be dead."

"So how do you plan to get away with this?"

"It isn't a crime to return from the dead. A quick DNA test will prove that Keiran was indeed my son, and I collect his inheritance. After I take care of my brother, there will be no one left to refute any of it."

"You won't touch my father," Keenan growled.

"Son, you won't be around to stop me."

"Mitch, take the money and go. I'll even give you a head start. That's my only offer," Keiran ordered.

"You think you can just stand there and puff your chest up at me? I am your father, you shit. You don't dictate to me. I made you," he roared.

"And a fine fucking job you did. You made me and then you sold me."

"You were always a means to an end and that end was money. I was supposed to marry and produce an heir. Your mother screwed that up when she ran off to be a whore for my brother!"

"What the fuck are you talking about?" Keenan asked. He was looking between Keiran and Mitch while I stood by in shock.

"Isn't that the reason you hate John so much, son? Because my *brother*," he sneered, "had forbidden Sophia from reporting you missing to the police so they could protect another child," he looked toward Keenan, "the bastard child she had with him."

Keiran's glare darkened while Keenan froze as the

aftermath of the catastrophic bomb Mitch had dropped knocked us all on our asses.

They're brothers.

Oh, fuck.

He had to be lying. He's told many lies before in order to get what he wanted. "Shut the fuck up, Mitch," Keiran warned.

"When Sophia left me, I had every hospital watched for any sign of her, so when Keenan was born, it led me right to her. Imagine my surprise to find her with my brother of all people. I wasn't even aware they'd met, but apparently, he'd come sniffing around and decided to play the hero."

"You were holding her hostage," I spoke aloud again, thinking about the housekeeper who was dismissed. It all made sense. "She didn't want to be with you anymore, did she? Leaving you meant ruining your plans."

"You're smarter than I gave you credit for," Mitch snidely replied. He turned his eyes that lacked any fatherly warmth to Keiran again.

"Tell him, Keiran. Tell him how Sophia died because she wanted to protect you and this little bastard. Tell him how you killed his mother. The mother you both share."

Keenan took a threatening step toward Mitch, but the two men grabbed his arm. "My mother ran off when I was seven," he said through clenched teeth.

"Nephew, it is amazing how money can spin a tale many ways and no one bats an eyelash. Just as I was able to play dead for the past ten years."

"You're lying," he gritted and turned to Keiran. "Keiran, what the fuck, man? Tell him he's lying!" It broke my heart to see a tear run down Keenan's face before he wiped it away with an angry hand. Keiran stood there, silent and unmoving. "You killed her? You killed my mom?" Keiran remained silent, but his un-flinching gaze was fixed on Keenan. "Answer me!" he roared.

This was the first and only time I had ever seen Keenan, who was usually the joker, so angry. Mitch's dark chuckle broke the brief silence.

"He can't. He shot her right in the head and didn't even bat an eyelash." He laughed again. A split second later, before any of us could react, Mitch was on the ground, and Keenan was pounding his fist into Mitch's face, creating a bloody canvas. I was thrown to the ground as dust and bullets flew. The sound of gunfire was deafening as all my senses went on alert just before shutting down. I couldn't make out anything or anyone. The lights from the vehicles must have been shot out as darkness and dust mixed.

Where was Keiran?

I hadn't realized I was screaming until someone appeared out of nowhere and clamped a hand over my mouth. Once I quieted, the hand was removed, and I heard footsteps running. As the dust settled, I could see two large bodies lying still on the ground and under them both was a pool of blood.

# CHAPTER THIRTY-TWO

KEIRAN WAS GONE. I hadn't seen or spoken to him in four days. I visited the hospital frequently, hoping he might be there and to look in on Keenan. After the near-fatal shooting, Keenan had pulled through surgery but slipped into a coma due to the trauma of his injuries. After receiving six shots to his body, one near his heart, and another causing one of his lungs to collapse, I wasn't surprised.

Mitch had gotten away while the two men unloaded into Keenan. Keiran managed to shoot both—killing one and wounding the other.

Unfortunately, with Keenan being left in a coma and a dead body in the middle of nowhere, we couldn't stop the town from talking. Word spread quickly about what had happened Monday night, and by Friday, I was more than happy to lock myself away for the next two days.

The only piece of Monday night they were able to keep quiet was my part in the kidnapping slash shootout. Keiran had called Quentin, who was waiting nearby to take me home before the police arrived.

The first night I tried as hard as I could to stay home alone, but knowing Mitch was still out there haunted me. My nervousness turned into fear, and my fear turned into paranoia. Every sound I heard was Mitch coming for me. He was around every corner. I was afraid of my own shadow before long. Willow knew all about what had happened that night, and after urging me to call the cops had failed, she convinced me to stay with her.

As I walked inside the house from school to grab more clothes, my phone rang. I considered ignoring it knowing it wouldn't be Keiran, but since Aunt Carissa wasn't home, I decided to answer just in case.

"Hey, Lake," Sheldon spoke into the line.

"You sound miserable." Ever since finding out what happened to Keenan, Sheldon had been living a former shell of herself. She also refused to see him in the hospital.

"Gee, thanks."

"Go see him, Sheldon. It will make you feel better."

"I can't," she said. Her voice cracked, and she sounded close to tears.

"Why not? He's your boyfriend, Sheldon. I don't understand—"

"No, you don't so drop it, okay?"

"Fine," I reluctantly agreed.

"So, how is he?"

"Jeez, you just told me to drop it!"

"I know what I said, I—" The next second, I could hear Sheldon sobbing on the other end of the line.

"Sheldon, what's going on with you?"

"He fucked her." I didn't immediately react because we all knew Keenan strayed often, but Sheldon always forgave him.

"Who?"

"Ms. Felders."

"The new chemistry teacher?" I shrieked.

She sniffled and said, "Uh huh."

"How... when?"

"Oh, you know the traditional way," she said with sarcasm. "I don't know when it started, but I have an idea. I knew something was fishy between the two of them when she started paying extra attention to him. I caught her one day with her hand on his chest when I went to ask her about my failing grade on a project."

"What did they say?"

"She laughed it off and said she was smoothing out a wrinkle in his shirt. Do you know how close I came to head butting the fuck out of her? I thanked her and told her from then on, I would be the one fixing his wrinkles."

"When did you find out? I mean... how do you know he really had sex with her? That's a little far-fetched even for Keenan."

"Apparently not. I saw the text messages between the two of them spanning about two weeks and confronted him about it after we left laser tag. We argued, and I kicked him out of my house. He must have gotten snatched right after," her voice finally broke on the last, and I knew she must have felt guilty.

"Sheldon, I know you think it's your fault, but it's not."

"I just can't help but think that if I had given into his bullshit just one more time, he wouldn't be fighting for his life right now."

"Sheldon..."

"I left him, Lake. I told him I hated him and wished he would die. Do you know how horrible I feel? I went to see him, you know."

That caught me by surprise. "When?"

"The next morning. Dash and I weren't told until then. I rushed straight there, I swear I did, but then I saw her. She was there, Lake. She went to see my man. Can you believe that bitch?"

"So what did you do?" I asked, picking up on her claim of Keenan. I knew she still loved him but was hurting too much to see it now.

"I left. It was the final nail in the coffin, and now we will never be able to forgive each other."

\* \* \*

MONDAY MORNING CAME all too quickly, and I still hadn't heard word of Keiran. I didn't know if he was even alive...

Did Mitch find him again?

At this moment, Keiran could be dead...

My mind brought forth an image of a broken and lifeless Keiran, and I would have collapsed if I weren't already seated. *Don't think about that.*

But I couldn't help but worry. His absence was driving me mad, and everyone seemed to be caught up in his or her own thing so I couldn't distract myself. How dare he put my life in danger and then just disappear like that? I could have lost my life... I could have lost him. It felt like I had already lost him. Mitch was still out there and knowing what he planned to do with his son was nerve wracking.

Lost in my thoughts, I turned into the school parking lot a little too quickly. There was a gang of students still in the parking lot, even though the first bell would ring soon. As I parked my car, I noticed a crowd of students in one spot. When I got closer, I could see through the slight opening, and I could see a familiar black muscle car and Keiran leaning against it. Quentin and Dash were blocking him from the crowd. I couldn't tell what was going on because everyone was talking at once. I walked closer to the circle and could just barely make out the various 'are you okay', 'how is Keenan', and 'what happened.'

My heart skipped at the sight of him. It had only been a week but the worry and the fact that I missed him made it seem so much longer.

I picked up my pace to get to him before he could disappear again and just as I got in the circle, Chloe Newman, one of the cheerleaders, threw herself into his arms and worse... *he caught her.*

I stood there and watched them. Pain rooted me to the spot as I died inside. But when I saw his hands grope her ass, I forgot about the pain and let my rage take over. Before I knew it, my hands were in her hair, and she was being yanked to the ground. The crowd erupted in chaos as I got on top of her and reared back my fist. Oh, you had better believe I was going for her perfect little nose, but my fist never connected with her face. My hand was caught, and I was yanked up and into a hard chest.

"What are you doing, Lake?" Keiran asked his voice neutral. He sounded bored.

"What am I doing? What are you doing?" I screamed and ripped myself away from him. I didn't care that I may have looked and sounded like a banshee. *What is he doing to me?* "You disappear for days and the first time I see you, I find you with your hands all over the nearest skank?" Said skank had already run off with her posse of skanks.

"It's not that big of a deal."

"The hell it isn't, asshole."

The familiar burning look in his eyes returned, and the vein in his temple began to throb again. "Let's go." He walked off, assuming I would follow. I did. I followed him to one of the empty classrooms they used to store extra desks.

"Where have you been?" I asked when he stared at me with a black look in his eyes. I haven't seen him this way in such a long time that I nearly forgot about the ferociousness of it.

He released an aggravated breath. "Look, I'm sorry I disappeared. How are you?"

"Pissed and I don't know... maybe hurt? Where were you?"

"I had to figure shit out."

"But how could you just leave Keenan alone like that?"

"He isn't safe as long as my father is out there, and he has John."

"But he needs you too, you're his bro—"

"Don't," he bit out. "Don't say that." The pain in his voice was unmistakable. I could only imagine how Keenan must have felt finding out the way he did. Keiran, however, didn't appear surprised that night.

"Did you know all this time?"

"Yes."

"How?" I asked incredulously.

"I saw her picture on Keenan's nightstand the day John brought me home. He said she was his mother." He swallowed and took a deep breath but didn't continue.

"What did they make you do?" I didn't feel the need to elaborate. There only one thing standing between us. He watched me intently, but I wasn't about to back down again.

"I guess it doesn't matter anymore, anyway." His tone was desolate, and I wondered what he meant by that. "I made my first kill for them when I was six."

"How? You were so young."

"It's amazing what you're willing to do when you're starving and don't know a way out. They used anything they could to control us. Before long, I stopped noticing the hunger pains or thirst, and the scars healed before I ever knew they were even there."

There were so many questions swimming in my head, but I didn't want to interrupt. His gaze was distant, and his entire body was so still.

"They started me off small. First, it was other kids they wanted me to punish until I made my way up to adults. After two years of training to be a murderer, I became one of their best students. I was a fucking eight-year-old kid. I stopped thinking and I stopped feeling. It kept me alive."

"That isn't living," I argued.

"How would you know?" he asked with anger, and I realized he was right. I wouldn't know—I was judging. It wasn't as if he had a choice.

"I'm sorry." He nodded and continued.

"She came in the middle of the night like a bad fucking dream—just like you except you were much more real. I spent weeks ignoring her while they beat her endlessly. She was so small and so innocent. I thought she was weak when she wouldn't do what she needed to survive. One day, I guess the hunger overrode her fear because one of the runners caught her digging in the trash for food and beat her. He beat her so bad that day, I finally did something I shouldn't have."

"What did you do?" I asked while fighting back tears for the picture he painted of the young, helpless child.

"I stopped him from caving her head with the heel of his boot as if she were nothing. Two years of work went down the drain because of one wrong move. I still didn't regret it, at least not at first. She clung to me after that and looked to me as her protector. Every day, I took her beatings and mine, and often, I was too weak to make any kills, so they became crueler. I began to hate her after a while. I blamed her for making me weak again when all she wanted me to do was care about her. I didn't want to so I don't know why I helped her. I just did."

He moved to sit in one of the desks and held his fists clenched out in front of him. "What happened to her?"

"One day, after a run, they told me I had a job to do, one that would cost me my life if I didn't do it. What they didn't know was that I didn't care if I lived or died, but I accepted anyway. They took me to a room I'd never seen before. Lily was there, waiting. She was naked and crying, and I saw the bruises and gashes all over her body."

"Why was she naked?" I was afraid of the answer, but I had to know. I needed to understand how deep their cruelty ran.

"They wanted me to—we had—they wanted me to fuck her for some sick fantasy that a lot of sick, old fucks were paying a shit load of money to get on camera."

"Oh, God, Keiran..."

"She looked so broken, and I could tell she had nothing left. I couldn't do it. Out of all the jobs and people I'd hurt, this was something I couldn't do. That's why I was relieved when she asked me to do it."

"Do what?"

"To save her."

"But you were in danger, too." He shook his head and looked up at me.

"I didn't care what happened to me."

"How could you have saved her?"

"The only way that mattered," he said cryptically, but I knew what he was saying. *She asked him to kill her.* "I took away her pain, and I took away her fear. I went to her, and I laid her down and closed her eyes. In that space of time, I tried to find another way, but in the end, I kept coming back to the same answer."

"You were only a child."

"I was never a child, Lake. For ten years, my decision has haunted me. When I saw you for the first time, I thought you were her, and then I thought I was hallucinating. You looked just like her. When I finally realized you weren't her, I knew I was being punished. You reminded me so much of her." He finally looked at me with a painful expression. "Are you here to punish me?"

"I never wanted to punish you, Keiran." *What am I saying?*

He shook his head. "I think I was punishing myself and looking for someone to blame."

"Did you love her?" It was crazy to feel jealousy for an eight-year-old, but the emotion he carried for Lily was strong.

"No."

"Because you don't believe in love?"

"Would you?"

"How did your father get you back?" I asked him rather than answer his question. I didn't know what to believe in anymore. "Wouldn't they have killed you when you ruined their plans?"

"I wasn't killed for disobeying them by a stroke of luck named Mario. It seems his only vice was child prostitution and pornography. He saved me from being killed and severed his business ties with his partner shortly after, but not before leaving me a way to contact him if I ever needed anything—but mainly if I wanted to work for him. I didn't fool myself to think he cared."

"And your father?"

"A couple of weeks after Lily died, I was snuck from the compound by one of the runners my father had in his pocket. I was with Mitch for a week before Sophia showed up—though I didn't know who she was—not at first. He told me who he was right away. I didn't know who she was until after she died."

"Did you really kill her?"

"Yes." I had been hoping somehow, Mitch was lying. That Keiran hadn't killed his mother. But if he didn't know...

"Why?" He looked up at me again, his eyes void of emotion or feeling.

"Why not?"

"Because she was innocent."

"Was she?"

"But—"

"There is no such thing as *innocence,*" he barked. "How many mothers do you know would let their child be taken without even trying?"

"So you killed her because of it?"

"I didn't know she was my mother when I put the fucking bullet through her fucking skull," he spat.

"Are you even sorry for it?"

"I don't regret what I can't fix. She's dead—you don't come back from that." He stood up hurriedly, and the momentum pushed the desk back a few feet. He was walking past me and had reached the door before I realized what was happening.

"Where are you going?"

"I'm done talking."

"But what about Mitch? He knows where you are now. He knows where all of us are."

"I know," he said as he turned his head around to face me but kept his hand on the door. "You were almost killed because of me. I do regret that, which means I can fix it."

"How are you going to fix it?" I asked suspiciously.

"I'm letting you go," he said and slammed out of the room.

* * *

I WAS LEFT standing alone in the dusty classroom. *I'm letting you go.* The reality of his words didn't hit me until I was left standing alone with the feeling of my heart breaking. Before Keiran, I didn't think a heart was capable of breaking so many times. After everything he'd done, do I just let him leave? Before I could stop myself, I stormed out into the hallway.

"So that's it then?" The hallway was full of people heading to their first class, and when I yelled down the hallway at him, they all stopped to watch us.

He turned back to face me. "That's all I'm willing to give you."

"You torment me for ten years, fuck me silly for the past two months, and make me fall in love with you. Then, if that's not enough, you almost get me killed because of your asshat dad, and you think you can just walk away because you think it's the right thing to do?"

"I don't give a fuck about what's right. It's safer this way."

"Says who?"

"Says my brother, who is lying in the hospital fighting for his life because of me!" he yelled. The hallway erupted with whispers and shocked sounds at his outburst. No one knew yet that Keenan and Keiran were actually brothers.

"So you're going to walk away from him, too?"

"If that's what it takes. He's still out there."

"Because you chose to save your brother's life!" He didn't react. I was right, and he knew it. I couldn't see much of anything that night, but I knew Mitch was close enough for Keiran to kill him easily. Instead, he concentrated on putting down the men who shot Keenan and so Mitch was able to get away. "You love your brother, Keiran... and you love me, or else you wouldn't care."

He shook his head and turned away. My breathing escalated at the same time my temper skyrocketed. *Fuck that.* I looked around and noticed Quentin holding a basketball and watching us with sad eyes. I walked up to him and snatched the ball away before he could stop me. The next second, it was flying through the air and hit Keiran's back. I was on him before he could turn around fully and pushed him with all the strength I could find, and even though I knew my strength didn't match his, I was too pissed and emotionally wrecked to care. I was willing to make a fool of myself for him. I had been for the last couple of months.

"You don't just get to walk away," I cried while beating on his chest. "You don't get to leave." My tears blinded me, and surprisingly, with each push, he moved a step back. "You can't," I whispered breathlessly. His head lowered until his lips were centered right above mine.

"I... don't... want... you," he ground out, and then pushed me away from him.

I lost my footing and fell to the ground. There were collective sounds of shock and laughter around us. I watched Keiran walk away and didn't notice when someone had lifted me off the floor.

I couldn't see anything but the sight of Keiran walking away from me. The need to escape and hide came when he was no longer in sight. I pulled away from the unknown hold and willed my feet to carry me down the hall and out the double doors to safety where I could die in peace.

* * *

THERE WAS NOWHERE else I felt safe enough to cry any more than in my grandmother's arms. I pulled into Whispering Pines, spitting gravel as I slammed to a stop. I didn't remember the drive there. I didn't remember much after running from school. All I could feel was pain. The weather had become even colder since the last time I was here, so the grounds were empty. I rushed through the lobby, not stopping to check in, and made my way to her room. When I reached my grandmother's room, I could hear familiar voices drifting through the cracked door.

"Oh, Mom. I just don't know what to do or say." *Aunt Carissa?* When did she get back? She wasn't due back until Wednesday.

"Honey, there isn't an easy way to handle this, but she needs to hear it. That child has been lost all these years. She thinks she hates them. Tell her the truth."

"Mom, how do I just tell her that her parents didn't abandon her? They didn't just die. They were *murdered.*"

# CHAPTER THIRTY-THREE

SOMEONE ONCE TOLD me pain didn't last forever. I remember hearing it after finding out my parents were missing.

Over the years, I found that to be complete bullshit. Pain was forever.

It was love that didn't last forever.

I looked out the window while listening to the phone conversation.

"Lake, when are you coming home? We miss you, and you know who is brooding again," Willow said. It had been a week since my fallout with Keiran. I never made it back home after overhearing my aunt's conversation with my grandmother about my parents.

"Yeah, dude is seriously out of control this time," Sheldon added, bringing me back to the present. "I caught him driving by your house yesterday."

After he had played me so brutally in front of the entire school, I did everything I could to forget him.

"And Dash says if you don't come home soon, he's rounding up a search party."

"Guys, Keiran must be worried about his brother."

"Yeah, but even Coach is talking about benching him. It's the first game of the season. The town is going to be pissed. Dash said there will be scouts out there, and he could blow his chances if he doesn't pull it together."

"Am I supposed to feel sorry for him? I think he made it pretty clear he didn't want anything to do with me."

"So you're just going to let him go?" Willow asked.

"Are we really having this conversation right now?"

"It's fine. You have to come home sometime."

"No... I don't. Look, I didn't want to say anything too soon because I wasn't sure what I wanted to do, but I think I'm going to finish the rest of senior year up here."

"What?" they both screeched.

"Lake, no." Willow sounded as if she were on the verge of crying.

"What are you thinking?" Sheldon asked with hostility.

"I think I need to get control of my life. I think it will be really good for me if I get away from Six Forks for a while, and I can't miss school. Guys... I already put in the transfer papers."

The line was silent for a moment before I heard Sheldon growl, "Fuck that," before hanging up.

"Lake, are you sure?"

"Yes, Willow. I'm sure. It's easier this way," I admitted. I guess she didn't have much to say after that because she ended the call. I rested my head against the back of the couch and thought about where the past two months had led me.

"You know running away from your problems never solves anything. They only catch up to you later." My godmother and my aunt's best friend, Karen, had come into the living room to sit next to me after I hung up with Willow. "I'm sorry I eavesdropped, but I couldn't help but overhear. It sounds to me as if you have people who care about you back home. Are you sure you want to give that up?"

"I don't think I'm giving it up, Aunt Karen. I'm just giving it a break."

After hearing the news about my parents, I woke up in a hospital for the third time in my life. Apparently, I passed out cold from shock and dehydration. They called it a mental meltdown.

My aunt didn't say any more about what I'd heard, and I didn't ask. I wasn't ready to know what had happened.

After the doctor had cleared me to go home, I started having a panic attack all over again. All I kept thinking was how I couldn't go back, and so my aunt and I came to an agreement that I needed a vacation. We were able to finagle a doctor's note excusing me from school for a few days. My aunt called up Karen, who agreed to watch over me. It was only supposed to be for a few days, but every time I thought about going home, my anxiety rose.

Keiran had finally done what I think he was always trying to do. He ran me away from home and everyone I loved. He could have Six Forks and the school, but he couldn't have my sanity.

"Well, if you ask me, I think this boy deserves the kissing end of my nine up his ass."

"Aunt Karen!"

"Hmmp! Whatever happened to the days when a boy simply bought a girl flowers, and if she was really special, he'd buy her candy before sex, too?"

"I think it died in the seventies," I laughed.

"Shame."

I'd told Aunt Karen all about Keiran and me the first night I was there. I felt guilty for confiding in her and not my aunt, but it just all came out. I knew sooner or later I would have to tell her. It wasn't fair for her not to know anymore. She took me in when I wouldn't have had anybody. I owed her so much, and I would start by giving her my honesty.

"Have you talked to Carissa yet?"

"No, not yet. I just need some time."

"Time doesn't wait for anyone, Lake—remember that."

We sat and talked for hours and before I knew it, night had fallen. Aunt Karen left to go make dinner, and as I was watching TV, the door opened and Uncle Ben, my godfather, walked in.

"Hey, Lake. Isn't it passed your bedtime?"

I laughed. "No, Uncle Bennie. I'm not eight anymore, but I do think it's past yours." He chuckled and ruffled my hair before rushing off to find his wife.

When he entered the kitchen, I heard her giggle like a schoolgirl with a crush and the unmistakable sound of heavy kissing. I always thought they were the most romantic couple I'd ever known.

Aunt Carissa, Aunt Karen, and Uncle Ben had been best friends since college. For Aunt Karen and Uncle Ben, it had been love at first sight, and they have been happily married since their senior year. Their only bad time was when Aunt Karen suffered two miscarriages before her body and the couple gave up on trying. It broke Aunt Karen's heart that she couldn't give him the children they always talked about, but Uncle Ben said she was all he ever needed.

It's been five years since her last miscarriage, and now they were talking about adopting.

I guess happily ever after was only meant for a few.

\* \* \*

My vacation was drawn to a halt the next day when I got a phone call from my aunt telling me there were detectives looking for me. I immediately panicked, thinking they somehow found out about my being kidnapped by Mitch and how much they might have told my aunt. I rushed back to Six Forks and drove straight to the station to recite the story Keiran told me to give about that night if anyone ever asked. I walked into the station with my nerves in my stomach and threatening to come up at any moment.

"Miss Monroe, so nice of you to pay us a visit," a detective who I believe said his name was Daniels spoke to me. He looked and acted like the typical asshat detective with thinning hair and a bushy mustache. He also tried too hard to be intimidating. If I weren't already so nervous, I would have laughed.

"My aunt said you were looking for me?"

"Yes, you missed your scheduled interview." *Shit, Trevor and Anya!* With Mitch returning from the dead, I'd forgotten about their disappearance.

"I'm sorry. I wasn't told…"

"A phone call was placed to your aunt, who notified us that you were out of town. Any particular reason why?"

"I'm transferring schools."

"I see," he wrote something down before looking back at me. "Tell me about your relationship with Trevor Reynolds and Anya Risdell.

"Nonexistent. We weren't friends."

"Why is that?" he asked with suspicion.

"Were you friends with every person you went to high school with?"

"No, but there must be a reason why one of them would allegedly attack you in a bathroom stall and receive a broken arm by Keiran Masters for the trouble."

"It isn't alleged because Trevor Reynolds did attack me. Instead of treating me like the criminal, you should be searching for him harder. He needs to be put away."

"We've called off the search." I didn't bother to hide my surprise as I stared back at him. "I can see this news surprises you."

"Why did you call off the search?"

"Because there has been a new development in the case. Trevor Reynolds and Anya Risdell were both found this morning."

"So why am I here?" I stood to leave, not really caring about the answer. I needed to get the hell out of there.

"Because they were both found burned alive in a field just outside of town. They're dead, Miss Monroe, and I think you know who did it."

Dead? *He didn't bring them back?*

"Who didn't bring them back, Miss Monroe?" the detective asked, and I realized I must have said it aloud. I slowly sat back down when I struggled with the realization of what I had to do. He didn't just kill them. He tortured them. I could practically smell their burning flesh as guilt ate away at my mind. "Lake?"

I finally met the detective's gaze when he called my name again. I knew what I had to do. "I have to tell you something."

* * *

I LEFT THE station feeling numb. What I'd done felt like the ultimate betrayal, but I also knew it was the right thing to do. I just never knew choosing right over wrong was so damn hard.

He killed them.

He killed so many.

He shouldn't be allowed to walk away from that. Right?

I didn't head straight back to my godparent's place. Instead, I went home because, truth be told, I had been feeling homesick. I hadn't decided to leave because it was what I wanted. I felt it was necessary because there was no other way I could stay away from Keiran. I was as addicted to him as he was to me.

*Is that why you turned him in?*

I shook off my thoughts and pulled into my driveway. My aunt's car was parked outside, and I was eager to see her and maybe finally catch up. I never got the chance to ask about her tour or tell her about the break in. I shut off the car to get out, but the sound of my ringing phone stopped me. I read the screen and saw Sheldon's name, so I quickly answered. Over the past couple of weeks, Sheldon had not been in the best shape.

"Hey, Sheldon."

"Lake, oh, God. He's going to die!" she sobbed brokenly into the phone.

"Sheldon, calm down. Who is going to die?"

"Keenan's only working lung is failing. The doctors said it doesn't look good for him, and if he doesn't get a lung soon, he will die."

Finding an organ donor was like winning the lottery. It could take months, the match had to be near perfect, and the perfect candidates were usually the parents.

"Sheldon, Keenan won't die. He's too much of a rebel for that. Did they test John to see if he's a match?"

"Yes, and they pulled his mother's medical records

from his birth to check for any record of family medical problems and all that other crap doctor's do." The line grew silent so I checked my phone to see if we were still connected.

"And?"

"John wasn't a match."

"Damn. He must have taken his mother's blood type. So how long does he have before it becomes critical?"

"Lake, you don't understand," she said, her sobs becoming heavier.

"What don't I understand?" Sheldon sounded near hysterical now.

"John's blood was type AB, and when they pulled Sophia's medical records they found out that her blood was type A."

I frowned when I couldn't make the connection. "I wasn't all that great with Biology, so you're going to have to help me out here."

"Keenan is blood type O. Parents with blood type AB and A can only produce a child with A, B, or AB."

"Oh, shit, so you mean—"

"John isn't Keenan's father."

"But that's insane! If John isn't Keenan's father, then it has to be—oh, God..."

"Mitch," Sheldon finished.

The End

# AUTHOR'S NOTE

THANK YOU SO much for purchasing *Fear Me*. Creating the characters and making the story come to life has truly been the best journey of my life. If you enjoyed it, please leave a review.

# ACKNOWLEDGMENTS

THE EASIEST PART about writing Fear Me is thanking the wonderful and dedicated people who have helped me along the way...

First, I want to thank God for blessing me with the courage to not only chase my dream, but to catch it.

Mama, thank you. There is so much I can say, but all of it would never fit on paper. I'll do any and everything to keep you proud of me. Oh, and if you read Fear me...Please don't tell me. It would be weird. I love you!

Deven, you have encouraged me in ways you will never know. Thank you for putting up with being ignored and all my crankiness. I hope I haven't neglected you too much while I wrote Fear Me. You are everything a girl could ask for...sometimes. You can still be such a guy sometimes.

Tiera, my very best friend and most likely the first person to buy Fear Me, thank you for all the support and love. You were the very first person I told when I decided to pursue my dream because I trusted you to be the one to encourage me the way I needed. Plus, your antics keep me going.

Tae, for the last time, I am not writing another Fifty Shades of Grey. Stop obsessing and meet your new book boyfriend.

Kimie, Sharee, Stephanie, and Kimmy I don't think you know how loved you are among the writing community. Pussycat Promotions will go extremely far with the dedication and love you show each person you work with whether it be authors, bloggers or PAs. Your names should be revered. I couldn't have done it without you ladies. With the teasers, cover design, cover reveal, and even beta reading, you guys have been there. Thank you so much.

To any new author out there looking for a promoter or even a friend, these ladies are who you need to see. They have many connections and know how to work them. You can find them on Facebook or their business website. They can and will meet all of your promotional needs.

Sharee, my beta reader, you put up with my doubts and second guesses to the very end and as my very first reader, I thank you for your honest opinion and the extra time you spent making sure Fear Me was written the way it was meant to.

Sabrina, Karina, and Dani, you ladies were the first authors I met who would even give me the time of day. Thank you so much for the support!

For all of the awesome blogs and readers that participated in promoting Fear Me, thank you!

Here's to Fear Me.

# ALSO BY B.B. REID

## *Broken Love Series*

Fear Me

Fear You

Fear Us

Breaking Love

Fearless

## *The Stolen Duet*

The Bandit

# CONTACT THE AUTHOR

Join **Bebe's Reiders** on Facebook!

**Twitter:** _BBREID

**Instagram:** _BBREID

www.bbreid.com

# ABOUT B.B. REID

B.B., ALSO KNOWN as Bebe, found her passion for romance when she read her first romance novel by Susan Johnson at a young age. She would sneak into her mother's closet for books and even sometimes the attic. It soon became a hobby, and later an addiction. When she finally decided to pick up a metaphorical pen and start writing, she found a new way to embrace her passion.

She favors a romance that isn't always easy on the eyes or heart, and loves to see characters grow—characters who are seemingly doomed from the start but find love anyway.

Fear Me, her debut novel, is the first of many.

61274769R00288

Made in the USA
Middletown, DE
09 January 2018